Other Books & Stories
by Lynn Bohart

NOVELS

Mass Murder

Grave Doubts

Inn Keeping With Murder

SHORT STORY BOOKS

Your Worst Nightmare

Something Wicked

Ms. Bohart is also published in
the anthology of short stories:
"Dead On Demand"

MURDER IN THE PAST TENSE

By Lynn Bohart

Cover Art: Mia Yoshihara-Bradshaw

Published by Little Dog Press

Disclaimer: This book is a work of fiction and while many of the businesses, locations, and organizations referenced in the book are real, they are used in a way that is purely fictional.

ACKNOWLEDGEMENTS

I now realize that writing a successful novel takes a village (not to steal a quote). It is a long and complicated process that certainly requires more collective knowledge than I personally possess. Therefore, my sincere thanks go to the following people:

First and foremost to my writing group (Tim McDaniel, Lori-Church Pursely, Michael Manzer, Timera Drake and Gary Larsen) who painstakingly read this book chapter by chapter over a period of several months, giving me invaluable feedback as the story developed. I'd also like to thank my 'beta' readers: Kathy Perrin, Karen Gilb, Bill Dolan, Chris Spahn, and Valerie O'Halloran, who read it cover-to-cover and helped to find weak spots and small mistakes. And lastly, thanks goes to Liz Stewart, who serves as my editor and does a thorough job line-editing every page.

Beyond the writing folks however, is a long list of experts and professionals who helped to vet this book. My personal thanks to Renton Fire Chief, Mark Peterson and Andy Speier, Battalion Chief of the McLane-Black Lake Fire Department and Thurston County SORT. Andy teaches search and rescue and gave me detailed information on the search and rescue aspects. Thanks also goes to the following: Dr. Dinesh Rao (India), forensic pathologist, who generously offered his advice on the forensics details; Dale Tallman, retired Seattle homicide detective, who vetted the police procedural aspects (and allowed me some literary license); Dr. Katherine Taylor, forensic anthropologist and King County Medical Examiner, who helped me with the cadaver dog and bone discovery information, and Rich Wagner, Baylis Architects.

Once again, I applaud my cover designer, Mia Yoshihara-Bradshaw for a fantastic cover. Please check out her website at: www.miayoshihara.com. I would also like to thank all the women who so lovingly offered to have their pictures grace the front of the book: Cindy Warden LaSance; Pat Auten; Chrystine Warden Dimitry; Sheila Lynn Horn Kaplan; Linda Madeira; Diane Clauder-Liefke; Lisa Hodgkin Thomas; Pat Butler Nolan; and Dana Whitney. Oh yeah, and there's one more – me.

Dedicated to my high school alma mater, Pasadena High School, and all the great friends with whom I graduated and who encouraged me in this endeavor.

MURDER IN THE PAST TENSE
May, 1967

Her body was stuffed into a duffle bag and tossed carelessly into the old well as if it were nothing more than a bag of garbage. Those doing the tossing waited to hear the thud when she hit bottom and then threw a few shovelfuls of dirt in behind her for good measure. Since the shovel was caked with her blood, it followed a moment later.

The night was unseasonably warm, and a rustling sound made them stop. Were they being watched? The taller one glanced around, but all was quiet. The parking lot was empty and all the windows at this end of the big building appeared dark.

Satisfied the noise had come from a rodent, he gestured to his companion to help him roll the well cap back to seal the girl into her makeshift tomb. Once their secret was safe, the two dark figures climbed into the long, black car and glided silently away.

Thirty-five feet below ground, the girl's once graceful figure lay twisted and broken like a forgotten Barbie Doll. The lovely forest green prom dress her mother had splurged on for that night was torn and stained, and her lustrous brown hair was soaked in blood. Her dreams of becoming a teacher were gone, along with the dream of marrying the boy she loved.

As a flurry of bats swooped down from the silent bell tower above, only memories of this once beautiful girl would be left behind to remind the world of such a heartbreaking loss.

CHAPTER ONE
Present Day

The image of the once proud Catholic monastery emerged from the Southern California morning mist like the war-torn ruins of Nuremberg. One-third of the sprawling complex had been demolished. And, like the bombed-out buildings in Germany, a jagged and ugly scar now marked the spot where the retreat center had been ripped away from the rest of the building.

The demolition crew had spent more than a week removing enormous chunks of concrete, scrap lumber and broken roof tiles. But the monastery had been built over the ruins of an old Spanish rancho, which had been destroyed more than a century before when a hillside had collapsed during a torrential rain storm. Buried in the mud, the rancho's hallways and courtyard had created ancient tunnels, discovered when the monks had dropped below ground to lay the foundation for the monastery's bell tower.

When the demolition crew was ready to fill in those tunnels, the work had to be stopped because they'd found the skeletal remains of two people killed in the century-old mudslide. A team of archaeologists were called in to catalogue and remove the bones.

When their work was complete, the contractors returned to remove patio tiles, laid when the monastery had been remodeled to include a retreat center. But the contractors were caught by yet one more surprise.

They found an old well.

The well had probably been part of the old rancho, covered over when the patio was built for the modern-day banquet room. To be safe, the workers shone a light inside and were surprised again when something metallic at the bottom glinted back.

The company's owner, Jock Peters, called for a volunteer. He wanted someone to be lowered into the well to make sure there wasn't anything of value hidden down there.

Steve Nicely raised his hand.

The crew brought in large sheets of plywood and laid them around the lip of the well. This would distribute weight around the old cistern. Then they backed up a skip loader and raised its bucket high, rigging a pulley system that would lower Nicely straight down the middle, strapped into a harness and wearing safety glasses.

Anxious to show up the older men on the crew, young Nicely flashed a broad smile as he made ready to go. Billy Cooper, the team clown, couldn't let the moment pass, however, and called out, "Hey, Nicely, got a will? Don't want to leave that pretty little wife with nothing!"

Billy chortled and jabbed his elbow into Kevin Olney's ribs.

"Yeah, Nicely," Kevin laughed. "And keep your eye out for those ghosts we keep hearing about."

The two men broke into a peal of laughter and started singing the theme song from *Ghost Busters!* The rest of the team merely chuckled as two guys lifted up a heavy rope.

"You ready, Steve?" Mr. Peters asked, handing him a flashlight.

Nicely nodded, though the acid churned in his stomach.

Mr. Peters gave the signal, and the men handling the rope started to let it out.

Nicely began his descent with a jerk and felt the last of his morning's breakfast refresh itself in his throat. The world disappeared one inch at a time. His anxiety rose with every inch.

When he passed the lip of the well and sank lower into the dark, dank interior, he glanced nervously around, remembering the rumors about ghosts. Maybe this hadn't been such a good idea.

He surveyed his surroundings in the disappearing light, and realized that he was in a space that was only four or five feet across. The air was heavy with dust, and a cloying, organic smell that brought a feeling of panic bubbling up in his chest.

But Steve Nicely was nothing if not stubborn. He would die of suffocation before he gave in to his fears or allowed anyone to suspect his weakness. So he sucked in several deep breaths and tried to focus his thoughts on his surroundings.

Sounds above became amplified as he went deeper into the shaft: the squeaking sound of the pulley as the rope slid through the metal roller, and the crunching of feet as the men moved back and forth up above. And then there was a rustling sound he couldn't identify.

He clicked on the flashlight and tried desperately to see below him. Were there rats? He hated rats. But all he could see was the cramped space right around him.

As a chill rippled across his shoulders, he focused straight ahead, trying to block out the sounds. His gaze scanned the walls, which were made mostly of clay bricks. And the lower he sank, the more the bricks began to sag under the weight of the ground above.

His throat constricted at the thought they had backed that heavy skip loader to within fifteen feet of the well.

What a fucking idiot he was, he thought. One wrong move and these walls could collapse. He'd been way too quick to raise his hand on this one.

By the time his feet touched the bottom, young Steve Nicely was practically hyperventilating.

Then, when he adjusted his weight and something snapped, he rebounded as if he'd been bitten by a snake. The beam from the flashlight bounced around erratically, casting ghostly shadows on the walls.

The acid was flowing freely into his mouth now, and he swallowed with difficulty. He closed his eyes and counted to three, forcing his mind to focus. Then he called up in a weak voice to let them know he was at the bottom.

Nicely took a deep breath, trying to lower his heart rate. He had to get control of himself; otherwise, he'd never live this down.

After another deep breath, he carefully skimmed the floor with the flashlight, keeping one hand on the rope that led to safety. He didn't know much about wells, so wasn't sure if the well had just dried up, or if it had been filled in up to the level where he stood. Either way, the bottom wasn't flat. The small space seemed to rise in the middle, and every time he shifted his weight, something crackled.

It gave him the creeps.

He finally moved over to the wall, where it was level, and the crackling stopped.

Nicely studied the uneven ground around him. When he noticed something protruding from the dirt next to his right foot, he froze.

Curious, he leaned over and used his fingers to dig it out.

It was an old army shovel – the kind troops could fold up and carry on their packs. Although made of metal, this wasn't what he'd been sent to find. It was supposed to be shiny. This shovel was Army green and as dull as his mother-in-law's personality.

Nicely dropped the shovel and rotated the flashlight slowly back and forth over the rest of the floor, hoping to find something important enough to spark a story or two at the Brewmeister Pub near his home. Finally, the light reflected off something a few inches in front of him. He scooted forward and reached out with his thumb and index finger to pull it out.

It was a small, metal heart attached to a heavy chain that was still imbedded in the dirt. This must have been what Mr. Peters had seen.

Nicely pulled on it, but it was caught on something hidden beneath the surface. Not one to give up easily, he leaned in and looped his fingers through the chain. With a tug, he pulled the chain one way and then the other.

Each time, something in the dirt moved, but the chain didn't budge.

Frustrated, he crouched down and placed the flashlight on the ground. Then he bunched up the chain in his hand and yanked on it, hard.

Whap!

A dirty skull popped out of the ground and nearly smacked him in the face.

Nicely flew backwards, landing on his butt. The skull rolled free, strands of long, dark hair trailing behind, a worm curling its way through the eye hole.

He stared wide-eyed at the skull, while its hollow eye sockets leered back at him.

Nicely tried to draw in a breath. But his lungs wouldn't expand.

He tried a second time. Then a third.

Finally, he sucked in a large gulp of air.

And that's when Steve Nicely's little girl scream echoed all the way up the well to chill the hardy men waiting above.

CHAPTER TWO

It was late Monday morning, three weeks before Christmas. Giorgio Salvatori was installing a kid safety gate in his kitchen, helping his wife get the house ready to open as a day care center after the first of the year.

He stopped a moment to flex the muscles on his right forearm and felt a deep burning sensation. He'd sustained two recent injuries to his arm, nearly in the same place. The first time someone had slammed his forearm with a hammer, nearly breaking the bone. The second time, he'd been shot.

Both injuries came as a result of his investigation into the murder of Mallery Olsen up at the old monastery in Sierra Madre, where he served as lead detective.

"How's your arm?" his wife asked, appearing from behind him.

She reached out and stroked the scar where the bullet had sliced through the skin. Her touch released a ticklish tingle up his arm.

"It's okay," he said, placing his other hand over hers.

He gazed for a moment into her gentle, brown eyes, noticing the first hints of age accenting her dark lashes.

"Well, don't tire it out," she said. "Some of this can wait."

"I'm fine," he replied. "And, no, it can't wait. We're on a schedule here."

He squeezed her hand in a sign of support.

"Okay," she said with a brief smile. "But don't overdo it."

Giorgio watched his wife return to the sink, thinking back to that night several weeks before when she had fallen down the stairs and lost their baby. The guilt he'd felt was mind-numbing, not only because he'd been the cause of the accident, but because he hadn't been exactly supportive of the pregnancy in the first place.

Giorgio made a decent living, but they already had two children; the thought of one more on a detective's salary had made him react to the news with less than his customary understanding and sensitivity. Angie had thought him a boor and ignored him for days.

In an effort to patch things up, he'd brought a dog home from the pound. In Giorgio's mind, it was a peace offering and would finally replace the dog they had lost years before in New York. But Angie hadn't seen it that way. To her, the dog was just one more "slob" to clean up after.

Eventually, they had worked it out and Giorgio had not only come to accept a third child, but even to relish the idea. And then Angie had fallen.

He'd been attacked by one of the suspects in the Mallery Olsen case, landing him in the ER. Angie fell in her hurry to get to him. The result was devastating. Angie had lost the baby and any possibility of having more.

So, once the Mallery Olsen case was closed, Giorgio had devised the plan to open a day care. As a former elementary school teacher, Angie had been thrilled. It wouldn't completely fill the hole left behind by the loss of a baby, but with Angie, it was all about kids.

"So, what are we getting the kids for Christmas?" Giorgio asked, thinking of his own children.

Angie turned. "Tony wants those night vision goggles they keep advertising on TV. And Marie wants a hair dryer."

Angie finished putting a last dish into the dishwasher and turned it on.

Giorgio rolled his eyes. "That girl is growing up too fast," he said. "Soon she'll want to wear makeup."

Angie laughed. "Oh, you're way behind the curve on that one."

"Seriously?" he said. "She's only nine years old!"

"Almost ten," his wife corrected him. "And she's also talked about getting her ears pierced."

"No way!" he exclaimed. "I…"

His wife raised a slender hand as if bartering a peace agreement. "Don't worry. I told her not until she was twelve, just like we decided," she said. "Listen, I need to go wrap a present. Marie is going to a birthday party this afternoon." Angie stepped past him, landing a brief kiss on his cheek. "And I've decided to go back to church next week."

"You sure?"

"Yes," she said, a tear forming. "If it was God's will when I got pregnant, then I have to accept that it was God's will when I lost the baby. I'll be okay, Joe. I have you and the kids. I couldn't ask for more." She brushed the tear away and patted his arm. "Now, I think you should take a break. I'm sure there's a football game on *somewhere* in the country."

He laughed. "Okay. You're the boss."

She tapped his nose with her index finger. "Yes, and don't you forget it."

She started to leave the room, when he grabbed her hand.

"You do know that it's Monday morning, and there isn't a football game being played *any*where in the country."

She smiled coyly. "Then you could go pay bills," she said with a lift to her delicate eyebrows. "They're all laid out on the desk."

"You did that on purpose," he said with a grimace.

Her eyes merely twinkled as she pulled her hand away and left the room.

He finished tightening the last screw on the safety latch, feeling a sense of accomplishment. His last project would be to build a dog yard for Grosvenor, the abused Basset Hound he'd rescued from the county animal shelter. Giorgio had acted on impulse that day, saving the young canine only a day before he was scheduled to be euthanized. And now the poor dog would be tortured daily by a bunch of screaming toddlers that would overrun their house.

Giorgio's cell phone rang just as he tucked his toolbox into a cupboard. It was his partner, Detective Swan.

"Hey, Chuck, what's up?"

"I know you'll be back to work next week, but I thought you'd like to be in on this," Swan said. "They just found another body at the monastery and called us in. I'm up there now."

Giorgio dropped into one of the kitchen chairs, a heaviness spreading across his chest.

"Where?" he murmured.

"An abandoned well. I don't think it has anything to do with the Mallery Olsen case," Swan was quick to say. "Apparently this body isn't much more than a bunch of bones. The demolition crew found it. We've called in the Sierra Madre Search and Rescue Team to help get it out. They just arrived. Anyway, I thought maybe you'd like a break from housework."

Giorgio smiled with relief. "Give me five minutes to change."

CHAPTER THREE

It was almost noon by the time Giorgio emerged onto his front step. He was greeted by a bank of storm clouds rolling in. He paused along the walkway to reposition a holiday reindeer that had fallen over on the front lawn. Then, he climbed into his police-issued sedan and started the engine.

Giorgio had moved his family from New York four years earlier, after his partner had been killed in a standoff with gunrunners, and Giorgio had suffered a bullet wound to the chest. Their destination, Sierra Madre, nestled at the base of the San Gabriel Mountains in the Los Angeles basin in Southern California. With only sixteen thousand residents, it's a town where people know each other mostly through school, scouting and other community activities.

The move was supposed to give Giorgio a more relaxed work schedule and a break from the horrific crimes that had become a part of his everyday life in New York. Until recently, Sierra Madre had been known largely for its enormous wisteria vines and the historic Pinney House, an old Victorian home that had been the location for several movies. But the murders connected to the Mallery Olsen case had suddenly given the town a sordid past that few would be proud of.

Now, here he was again, about to head up Sunnyside Avenue to view another body on the grounds of St. Augustine's Monastery.

As Giorgio backed out of his driveway, he thought it was too soon to be going back to the place where he and his brother Rocky had confronted the killer. The place held unpleasant associations for both of them. It was in the bell tower that he and Rocky had found evidence of a decades-old pattern of sexual abuse when the monastery included a boys' school. The big bell tower had been torn down by order of the bishop, but everything else would still be there.

It was enough to make Giorgio take an apprehensive sigh as he headed up the street.

St. Augustine's sat alone at the foot of the San Gabriel Mountains, with two hundred acres of land around it. Some of it was garden. Some of it was a grove of walnut trees. And the rest was open field.

As his car approached the massive mission-style building, Giorgio couldn't help but wonder about Christian Maynard – or rather his ghost.

Giorgio had always had hunches, and most of the time, those hunches came true. Yet he had never believed in things like ESP or ghosts, and had in fact dismissed the ideas. But during the case, he'd been confronted over and over again with the image of a young boy who had hung himself on the monastery property in 1943. In the end, the boy had actually helped with the investigation, pointing Giorgio in the right direction for critical clues, making him reluctantly accept the possibility of the paranormal.

He arrived to find the street to the monastery blocked off to normal access. A patrol officer waved him through. The west side of the religious campus had been the location of the retreat center, where Mallery Olsen's body had been found. It had also formerly been the site of the old boys' school. But now, with demolition underway, it was organized chaos, surrounded only by piles of rubble.

In addition to the police, there were local news reporters, the coroner's van, and about twelve members of the demolition crew, all watching a group of firemen and rescue team members work around the well. A fire truck blocked the drive that wound around to the far side of the big building, and a group of monks stood watching quietly in the background.

This was all too familiar, and Giorgio felt a flutter of unease cross his chest.

Swan's intimidating figure greeted him as he emerged from his car. Swan had wrestled in college and was built like a linebacker. Yet, he had the disposition of a priest.

"You're just in time, Joe," he said. "They're going to extend the aerial ladder over the hole, and then they'll lower a guy down."

He pointed to the fire truck. A brisk breeze had risen, blowing dirt from the demolition site into mini tornadoes around the demolition site.

"Shouldn't we be the ones to go down?" Giorgio asked.

"Maybe. But I guess the well is pretty compromised. They just dropped an air monitor down to make sure there's enough oxygen down there."

The two men walked across the paved driveway and up onto the dirt where the team was working. Sierra Madre Search and Rescue was well-known in the area, and since this was a small town, emergency personnel often trained and responded to calls together. Giorgio nodded to a couple of the guys he knew.

They approached the fire chief who stood with his arms crossed, watching the men work. The chief greeted Giorgio with a grim smile.

"Your car must be on autopilot for this place," he said, using his fingers to stroke his moustache.

Giorgio chuckled politely. But it wasn't funny. He'd spent far too much time up here, and the end result had been pretty grisly.

At the thought, he glanced past the well to where the bell tower had once stood. It was the last place he'd seen the ghostly image of the boy. But the tower and the secret room with its shackles and old mattress were gone. Giorgio couldn't help but wonder if the boy's spirit was gone, too. He hoped so.

"The crew chief, Jock Peters, is over there," the chief said, bringing Giorgio's attention back.

The chief pointed to a tall, thin man in gray slacks and a heavy denim jacket.

"He said they lowered one of his guys down earlier because they saw something metallic at the bottom." The chief shook his head. "These guys are idiots. Someone could have been killed. But they've already had to stop the project once because it's considered an archaeological site, so they thought they'd better check it out."

"And they found a body?" Giorgio said.

"Just a skeleton," the chief replied. "I guess it scared the hell out of the kid that went down. At first, they thought maybe it was left over from the Spanish rancho days. But the guy who found it said he found a metal chain and a heart pendant with it, plus a heavy zipper buried in the dirt. Maybe from a duffle bag. That's why you guys were called. A heart pendant and a duffle bag sounds way too modern. And I don't think the rancheros had zippers," he said with a sardonic smile. He raised his eyebrows and then turned and spit onto the ground as if to make a point.

17

One of the rescue team members appeared at Giorgio's elbow. He was already fitted into a harness and a helmet.

"Wanna be the one to drop down there, Joe? I'd be happy to give up my spot. I know how much you like finding dead bodies."

The guy in the harness was Pete Colbert. He was in his late thirties and sported a goatee. He'd also been Giorgio's instructor when Giorgio participated in a search and rescue training class the year before.

Giorgio smiled. "Didn't you tell me once that I ought to stick to detecting?"

The man's lips separated into a grin, exposing a chipped front tooth. "Damn straight. That way you can stand around while we do all the tough stuff."

He winked and started to walk away. Giorgio stopped him.

"Hey, Pete, wait a minute. You got a camera? You'll need to record the area before you pull the body."

Colbert tapped a pocket in his cargo pants. "Right here. But you realize that if she's all bones, she isn't going to come up in one piece."

Giorgio shrugged. "Do the best you can. And get shots from all angles, including the position of the bones, if you can."

Colbert nodded. "I know the drill. I'll bag and tag everything."

Giorgio smiled. "You'd make a decent detective."

Colbert grinned this time. "Never!"

"Okay, but be careful down there. I'd hate to have to come save your sorry ass if you get into trouble," Giorgio quipped.

The man chuckled. "Right. I'll tell the guys to send *you* down in case there's an S.O.S."

He walked away, laughing.

Giorgio folded his arms across his chest, feeling his muscles flex. The slow pace of a small town had left him a little flabby, something he'd noticed when the Mallery Olsen case broke. So after that case closed, he'd started working out again. He could already feel the difference, making him wish he was the one strapping on the harness and dropping into the well instead.

A rescue team member approached the well and dropped a ventilation hose down. It was attached to a small orange fan that began to blow fresh air into the shaft.

"They worried about the air quality?" Giorgio asked the chief.

"We're worried about everything," he replied. "The well is about thirty-five feet deep. Pete will carry an air monitor with him, just in case. If the air changes, he'll let us know and we'll pull him up. We're not taking any chances."

A fireman had climbed into the big rig parked at the curb and fired up the engine. He backed it up about fifteen feet. A second fireman was at the rear of the ladder on a turntable, moving a lever. The ladder began to extend until the tip of it hovered just above the opening to the well.

When it stopped, he climbed out to the end of the ladder and attached a huge hook and pulley system for two ropes. Both ropes were then stretched back and looped through a second pulley anchored at the base of the ladder. One was equipped with a lifting bridle designed for small spaces.

Pete Colbert moved to the back of the truck and was securely attached to the first rope. He nodded to two firemen who handled the ropes back by the base of the ladder. One of them released the safety lock on the pulley, and they pulled back so that Pete's feet left the ground. A few seconds later, he was hanging over the center of the well. The two men controlling the rope began to lower him into the opening.

"Why the big rig?" Swan asked, nodding toward the fire truck.

"We want him going right down the middle so he doesn't hit the sides of the well," the chief said. "It's very unstable. That's why we're all standing back. We don't want any more pressure up close." He nodded toward the sheets of plywood that lined the perimeter of the well opening. "At least the demolition guys had enough sense to put down the plywood." He rolled his eyes again, and his moustache twitched in mock appreciation for their effort.

Swan nodded and they all waited patiently while Pete descended through the opening. It was only a minute or two before they heard the crackle of the radio.

"At bottom," he said.

The firemen stopped extending the rope.

"Give me a few minutes," he said, his voice breaking up.

As everyone waited above, there were intermittent bursts of light as Pete took pictures. When those stopped, Giorgio supposed he was beginning to unearth the remains. A couple of minutes went by. Then there were more bursts of light. Ten minutes later, Pete's voice could be heard asking for the litter.

Within seconds, the small boat-shaped device was lowered vertically through the opening of the well. As it slid past, a sudden breeze came up, blowing it sideways. It hit the edge of the well, dislodging a few bricks, which dropped into the depths.

Everyone paused and held their breath. A moment later the radio spurted.

"I'm okay," Pete said. "Keep it coming."

It was a good five minutes before Pete's voice finally sputtered on the radio again.

"Bring the litter up," he said.

When the litter reappeared, it was filled with a body bag. The cradle was raised all the way to the ladder, and then one of the firemen pulled it up and over, before releasing it to slide down to another waiting team member.

"God, these guys are good," Swan mumbled, watching them.

"Yeah," Giorgio agreed. "Just think if that had been a live kid down there."

It was another minute before Pete's yellow helmet appeared at the top of the well. His face and boots were dirty, but he was safe. By the time he was climbing down the ladder, the litter had been placed on the ground.

"Now it's your turn," the chief said to Giorgio. "We don't do dead things."

Giorgio snapped on a set of gloves and approached the small bundle. He and Swan crouched down and unzipped the body bag to find a bunch of bones with dry dirt still clinging to them. Bagged separately was a heavy, rusted zipper and two metal grommets with short strands of thick cotton thread attached to them.

The bones were completely bare; there were no strings of cartilage or swaths of skin left. The bagged skull sat off to one side in the cradle. Also separately bagged was what appeared to be the plastic toe box and spiked heel of a woman's shoe.

A few large patches of a faded deep green polyester fabric was stuck to what looked like rib bones. And at the bottom of the litter, were the bagged pieces of a rigid plastic hairband. One piece of the hairband still had a small plastic flower attached. Its original dark pink coloring had faded to white in most places. Next to it was the bag holding the heavy metal chain with its heart pendant. Alongside that was one dangly heart earring.

The Army shovel lay next to the remains, also bagged.

Giorgio picked up the skull and peered at it through the plastic bag, turning it over in his hands. A moment later, he waved in the technician from the coroner's office.

"Don't you want to see the rest of her?" Pete asked.

He had jumped off the fire truck and was standing at Giorgio's shoulder, pulling off the harness. Giorgio glanced up at him.

"Don't need to," Giorgio replied.

"Why not?"

Giorgio placed the skull back in the body bag.

"Because this just became a crime scene," he said with a sinking heart.

"You know it's a crime because she was put in a duffle bag?" the chief asked.

Giorgio turned to him.

"That and the big hole in the side of her head."

CHAPTER FOUR

That night, the storm that had threatened all day finally blew in. It rattled windowpanes and littered the lawn with leaves.

Giorgio lingered downstairs after Angie went to bed, watching the news and feeling unsettled about the skeleton found in the old well at St. Augustine's. The story was sensational enough that even the cable news stations carried segments on the recovery.

Mia Santana, the reporter who had dogged Giorgio all through the previous investigation, gave a rousing report of the day's activities, including interviews with Steve Nicely and a couple of the rescue team members. Nicely dramatized his shock when the body's skull first popped out of the ground, and then Ms. Santana described the broken headband and heart necklace. And, of course, the young reporter felt compelled to speculate as to whether the discovery had anything to do with the recent Mallery Olsen murder since it was found on the monastery grounds.

Giorgio watched the news accounts with varying degrees of unease. He knew that, logically, the cases couldn't be connected. After all, this skeleton had lain undetected in an abandoned well under a concrete patio for decades. Mallery Olsen had been killed in October.

And yet…he didn't believe in coincidences.

Giorgio turned off the TV and was just about to follow Angie upstairs, when the phone rang. He picked it up in the hallway and heard a familiar voice.

"Hey, they're gonna spring me tomorrow. Can you pick me up?"

It was Rocky, Giorgio's younger brother. He'd spent the last thirty days in an alcohol treatment center. Rocky had lost his fiancé to a brutal rape and murder in New York right after Giorgio moved to California. The loss had turned Rocky inside out. A year later, he'd followed Giorgio to the sunshine state, landing a job with the Monrovia Police Department, just south of Sierra Madre. But by that time, alcohol had already become his constant companion. Rocky hid it well, but his normal jovial attitude had become more nervous and on edge. Eventually, he started making mistakes, and the Monrovia PD put him on administrative leave.

While on leave, Rocky had helped Giorgio with the Mallery Olsen case, but had been shot in the process. Once the case was over and he'd recuperated, he'd been offered a job in Giorgio's department in Sierra Madre. It was the incentive he needed to check himself into rehab.

"Sure, what time?" Giorgio responded.

"Five o'clock is check out," Rocky said. "But it wouldn't kill me if you were a little early."

A rush of wind whistled past the house, making the windows and door shudder. Giorgio looked up to the front window as he answered, "I can do that. How about 4:30?"

"That's good. By the way, I saw the news. Helluva thing finding that skeleton at the monastery. There's no chance that it's…"

"No," Giorgio said, cutting him off. "It doesn't have anything to do with Mallery Olsen. All we found today was a bunch of very old bones."

"Still," Rocky said. "Weird. Can't have made you feel too comfortable driving back up there."

Giorgio was distracted by the wind for a moment, lost in the memory of the big storm that had practically swallowed up the monastery the night Olsen was killed. It was the same night he'd first seen the boy.

"You still there?" Rocky asked.

Giorgio flinched. "Yeah, sorry. It's really blowing outside."

"Yeah, here, too," Rocky said. "Anyway, I'll see you tomorrow."

"Yeah, see you tomorrow," Giorgio replied.

He hung up and glanced out the small window in the front door, watching the tops of the trees across the street whipping back and forth. He reached for the wall switch and turned off the light and began to climb the stairs.

He was only halfway up to the second floor, when a rolling gust of wind buffeted the house, forcing the front door open with a bang. He spun around just as a swirl of leaves and dirt blew in, along with something that clinked when it hit the floor.

He rushed back down the stairs and pushed the front door closed, making sure this time that it was latched and locked. Then he turned to study the mess on the floor.

A scattering of leaves and twigs covered the area right in front of him. And sitting right in the middle of it all, was a copper coin.

He bent down and picked it up.

The coin was larger than a penny and had been stamped with the image of a shoreline on one side and the words "Big Bear Lake" on the other. It was a souvenir of some kind.

A chill snaked its way down his back, and he turned back toward the front door.

On the night Mallery Olsen was found hanging by her bra strap in a supply closet at the monastery, a burst of wind had blown a metal button down the walkway outside the theater, just as he and Rocky were about to leave for the crime scene. The button had bounced off the curb and landed at Giorgio's feet. It had been stamped with a Latin cross. And that very same night, the large, wooden door at the monastery had blown open only moments before he'd seen the ghost of Christian Maynard for the first time.

"Shit!" he murmured.

He rushed to the front door and threw it open again, stepping onto the front steps.

Outside, the wind seemed to thrash the neighborhood. Trees bent to the wind. A garbage can lid came rolling down the street. And the corner streetlight flashed off and on as if it had a short.

The same thing had happened the night of the Olsen case.

He glanced up at the streetlight, thinking the night was alive with the storm. Again.

But there was no boy.

He riveted his head back and forth, looking up and down the street, but there was no one about. Anywhere.

Giorgio waited a full minute, his heart hammering in his chest. But the boy didn't materialize.

Still, he didn't believe in coincidences.

CHAPTER FIVE

With the discovery of the skeleton, Giorgio decided to go back to work early.

The next morning, he pulled around to the back of the Sierra Madre PD, where all the officers parked. The parking lot was populated with a small swarm of local press and TV news reporters. He spied Mia Santana standing near the back door of the building as he pulled into a parking space, her ever-present camera man lurking behind her.

As soon as Giorgio killed the engine and stepped from the car, a young man shoved a microphone in his face.

"Who's the woman in the well?" the man blurted.

Giorgio gently pushed the microphone away and sidestepped from in between the parked cars, giving himself time to think. While he had ignored pleas from the press for information during the Mallery Olsen investigation, this case was different. Whoever this woman was, she'd been dead a long time. Maybe the news reports would help.

He stopped and turned to the man who still had his microphone extended. "We don't know who the woman is yet. She's a Jane Doe at this point."

"So what steps will you take to find out who she is?" the man asked.

"The body has been sent to the county morgue," he replied. "They'll do the forensics work."

"Is there DNA evidence?" a female voice shouted above the rest.

Giorgio turned to find Mia Santana pushing ahead of the other reporters, her microphone aimed directly at Giorgio.

"We don't know yet," he said patiently. "The coroner will have to tell us. Now if you don't mind," he said, attempting to step past her.

"Detective," she persisted, blocking his path. "Does this have anything to do with the Mallery Olsen case?"

He stopped, glaring down at the petite brunette. "I don't see how it could. Excuse me."

He shouldered his way through the group of reporters and climbed the few steps to the back door of the police station.

The rear hallway passed two small interrogation rooms and opened up into the squad room. A fake Christmas tree and some fake garland had been draped across the reception counter to give an air of holiday cheer. A few people greeted him as he entered, and he acknowledged them with a nod. He turned left and hurried to the far end of the hallway, where he shared an office with Detective Swan.

"Damn!" he said to Swan when he walked into their office. "It's a feeding frenzy out there."

He threw his jacket over the back of his chair and went to the coffee pot that sat in the corner.

"Can't blame 'em," Swan said, moving a chess piece on the game board set up by the back window. Swan was always in the middle of a chess game with someone, and they communicated through the internet. "They want to know if it's connected to the Olsen case. After all, it's only been six weeks or so," he said, returning to his desk.

"I know," Giorgio replied, pouring a cup of coffee. "But it would be nice if just once they'd give us five minutes to do our job."

He sat behind his desk and came face to face with a stuffed Santa, secured to a metal base.

"What the heck is this?" he snarled.

Swan laughed. "Merry Christmas. I thought you might need some cheering up, especially since you had to come back early. Push the button."

Giorgio shot him a surly look and reached out to push a small button at the base of the stand. The doll began to wiggle its butt and sing *All I Want for Christmas Is My Two Front Teeth*.

Swan burst into laughter, while Giorgio grimaced.

"Gee, how can I ever thank you?" he said.

He flicked the button off and pushed the Santa to one side.

Swan was still chuckling and said in between laughs, "You know the captain is still looking for someone to play Santa at the kids' breakfast next week. You're the best actor we have in the department."

"I'm the *only* actor we have in the department,'" Giorgio said. "But I don't play department store Santas."

Giorgio sat on the board of the community theater group and was one of their leading actors. In fact, he was scheduled to play Teddy Roosevelt in the upcoming production of *Arsenic and Old Lace.*

Swan took a deep breath to keep his mirth in check. "Okay, so what's the order of the day?"

Giorgio took a swig of coffee and sighed.

"There isn't too much we can do until we get preliminary findings from the coroner's office. But we *can* search cold cases going back ten or twenty years. I think I'll also see if Drew can find out when that well was covered over at the monastery."

Drew McCready was their tech whiz and did most of their research.

They got to work while the press milled about outside. By noon most of the reporters had drifted away. At 3:30, a tall, good-looking man with dark hair interrupted them. He was wearing jeans, cowboy boots and a chambray shirt.

"Jeez, is this the famous crime-busting team of the Sierra Madre Police Department?"

Both Giorgio and Swan looked up. Swan laughed, and Giorgio rolled back in his chair and got up. He strode over and gave the man a half hug and a solid pat on the arm.

"Hey, little brother. I was just about to leave to pick you up."

The man smiled, exposing a perfect set of white teeth, his dark eyes dancing.

"I couldn't take it anymore. I decided to break out of that place and come get my paperwork done here."

"So you start tomorrow, Rocky?" Swan asked.

"Yeah, if the captain will let me."

"Hell," Swan said, rolling his eyes at the two of them. "Two Salvatoris working here at the same time. I might have to retire early."

"Don't worry," Rocky said. "I'm the easy-going brother. You'll *like* working with me."

He and Swan chuckled, while Giorgio grimaced and returned to his chair.

"Keep talking like that and I'll see you get assigned to patrol."

Rocky laughed half-heartedly and shook his head. "Right now patrol looks pretty good to me." He shoved his hands into the pockets of his jeans. "Besides, I guess I'm gonna have to prove myself, anyway."

The mood in the room darkened momentarily as an awkward pause hung in the air.

"Don't worry," Swan said, picking up the moment. "Your brother's bark is far worse than his bite." He got up and approached Rocky. "And most of the guys around here...they've got demons of their own."

He gave Rocky a reassuring pat on the arm and crossed out of the office into the hallway.

"How do you feel?" Giorgio asked, once Swan was out of earshot.

Rocky was over six feet tall with the kind of George Clooney good looks Giorgio could only dream about. They shared some family resemblance; Rocky took after their father, while Giorgio took after their mother. That meant Rocky was tall, with broad shoulders and a lanky physique, while Giorgio was three inches shorter and had a tendency to put on weight. According to his wife, Giorgio's best features were his dark, brooding eyes, which she said were all he needed to get her in the *mood*.

Rocky moved into the room and took the chair across the desk from his brother.

"I feel okay," he said, folding his hands into his lap. "They say you're never cured, so I'll always have to be careful, but I feel better than I did."

"That's good. We missed you."

"Yeah? Well, I missed Angie's fried chicken," he said.

Giorgio smiled. "I'll tell her. How about tomorrow night? Six o'clock?"

Rocky smiled. "Done. By the way, how's she doing?"

Giorgio paused and dropped his gaze to the desk for a moment, his fingers toying with a pen. "She's okay. We've had our moments, but getting the house ready for the state inspection for the day care center has helped a lot. It's not going to totally fix things, but you know Angie... Put a kid in her lap and she's happy."

"That's good," Rocky said. "I'm glad. So, any news on your find up at the monastery?" Rocky asked, changing the subject.

"No. We're still waiting on the coroner. All we can do right now is search old cold cases." Giorgio began clicking the end of a pen. "Your timing is perfect, though. Swan's dad died a few weeks ago, and he's scheduled to take some leave and help his mom clean out the house."

"Sounds good." Rocky stopped. "I mean, not that his dad died, but…"

Giorgio smiled. "I knew what you meant. It's not too soon for you though, is it? To get back on another murder case?"

Rocky glanced up at his brother.

"Sorry," Giorgio said, dropping his head. "That was stupid."

"No, it's okay, Joe. One of the things my therapist told me is that I have to talk about it…about Rebecca and what happened to her. Let's face it, the fact that her killer got away is one of the things that… drives me to drink. But I'll have to accept that the bastard may never be caught. It's the only way I'll heal."

Giorgio sat back and took a deep breath. "How the hell do you talk about something like that," he said quietly.

"I don't know. But I have to try," Rocky replied. "And you're going to have to listen."

The two brothers stared at each other. The moment drew out until Giorgio recognized the need for rescue.

"Okay, but not here. Not in this environment," he said, glancing around.

"I know," Rocky said with a wave of his hand. "Don't worry. I'm not about to bare my soul around here. But I *am* a cop. Just like you. And I want to find the son of a bitch that killed her. And then, if I'm lucky, I'll get to kill the mother fu…"

"Well, *that's* a wish I hope you get," Giorgio interrupted him. "C'mon, let's get you signed in." He stood up. "I'll walk you down to HR."

CHAPTER SIX

It was late morning the next day. Rocky was taking part in orientation, while Giorgio and Swan continued to search the databases. Officer McCready, the twenty-nine-year-old, red-headed techie, came into the office with the coroner's preliminary report and handed it to Giorgio.

"Looks like the bones found in the well belonged to a teenage girl," he said. "No more than sixteen or seventeen years old."

Giorgio skimmed the report, reading out loud for Swan's benefit.

"According to the M.E., she's been in the hole for some forty to fifty years. Her neck was broken, but probably from the fall. Most of the fingers were broken and a couple of ribs, but he thinks that happened when the demolition guy found her and stepped all over her." Giorgio stopped and rolled his eyes. "Anyway, he believes the most likely cause of death was the blow to the head. And, so far, the most reasonable culprit is the shovel." Giorgio sighed and put the report down. "But after all this time, there isn't enough of a blood trace on the shovel to get a DNA sample. Besides, DNA wasn't even used to help solve crimes until the early '90s."

"Which means CODIS wouldn't have anything in the database to match it against anyway," Swan said.

"Right. I suppose they can still get DNA from the bones, hair or teeth. But we still won't have anything to match it with," Giorgio mused. He leaned back in his chair and tapped the report. "But since she had her teeth, why don't you see if you can track down dentists from that time period?" he said to McCready. "Maybe we can match them to old dental records."

McCready grimaced. "That should be easy," he said as he left the office.

"What about the big zipper that was found with her?" Swan asked.

"The M.E. thinks she may have been encased in a canvas bag." Swans eyebrows arched.

"So, like a duffle bag?"

"Yeah," Giorgio replied. "Just like that."

By that afternoon, McCready had found that only two dentists had practiced in town back then; both had long since died. Several other dentists from the surrounding area were possibilities, but they had retired or moved away, making accessing dental records almost impossible.

Now that they had a more accurate time period, Giorgio and Swan started searching through old missing person's cases, branching out to surrounding cities. They had a couple of good possibilities, but couldn't pin down an ID without more information.

So, when a tall man in his early seventies appeared at the office doorway that afternoon and said, "I know who that girl is," Giorgio felt Providence had smiled on them.

Their visitor had a deeply lined face, pale blue eyes and a scar that ran across his chin. He carried a cardboard box in his hands.

"I'm Detective Salvatori," Giorgio said, standing up and gesturing to the chair at the side of his desk. "Why don't you sit down?"

The man came forward and placed the box on the corner of the desk. He shook Giorgio's hand and then lowered himself into the wooden arm chair. Swan came over and perched on the opposite end of Giorgio's desk.

"I'm Detective Swan," he said, offering his hand.

The man twisted around and grabbed it, gave it a good shake and then let it drop.

"My name is Cal Birmingham," he said. "Detective Cal Birmingham – retired," he emphasized at the last second.

Giorgio raised an eyebrow and gazed at the box. "I recognize your name. I've seen it on some of the old case files. Can we record you?"

"Sure," the older man said.

Giorgio nodded to Swan, who pulled out a little handheld recorder. Swan spoke briefly into the device, identifying the case number and who was participating in the interview. He placed it on the desk in front of Detective Birmingham.

"Tell us about it," Giorgio said to the detective.

"I was a young cop back then. Pretty new to the force. I'd only been here for a couple of years. It was May of 1967. Her name was Lisa Farmer, and she lived in a duplex up in the canyon with her mother…you know, Bailey Canyon. Anyway, she was a senior at Pasadena High School and had gone to the prom with her boyfriend, a guy named Ron Martinelli. After he dropped her off at home that night, no one ever saw her again. Until now, that is," he said, bringing his hands together in his lap.

"How do you know the bones we found are hers?" Giorgio asked, leaning forward.

"I saw that female reporter on TV interview the guy who found her. He mentioned the rose headband and the necklace."

Birmingham reached into his shirt pocket and pulled out his wallet. From an inside sleeve, he withdrew a faded, creased picture and handed it across the desk to Giorgio.

Giorgio took it and gazed down at the head shot of a young, dark-haired beauty with a broad smile. She was wearing a flowered headband and a heart necklace.

"Pretty girl," Giorgio mused, handing it over to Swan.

"Yes," the big man agreed. "She was. And from all accounts, she was really nice, too."

Birmingham leaned forward, removed the top of the cardboard box and pulled out a grainy 3x5 Polaroid picture of a boy wearing a tuxedo and the same girl dressed in a dark green dress. The boy was about to pin a corsage on her shoulder and grinned stupidly at the camera.

"Her mother took that picture just before they left for the prom that night. You can see the headband and the necklace again."

Giorgio studied the old photo. The colors had faded, but the flower on the headband definitely looked like what they'd found with the skeleton. The girl in the photo was wearing high heels, a dark green prom dress, and encircling her neck was a thick chain necklace with a silver heart pendant. Giorgio felt a faint rush of adrenalin at a possible identification.

"Can I get you a cup of coffee, Detective Birmingham?" Giorgio asked.

He shook his head. "No, thanks. I just need to relate what I know and let you do your work. I kept these records in my basement all these years and I thought you might need them. I'm not sure what you'll find in the department after forty plus years."

"Please, go ahead," Swan said, pulling up a chair opposite their guest.

The man took a deep sigh. He crossed one leg over the other, drawing attention to his well-worn jeans. A tuft of gray chest hair poked out of the collar of his blue denim shirt.

"As I said, I was pretty new to the force, but I was the only one here with a college degree – other than our captain. Back then, we didn't have any detectives. We were too small. When the girl went missing, it became a big deal. Her boyfriend was the son of our most prominent citizen – Royce Martinelli. He owned a lot of property around here. Actually, all over the basin. Office buildings. Apartment complexes. You name it. The captain wanted to treat this case with all the seriousness it deserved, so he assigned me to investigate. Even gave me a new title – Detective," he said with a smile. "Anyway, Martinelli's son, Ron, was a star athlete at Pasadena High."

He paused and shook his head slightly at an undisclosed memory.

"And let me guess, Lisa came from the other side of the tracks," Giorgio said.

"Right," he said, looking up solemnly. "As I said, she lived in a small duplex with her single mom. Not such a common thing back then. Divorce was pretty rare, and those who got divorced were often looked down on. But from what the mother said, Lisa had been sexually abused by her step-father when she was in her early teens, and when her mom discovered it, she kicked the bastard out."

"So the mother had been married before?" Giorgio asked.

"Yes. The first husband committed suicide. So the poor woman carried a double stigma."

"And the step-dad never went to jail for the abuse?" Swan asked.

Detective Birmingham glanced over at him. "Back then, those kinds of things were swept under the rug. No one wanted to talk about them. And it would have been the girl's word against his, anyway. But the mother suffered a lot of guilt about it, I guess. I think that's why she drank."

"So, Lisa didn't have much supervision?" Swan speculated.

"No. But I guess she was a good kid. She slept around a bit, but once she started dating Ron, I think that stopped. They were pretty serious — he told us he wanted to marry her."

"Did his father know that?" Giorgio asked the obvious question.

"Not about how serious they were. He allowed his son to date her, I think, because he thought the kid was just getting his rocks off, you know? So it didn't matter. The father told me at the time that if he'd known how serious the relationship was, he would have stopped it."

"Any chance he might have stopped it by making her disappear?" Swan interjected.

The old man leaned back, thinking. "I've wondered about that for over forty years. I just don't know. Back then, we didn't have a body. No one knew what happened to her. She just up and disappeared. Then, a few days after she went missing, there was a phone call; it was an anonymous tip to search all the student lockers at the high school."

He paused again and Giorgio glanced up at Swan.

"And?" Giorgio encouraged him to continue.

"We found her underwear and one of the shoes she'd worn to the prom in little Jimmy Finn's locker. Her left shoe. Jimmy was a year behind her in school and kind of slow. He lived next door to Lisa and was known to have a crush on her."

"What happened?" Giorgio asked.

"He was arrested. His family didn't have any money so they assigned a public defender. Some kid right out of law school." He paused, as if what he was about to say was difficult. "And, also, Jimmy was black. Even though things were changing between blacks and whites back then, the Civil Rights Act had just been passed a few years earlier. People hadn't learned tolerance, yet. And the fact that he was known to have had a crush on a white girl…well, people rushed to judgment. He was also retarded. Maybe not exactly retarded," he said with a shrug, "but certainly slow. And he couldn't explain how those things got in his locker."

"So, he went to prison?" Giorgio prodded him

"Yeah. Died there, too, from what I heard. Hung himself. Like I said… the kid didn't have a chance."

"So what happened to the boy…Ron?" Giorgio wanted to know

"The family moved to Pasadena less than a year after the girl disappeared. Too much publicity, they said. But if his dad was a bigwig here, he became an even *bigger* wig in Pasadena. I kept track of them for a while. They lived in a fancy home just off Colorado Boulevard. The father became President of the Tournament of Roses organization and sat on the board of PCC – Pasadena City College," he clarified. "I think he was even on the board of the museum. Anyway, the old man is gone now. He died of a heart attack several years back. The kid runs the company today with his cousin. I believe the mother is still alive, though. Boy, was she a piece of work." He shook his head at the memory. "Talk about the Ice Queen…it was all about appearances for her. That's all she cared about. The old man, too. They didn't care a whit about the missing girl. They only cared about how the investigation would make their family look." He glanced up at Giorgio with a sigh and stood up. "Well, that's the story. You'll find all my notes in the box. Plus, I'm sure the department has a file somewhere, if you can find it."

"Thanks for coming in," Giorgio said, standing as well. "But if you don't mind me asking, why did you carry her picture in your wallet all these years?"

The older man put a hand to his pocket where the picture had resided, as if touching the photo one last time.

"Because I wasn't much older than her, I guess. I was only twenty-six at the time she went missing, and I felt like I got to know her during the investigation. I interviewed her mother, the boyfriend, and lots of her friends. It became personal to me. But to the department and the city, it seemed more important to protect the Martinelli family than to figure out what happened to this beautiful girl. And in all the years I worked here, that was the only murder we didn't solve." He dropped his chin and gave a short, derisive laugh. "Well, let's face it…there weren't too many murders in this town. We had several runaways, but not many murders," he said, looking up again. "Of course, we didn't know for sure that this *was* murder, but we all suspected it. I held out hope that someday I'd see her walking down the street and that she'd had a chance to actually grow up and have a life. I guess that's why I kept the picture. Just in case."

He gave Giorgio a haunted look. This man had bonded with this girl, Giorgio thought, even though he'd never met her.

"Anyway, I put a slip of paper in there with my contact information in case you need anything else," he said, gesturing to the box.

Giorgio reached out and shook his hand. "Thanks."

The old detective started for the door, but Giorgio stopped him.

"Detective Birmingham, even though a jury convicted Jimmy Finn… I get the sense that you brought these records to us for another reason."

The old man stopped and stared into space for a moment. Then he glanced at Giorgio.

"Things are different now. Technology is better, and you guys are trained detectives. *And* you have a body."

"But it sounds like the case was closed years ago," Giorgio said, with a skeptical edge to his voice. "What do you expect us to do?"

"Find out what *really* happened."

CHAPTER SEVEN

"So, whaddya' think?" Swan asked after the retired detective had left.

Giorgio's adrenalin was pumping. The detective had presented them with a challenge. He reached into the box and eagerly pulled out file folders and loose sheets of paper.

"I say we do a little digging. They closed the case without ever having found the body. And according to Detective Birmingham's own account, it seemed like they conducted a cursory investigation leading to the arrest of a kid that couldn't defend himself. Maybe having the body changes things." Giorgio looked up at his partner. "Why don't you ask Drew to see what he can find out about the girl's mother? If she's alive and hasn't seen the news, then we owe it to her to let her know we think we've found her daughter. Maybe we can also get something of hers to match the DNA. We also need Ron Martinelli's address."

Swan nodded. "I'll go talk to him."

When Swan returned, they took the next hour to study Detective Birmingham's files. McCready provided an address for Lisa Farmer's mother and they headed out to meet her.

It was late afternoon by the time they made it to the rundown apartment building in Burbank, a city known to some as the "Media Capital of the World." Giorgio had never been to Burbank, and as they rolled down the streets, it was clear that while the city might be home to many of the major film studios, the city was more working class than Hollywood or Beverly Hills.

The two detectives entered Mrs. Farmer's apartment building on the ground floor and tracked down a long, dim hallway that smelled of cigarette smoke and urine. A small woman dragging an oxygen tank by her side answered the door when they knocked.

"Mrs. Farmer?" Giorgio asked.

"Yeah," she replied, stopping to cough.

"We're with the Sierra Madre police," he said, pulling his jacket aside to show the badge attached to his belt. "I'm Detective Salvatori, and this is Detective Swan. May we come in?"

Her gray eyes shot him a curious glance, and then she stepped back to allow them into a shabby living room. Giorgio's nose twitched at the odor of rancid cat food and dirty cat litter. A fat tabby glared at them from a cluttered kitchen counter. Scattered around the room were several ashtrays overflowing with cigarette butts. There was no Christmas tree and no holiday decorations.

Mrs. Farmer had not aged well. Her skin sagged and had the mottled look of a heavy drinker. She also breathed through two rubber tubes stuck into her nostrils.

She didn't offer them a seat, but rather remained standing in the middle of the room as if to challenge the reason for their visit.

"Mrs. Farmer," Giorgio began awkwardly, "we're here to discuss your daughter, Lisa."

She snorted and dropped into a nearby rocker, her baggy housecoat flopping open to reveal a pair of crimson polyester slacks. "What can you tell me that I don't already know?" she rasped, inhaling the oxygen as she spoke.

Giorgio chanced a glance at Swan. Swan took out a small pad of paper and a pencil to take notes.

"I take it you haven't been watching the news," Giorgio said.

She threw out a scrawny arm to gesture around the room. "Do you see a television here?" she said. "I ain't got money for no TV."

"I'm sorry to have to tell you this way," Giorgio said. "But we found a skeleton in an abandoned well, along with some things that may have belonged to your daughter."

She settled a vacant look in his direction, and it appeared as if she'd momentarily stopped breathing. Then the glisten of a tear formed in the corner of one eye.

"Where?"

"At the monastery in Sierra Madre. They were excavating the property after part of the building was torn down. There was no identification on the remains, but the bones are forty to fifty years old and we know it was a young girl. Detective Cal Birmingham came to see us and gave us the box of evidence from back in 1967."

"Detective Birmingham," she murmured to herself, glancing down at the floor. "He was a good man. He cared about my daughter." She looked up at them as if really noticing them for the first time. "I'm sorry. Please sit down."

She gestured to the lumpy sofa behind them. Swan sat down, perching as far forward on the frame as possible. Giorgio removed the baggie with the girl's necklace from his coat pocket and handed it to Mrs. Farmer before he also sat down.

"I was wondering if you can identify this necklace?" he asked.

She looked at the baggie for a long moment and held her breath. Then, she slowly drew it close to her face and began to weep.

"I gave this to Lisa the afternoon of the prom as a combination birthday-graduation present," she cried. "We didn't have much money. I worked at Kmart and they had these gift sets on sale. So I bought it for her. A necklace and a pair of earrings. She was so happy when I gave it to her. It's not real silver," she said with a look of apology, "but she didn't care. She said it was the best present she ever got."

A sob caught in her throat, and she began to cough again. Once the coughing subsided, she continued.

"Did you find the earrings?" she asked hopefully, her watery eyes searching his.

"Just one earring," Giorgio said.

"Oh," she murmured with disappointment. "Maybe she lost the other one," she almost whispered.

Or maybe the killer had pulled it off and saved it, Giorgio thought to himself. Giorgio and his partner had worked a case in New York where a serial killer had saved one piece of jewelry from each of his thirteen victims. It was one of the things that had helped convict him.

"I never really thought I'd see her again, you know," she said wistfully. "I guess I always knew she was dead, even though people kept telling me there was still hope."

"Mrs. Farmer, did you believe Jimmy Finn was capable of hurting your daughter?" Giorgio asked.

"No," she said, shaking her head, the loose folds under her neck flapping. "He adored her. And he liked Ron, too. That was her boyfriend. Jimmy was slow, you know? I mean, he could function okay, but it was like he just couldn't form his words too good. He wasn't a big kid, either. Lisa musta been a good two inches taller than him. She was almost five-foot seven. I always wondered how he coulda hurt her. But no one listened to me. Then when they convicted him, I didn't know what to think."

"What about her father?"

The question made her constrict as if she'd just had an angina pain in her chest. "Step-father, you mean," she said.

"Yes," Giorgio nodded.

"I don't know," she said tersely. "The police questioned him back then and said he had an alibi."

"Do you know if he's still alive?"

She shrugged her narrow shoulders. "I suppose. I haven't heard anything different."

"Do you know where he might be living?" Swan asked.

"I haven't seen him since he showed up twenty years after Lisa disappeared. I don't know why. He just showed up on my doorstep all of a sudden. He'd gotten remarried and said he owned a junk yard down in Whittier someplace. That's where he grew up." She took a deep breath to inhale the oxygen, sputtered a bit and then continued. "If you've read the file," she said, "then you know that he abused Lisa when she was thirteen. I didn't know it was happening until I noticed a change in her behavior. She was angry all the time and wouldn't talk to me. At first, I thought it was just the teen years, you know? Anyway, Butch worked the graveyard shift back then and was home during the day."

"So he was there when Lisa got home from school?" Giorgio asked.

She glanced at him with a deep-seated hatred in her eyes. "Yes."

Giorgio noticed that her hands had begun to shake, and she hooked her fingers together as if to keep them from getting away from her. After a moment, she released her right hand and found a tissue in the pocket of her housecoat and used it to wipe her eyes.

"I actually walked in on them one day," she said in a low voice. "I came home early from work because I wasn't feeling well and found them."

This time, a sob actually escaped her throat, and she had to stop again.

Giorgio allowed her to proceed at her own pace. He'd learned a long time ago not to push too hard in situations like this. People processed pain differently.

"I kicked him out," she finally said. "Back then, you didn't talk about things like sex abuse. That was private, family business," she said, twisting her mouth into a frown. "You just dealt with it yourself. There weren't organizations like there are today. People just suffered alone."

"And then Butch showed up not too long before she disappeared. Is that right?" Giorgio asked quietly, remembering a note in the file.

She nodded, using the tissue to wipe her nose. "Yes. It was only about a week before the prom. Her birthday was just a few weeks away. He showed up at the house just before she was supposed to go out with Ron. He said he had a present for her. But she didn't want it. She wouldn't even talk to him. I told him to get out. We all got into a big argument, shouting at each other. He called her a fucking whore and then stormed out the door."

"The file says that your ex-husband's alibi for the night of the prom was a buddy of his," Giorgio said. "Where was Butch living at the time?"

"In Whittier, I think. Like I said, he has family there."

"And the buddy corroborated his story?" Swan asked.

"I suppose. They said that on the night she went missing, they were at his house watching TV or something. I remember he used to like to watch *Bonanza*," she said with a shrug.

"Did you know this buddy of his?"

"No," she shook her head. "He was a high school friend of Butch's, I think."

"Mrs. Farmer, is there anything you can tell us about the night your daughter went missing that might be helpful?" Giorgio asked.

She dropped her hands to her lap, cradling the baggie with her daughter's necklace inside.

"No. I drank a lot back then. I'm sure they told you that. What Butch did to Lisa destroyed our family. Then there was my first husband…I felt so guilty for…for all of it. So when I came home from that thankless job, I would hit the sauce pretty hard, especially on nights when Lisa was gone. When she was home," she said, tears beginning to flow again, "she would take care of me. We'd talk until all hours of the night, dreaming about the day when she'd get married."

"So you didn't see or hear anything suspicious that night?"

"No," she said, disintegrating into tears again. "Maybe if I hadn't been drunk," she sobbed. "Maybe if I'd been a better mother."

"Mrs. Farmer," Swan interjected. "Take a moment and think. Sometimes people see or hear things that at the time don't seem that important. Were you aware of your surroundings at all that night?"

She took a deep breath, sucked up a sob and thought for a moment. Then she nodded.

"Yes. I told the police that I heard a car around midnight. We lived on a dead end street, so cars didn't come up there very often. You didn't come onto our street unless you were coming to see someone. I thought that maybe it was Lisa coming back from the prom. I was on the sofa and glanced out the window and saw a big, dark car, but then it was gone…and, well…when Lisa didn't come into the house, I heard a dog barking, but then I passed out again. But the police didn't believe me. One of them even asked if I was just dreaming."

"Nothing else?" Giorgio asked. "Anything out of the ordinary? Something that didn't seem monumental, but made you pause?"

"No," she said, tearing up again.

"What happened when you woke up the next day?" Swan asked. "What did you do?"

She glanced over at him, as if he'd asked a question no one had ever asked before.

"I…uh, woke up on the couch," she said, furrowing her brow. "Let's see. It was late – already ten o'clock, I think. I thought Lisa was still asleep, and so I decided to surprise her with breakfast. I made as much noise as I could, hoping to wake her up," she said, smiling briefly at the memory. And then the smile faded. "But she didn't get up. So I went out into the backyard to get the paper." She turned to Giorgio. "Our paperboy, Billy, always rode down the alley and threw the papers into the backyards because all the backyards had fences. He said it was safer."

"Why is that important?" Giorgio asked, watching her closely.

"Because our back gate was open." Her expression changed to a look of mild surprise. "We'd actually had a dog up until a few months before, and so we'd trained ourselves to always latch the gate so the dog wouldn't go after Billy. But the gate was open that morning."

"And no one ever asked you about that?" Swan asked.

"No," she said, shaking her head. "Once they knew I'd been drinking, they only asked me about Lisa, her friends, her habits –

things like that. No one seemed to care what I might have seen or heard."

"When Lisa was going to be out late like that," Swan continued, "would she have come into the house from the backyard?"

"Yeah," she replied. "She knew I often fell asleep in the front room, so she would come in through the back door so she wouldn't wake me."

Bells were going off in Giorgio's head. It appeared the girl might have made it home that night, but just not into the house. If she had, that might corroborate the boyfriend's story that he had dropped her off.

"Did you notice anything else about the backyard that might be helpful?" Giorgio asked, keeping his fingers crossed.

She dropped her chin and seemed to sink into herself as she thought. But then, she relaxed.

"No," she said. "Nothing."

"All right. Thank you, Mrs. Farmer," Giorgio said. He stood up and pulled out his card and handed it to her. "Please call me if you think of anything else."

She took the card and looked up at him gratefully. "Thank you for finding my little girl," she said with such a plaintive look that Giorgio felt his heart melt. "At least now, she can be buried properly."

Giorgio nodded. "I'll let you know when we can release her remains. We're just tying up loose ends."

He reached out a hand for the necklace, which she still held in her lap. She glanced up at him without relinquishing the jewelry.

"Detective, you haven't told me how she died."

He retracted his hand. "We don't know for sure yet. She may have fallen into the well...but it appears that she was hit on the head with something."

She nodded and reluctantly handed the envelope back. "I understand."

"Thank you," he said. "I'll see that you get it back when we're finished."

They moved towards the door, when Giorgio stopped and turned.

"By the way, is there any chance you might still have something that would have your daughter's DNA on it? Something personal like a hair brush?"

She had risen from her chair and stood hunched over, grasping the oxygen tank by her side.

"You're going to think I'm crazy," she said, turning. She shuffled to an old desk in the corner, opened a drawer and removed something.

"The night before Lisa disappeared," she said, coming back. "She'd been watching TV in the living room sucking on a lollipop." She held a white cloth in her hand. "I found the sucker the next night. It was stuck to the table next to the chair she always sat in." She glanced over to the window as if she were still in her old home. "I just stared at that lollipop for what seemed like hours, crying. Because I could see her, you know? Sitting in that chair, her knees pulled up to her chest, sucking on that stupid sucker. And I couldn't throw it away. I just couldn't." She turned back to Giorgio and held out her hand.

In it was a small white handkerchief. Inside the handkerchief was a cracked red sucker that had partially disintegrated, the sugar congealed into small globs around the edges. Giorgio reached for the handkerchief, but she didn't let go.

"Every time I've looked at that piece of candy over the last forty-some years, I've been able to picture her that night. Happy. Contented. Her whole life in front of her. And now you're going to take it away from me," she said in a wispy voice. "I'll never get it back."

Her anguish made his chest swell. He quickly coughed and said, "I promise…that I'll get the necklace and whatever else I can back to you. And I'm going to try and find out what really happened to your daughter."

She looked up at him with a question in her eyes. "Do you have children, Detective?"

He nodded. "Yes. Two," he said.

She stared at him for a long moment, as if to cement the promise he'd just made into his soul. Then she nodded and let go of the handkerchief.

"I believe you."

CHAPTER EIGHT

It was too late that afternoon to make an appointment with Ron Martinelli, so they called it a day and Giorgio headed home for the aforementioned fried chicken dinner with Rocky. After dinner, the brothers volunteered to take the kids shopping for a Christmas tree, so they all piled into the Salvatori Suburban and headed downtown.

They found a crowded tree lot run by the Boy Scouts in the parking lot of the community pool on Sierra Madre Boulevard. Stands of Noble Fir, Scotch Pine and Blue Spruce trees were laid out in rows, highlighted by strings of colored Christmas lights.

There were dozens of people browsing, and the kids scrambled out of the car as soon as Giorgio killed the engine.

"Hey!" he called after them. "Take Grosvenor with you."

Tony raced back to the car, opened the door and grabbed the dog's leash. A moment later, they had disappeared into the forest of trees, while Giorgio and Rocky sauntered behind.

"So what are you looking for?" Rocky asked as they approached the first line of trees.

"Tony wants a big tree," Giorgio replied, heading straight for the stand that sold hot apple cider and hot chocolate.

"A big tree?" Rocky chuckled. "Remember that year dad talked us into going out to that tree farm in upstate New York?"

Giorgio laughed. "Yeah, he found the biggest tree there and convinced mom that it would fit into our living room."

"God, I was only eight or something," Rocky said, following Giorgio to the refreshment stand. "I just remember that monstrosity of a tree looming over me in the dark. I couldn't even see the top of it. And mom kept saying, 'Robert, it's not going to fit. I'm telling you, it's not going to fit.'"

He imitated his mother's high-pitched voice, which got Giorgio laughing.

"It took him forty minutes just to cut the damn thing down," Giorgio said, chuckling.

"Right," Rocky cut in with a snort. "And then, of course, it didn't even fit onto the top of the car."

The brothers shared a moment of laughter as Giorgio ordered two hot chocolates. An attractive woman in her thirties walked past them, holding the hand of a little girl. She turned an appreciative eye towards Rocky as she passed.

"Poor dad," Giorgio murmured, paying for the drinks. "He had to cut off so much of that tree, that in the end it was just this fat bunch of pine needles in the corner of the living room, and mom..."

"Dad!" Tony called out in alarm, running up with his sister right behind. "Grosvenor tried to bite someone!"

Tony was having trouble catching his breath. Marie stopped behind him with her arms folded across her chest and tears in her eyes.

"There was this man," Tony rattled on.

Giorgio squatted down. "Slow down, Buddy. Tell me what happened," he said, glancing at the dog.

Grosvenor was panting, even though the night air was cold.

"A man started talking to us about the Christmas trees," Tony said breathlessly. "Then he squatted down, like you are now, and told Marie how pretty she was."

Giorgio looked over at Marie, who dropped her chin.

"Then what?" Giorgio said, his voice taking on a hard edge.

Tony glanced at his sister.

"He reached out and touched my chest," she said with a whine.

"He said, 'look at that, you'll be a woman soon,'" Tony reported. "And that's when Grosvenor lunged at him! He almost took the guy's hand off."

Giorgio immediately stood up and looked around, his adrenalin pumping.

"What'd this guy look like?"

"He was wearing a dark stocking cap," Tony said. "And had really dark eyes."

"Rocky," Giorgio snapped. "You take Tony. I'll take Marie."

His brother didn't need any additional instruction. Rocky grabbed the boy's hand, while Giorgio took Marie's. They tossed their hot chocolates into a nearby trash can and split up.

"Marie, tell me if you see him," Giorgio said.

They wove in and out of the tree lines, searching for the man in the stocking cap. They even searched the area in back, where the owner's RV was parked, but saw no one in a stocking cap.

Giorgio reported the incident to the two men who worked there. As he and Marie were returning to the refreshment stand, Giorgio noticed the tail lights of a car peeling out of the far end of the parking lot. He watched it disappear up the street, unable to see the license plate. But the car had a boxy shape and a spare tire attached to the rear. Maybe a jeep, Giorgio thought.

"Did you find him?" Rocky said, appearing to Giorgio's left.

"No," Giorgio said.

"Think we ought to report it?" Rocky asked quietly.

Giorgio looked down at the kids, who both had worried expressions. Marie was squeezing his hand so hard, it hurt.

"I think we'll call it a night," he said. "I'll file a report in the morning." He leaned down. "We'll get the tree this weekend, okay? Then mom can come, too."

Neither child objected. They seemed content to just go home.

On the way home, Giorgio praised the kids, telling them they had done exactly what they should have. Once they were inside the house, Tony and Marie went immediately to their bedrooms, while Giorgio reported the incident to Angie. She paused momentarily, tears appearing in the corner of her eyes.

"We'll talk later," she said. She ran upstairs to be with Marie.

"Hey," Rocky said, catching Giorgio's attention. "She'll be okay." He placed a reassuring hand on his brother's shoulder. "Marie is tough. And kudos to Grosvenor…again. That dog is proving to be the family hero."

Rocky was referring to a couple of instances in the Olsen case when Grosvenor had come to the rescue.

"Yeah," Giorgio said absent-mindedly.

"Listen, I'm going to go," Rocky said. "Call me if you need me."

"Yeah, thanks," Giorgio said, bringing his attention back to his brother. "I'll see you tomorrow."

Giorgio closed the big front door after his brother had left, his thoughts focused on one thing – the man in the stocking cap and how he would prevent it from ever happening again.

CHAPTER NINE

Giorgio woke with a jolt early the next morning. It was only 4:00 a.m., and he'd been ensnarled in a complicated dream in which a man in a stocking cap chased three young women down a long, winding road. Giorgio ran with the girls, until a tree branch slapped him across the face, making him flinch. His hand reached for his cheek, and then he tripped and fell, jolting him awake.

He lay in bed, his heart racing, the lingering sting of the tree branch on his right cheek. His fingers sought it out, but there was no welt, just the rough stubble of beard he'd have to shave in the morning.

He turned towards Angie. She lay with her back to him, sound asleep.

Now wide awake, he pulled back the covers and swung his legs out of bed. Grosvenor was comfortably curled up in a dog bed by the wall. He raised his head when Giorgio's feet touched the floor.

"C'mon, Boy," Giorgio whispered. "Let's go get a snack."

Giorgio slipped his feet into some moccasins and shuffled past the window. He glanced down into the yard. The light above the garage illuminated the driveway and part of the side yard, but all was quiet. Remnants of the dream had him searching for the girls, but of course, there was no one there.

And yet…he felt *something* had awakened him – something other than a bad dream.

He headed into the hallway with the dog at his heels.

They quietly descended the staircase and skirted the foot of the stairs. Prince Albert, the suit of armor he'd liberated from the local theater, stood against the wall, guarding the second floor. Giorgio patted the prince on his metal head and turned for the kitchen, when he stopped. He opened the drawer in the hall table and found the strange coin that had blown in the door the night the door had blown open. He went to the kitchen, clutching it in his fist.

He flipped on the light, squinting at the brightness.

He glanced around at the white tiled counters, black and white checkered floor and chrome appliances, thinking that standing here felt like having Angie's arms wrapped around him. Their kitchen was filled with memories of family dinners, family arguments, family games, and lots of laughter. It felt good, and the fog of the dream began to lift.

He dropped the coin on the red Formica table and went to the refrigerator to grab a package of roast turkey. He found a box of crackers in the cupboard, and a moment later, there were four meat and cracker sandwiches sitting on the counter.

Giorgio was about to pop one into his mouth when he glanced down at Grosvenor. The dog's soulful eyes pleaded with him, as a glob of drool slipped out the side of his long snout.

Giorgio laughed. "Okay, I did say *let's* go get a snack," he said.

He bent over and gave one of the cracker sandwiches to the dog. With one chomp, Grosvenor promptly swallowed it whole.

"Damn!" Giorgio said. "Did you even taste that?"

Giorgio straightened up and was about to take a bite of his own, when he happened to glance through the kitchen window above the sink.

His hand froze halfway to his mouth.

The kitchen window looked across the street to his neighbor's driveway. Standing under a tree, near the curb, was Christian Maynard, dressed as he always was, in dark knickers and long stockings, a white shirt and suspenders. It was the same attire he was wearing when he'd hung himself at the monastery several decades before.

The first time Giorgio had seen the boy, his image had appeared at the head of the stairs at the monastery. The image had disappeared so quickly, Giorgio thought it was his imagination. But after several more sightings, he had finally been forced to accept that not only was he seeing the ghost of this young boy, but the boy was trying to help him.

Once he'd come to terms with the apparition, he'd also tried to assist the boy. When he and Rocky had found the secret room in the bell tower, complete with shackles and an old mattress, the discovery confirmed rumors of abuse by the priests when that half of the building was a boys' school. It was enough to make Giorgio approach the new Bishop and suggest that the tower be torn down. Giorgio had assumed that as a result, Christian's spirit would go wherever dead people are supposed to go.

But here he was again.

Giorgio moved over to the sink, his heart racing. He stared at the boy's unearthly image as it hovered a few inches above the curb. The boy didn't move, watching Giorgio, as he always did.

"What are you doing up?"

Giorgio spun around and dropped the crackers and turkey onto the floor. Grosvenor lunged quickly to gobble them up, as Angie moved from the doorway into the kitchen. The drape of her sleeve whirled past the coin and swept it off the table onto the kitchen floor with a *ping*.

"What was that?" she said, leaning over to pick it up. "It looks like a souvenir of some kind."

Giorgio just stood there. He had no idea what to say. Clearly, Angie hadn't seen the boy's apparition. But now he might have to explain the coin.

"Um…" he stuttered. "I…um…"

Angie looked over at him, her brown eyes furrowed. She handed the little piece of metal over to him. "Is this something the kids picked up?"

She pulled her robe tighter around her slender waist and turned to the refrigerator. Giorgio stood there mute, staring at the coin in his hand.

As Angie grabbed a carton of milk and went to the cupboard for a mug, he mumbled, "No, I uh, found it on the lawn today. I just had it in my pocket."

He felt his nose growing at the lie, but what else could he say?

She turned while she poured herself a half cup of milk.

"You mean you had it in the pocket of your pajamas?" she said, nodding to his pants legs.

She put the cup of milk into the microwave and turned it on. He glanced down at his pajama bottoms. His pajamas didn't have pockets.

"No. My jacket. I just grabbed it on my way downstairs and laid it on the table," he said dumbly.

"Well, never mind. I was having trouble sleeping, too," she said, tapping her fingers while she waited for the milk. "I couldn't stop thinking about what happened tonight. I know we've taught the kids well, but…"

He recognized an opportunity to change the subject.

"We *have*, Angie," he said, stepping forward. "They did what they should have done. They stayed together. They had Grosvenor…"

She looked up at him, a worried expression marring her pretty features. "But they talked to him, Joe," she said. "They talked to that man. We've told them countless times not to do that."

He pulled out a chair and sat at the table, placing the coin on the table. It really did appear to be a souvenir, the kind you buy at any souvenir store in popular tourist sites.

"Giorgio," Angie said.

He snapped his head up. "What?"

She sighed and pulled her cup out of the microwave.

"I was saying," she emphasized, "that we need to have a talk with them. We need to stress the importance of not talking to strangers again."

He fingered the medallion, rolling it back and forth on the Formica table top. His focus was split between the situation with his children and the strange medallion in his hand.

"It sounds more like *he* talked to *them*," he replied. "I don't want to make them paranoid."

Her eyes suddenly blazed. "I think a little paranoia would be good right now, don't you? Someone touched our daughter tonight, Joe!"

"I know, Angie," he said, getting up and going to her. "I'm as upset about it as you are. Let's talk to them again, but let's couch it in terms of ways to stay safe. Situations to avoid. It was as much my fault as theirs, but I thought they'd be safe since they were together and had Grosvenor."

She seemed to relax against the counter. "Well, thank God Grosvenor was there. Okay. I agree. Maybe I'll even talk to Marie's teacher and see if she can address this sort of thing in class."

He kissed the top of her head. "We won't let anything happen to either one of our kids."

She smiled briefly. "I know. And now the house is going to be overrun with a bunch of new kids," she said with a brief smile. "Will you have time to finish up this weekend? I know how you get when you get on a new case."

"This is an *old* case; we just have to follow up some loose ends. I should have plenty of time this weekend."

She gazed at him for a moment, as if weighing the truth of his words.

"Okay," she said. "But I'm going to hold you to that. Don't stay down here too long." She brushed her lips against his and left with her mug of warm milk.

He waited until he heard her climb the stairs, and then he hurried back to the window.

Young Christian Maynard was gone. Giorgio craned his neck to look up and down the street, but the boy was nowhere to be seen. He glanced at the stamped medallion in his hand.

What the heck did it mean?

The metallic button that had skipped down the sidewalk the night Mallery Olsen died had had a Latin cross on it; it clearly represented the Catholic monastery where she'd been killed. When he had held the button that night, it had given him chills. He saw it as an omen, a sign. And in the end, it had been. This medallion was having the same effect on him, which meant that it must have something to do with Lisa Farmer's murder. But what?

He stared across the street at the now empty curb.

If Christian Maynard was back, he was sure to find out soon enough.

CHAPTER TEN

It was 4:00 a.m., and the man in the stocking cap had watched the home on Pendleton Drive until he was sure the inhabitant of the house was asleep. He knew the neighborhood and had cut through the backyard of the house next door to get where he was, the weapon tucked neatly in his pocket. He waited behind a bush at the side of the property, indulging in a string of cigarettes, his car parked around the corner.

It had already been a good night. He'd followed the detective to the Christmas tree lot earlier in the evening and approached the little girl just out of fun. He didn't think the detective would get anywhere close to the truth about Lisa Farmer, but why not distract the family just in case? Sometimes it was enough to throw a monkey wrench into everything. Besides, the little girl *was* very pretty. Maybe he'd revisit her in a few years.

He drew in a lungful of smoke and then exhaled. The early morning air was crisp, and the upscale neighborhood in Pasadena was sound asleep.

He knew the old guy who owned the house and knew that he suffered from a variety of ailments that forced him to rely on sleeping pills at night.

But he had a plan.

So, when the time was right, the man in the stocking cap took out his cell phone and dialed a number.

"Mrs. Simpson? This is Officer John Bundy," he said, when the housekeeper answered. "Your daughter has been in an accident. We just took her to Santa Monica Hospital."

He chuckled silently at the hysterics on the other end of the phone.

"Calm down, Ms. Simpson. We'll meet you at the hospital," he said and then hung up.

Less than five minutes later, the housekeeper came barreling out the front door, jumped into her car and took off up the street. The man in the stocking cap smiled.

The old man was alone now, and the house remained dark and still. The street was quiet.

The man's dark, piercing eyes followed the roofline of the big home. It was wired for security, as all the homes were in this neighborhood. But a phone call had given him the information he needed to disable the alarm system. Now, all he had to do was walk inside and get the job done.

He dropped his last cigarette to the ground and snuffed it out. Then he snuck down the long driveway to the back and carefully opened a side gate. Most of the backyard was patio and pool, so he quickly traversed the pool deck to a back door, leaving no footprints behind. He jimmied the lock on the kitchen door and slipped inside.

It was prudent to pause for a moment and listen, just in case. But there were no sounds except the ticking of a wall clock above the sink.

With his adrenalin flowing, he crossed through the large kitchen and crept into the stately dining room. Out the door into the foyer, he turned left and he was in the living room. The heavy front curtains were closed, so he felt comfortable turning on a flashlight.

With carefree abandon, he began pulling things off the shelves and out of drawers. Books, lamps and collectibles went crashing to the floor. He wanted it to look like a random break-in. Every few seconds, he'd stop and listen and then start up again.

After only a minute or two, he heard what he wanted to hear – the old man's voice.

"Who's there? Roberta? Is that you?"

The intruder pulled the gun from his pocket and attached the silencer, and then tucked it back into his jacket. He removed the stocking cap and stuffed it into his belt and then moved to the entrance of the living room and stepped into the foyer.

"Don't shoot, Alex. It's just me," he said, holding up his hands. He chuckled as if this was a casual visit.

The old man stood at the banister at the top of the stairs. He leaned over the railing, peering down into the darkened foyer.

"What are you doing here? Where's Roberta?"

The intruder moved to the foot of the stairs and began to climb to the second floor.

"She had to go to the hospital. Her daughter's been in an accident. I came to tell her." He kept climbing, coming closer and closer to the old man. "I can help you get back into bed."

"I don't need help," the old man snarled. "You need to go. I'll call the police."

"The police?" the intruder said with a laugh. "For heaven's sake, Alex. Let me help you back into bed."

"I said no!"

The old man started to turn for his bedroom. That's when the intruder skipped up the last few stairs.

"Wait, Alex. We need to talk."

The old man turned around as if to say something, but found the intruder's gun pointed at his chest.

"Wait. What are you doing?" the old man sputtered. "I wasn't going to say anything…"

The gun fired, hitting the octogenarian in the chest. He staggered backwards against the wall. He hung there for a brief second, his eyes opened wide. He slid to the floor, leaving a trail of blood to mar the floral wallpaper behind him. His body landed with a thud, and he remained there, slumped to one side, his eyes staring straight ahead.

The intruder stepped forward, but the old man didn't move. Two fingers at the carotid artery confirmed that he was dead, so the intruder stepped back.

"There you go, Alex. Better than a sleeping pill. Don't you think?"

A few minutes later, the intruder was back in his car, with a feeling of deep satisfaction.

Now if only the job in Seattle would go as well. He didn't have as much confidence in that one. But if the kid didn't screw up, they were safe once again to pursue the little hobby he'd come to depend on.

CHAPTER ELEVEN

The next day, a gaggle of local reporters milled about the police station parking lot again. Giorgio parked on a side street this time and was about to enter the building by a side door, when Mia Santana called out to him.

"Detective," she yelled, running down the sidewalk. "Do you have a minute?"

He turned away, intent on ignoring her, but then thought better of it; it would help to have the media on their side. He turned back and gave her a quick smile.

"Ms. Santana," he said. "What can I do for you?"

She stopped short, her expression cautious.

She was a petite brunette, with large brown eyes, a full mouth and long dark hair pulled into a loose pony tail. She had her microphone out, and her cameraman was poised and ready to shoot from behind her. Giorgio put up a hand.

"Sorry. Not on camera," he said.

She paused and then turned. "Turn it off, Randy," she said. She turned back to Giorgio. "Okay, do you know yet how the girl was killed?"

"Not for sure. I expect we'll get a full report today or tomorrow."

"Rumor has it that it's Lisa Farmer. Can you confirm that?"

He allowed his eyebrows to shoot up momentarily.

"Where did you hear that?"

"You're kidding, right? It's my job."

He rocked back on his heels a bit, thinking about how to answer.

"The DNA test will confirm whether it's Lisa Farmer."

"What about the flower and jewelry?" the young woman asked.

"That too," he nodded.

He avoided any mention of his conversation with Lisa's mother. No doubt the press would track her down before long, but there was no reason for him to destroy what little privacy she had left.

"Jimmy Finn was convicted of her murder years ago," Ms. Santana said. "Is there any reason to doubt his guilt after all these years?"

"I can't say. We're only following up on a few things left over from 1967. Due diligence and all of that," he said.

"Have you talked with Ron Martinelli?" she asked.

He smiled. "I have to go," he said. Without further comment, he turned and went inside.

He used the main hallway to cross from one side of the building to the other, passing through the small squad room to his office at the far end. When he entered, Swan was talking with Officer McCready.

"I was just telling Chuck that I looked into when that patio was laid up at the monastery," McCready said, as Giorgio took off his coat and threw it over a hook on the wall. "Believe it or not, it was back in 1967."

Giorgio's eyebrows arched. "Well, isn't *that* a coincidence?"

"Yep," McCready agreed.

McCready had a round face, a splash of freckles across his nose, and short, spikey red hair that made him look like he was in high school.

"When the monks and church elders decided to rent out parts of the monastery for things like weddings and conferences," he said, "they needed a place for people to sit during the spring and summer. So they had the patio built."

"Too bad that won't tell us when the girl was dumped into the well," Swan said.

"No," Giorgio said, "but it narrows the field, and it gives us one more reason to believe this really is Lisa Farmer, since she went missing in 1967. Did you find exactly when the concrete was laid?" Giorgio asked McCready.

The young cop shook his head. "No. All I found were building plans and the permits from March of that year."

"Well, we had luck with the architect that designed the monastery additions last time round," Giorgio said. "See if you can find whoever constructed the patio."

Giorgio was referring to Elvira Applebaum, who also ran the child care consortium that would help license Angie's new business.

Elvira's father had been the architect who had designed the addition to the monastery that would become the boys' school and then the conference center. It was Ms. Applebaum who gave Giorgio the key needed to unlock some important doors at the monastery during the investigation up there. Giorgio didn't hold out much hope that he'd be so lucky again, but then, you never knew.

"Listen, I have to make a report on something that happened last night," he said to Swan. "Rocky is doing his weapons retest, so how about you and I go see the boyfriend, young Ron Martinelli?"

"Who won't be so young anymore," Swan quipped.

"True," Giorgio agreed. "Let's go see middle-aged Ron Martinelli."

Giorgio filed a report on the incident at the Christmas tree lot, and then he and Swan left for the Martinelli Property Development Company. It was in a large, two-story building near the Tournament of Roses headquarters in Pasadena.

They entered a spacious lobby with huge plate-glass windows and a slate floor. A floor to ceiling fountain flanked by chrome and leather furniture took up one corner, and an enormous, fully decorated Christmas tree filled the center of the room. Giorgio lifted an eyebrow in Swan's direction at the opulence.

A young woman sat behind a rich cherry wood counter against the wall. Above her in brass letters, a sign read "Martinelli Property Development Company." Right next to that was "Martinelli Real Estate." She looked up with a smile.

"May I help you?"

"We'd like to see Mr. Martinelli. And no, we don't have an appointment," Giorgio said before she could get the words out. "We're here on official business."

He pulled out his shield. Her brown eyes lost their friendly luster and grew wary.

"Of course," she nodded. "But do you mean Mr. Ron Martinelli, or Mr. Fritz Martinelli?"

Giorgio paused. "Ron," he replied.

"Just a moment," she said.

She picked up the phone and told someone on the other end that the police were there to speak to Mr. Martinelli. She hung up.

"Miss Brinson will be down in a moment."

"Thank you," Giorgio said.

She wasn't joking. A few seconds later a woman in her thirties appeared at the head of the staircase. Giorgio made an assessment as he watched her descent. She was attractive in an efficient sort of way: Blond hair cut just above the ears. A tight-fitting black pant suit with a blue blouse. Pearls at her neckline and a pair of blue tortoise-shell glasses. The fact there were police in her lobby didn't seem to unsettle her. She held his gaze without ever once looking down, one slender hand sliding down the bannister as she came. Once she'd reached the bottom, she approached him with a warm smile.

"I'm Julie Brinson, Mr. Martinelli's assistant," she said, crisply. "He's just finishing up a meeting. Perhaps I can help you."

"I'm Detective Salvatori with the Sierra Madre Police Department. This is Detective Swan. I'm afraid that we really need to speak with Mr. Martinelli," Giorgio said. "We can wait."

Giorgio had been forced to investigate enough business owners and CEOs to have a strong distaste for sifting through the layers of protection they put in place to isolate themselves from the rest of the world.

"The Sierra Madre Police Department?" she said with a slight lift to her voice. "Perhaps I can tell him what this is in reference to." Her eyes shifted to Swan, and then back to Giorgio.

"You can tell him it's in reference to the murder of his high school sweetheart," Giorgio stated.

Her eyes betrayed her surprise, but just for a moment. Then the sense of business calm returned.

"I see," she said. "Please, follow me."

She turned and headed back to the stairs. They followed her to the second floor, watching the rhythmic swing of her slender hips as she climbed each step. There was no attempt to engage them in conversation. There was no need. They weren't clients. She let her hips do the talking.

They reached the top of the stairs and turned left down a carpeted hallway. They stepped through double doors that led to an expansive reception area, where another attractive young woman was just fielding a phone call.

"If you'll just wait here," Ms. Brinson said, "Patty will let you know when Mr. Martinelli is available."

Patty nodded, while she listened to the caller and made a note.

What was it with women? Giorgio wondered as he watched the receptionist. They could multi-task better than most men. Angie was like that. She could fry bacon, get the kid's lunch boxes ready, and kick Grosvenor away, all without batting an eye. He could barely tie his shoes, one shoe at a time.

As Ms. Brinson disappeared into the inner office, Giorgio and Swan took seats across from the reception desk and settled back to wait. They didn't have to wait long, however; notification of their visit brought Martinelli out very quickly.

The door opened and a man in his mid-sixties emerged, dressed in an expensive tan suit and green silk tie. He was approximately 5' 11" and his hair was cut extremely short, probably to balance the fact that his hairline had receded up to the middle of his scalp. His brown eyes were quick and attentive, and he retained a look of health and vigor, although his face showed lines of age.

He approached them with a tense expression. "I'm Ron Martinelli. Pam tells me you're here about Lisa. Please, let's go into my office," he said, gesturing with his left hand.

Giorgio noticed the heavy gold watch on his wrist. With a rigid turn, Martinelli led them into his office, where Ms. Brinson stood off to one side.

"We'd like to speak to you alone, if you don't mind," Giorgio said, eyeing the assistant.

Martinelli circled his desk to stand behind it. "You can speak freely in front of Ms. Brinson."

"I don't think so," Giorgio countered. "This is a police matter. We need to speak to you alone."

Martinelli started to object, but she put up a hand. "That's fine, Ron. I'll be in my office if you need me."

She left for her office through an adjoining door, and Martinelli offered the two men a seat.

"What's this about Lisa?" he said, sitting behind the desk. "Is there some new information about her disappearance?"

Giorgio glanced at Swan. "You haven't seen the news?"

"I just got back from Florida. What news?"

"We believe we've found her remains," Giorgio said.

Martinelli inhaled, his eyes growing wide. His fingers reached out for a pen lying on the desk. He picked it up and began rolling it between his fingers.

"Where?"

"Some landscapers found an old well on the property of the monastery up in Sierra Madre. At the bottom was the skeleton of a young girl. We found a faded pink flower headband and a heart necklace with the body."

Martinelli inhaled again and held it this time. His eyes glistened as tears threatened. He opened his eyes wide to control the onset and then dropped his chin. After a moment, he said, "My God, she was there all the time. So close. And we didn't even know it." He lifted his head and looked at Giorgio through wet lashes. "What happened? How did she die?"

Giorgio glanced at Swan again, allowing him to take over.

"It appears she may have been struck on the head. They found an old army shovel in the well with her."

At the mention of the army shovel, Giorgio noticed a quick flash of recognition in Martinelli's eyes, but then it was gone.

"Did you know anyone who owned an army shovel back then?" he asked.

Martinelli laughed a mirthless laugh as he opened a drawer and drew out a tissue.

"We all did," he said, wiping his eyes. "Well, any of us who were in the Boy Scouts. We used them for making camp."

"I see," Giorgio said. "Can you tell us what happened that night? We've read the case file. But we'd like to hear it from you."

Martinelli stared at them a moment and then got up and turned to look out the big picture window behind his desk. It looked out onto a canopy of trees and a stretch of green lawn.

"It was prom night...1967," he said as if the memory of that night had just reformed in his mind. "I picked Lisa up around six o'clock. I had borrowed my dad's car and took her to dinner at the Northwoods Inn in Pasadena," he smiled. "From there we went to the prom at the Huntington Sheraton." He turned back, his hands in his pockets, his nervousness abated now that he was walking down memory lane. "We left the dance around eleven o'clock and..." He stopped.

Giorgio had the distinct feeling he was contemplating something. To lie? To tell the truth?

"The temperature was mild that night, so we went to the park and...well, we had sex." Martinelli said with a shrug. "Then I took her home."

"What time did you drop her off?"

"Just before midnight."

"What happened the next day?" Giorgio asked.

"I went to church with my parents. I tried calling Lisa when we got home, but no one answered." He looked up at the detectives. "Her mother drank a lot, so I didn't think much about it. But by noon, she was calling our house wondering where Lisa was."

His throat seemed to close around the words, and he reached over and grabbed a bottle of water on his desk. He opened it and took a swig. A bead of sweat glistened at his brow.

"By Monday, her disappearance was all over school. Everyone was hammering me, wondering what I'd done to her," he said.

"They thought you'd harmed her?" Swan asked.

Martinelli sat behind his desk again.

"Not necessarily. A lot of my friends figured we'd gotten into a big fight, and she'd just run off. But we hadn't fought. The police department was pretty small back then, and they didn't even look into it until Monday night. By that time, it was clear that something had happened to her, and they opened an investigation. And of course, I was their primary suspect, and I didn't have anyone to corroborate my story."

Martinelli shrugged his broad shoulders again as if it was no big deal, but the tense muscles around his mouth said otherwise.

"What about Jimmy Finn?" Swan asked.

Martinelli's eyes seemed to shrink back into his head at the name. "Jimmy had a crush on Lisa. Everyone knew it. He lived next door to her in a duplex up near the canyon. She was always nice to him, but that's as far as it went. As far as I knew, he'd never done anything inappropriate towards her -- she would have told me. I mean back then, white girls didn't date black guys. Well, not many, anyway. So if he'd so much as suggested anything, Lisa would have said something."

"So you don't think he killed her?" Giorgio said.

"I don't know. I don't know why he would. But then I don't know why anyone would..." He dropped his head again and clasped his hands. "She was just a really nice girl, Detective. She may not have been from a wealthy family, but she was smart and funny, and she wanted to be a teacher." He paused and sighed deeply. "She would have made a great teacher," he said, almost to himself.

"How do you think her belongings got into Jimmy's locker?"

He glanced up, recognizing the edge to Giorgio's voice.

"I didn't put them there, if that's what you're thinking. I don't know how they got there, and I would never have hurt Lisa."

"How did Jimmy react when they found those things in his locker?" Swan inquired.

Martinelli thought back to that moment. "Two police officers came to the high school. We all went to PHS – Pasadena High School," he clarified. "It was at the first lunch break, and they started going through lockers. We didn't know why. We just saw the cops, so the kids all gathered around and watched. I remember Mr. Franken, the drama teacher, tried to get kids to break up and move on. We didn't know what they were looking for, though, so it was better than watching a John Wayne movie. At least, until they opened Jimmy's locker. They pulled out Lisa's shoe…and her underwear." He swallowed, as if his throat had tightened again. "And, my world kind of fell apart."

"Was Jimmy watching with everyone else?" Swan prodded him.

"Yeah. He just stared at the officers. He was kind of slow, you know. One of the guys on the football team pushed him forward, and he kept staring at the underwear without saying anything. The cop asked him if it was his locker, and he said yes. But when they asked him how the shoe and underwear got there, he just kept shaking his head and saying, 'no, no, no.'"

"What did you do?" Swan asked.

He sighed with remorse. "I lunged for him. I was pissed. I actually caught him by the shoulder and wrestled him to the ground. The cops had to pull me off."

"So you thought he did it?" Giorgio asked.

"At the time I did. I mean, there was that evidence."

"But not now?"

"Like I said, I don't know. It just didn't seem like him. But he got convicted, and then I heard Jimmy died in prison. So maybe we'll never know."

"What about Lisa's step-father? Did you ever meet him?"

"No. Lisa never talked about him. I didn't even know about the …you know, what he did to her, until the investigation. She was a very private person."

"Is there anything else you can tell us?" Giorgio asked. "Kids who didn't like her? Other boys who might have bothered her? Girls who maybe were jealous of her relationship with you?"

He just shook his head. "No. I admit that I was probably a good catch back then. I was on the football team, and my dad was obviously wealthy. But kids were pretty cool about our relationship. And Lisa was well-liked. She was even on the drill team. That was a pretty elite group of girls."

"Elite?" Swan asked.

"Yeah. The drill team was very competitive, and all the girls wanted to be on it. Lisa loved wearing that stupid red and white uniform," he said, his face relaxing into a smile. "But she didn't have the money to buy it, so I paid for it." He looked uncomfortable for a moment. "I never told my parents, though."

"Did your parents approve of your relationship?" Giorgio asked.

Ron Martinelli grimaced. "No. They tolerated it. My mother, just barely."

"And they were both home the night she disappeared?" he asked.

Martinelli stiffened at the question. "Mother was, yes. My father was out of town."

Giorgio perked up. "But you just said you went to church the next day with your parents – plural."

"Yes…um…we did," he stuttered. "My father came home late that night. He wasn't supposed to be home for several more days, but…uh, he was there when I got home."

Giorgio regarded him quietly and then stood up. "Well, if you think of anything else, please let us know."

He handed over his card and moved to the door. Martinelli followed, stepped in front of him and opened the door.

"So, you're opening a new investigation?" Martinelli asked. "You don't think Jimmy did it?"

"I think Lisa Farmer deserved a better investigation," Giorgio said.

As they stepped into the reception area, another man was standing at the front desk. He was taller than Ron Martinelli, and had dark, heavy features. Ron saw him, paused, and then moved forward.

"Detectives, this is my cousin, Fritz Martinelli. He runs the real estate half of the business."

The other man was dressed in crisp slacks and a polo shirt. A gold chain glittered around his neck. He was about the same age as Ron, tan and physically fit. He regarded the two police officers with caution.

"Police? What's going on?" he asked.

"They think they've found Lisa's body," Ron said. "After all these years. Up at the monastery."

Fritz Martinelli's thick eyebrows lifted in mild surprise. "Really? Well, we all *thought* she was dead," he said unsympathetically. "Took a long time to find her, though."

"Yes," Giorgio said, thinking this guy could use some sensitivity training. He glanced at Ron. "We'll be in touch."

CHAPTER TWELVE

Giorgio and Swan returned to their car, and Giorgio pulled out his cell phone to call McCready.

"Hey, I need the current address for Ron Martinelli's mother," he said.

He waited while McCready found what he was looking for. A moment later, the young cop came back on the line with the information.

"By the way, I found the company that did the construction up at the monastery back in 1967," McCready said. "They're still in business over in Monrovia."

"What's the name?

"Aladdin Construction."

"Okay, why don't you head over there and talk to them. Find out if they still have records from when the patio was constructed and if anyone knew about the well. Also, we need to know if Lisa Farmer's step-father is still alive. And see if the duplex the Farmers lived in still exists."

"Will do," McCready said.

When Giorgio hung up, Swan glanced at him. "Where to now?"

"Let's go see the Ice Queen," he said with a smirk.

Claire Martinelli still lived in her big Craftsman-style home in Pasadena, off Colorado Boulevard. The home was set back from the road, with sweeping lawns and a long, circular drive that ended in a large parking area in front of the veranda. The property was protected by a walled perimeter and heavy iron gates.

They had called in advance and were buzzed in when they announced themselves at the gate. A young Latino woman wearing a crisp uniform met them at the front door and showed them into a swank living room, with a big picture window overlooking the front gardens. A tastefully decorated Christmas tree stood in one corner, while a grand piano stood in the other. The piano was accented with green garland, red bows and a display of family photos.

Giorgio took a moment to survey the photos. He ID'd younger versions of both Ron and Fritz Martinelli, and two older men who looked enough alike to be brothers. One was probably Royce Martinelli, and the other was his brother, Fritz Martinelli's father. According to the file, his name was Edmond.

"Detectives," a strong voice said behind them.

They turned to find a woman in her eighties sitting in a motorized wheelchair. Wheelchairs often diminished an individual's presence, but not so with Claire Martinelli. She appeared to be a tall woman and sat straight as a rod. Her gray hair was pulled back from an angular face, exposing high cheekbones and sharp brown eyes. She was dressed in an expensive gray pants suit, with a silk blouse and a string of heavy pearls at her neckline. Large pearl and diamond earrings graced her earlobes. There was nothing frail about this woman, other than her inability to walk. There was nothing casual about her, either. This was a woman who still commanded attention and wanted them to know it.

"Please," she said, gesturing toward the sofa. "Sit down. I'll have Rita bring us something to drink."

She turned to the girl who hovered in the background and flicked her wrist. The girl disappeared down the hallway.

Claire Martinelli pressed a button on the arm of her chair and wheeled into the room. Giorgio and Swan sat at opposite ends of a pristine Queen Anne sofa.

"I understand you're here to ask some questions about Lisa Farmer. I heard on the news that someone finally found her body after all these years. I'm afraid I won't have much to say. As I told the police back in 1967, I was asleep the night she went missing."

"Yes, Ma'am," Giorgio began. "But we'd like to hear it for ourselves."

Her eyebrows arched. "I think you just did."

Giorgio paused. Claire Martinelli was clearly used to controlling her environment, and he had just invaded her space. She didn't like it. He would have to tread lightly.

"Let me be more clear," he said with an apologetic nod. "Can you tell us what you did earlier that night?"

"I thought the man who was responsible was put in jail years ago. Why are you bothering to ask questions now?" she retorted.

"From what we can tell, there wasn't much of a case against him. No direct evidence."

She laughed derisively, her upper lip curling. "I beg to differ. They found her underwear in his locker. What do you call that?"

"That's circumstantial evidence. Someone else could have found a way to put those things in there."

"Oh for heaven's sake, why would anyone do that?"

Rita interrupted them by returning with a tray of glasses, ice and a pitcher of lemonade. She set it down on the coffee table and quickly poured a glass for her employer. Mrs. Martinelli took it and then flicked her fingers again. Rita poured glasses for her guests. When the girl was finished, she quietly left the room.

Swan picked up his glass and took a drink, while Giorgio continued.

"Mrs. Martinelli, just a moment ago you said they had arrested the *man* who was responsible for Lisa Farmer's disappearance."

She flinched. "Did I? Well, he'd be a man by now, wouldn't he?"

"Actually, we understand that Jimmy Finn is dead," Giorgio said. "He died in prison."

She paused again, as if she hadn't known that. She recovered quickly.

"So much the better," she said, with a flip of her head. "I've always thought we spend far too much money on our prison system."

Giorgio wasn't sure if her callous attitude was real or manufactured. But he was more curious about what it was meant to convey.

"If you could just tell us what you did the night Lisa Farmer disappeared," he said, knowing that he was pushing her.

She took a sip of lemonade and placed the glass on a coaster on a side table. "I hardly remember every detail about a single night over forty years ago, Detective."

"I understand. But please, if you would, try. We know your son left around six o'clock to pick Lisa up for the prom. Did you see him leave that night?"

"Of course. I took some pictures of him dressed up in his tuxedo."

"Do you still have one of those photos?"

She lifted her eyes to meet his. "Yes, I believe I have one in one of our photo books."

She reached over and grasped a small bell and rang it. Rita appeared so quickly, it was as if she had been waiting down the hall. Mrs. Martinelli asked her to find the big green photo album in the family room.

"Did you approve of Lisa, Mrs. Martinelli?" Giorgio asked after the girl had left.

Her eyes flashed momentarily. "Neither my husband nor I approved of his dating that girl. She was from up in the canyon, and her mother was a drunk. But Royce said Ron was just sowing wild oats, and so we allowed it."

"Had you ever met Lisa?"

"No. Of course not. My son wasn't allowed to bring her to the house. What would our neighbors have thought?"

"You lived in what's known as the Pinney House back then, is that right? On Lima Street?"

"Yes. It was a beautiful old Victorian. I believe it's a bed and breakfast now."

Rita returned with a large, faded photo album and handed it to her mistress. Mrs. Martinelli flipped open the pages until she came to the page she wanted. She extracted an old color photo of her son and held it out for Giorgio. The picture showed a young Ron Martinelli standing in the hallway in front of a room with a desk and a tall bookcase in the background. Giorgio studied the photo for a moment and then handed it to Swan.

"May we hold onto this temporarily? I'll see that you get it back."

"If you must," she said, stiffly.

"So, Ron left to go pick up Lisa. What did you do that evening?" he continued.

"My husband was out of town. As I recall, I had dinner and watched some TV. I was getting ready for bed when Ron came home," she said, placing the photo album on the side table.

"So you *did* hear him come in?"

Those blue eyes darted away, and she busied herself reaching for her lemonade again. She took a drink before continuing. Giorgio loved watching people attempt to cover their lies.

"I'm not sure whether I heard him come in," she said with hesitation. "I think perhaps that I was already *in* bed."

"The police report says that you originally said you were sound asleep by ten o'clock. Ron says he didn't get home until after midnight."

"I misspoke just now, Detective," she snapped. "After all, it's been over forty years. You can't expect me to remember every little detail."

She lifted her chin as if to emphasize her point.

"I'm not accusing you of anything. Your husband also came home unexpectedly that night, is that right?"

Her expression tightened. "Yes. Why is that important?"

"Where had he been?" he pressed her.

Her demeanor became guarded. "Why does it matter?"

"It might not," he said. "But it's good to have all the information."

She waited a moment, and then said, "He'd been on a ten-day fishing trip. But I think he said the fish weren't biting."

"I see. And so what did you do the next day?"

She took a deep breath, as if it took every ounce of her patience to put up with this intrusion.

"We went to early church service and then went out to breakfast."

"Did Ron mention anything about the night before?"

She was clasping her hands in her lap, and he noticed the long, strong fingers of her left hand, along with her expensive wedding band set.

"I believe I asked him if he had had a good time," she said.

"And?" Giorgio prodded her.

"He said yes."

"Did he say what they did after the dance?"

"I beg your pardon," she snapped, her eyebrows lifting.

Giorgio realized she thought he was referring to any intimacy between the couple, but he kept quiet to let things fall where they may. She seemed to make a decision.

"Ron didn't discuss his girlfriends with us," she said.

"Where were you when you heard about her disappearance?"

"Oh, for heaven's sake," she exclaimed, throwing a hand out to the side. "How should I remember that?"

"Was it Ron who told you that she'd gone missing, or your husband? Or perhaps you didn't know until the police showed up on your doorstep."

He imagined that the police had never showed up on their doorstep. Most likely Sierra Madre's most influential couple had been *invited* to come down to the station.

"Really, Detective. This all seems superfluous. After all, this case was closed decades ago. You're just wasting your time – and mine," she said with emphasis.

"Mrs. Martinelli, your son was the primary suspect for a time. By his own account, he didn't have anyone to back up his story that he dropped Lisa off at home."

She stiffened. "His *story*? My son had nothing to do with her death," she almost spit. "Don't you dare try to sully his name."

"I have no such intention," he replied calmly. "But I need to know what you know. Was there anything about his behavior that raised your suspicions? Did he say or do anything out of the ordinary?"

"No," she said with a raised voice. "I told you. My son didn't do anything wrong."

"What about his friends? Had any of them ever dated Lisa? Would they have been jealous of Ron?"

"Everyone was jealous of Ron," she spat. "The kids in his class. The rest of the football team. Even the girls. But he never saw it. He coddled his friends. Thought they all had his best interests at heart. But they didn't. Especially that Joshua Springer, who tried to get him expelled."

"Expelled? What for?"

Giorgio's interested was piqued. The Ice Queen was wound up. All Giorgio had to do was let her go.

"Joshua Springer was the second string quarterback. He barely got to play during his junior year and desperately wanted Ron's position. So he talked a friend into getting Ron to give him some answers on a test at the beginning of the senior year. And then someone told the teacher and Ron was called into the principal's office and suspended for three days."

"How do you know Ron was set up?" Swan asked.

"Because Joshua's girlfriend eventually told him that it was Joshua that set him up and then snitched on him. Fortunately, the school couldn't afford to lose Ron on the team, so he was allowed to play."

"Do you know if the police ever talked with this Joshua Springer?" Swan asked.

She snorted. "I have no idea. They arrested Jimmy Finn and things quieted down. That's all I cared about," she said. "It's time to let that girl rest in peace, Detective." She pushed a button and began to back the wheelchair towards the hallway. "Now, if you'll excuse me…"

Giorgio glanced over at Swan and they both stood up.

"Do you happen to know if Joshua Springer still lives in the area?" Giorgio asked.

"Last I heard he drank himself to death," she spat. "Good riddance, I say. But his horrid father is still around."

"Why do you say that?" Giorgio asked.

She turned back to him, her eyes ablaze. "As far as I'm concerned, his father was the mastermind behind that incident with the test. Joshua wasn't smart enough to think up anything on his own. Alex Springer ran against my husband for the school board when we lived in Sierra Madre and said some of the most hateful things. But despite the lies, Royce won. I just couldn't believe it when Royce hired him a month or so later."

"To do what?" Giorgio asked.

She exhaled in exasperation. "Royce hired him to manage all of our apartment buildings. I couldn't believe it, but Royce said he was a brilliant manager, and if anyone could turn that part of the company around, Alex could."

"And did he?" Giorgio asked.

She paused, considering her response. "Yes. He made us a lot of money. But I swear, if that young Negro boy didn't kill Lisa Farmer, I'd bet my diamond bracelet that Alex Springer was the one who did."

"Why do you think Alex Springer would want to kill your son's girlfriend?" Swan asked.

She shot Swan a look that was meant to belittle his intelligence.

"To embarrass Royce, of course."

CHAPTER THIRTEEN

Giorgio called McCready again and got the address for Alex Springer. He programmed it into his GPS, and they made their way to East Walnut Drive in Pasadena and turned south towards the Museum of California Art.

As they entered Springer's neighborhood, they rolled down streets lined with large oak trees and big, stately homes set back from the road. Most had wide, sweeping lawns; some even had security gates.

They turned a corner onto Pendleton Drive, counting down the house numbers, until they were stopped by a police cruiser and an officer in uniform. Alex Springer's home was the next house on their left.

Giorgio rolled down the window and showed the officer his badge. The officer arched his eyebrows.

"What's the Sierra Madre PD here for?" he asked.

"We're here to talk to the gentleman who lives at 1818 Pendleton Drive."

The officer stuck his thumbs into his belt. "Don't think you'll be talking to him," he said, rocking back on his heels. "He was dead when we got here."

Giorgio threw a quick glance at Swan. "What happened?"

"Looks like a home invasion," the officer replied matter-of-factly, glancing back up the street.

"That's 1818 right there."

He pointed to a big colonial-style home with white pillars holding up the front portico. An ambulance was just pulling out of the driveway and drew alongside Giorgio's car. The officer waved it by and Giorgio's eyes tracked the red and white van as it turned the corner and left.

"The old guy that lived there was shot in the chest," the cop said.

Giorgio glanced at Swan and back again. "I need to speak to the officer in charge."

"Okay. Pull up over there," he said, gesturing to his left. "And then ask for Lieutenant Pearson."

Pendleton Drive curved out of sight under a canopy of trees about 100 yards away. Giorgio pulled up in front of a red brick house across the street from Springer's home. Three women stood in front of the house, arms crossed, watching the activity with grim faces. A young boy stood at the curb.

Giorgio got out of the car, noticing the women and the little boy.

"I doubt they've ever seen anything like this in *this* neighborhood," Swan said cynically.

"No," Giorgio agreed. "My guess is that there will probably be a run on updated security systems after this."

Three police cars were parked in Springer's driveway, along with the coroner's van. He and Swan strode up the driveway as the ME and his assistant were climbing into their vehicle. The two Sierra Madre officers climbed the porch steps, but were stopped at the front door by a burly officer in uniform.

Giorgio asked to speak to Lieutenant Pearson. A few minutes later, a thirty-ish woman with a decent figure and short, brown hair came out and shook his hand. She was dressed in a dark pantsuit and thick, rubber-heeled shoes. She wore her badge on a lanyard around her neck.

"I'm Lieutenant Pearson. I'm a bit busy here. What can I do for the Sierra Madre PD?" she said in a husky voice.

"We were coming to interview Mr. Springer," Giorgio said to her. "It has to do with an old case we're working on."

She regarded Giorgio a moment and then said, "The body found up at that monastery?" When Giorgio nodded, she said, "I saw it on the news. Okay, let's step over here." She moved to one side to allow another officer to move past them. "Well, I doubt this guy was your perp for that one," she said. "He was in his mid-eighties and walked with a cane."

"The body we found is over forty years old," Giorgio said. "So Springer *could* have been the perp back then. But we were just looking for some information from him."

"Well, this looks premeditated," she said, nodding toward the house. "Someone called his housekeeper early this morning, telling her that her daughter had been in an accident and was all the way over at Santa Monica Hospital. Of course, she took off, leaving Mr. Springer alone. Whoever this was broke in through the kitchen door."

"What about an alarm system?" Giorgio asked, glancing around. "These are all pretty expensive homes."

She nodded. "The line at the back of the house was cut."

She had her hands on her hips and seemed to be considering something. Finally, she said, "Let's get you checked in and I'll take you inside."

Giorgio and Swan put on the blue paper booties they found in a box at the front door, checked in with the duty officer and then followed Detective Pearson into the foyer of the home. A large chandelier hung from a vaulted ceiling and a big staircase curved up to the second floor along the left wall. To their right was the living room, where two forensics people were dusting for prints. The floor was littered with broken glass, books and random papers.

"Up here," Pearson said.

She led them up the stairs to where a streak of blood ran down the wall just to the left of a bedroom door.

"He was found here, slumped against the wall," she said, pointing to the spot where Springer had died.

Giorgio glanced around. "Weird," he mumbled. "If he'd been shot from downstairs," he said looking over the railing, "he would have either just crumbled or maybe fallen backwards onto the floor. But this looks like he fell back against the wall."

"You're thinking his killer came up here," she said. "Me, too. He had gun powder residue on his pajama top."

"Which meant he was shot at close range," Swan said.

"Right," she said, glancing at him. "Springer must have heard the commotion downstairs and come out onto the landing," she speculated, pointing to the railing.

"But why was the thief up here?" Giorgio said, looking around.

She shrugged. "Well, either he was looking for something downstairs and didn't find it," Pearson began.

"Or he knew Springer and purposely came upstairs to kill him," Giorgio finished her thought.

"But then why trash the living room?" Swan asked.

"Maybe to make it look like a break-in," she said.

"Was anything stolen?" Giorgio inquired.

"All the big electronics are still there," she said. "We don't know, yet, whether anything else is missing. The housekeeper found him when she came back from the hospital and is pretty upset. We'll get her to ID anything that might have been taken."

"What about the rest of the rooms?" Swan asked. "Anything else disturbed?"

She shifted her eyes to him. "No. It looks like the killer came in through the kitchen and went directly to the living room. Then killed Springer and left. The ME thinks he's been dead about six to seven hours."

Giorgio stuffed his hands into the pockets of his jacket. "Convenient," he muttered.

"You think this has something to do with your case?" the Lieutenant asked, her eyebrows curling into a question.

"What happened to the housekeeper's daughter?" Giorgio asked.

Pearson shrugged. "It was a ruse. Someone clearly wanted her out of the house."

"Then this wasn't just convenient," Giorgio said. "It was planned. It seems someone went to great lengths to make sure Springer was alone. I doubt it was just a thief."

The Lieutenant stared at him a moment and then said, "Did anyone know he was on your radar?"

"No," Giorgio shook his head. "We just found out about him today. But he was well known to one of the families involved in our case. And as you just said, the case has been all over the news. Did any of the neighbors hear anything?"

"We haven't canvassed every house yet," Lieutenant Pearson said. "But so far the neighbors close by say they heard nothing." She stood in thought for a moment and then straightened up. "I'll be sure to keep you in the loop, Detectives. And I hope that if you find out anything that would be material to this investigation, you'll give me a call."

"Absolutely," Giorgio said, producing his card. "Thanks."

"Lieutenant!" a voice called from below.

A young man dressed in a dark suit and tie skipped up the stairs. "We found these under a tree in the side yard."

He held out a gloved hand, in which he held three cigarette butts, each bagged separately. The lieutenant leaned over, opened one of the bags and sniffed the contents.

"Smells pretty fresh," she said. "Get them to forensics."

She turned to Giorgio. "Looks like someone might have been waiting outside. If so, we'll get some DNA. I'll be in touch," she said and the three of them returned to the foyer.

Giorgio and Swan returned to the car and slid inside.

"Well, that certainly changes things," Swan said.

"Sure seems to," Giorgio replied.

"Of course, if Springer was anything like what the Ice Queen said, he could have a lot of enemies," Swan said.

"Who just happened to choose now to take him out?" Giorgio said with a raised eyebrow.

Swan shrugged.

"Timing is everything," Giorgio said, glancing up at the big house. "And the timing on this stinks."

CHAPTER FOURTEEN

As he and Swan left Pasadena and headed back towards Sierra Madre, Giorgio got a call from McCready.

"Good news," McCready said. "Jimmy Finn isn't dead."

Giorgio flashed a look at Swan. "Do tell."

"Apparently he did hang himself in prison about thirty years ago, but they cut him down in time to save him," McCready continued. "He was on life support for a while, but finally woke up. They put him in a psychiatric ward. He was released about eleven years ago and has been living in a halfway house ever since."

"Have an address?"

"Sure do," McCready said.

The young cop read off the address, and Giorgio repeated it for Swan.

"Okay. Good job. We're going to get a late lunch and head over there."

The halfway house was an old, two-story, run-down motel in West Covina. They checked in at the office, where the Christmas decorations consisted of an aluminum tree decorated with about six glass ornaments. They asked if they could see Jimmy Finn. The manager pointed across an overgrown courtyard to an upstairs room.

As they traipsed across a weed-infested lawn, they passed a woman turning circles outside one of the doors. She was dressed in her bathrobe and talking to herself. When they found the stairs leading to the second floor, Giorgio almost bumped into a man tucked around the corner, sucking on a cigarette. Giorgio excused himself, side-stepped the man, and waved a hand in front of his face to dispel the smoke before springing for the bottom step.

They knocked on #23 and waited a moment. When Jimmy Finn answered the door, the dank aroma of grungy clothes and body odor billowed out, momentarily taking Giorgio's breath away. He showed his badge and introduced himself.

"Why…why are you here?" the little man asked.

"May we come in?" Giorgio asked. "We just need to talk with you."

Finn was indeed a small man – not more than 5' 4" or 5' 5"tall and with a slight build. Like Ron Martinelli, he would be in his early sixties now, but time had been far harsher to him. His face was deeply lined, and he had several scars across one cheek. His hair was cut short and peppered gray, and he had a cauliflower ear. As he stepped back to allow them inside, he listed to one side, as if one side of his body was weak or injured.

The room was depressingly blank. It had pea green walls and a carpet that looked like it had never been shampooed. Dark stains were visible all across its surface, and it was frayed in places, showing the thin padding underneath.

The only places to sit were the sagging sofa and the chair Jimmy had taken – an old patio rocking chair. An old box TV sat on a chipped wooden table, while a three-shelf bookcase, devoid of any books, leaned against the wall.

When Giorgio introduced himself and why they were there, Finn's dark eyes betrayed no recollection of the case.

"Mr. Finn, do you remember going to prison?" Giorgio asked, hoping to make a connection.

The little man nodded with a blank expression.

"Do you remember why?"

"They thought I killed that girl," Finn said without emotion, starting to rock back and forth.

"Lisa Farmer. And did you?" Giorgio asked.

"Course not. I never killed nobody," he replied simply

Finn was still rocking back and forth, staring at them, his fingers tapping the arm of the chair.

"Do you know who did?" Giorgio asked.

"How would I know?"

"May we sit down?" Giorgio asked, pointing to the worn sofa.

"Suit yerself," he said.

This wasn't going to be easy. Finn was clearly in a diminished capacity. Whether more diminished than when he was eighteen years old, Giorgio didn't know.

"Mr. Finn…may I call you Jimmy?" Giorgio said, perching on the edge of the sofa.

He nodded. "Sure."

"We believe we've found Lisa's body."

There was an immediate change in the man's facial expression. His dark eyes suddenly lit up, and he seemed to come to attention. But he remained silent.

"Her body was found in an old well, up at the monastery in Sierra Madre," Giorgio continued. "Would you know anything about that?"

Finn shook his head slowly, and Giorgio noticed that his eyes had begun to glisten. And then he suddenly dropped his gaze to the floor and stopped rocking.

"We're trying to find out what really happened, Jimmy."

Giorgio paused, letting this sink in. It may have been the first time anyone had ever expressed doubt that he had committed the murder.

The small man got up suddenly, crossed his arms over his chest and began to pace back and forth. Giorgio and Swan watched him for a moment.

"Jimmy, did you put Lisa's belongings in your locker?" Swan asked.

He stopped pacing and looked over at Swan and shook his head.

"No, sir," he spat in military fashion. "I didn't know nothing about that." Then he began
pacing again and mumbling to himself.

"Jimmy, please try to help us," Giorgio said. "Why did they think you might have killed Lisa?"

"I liked Lisa," he said, still pacing. "I would never hurt her. Cheryl, maybe. But not me."

Giorgio looked at Swan. "Who's Cheryl?"

"My girlfriend. I had a girlfriend. She didn't like Lisa. She was jealous all the time. Her brother told me to leave Lisa alone, or he'd hurt me."

"Whose brother?" Giorgio asked.

"Cheryl's brother. He didn't like her, neither."

His pacing picked up speed, as if this memory made him nervous.

"Jimmy," Giorgio began. "Do you remember Cheryl's last name and where she lived?"

"Sure. I'm not stupid. I'm not *stupid*!" he almost yelled, stopping and staring at them. "People think I'm stupid. But I'm not."

"What was Cheryl's last name?" Swan asked quietly. "That would help a lot."

"Lincoln. Her last name was Lincoln."

"What was her brother's name?" Giorgio asked.

Jimmy's brows furrowed as he concentrated. "Leroy. He wasn't very nice. He used to hit *his* girlfriends. He told me that's what men do to keep their women in line. I never hit Cheryl."

"Do you have any idea where either one of them are today?" Giorgio took the long shot.

He shook his head. "No. I went to prison."

He said this as if it had been the end of his life. And in a way, it had been.

"Jimmy, you told the police you were home alone the night Lisa disappeared. Was Cheryl with you?"

He looked up at Giorgio, his dark eyes pinched in thought. "She was there," he said.

"But we read the file. And according to the file, you told the police that you were alone."

He shook his head slightly, as if clearing his head. "She was there, but then she left."

Giorgio had to tamp down his impatience and work *with* Finn and not against him. He tried a different tactic.

"Did you hear anything, or see anything unusual after Cheryl left that night?"

Jimmy was still standing with his arms crossed, tense and anxious. Finally, he let his hands drop to his sides.

"We had a dog – Skipper. He started barking."

"Did he bark often?" Giorgio asked.

"No. Only when people came into the yard."

Swan and Giorgio exchanged quizzical looks.

"Into *your* yard?" Swan asked.

"Or Lisa's. He was a little dog and would get up onto the kitchen table and look out the back window. He could see into Lisa's yard."

"You think he might have been barking at someone in Lisa's yard?" Giorgio asked, trying to confirm.

"Yes. He always barked when she came home late at night."

"Do you remember what time this was, Jimmy? It's important."

"Maybe midnight. I just turned off the TV."

"And Cheryl was gone?" Swan said.

Finn seemed to have relaxed a bit and returned to his rocking chair.

"Cheryl left early. I watched TV by myself. I liked Lisa," he repeated. "I liked her a lot."

"Did you see anyone outside that night?" Swan asked.

"No," he shook his head. He held his hands in his lap and was clasping them tightly. "My mother was yelling at me. She wanted Skipper to be quiet."

"And so you went into the kitchen to get the dog?" Giorgio prompted him.

"Yeah. I grabbed him and pulled him off the table."

"Can you remember anything else about that night?" Giorgio said.

"A car," he said right away. "There was a car behind the house."

A virtual concert of bells went off in Giorgio's head. He paused and looked at Swan.

"Could that have been Ron Martinelli's car, dropping Lisa off after the prom?"

Finn began to rock back and forth again.

"No. This car was parked. Ron always dropped Lisa off at the street, and she would walk down the alley. I used to wait and watch her come in the back gate. Ron never drove down the alley."

"This car you saw…could you tell what color it was?' Swan asked.

His eyes squinted in thought. "Dark. Black, maybe."

"And it was parked? And the headlights were off?" Giorgio prodded.

"Yeah. It was parked. Ron never parked back there."

There was absolutely no animosity in his voice as he spoke about Ron, telling Giorgio that just as Lisa's mother had said, Finn must have liked Ron Martinelli.

"Why didn't Ron drive into the alley?" he inquired.

"Because the alley came out onto a different street."

"And you lived in a cul-de-sac?" Giorgio said.

He looked up as if he wasn't quite sure what that was.

"Your street ended in a circle," Giorgio clarified.

He nodded. "Yes."

"So Ron would drop her off, turn around and go back out the same way he'd come in?"

"Yes," he said.

"And you don't know who might have parked in the alley?"

He thought for a moment and then shook his head. "People weren't supposed to park back there. It's too narrow."

"Jimmy," Giorgio began. "Did the police ever ask you about any of this?"

He was rocking and rubbing the palms of his hands together. "I don't think so," he said.

"They said I killed her."

"Is there anything else you can remember about that night? Anything that might help us?" Giorgio asked.

The little man stopped and stared at him.

"I wouldn't hurt Lisa," he said simply.

CHAPTER FIFTEEN

The kid drummed his fingers on the steering wheel. He was watching the entrance to the nursing home in North Seattle, thinking about how to approach his task. His heart was racing, and his eyes flitted back and forth to take in his surroundings, as he toyed with a blond wisp of hair that draped down his cheek. There could be no mistakes. There were people counting on him, and this was the first time he'd been trusted with a solo operation. The trouble was, he didn't have a plan.

He was parked across the street, studying the building. There was a parking lot to one side of the building, at the end of a circular drive. A big dumpster sat against the building about halfway back in the lot. Out front, there was a metal bench to one side of the main entrance. The bench was set back from a concrete walkway that wrapped around the building and extended all the way to the parking lot.

As his gaze followed the walkway, a plan finally began to form in his mind, and he fingered the loaded syringe in his pocket. The day was unseasonably warm and clear for Seattle — something he thought could work in his favor. Doing the job inside the building was a big risk. Too many people. Too many eyes. But if he could get the old man outside, well that was a different matter. He knew some basic information about the guy. He had been a big drinker and a chain smoker for most of his life. It's why he was in the nursing home now and wasn't expected to live much longer.

The kid reached for the open pack of cigarettes on the dashboard and stuffed them into his pocket – right next to the wrinkled photograph he'd grabbed out of a family picture album the day before.

He was ready.

He started the engine and pulled away from the curb. He turned down the short side street that ran along the west side of the building. The old van bounced over a speed bump and into the parking lot. He pulled into a space near the street and turned off the engine.

The door creaked when he opened it and groaned when he slammed it shut. With quick steps, he traversed the walkway and entered the building through the automatic front door.

A young woman sat behind a half-moon desk in the middle of the lobby. She was staring at a computer screen. Two elderly men with canes stood chatting off to one side, and a middle-aged couple to his left were hugging each other.

He adjusted the fake glasses he'd bought at a drug store and approached the desk.

"Excuse me," he said pleasantly.

The young woman looked up. She had big brown eyes and apple cheeks.

"Yes?" she said. "May I help you?"

"I'm here to see my great uncle," he said. The initial lie rolled off his tongue with ease, giving him confidence to continue. "Carson Montgomery?"

Her eyes shifted to the computer screen, and she punched in something on the keyboard.

"Ah, let me see. Just a moment," she murmured. "Here we are. Yes, Mr. Montgomery. He just had lunch, so he's back in his room." Her gaze rested on him now. "Is he expecting you?"

"Um, no," he said, shifting uncomfortably. "I haven't seen him since I was a little boy. I'm just passing through Seattle and wanted to say hello."

"May I see some ID?"

He reached into his pocket and pulled out his wallet.

"Here," he said, holding up a driver's license. It wasn't actually him, but close enough he thought she wouldn't notice. But just in case, at the same time, he grabbed the picture he'd been carrying and drew it out. "But this might help more," he said, immediately switching her attention to the faded photograph. "This is a picture of me and my uncle when I was young."

She took the picture and stared at it.

"I was only six. He used to take me to the beach." The kid smiled at the false memory as if it were just yesterday. "We had some great times."

She looked at the picture of Montgomery and his own son, and then up at the young man in front of her.

"Anyway, I'm only passing through, so this is my one chance to see him before…" he stopped and dropped his chin as if it pained him to go on. "I know he's not well."

He looked at her with a plaintive expression. She melted.

"Okay," she said, handing the photo back. "Why don't you sign in, right there," she said, pointing to a registration book.

He reached out and grabbed a pen and scribbled the phony name that was on the driver's license in the space provided.

"Thanks," he mumbled. "This means a lot."

The girl gave him a broad smile. "No problem. Your uncle is in room 32." She turned and pointed behind her. "Just take that hallway to your left. It's about halfway down. He has a roommate who usually naps after lunch, so you'll need to be quiet. Mr. Montgomery is in the second bed."

A nervous jolt rippled across the young man's chest. Dammit! A roommate. He hadn't thought of that.

"Sure, no problem," he purred. "Thanks again."

He tapped his fingers twice on the registration book and then skirted the counter, heading for the hallway. He passed a rec room on his left, where a number of people played cards or board games. Sitting just outside the door was an empty wheelchair. He glanced around. No one was watching, so he grabbed the handles and spun the chair around in front of him and headed into the hallway.

He left the wheelchair in the hall and pushed open the door to #32. A wizened old man with a tuft of white hair dozed in the first bed, snoring softly. The curtain was pulled halfway around the foot of his bed.

The kid grabbed the edge of the thin drape and slid it the rest of the way around. The curtain rings bounced along the metal rod until it completely blocked the old man from view.

Then, the kid stepped past the first bed and found an old man with thick gray hair propped up in the second bed, watching the TV. He looked up with a curious expression.

"Who are you?" he said.

The boy came around to the far side of the bed.

"I'm Freddie's boy." He smiled as he moved closer to the head of the bed, and then leaned in with a whisper. "Shhh, I don't want to wake your roommate," he said in a low voice. "Here, take a look at this." He pulled out the photo again. "That's you and your son at the beach," he whispered. "Remember? You visited my uncle's place down in San Diego one year."

"So you're Freddie's boy?" the old man said, looking up at him. "So Freddie is all grown up. How is your dad? I haven't seen Freddie since he was in high school." As soon as the old man said it, he seemed to grow cautious. "Why are you here?" he said.

"My dad and I are just passing through town and wanted to say hello."

"Where is he?" the old man asked, looking over the kid's shoulder for the boy he once knew.

"He's having a cigarette outside."

"A cigarette?" Montgomery said, his eyes lighting up. "Man, I wish I could join him."

"Well, why don't we go outside? The sun is out and it's pretty warm out there."

The old man smiled. "A smoke?"

"Sure. No one needs to know," the boy said, conspiratorially. "We could go sit on that bench out front. Besides," the kid said, patting his coat pocket. "I might have a pint of something here to take the edge off." He gave the old man a Cheshire cat smile.

A slow smile spread across the old man's face. "Okay. You got some wheels for your dad's old friend?"

"Be right back."

The kid hurried to the hallway and grabbed the wheelchair. He took it back and helped the old man out of bed and into the chair, wrapping a blanket around him. He was about to push the chair forward, when the door opened and someone stepped inside the curtain next to them.

"Hi, Mr. Cornwall. It's time for your sponge bath," a female voice said.

Carson Montgomery chuckled. "Well, that'll keep 'ole Cornwall busy. Let's get this buggy rollin'."

They rolled past the first bed. The kid could see the backside of the nurse as she spoke to the old man named Cornwall.

The kid quickly opened the door and hurried into the hallway. As they passed the front desk, the young woman with apple cheeks looked up. She was about to say something when the kid shot her a big smile.

"Just goin' outside for some fresh air."

Mr. Montgomery gave her a casual wave over his shoulder, and they trucked right out the front door.

The kid didn't stop at the bench that sat in front of the building, but kept going around the corner and toward the back parking lot.

"Where's your dad?" the old man asked.

"He must be at the car. He'll be really glad to see you. Here take one of these," he said, tossing his carton of cigarettes into the old man's lap.

They passed a big bank of tinted windows, and rolled into the parking lot. The kid passed right by the van and kept going until he was on the other side of the dumpster.

With a quick rotation of his head, he checked the parking lot to make sure there were no prying eyes. Then he whirled around and backed up to the wall, extracting the syringe from his pocket in one swift movement.

"Hey, what the heck are you doin'?" the old man demanded, dropping the unlit cigarette. "What's going on? Where's your dad?"

"Still in California, old man."

And with that, the kid used his left hand to cover the old man's mouth and jabbed the syringe into the leathery folds of Carson Montgomery's neck, depressing the plunger to deliver the angel of death.

Montgomery squirmed, but suddenly groaned and slumped sideways, his head dropping forward.

The kid reached out and pressed two fingers against the carotid artery, and then removed the syringe. Half a second later, he stripped off the blond wig he'd picked up at a cheap outlet store and jogged back to the van.

As he opened the van door, he tossed the fake glasses under a car, jumped in and sped off. Half a block away, he rolled down his window and tossed the syringe into the street.

Oh, those pesky druggies, he thought to himself with a smile. *Always littering the streets with their drug paraphernalia.*

CHAPTER SIXTEEN

Giorgio dragged himself home at 7:15 that night. He'd met with the captain and reported his suspicion that Alex Springer had been murdered because of something he knew about the Lisa Farmer case. Since Swan was due to take the rest of the week off, they'd spent the remainder of the afternoon writing up notes and attempting to run down leads on Cheryl Lincoln, Jimmy Finn's girlfriend, and her brother, LeRoy. By the time he got home, Giorgio was starving.

His nostrils flared at the smell of oregano, bell pepper and onions when he stepped through the front door. He didn't know if it was spaghetti, ribs, or something else, but he didn't care. He threw his jacket over Prince Albert's helmet and headed for the kitchen.

Raised voices greeted him when he passed the den. It was Tony and Marie, arguing over something. He made a quick left turn into the kitchen, choosing to let them sort out their differences by themselves.

"You're home late," Angie said. "The kids have already eaten, but I waited for you. Do you have rehearsal tonight?"

"No. The first read-through is scheduled for next week," he said. "They're still cleaning up after the fire."

As soon as he said it, he glanced nervously at his wife. It was the fire and the attack on Giorgio during the Mallery Olsen case that had sent him to the hospital, and caused Angie to fall down the stairs. When she lost the baby, it had been a dark time in their lives. The shadow hadn't completely lifted for either one of them.

"We're working that cold case," he said to change the subject. "And Swan leaves tomorrow to help his mom clean out her house."

Angie turned and gave him a frown. "That's right. Didn't you say Rocky might step in to help you?"

"Yeah. He's been going through orientation," he said, opening the refrigerator.

He pulled out a beer, popped the top and sat at the kitchen table. Angie leaned over and opened the oven, pulling out a pan topped with aluminum foil. Giorgio felt the sour taste of saliva flooding his mouth.

"What's for dinner?"

"Chicken cacciatore," she replied.

"Smells great," he said.

Just then, Grosvenor lumbered in and pushed his nose against Giorgio's leg.

"Hello, little guy," he said, stroking the dog's head. "Hey, listen Ange, I'll work on those kiddie latches tonight. We'll get everything done by this weekend."

"Never mind. It doesn't matter anymore," she said with a distinct drop in her energy level.

She placed the pan of chicken on the tiled counter and turned to him, her mouth set in a straight line.

"What do you mean?" he asked.

"Elvira called today. She spoke to the state inspector, and she doesn't think they'll clear us for a license."

"What? Why not?"

He lowered the can of beer to the table, forgetting the dog for the moment.

"Two reasons," she said with a disappointed sigh. "We have firearms in the house, and…"

"But I keep them locked up," he said, cutting her off. "No one can get to them."

"I know," she said, coming to sit across from him. "But there can always be accidents. Then, there's Grosvenor."

"What about Grosvenor?"

He felt his blood pressure rising.

"I had to divulge his history, and the fact that he's been abused *and* been to dog therapy," she said with a sigh. "According to Elvira, their attorney says we're just a lawsuit waiting to happen."

She took a deep breath, and Giorgio recognized the pending onslaught of tears. He reached out and grabbed her hand.

"Hey, Ange. It's okay. I'll… I'll talk to them about the guns. I'm a cop. I can work this out."

Her eyes fluttered up so that her gaze rested on him.

"And what about Grosvenor?"

He paused and looked down at the brown and white spotted dog who sat with his tail curled around his long body. He didn't know what to say about Grosvenor. The dog was a part of the family now. How in the world could they get rid of him?

"I was really counting on this, you know?" she said in a small voice. "We're so close to having the house ready, too."

A tear rolled down her cheek, and she reached up and swept it away.

"I'll make it up to you, Ange," Giorgio said, squeezing her hand. "I'll... I'll figure out something," he said, lamely.

He stopped because he didn't know what else to say.

"No, Joe. It's okay," she said, reaching out to wrap her fingers around his. "I appreciate all you've done, Joe. Really, I do. And I love the two kids we have – I love them to death. In fact, after what happened with Marie, maybe it's just better that I focus on them. Really," she said, tears glistening. "I'll be okay."

He stared at her for a moment and then got up and crossed around the table, pulling her out of the chair. He drew her to him, wrapping his arms around her and burying his face in her auburn hair.

"I'm sorry, Ange. I wanted this to be perfect for you."

"I know," she whispered into his shoulder. "But we'll be fine." She patted his arm, as if she were comforting *him*. Then she pulled away, wiping the moisture from her face. "After all, having Grosvenor is like having another kid in the house anyway." She smiled up at him. "I'll be okay, Joe. Now, go wash up for dinner." When he didn't move, she pushed him away. "Go."

He took her face in both hand and gave her a kiss. Just then, the phone rang. He touched his nose to hers, and left the kitchen to pick it up in the hallway.

"Hello," he said into the mouthpiece. "Hello," he said again when no one answered.

Still nothing.

He looked suspiciously at the phone as a chill rippled across his shoulders.

He replaced the receiver and crossed the hallway to the den, where he found Tony and Marie wrestling on the floor. The argument had apparently been resolved, and the raised voices had been replaced with squeals of laughter. Grosvenor had followed him out of the kitchen and suddenly the three of them were fighting for control of a squeaker toy.

"Hey, it's a school night," he half-bellowed, stopping the action on the floor. "What about homework?"

"All done," Tony said, looking up from where Grosvenor's rear paw was stuck in his face. "I only had my diorama to finish."

"And I got most of mine done at school," Marie chimed in, rolling away from the dog.

Marie was a miniature version of her mother. She had honey-colored skin, and big, round eyes. Tony was a few inches shorter, with the same smooth skin, but shared his father's brooding, dark brown eyes.

Giorgio stood for a moment, watching them as if he didn't believe them. Then he grunted,

"You okay, Marie?"

She glanced up. "Yeah," she said quietly. "I'm fine, Dad."

He nodded. "Okay, as is everyone."

The children smiled and re-engaged with the dog, and before long, the three of them were rolling on the floor. Giorgio shook his head.

"How could anyone think you wouldn't be good with kids," he murmured to himself, watching how gentle Grosvenor was with them.

Then he went down the hallway to the guest bathroom to wash his hands.

÷

It was eight-thirty and the entire family was in the den watching TV when the phone rang.

This time Angie went into the hallway to answer it and came back to get Giorgio.

"Joe, it's for you. I don't know who it is."

He lifted himself out of his big leather chair, displacing Grosvenor, who had draped his snout over his foot, and went into the hallway. When he took the phone and said hello, a hushed voice greeted him.

"I know something about the murder of that young girl," the voice said. "We need to meet."

"Who is this?" Giorgio asked, remembering the earlier call.

"Look, I'm taking a chance here. Let's meet, and I'll tell you what I know. I'll be at the Prairie Diner in Arcadia in half an hour. Just get a table. I know who you are."

The line went dead.

Giorgio told Angie he had to go out, grabbed his weapon and badge and headed out to the car. As he backed out of the driveway, he noticed a dark Jeep Wrangler parked across the street. The flare of a cigarette inside signaled that someone was behind the wheel.

Giorgio drove down Sunnyside, glancing in his rearview mirror. His cop's intuition made him wonder why someone was sitting in the car in the dark. As he watched, the car's headlights flashed on and the car pulled away from the curb going the opposite direction. Giorgio relaxed.

It was nine o'clock when he parked across the street from the Prairie Diner in Arcadia. Huntington Drive was a main thoroughfare through many of the towns in the valley, so the street was busy, even this late.

The diner was small and sat between an antique store and a pawn shop. It had only a small front window that was almost completely obscured by curtains and a big flashing neon sign, depicting a green buckboard that kept flashing on and off.

It was December, so the night was cool, and yet the sidewalks were peppered with people. Several store windows were outlined in red and green holiday lights.

Giorgio got out of the car and crossed the street, looking up one side and down the other out of habit. He mentally took note of the cars parked along the curb and people loitering in doorways and on the street corner, just in case he had to remember details later on.

He pulled open the door to the café and was greeted with a darkened interior and the smell of hot oil. The order counter stretched across the back. Beyond that, a short order cook was busy moving back and forth filling orders and flipping something on a hot grill. A young waitress approached the counter and pulled off two plates filled with food. She turned and delivered them to a table in the corner.

The tables were covered with green plastic tablecloths, accented with cheap white vases that were filled with red silk Poinsettias. The place was half full of patrons engaged in conversation and consuming their meals.

Giorgio glanced around, looking for a table with a single man who might be watching for him. But there was none, so he took the first table to his right and sat facing the door. A moment later, the young girl came to take his order. He asked for a soda and some fries and she left.

The door opened and four kids came in laughing and texting on their cell phones. They took one of the tables in the center of the room. The door opened again, and a man in his forties entered. Giorgio came alert as the man glanced at him, but then headed for the counter.

Giorgio's waitress returned with his order. He was just about to squirt some ketchup onto his plate, when a second man suddenly appeared in the seat across from him.

"Thanks for coming," the man said.

Giorgio stopped, the ketchup bottle held mid-air.

The man was probably in his mid-to late fifties and built square, like a football player, but without the muscle. He had sandy blond hair, a full face and a receding hairline that gave him a broad forehead. And he had on an apron.

"Are you the cook?" Giorgio asked.

"No. My name's Monty," he said, nervously. "I own this place. But I help out in the kitchen when it's busy."

Giorgio glanced down and finished squirting the ketchup onto his plate and then put the bottle back onto the table. He picked up a fry, dipped it into the rich red sauce and popped it into his mouth.

"Was that you who called earlier and hung up?"

The man's shoulders slumped. "Yeah. Sorry. I just…this is hard."

"Okay," Giorgio said, swallowing. "Why am I here?"

Monty's eyes darted across the room, as if he thought someone might be listening.

"Look, I heard on the news that you found that girl up at the monastery. The word is that it's Lisa Farmer."

"What do you know about her?"

The man began wringing his hands.

"I was just a kid back in 1967, just ten years old. But my dad worked at the high school. He was one of the janitors. I heard him one night. He took a phone call from someone. I don't know who it was, but it made my dad really nervous."

"Whoa, slow down. He took a phone call. When?"

95

"I think it was a couple of nights *after* the girl went missing. I don't remember exactly. I was pretty young. But her disappearance was a big deal back then. *No*body ever just up and disappeared," he said to make a point. "Anyway, my dad didn't know I was there. Our phone was in the kitchen and I was in the hallway. I remember him getting pretty upset. It sounded like someone asked him to do something he didn't want to do, and he was trying to get out of it. He kept saying, 'I can't do that. You can't ask me to do that. I could lose my job, go to jail.'"

"And you don't know what he was talking about?"

"No." The man paused, wringing his hands again. He sighed. "Except that my dad was the one who ran the locker check the next day at the high school. He's the one who found the girl's underwear in that kid's locker."

When he said this, his shoulders slumped as if he had carried years of suspicion, and perhaps disappointment about his own father. It had also seeped into the tone of his voice, which had almost no breath behind it. This was a guy who had grown up suspecting his dad of something immoral, if not illegal.

"And you think your dad may have had something to do with that?"

He began to squeeze his hands together as if he were squeezing water out of a dish cloth.

"I don't know. I asked him about it once, when I was older. We'd heard that the kid who got arrested hung himself in prison. My dad got very angry and said never to mention it again. He was drinking pretty heavily by that time, so I let it go."

"Is your dad still alive?"

"Yeah, but my mom finally left him when I went off to college. I haven't seen him in a long time."

"Had he always been a big drinker?"

"No. Not at all. He didn't really start drinking until Jimmy Finn went on trial for Lisa Farmer's murder. He was called to testify, you know? Because he found the stuff in Jimmy's locker."

"Did your dad ever talk about the trial?"

"Only once. He was pretty drunk at the time. It was the day we found out that Jimmy would be going to prison. They tried him as an adult because he was almost eighteen. Anyway, my dad kept saying over and over again, 'That kid's in prison because of me.'"

Giorgio shrugged. "He could have meant that Jimmy went to prison because he'd found what was hidden in the locker. Maybe he felt responsible."

Monty shook his head. "I don't think so. He said it like he was guilty of something – like he'd done something wrong."

"And you have no idea who called your father that night?"

"No."

"Have you spoken to your father lately?"

His entire body seemed to deflate. "No. My dad changed after that. Like I said, he started drinking pretty heavily and hanging out at bars a lot. He stopped coaching my Little League team and would nag my mom about the littlest things. It was like something was eating his insides, but he'd never say what it was." Monty looked up at Giorgio, disappointment etched in the lines on his face. "He was never the same."

"Okay," Giorgio said, pushing his plate away. "We'll follow up. Here," he said handing his card to the man. "I'll need to know your dad's full name and where he lives now."

Monty took the card and held it between both hands. "I've lived with this my whole life, you know? – wondering if somehow my dad had anything to do with that girl's death." He lifted his eyes to meet Giorgio's. "God, I hope I'm wrong. And I hope he won't hate me for telling you this."

"We won't know until I talk to him. I need his name and where I can find him," Giorgio repeated.

The restaurant owner sighed as if he still wasn't sure he should rat out his old man.

"Carson Montgomery. He's in the Cascade Nursing home up in Seattle."

CHAPTER SEVENTEEN

Giorgio returned home after his meeting with Monty Montgomery, his mind racing. Questions now loomed as to whether or not young Jimmy Finn had, in fact, put those things belonging to Lisa Farmer into his locker. And if he hadn't, who had? Those questions kept him from falling asleep until long after midnight.

The clink that rattled the windowpane hours later woke him with a start, pulling him out of a deep sleep. His eyes opened to a dark room. A brisk breeze rustled the elm tree next to the window.

He glanced at the alarm clock next to the bed. It was 3:00 a.m. When a second ping hit the window, he pulled himself out from under the covers and stood up, careful not to wake Angie. He moved quietly to the window and pushed the curtain aside, thinking it sounded as if someone had thrown a couple of pebbles at the house. Since Marie was way too young to have a suitor, he was more than a little curious as to what it might be.

Outside, the floodlight mounted to the detached garage spilled a pool of light across the driveway, and street lights lit the front half of the driveway.

Giorgio's eyes scanned the area outside the window, wondering who or what had caused the noise. It was hard not to consider the ghost of Christian Maynard, but there was nothing there, except the roll of fencing waiting to be turned into Grosvenor's dog yard.

He was about to chalk it up to the tree and go back to bed, when something almost out-of-sight at the corner of the garage made the hairs on the back of his neck stand on end. Tucked under the oak tree was the dim image of Christian Maynard, shimmering in the dark like a glow bug.

Giorgio swallowed a ball of spit, and his heart kick-started with a thump.

Now what? There had to be a reason the boy was here again. Each time Christian had appeared in the past, he was trying to convey some information. From the first time the boy had unlatched the window on the second floor of the monastery, to the night in the graveyard when he showed Giorgio where to find a time capsule that would lead them to the answer they were looking for, the boy had purposely provided clues.

Giorgio turned to check on Angie, the adrenalin thrumming through his veins. She seemed to be slumbering peacefully, so he quickly slipped into his pants, threw on a shirt and grabbed his shoes. He was just about to exit into the hallway when Angie groaned.

"What's wrong, Joe?" she murmured.

She was just a pile of blankets in the dark. He stopped.

"Grosvenor needs to go out. I won't be long."

"Okay," she mumbled again. "Put a jacket on. It's cold out."

"Okay," he whispered with a brief smile.

He snapped his fingers at the dog, and Grosvenor looked up from his pillow. He hefted himself up and lumbered over, head down, ears dragging. Giorgio took him by the collar and pulled him into the hallway and closed the door.

"C'mon, boy. You have to go out. You just didn't know it."

They descended the stairs and Giorgio grabbed the dog's leash off the coat rack that hung by the front door. He clipped on the leash, put on his leather jacket and unlocked the front door.

The night was chilly and there was a thin fog hanging in the air. The house across the street still had their Christmas lights on, but their blow-up Santa and Snowman were mere puddles of color on the lawn.

Giorgio followed the walkway back to the garage. Christian had been standing in between the tree and the garage. The space was empty now.

Damn!

Giorgio moved over to allow Grosvenor to water the grass. When the dog finished, Giorgio looked around, wondering where the boy had gone.

He was startled to see the boy's hazy image about three-quarters of the way down the driveway. Giorgio stuck his left hand into his coat pocket, absentmindedly fingering the brass button he'd picked up in the theater parking lot the night Mallery Olson had died. He'd carried it with him all this time.

"What do you want?" he said to the boy in a hoarse whisper.

The boy didn't answer. He never did. Perhaps he couldn't. Giorgio didn't really know how all of this worked. But the boy was gesturing now with his right arm, as if he wanted Giorgio to follow him. Then his image faded – evaporating into thin air.

"Damn," Giorgio mumbled.

He hurried to the sidewalk with Grosvenor in tow, glancing from left to right, looking for the boy.

Shit, there he was at the corner of Grandview and Sunnyside. *What the heck?*

There were no cars or pedestrians out, so Giorgio relaxed and turned south, wondering where Christian was taking him. He crossed to the south side of Grandview and then followed the boy east.

The sidewalk was lined with trees and bushes, so he allowed Grosvenor to stop every so often to mark his territory. The boy kept appearing at each street corner, drawing Giorgio farther and farther east.

By the time they'd gone four long blocks, Christian disappeared altogether. Giorgio was left standing under a street lamp, looking around as if his date had left him at a party. A car rumbled by, making him look down at Grosvenor, as if he were waiting for the dog to finish something.

When he glanced up, he happened to read the street sign.

A full blown chill snaked its way down his back and he shivered.

He was standing on the corner of Lima Street and Grandview. The Pinney House, where Ron Martinelli's family had lived at the time Lisa Farmer went missing, was only a half a block away.

Giorgio turned south on Lima, walking past small, tidy homes and low-hanging trees. The line of trees ended at the edge of a big property with a broad front lawn.

The Pinney House was set far back from the street on about a half an acre of land, sitting in elegant contrast to all the surrounding homes. The old home was a landmark in the area. Giorgio had looked up its history. It was a three-story, huge Victorian built as a hotel in the late 1880s, complete with a turret and a veranda that ran the entire width of the building. Over its one-hundred-plus-year history, it had served as a sanatorium and a boarding house. There had also been many individual owners, one of whom was the Martinelli family back in 1967. Currently, it was a bed and breakfast.

The dramatic Queen Anne, with its oriel tower and gingerbread cutouts, was all decked out for the holidays. Garlands were draped along the white picket fence. Multi-colored light strands lined the porch railing and a large wreath hung on the front door. Several of the bushes in front of the porch were also covered in a spray of colored lights.

Giorgio viewed the grand old building with suspicion as it sat quietly and eerily in the surrounding dark. Why had the ghost of Christian Maynard brought him here?

He approached the white picket fence and glanced around again, wondering if the boy would make himself known. And then, there he was, standing right on the front porch.

Giorgio flinched inwardly. Now what the hell was he supposed to do?

The rumbling of occasional cars up on Grandview sounded distant and forlorn. He glanced around and then cautiously climbed the few steps to the curved walkway and approached the elegant staircase that led to the building's front door. He stopped there.

He couldn't go any farther. It was the middle of the night. And if he was caught on the grounds, he could be charged with trespassing. He glanced around again, unsure of what to do.

The boy's image flickered in the low light and then faded. Giorgio waited at the bottom of the steps for the boy to return.

A minute went by. Then two.

No Christian Maynard.

Giorgio had been deserted.

His common sense finally got the better of him, and he retreated to the curb.

When he took a final look at the grand old Victorian, he couldn't help but wonder why the boy had led him there in the first place.

CHAPTER EIGHTEEN

It was only a few hours later that Giorgio beat Swan into the office, his need to solve this case overriding his need for sleep. The meeting with the janitor's son and the trip to the Pinney House had energized him.

Jimmy Finn's girlfriend remained a loose end that Giorgio needed to tie up. He resumed the search to find current addresses for either Cheryl Lincoln or her brother, Leroy. The fact that Cheryl might have married would make the search more difficult, but he found seven Leroy Lincolns in the San Gabriel Valley. He gave McCready the task of trying to figure out if any of them had a sister named Cheryl.

Giorgio met with the captain as soon as he arrived, and asked about the possibility of taking a trip to Seattle to interview Carson Montgomery.

Captain Alvarez was a short man in his fifties, with salt and pepper hair slicked back on both sides. He'd served for many years with the Los Angeles PD, coming to Sierra Madre, like Giorgio, in search of a slower pace.

"Can I speak to you?" Giorgio asked, entering the office.

"Of course, Joe," the Captain said. "What's new on the Lisa Farmer case?"

"That's what I'd like to talk about. I got a phone call last night to meet with a man who says his father was the janitor who conducted the locker search at the high school back in 1967."

Captain Alvarez sat back in his chair, his hands in his lap. "So?"

"This guy was only ten years old at the time, but he says he heard his father on the phone the night before the locker search."

The captain's dark eyes flashed momentarily in anticipation.

Giorgio continued. "His father got a call from someone who asked him to do something he didn't want to do – something his dad said he could get fired for, maybe even go to jail."

"And the next day, there was the locker search in which the missing girl's underwear turned up," the captain said.

"Right. The son says his family was never the same. His dad started drinking and his parents split up. And when he asked his old man about it once, he was told to never mention it again. Eventually his dad moved to the Seattle area. He's up there now in a nursing home."

"And you want to fly up and talk to him?" Captain Alvarez said.

"We don't have a connection yet with this guy and anyone associated with Lisa Farmer's disappearance. I need to know who called him that night and what they asked him to do," Giorgio replied.

The captain's hands were clasped in his lap, and one thumb was pressing against the other. Finally, he said, "You realize that someone has already served time for this crime?"

"Yes, sir. But I think it may have been the wrong person. You heard that Jimmy Finn is alive, didn't you? We interviewed him yesterday, and he just doesn't fit the profile. He's docile. He doesn't even seem angry that he was sent to prison. Then there's Alex Springer's death. I don't know yet how he's connected, other than he worked for the Martinellis, but it's just too coincidental. And I don't..."

"Believe in coincidences," the Captain finished his thought, nodding. "I know." The captain studied Giorgio for a moment. "You feel good about this one, Joe? Because it's out of our jurisdiction, and I'll have to justify the expense."

Giorgio nodded. "I have a feeling captain."

The captain considered his comment. "Okay. Go. But for now, keep the media off this."

Giorgio nodded. "Thanks."

Giorgio found the number for the Cascade Care Facility in North Seattle and called to explain a visit that afternoon. He spoke to the manager, Joann Felton, but her response stopped him cold.

"I'm so sorry, Detective," she said. "But Mr. Montgomery died yesterday."

"What do you mean?" Giorgio demanded, his heart rate increasing. "How?"

"Well, he had congestive heart failure, so I assume it was his heart."

Giorgio paused, his thoughts spinning. *Another convenient death.* "You assume?!" he said.

"Well, yes. He was under a doctor's care and his prognosis wasn't good. So, even though he went a little sooner than we thought, his death wasn't unexpected."

Giorgio was about to say thanks and hang up, when he thought of something.

"Did anyone come to visit him yesterday?"

She paused. "Well…um…I'm not sure that's information I should give out."

"Mrs. Felton, let me be clear," Giorgio said, keeping his anger in check. "I was coming to interview him as part of a murder investigation. So it's important I know if someone came to visit him yesterday."

She sputtered on the other end of the phone. "Um…yes. A young man came to see him. In fact, that's the only thing out of the ordinary about all of this."

The hairs on the back of Giorgio's neck came to attention. "What do you mean, out of the ordinary?"

"The young man took Mr. Montgomery out for some fresh air, but never brought him back. We didn't find him for over an hour."

"Where the hell was he?"

"He…uh…was in a wheelchair out in the parking lot. That's why we had trouble finding him. I think he must have died while the young man had him outside, and the boy probably panicked and took off. He's not in any kind of trouble, you know. Our patients come to us at the end of their lives, but it can be frightening when it happens. He might have thought it was his fault."

"Were the police called?" Giorgio interrupted her.

"Well, no. We didn't think there was any reason. As I said, he had heart trouble. I…uh…I hope we didn't make a mistake."

"I'm on my way up there," Giorgio snapped. "I'll need to speak to your staff."

"Of course. We'll be happy to speak to you, but… I don't understand. Mr. Montgomery was very ill. I'm sure his heart just gave out…"

"Mrs. Felton, I'll be on the first plane up there, and I'm calling the Seattle police right now. You can probably expect a visit from them as well."

He hung up and found the number for the Seattle Police Department. When he explained why he was calling, he was immediately put in touch with a Detective Abrams. Giorgio explained the situation.

"Shit," Abrams said with a sigh after hearing the story. "Do you know where the hell they took the old guy?"

"No. Probably to a funeral home," Giorgio replied. "Anyway, I'll be on the first flight I can get."

"Okay, we'll track him down and get him to the Coroner's Office. Grab a cab to the downtown station. I'll be looking for you."

÷

Giorgio's flight arrived at SeaTac airport at 12:35 p.m. The sky was a slate gray, although there was no rain in the forecast. He'd taken an umbrella anyway. He actually had an uncle who lived in the Seattle area and had visited several times. Most of the locals didn't carry umbrellas, but Giorgio didn't like to get wet.

He'd flown on an open ticket, hoping to return that evening. Traveling light with only a briefcase and his weapon, he grabbed a cab and had the driver make a beeline for the downtown Seattle PD.

Giorgio glanced out the taxi cab's window as it sped north on Interstate 5 toward the city, passing intersecting freeways and two big sports arenas. The Puget Sound glinted in the background.

The cab driver dropped him off right in front of the Seattle PD in downtown. It was almost 1:20 p.m. by the time he walked into the busy lobby. The chaos reminded him of his days with the New York Police Department.

When he introduced himself to the sergeant at the front desk and asked for Detective Abrams, he was asked to wait. A few minutes later, a tall, athletic man in his late twenties or early thirties appeared and extended his hand.

"Sean Abrams," he said. "Let's grab a room."

Abrams was tall and had the rugged good looks of an action hero. But this guy walked with the kind of confidence that comes from a lot of physical training.

Abrams led Giorgio down a long hallway to a conference room and offered him something to drink. When the detective returned and handed a can of soda across the table, Giorgio noticed a U.S. Army Ranger tattoo on his forearm; that explained the air of confidence.

"We found Montgomery," Abrams said. "You were right — they sent him to a local funeral home. He's at the county morgue, now, and we're waiting for an autopsy. So, tell me more about this case you're working on."

Giorgio relaxed back in his chair. He didn't have any reason to hold back. Montgomery's death was Abrams' case, and all Giorgio could do was try to learn as much as he could.

"We found the skeleton of a girl in the well of a Catholic monastery in town," he said. "We're pretty sure it's a girl that disappeared the night of her high school prom back in 1967. The body was never found, but they pinned the rap on a young kid who couldn't defend himself."

"Evidence?" Abrams asked.

"Just circumstantial. They found the girl's underwear and one of her shoes in the kid's locker. Carson Montgomery was the janitor at the high school back then. He conducted the locker search."

Abrams was tapping the eraser of a pencil on the table.

"So, you came up here to find out if Montgomery knew anything?"

"Actually, more than that," Giorgio nodded. "His son contacted me last night and told me that the night before the locker search his father got a phone call. He says he overheard his father say something to the effect of 'I can't do that. I'll get fired. I could even go to jail.'"

Abrams' eyebrows arched over hooded blue eyes. "So…someone was asking, or maybe *telling*, him to do something he didn't want to do."

"Right," Giorgio said. "And the very next day the police get an anonymous tip to conduct a search of all of the lockers on the high school campus, and it was Montgomery who opened each locker. The son said his father changed after that. He started drinking heavily and retreating from the family. He and his mother eventually split up and Montgomery moved up here. I came up to find out who called him that night and why."

Abrams furrowed his brow while he continued to tap the pencil. "And now your potential witness is dead."

Giorgio shrugged. "What are the odds?"

"Too great," Abrams said.

"Have you heard anything from the M.E. yet that would pin this as murder?" Giorgio asked hopefully.

Abrams pursed his lips. "Naw, she just got started, so nothing about the body itself. But we called the manager at the nursing home and apparently he was found in a wheelchair behind a dumpster in the parking lot."

"Behind a dumpster?" Giorgio said with alarm. "She left that part out on the phone."

"Yeah, some kid claiming to be his great-nephew had come to visit him and took him outside for some fresh air. Neither one of them came back. Forty-five minutes later, they went looking for Mr. Montgomery and found him dead as a doornail. We asked the M.E. to put a rush on it, so hopefully we'll know more this afternoon."

"Have you been out to the nursing home yet?" Giorgio asked.

Abrams shook his head. "No. I got called in on another case for a lineup. So how 'bout we take a trip out there together now?"

Giorgio nodded. "Sounds good."

It took them only twenty-five minutes to make the drive to the Green Lake neighborhood, in North Seattle. They were greeted by Joann Felton, the nursing home administrator Giorgio had spoken to on the phone. She was tall and in her mid-forties.

"Nothing like this has ever happened," she said nervously as she settled behind her desk. "We have very strict rules about the patients and their visitors. But I have a new girl at the front desk, and she, well, she let the boy through. A young man, really," she corrected herself.

"What did he look like?" Giorgio asked.

"Just a moment. I should let you talk to Irene."

She picked up the phone and asked Irene to join them. A moment later a girl in her twenties stepped into the office. She was dressed in dark slacks and a green sweater and had her hair pulled back into a pony-tail.

"Irene," Ms. Felton said, "these officers would like to ask you a few questions about that young man who came to see Mr. Montgomery."

She glanced at them nervously.

"Sure," she said, clasping her hands in front of her.

"Can you tell us what he looked like?" Detective Abrams asked.

"He was medium height and kind of skinny. Um…"

Her eyes flitted over to her boss and back again.

"That's okay," Abrams said. "Just take your time. You're not in any kind of trouble."

"Okay. Um…he was…he had blond hair…long…pulled back in a pony-tail. But he had dark eyes and his lip was pierced."

"Where?" Abrams wanted to know.

"Here," she pointed to the corner of her bottom lip. "I also think he had a tattoo."

"Could you tell what it was?" Abrams asked, taking notes. "Think hard."

"No," she said, shaking her head. "He wore a turtleneck, but I saw just the tip of some ink above the neckline."

"Who did he say he was?" Giorgio asked.

"He said he was Mr. Montgomery's great nephew and that he was just passing through Seattle and would only be here a short time. He knew his uncle was ill, so he was really hoping he could see him. It was right after lunch, so I knew Mr. Montgomery would probably be awake. I told him I'd need some ID, and he showed me a driver's license and an old picture with Mr. Montgomery."

"Could you recognize Mr. Montgomery in the picture?" Abrams asked.

She fidgeted and glanced at the floor. "I…uh…it was a really old picture. You know, like one of those Polaroid pictures. So it was pretty faded. But it looked like Mr. Montgomery. And there was a blond kid sitting on his lap."

"What was the name on the driver's license?" Giorgio asked.

She paused and shot a glance at her boss. "I don't remember. He showed it to me so quickly and then he got out this other picture. I'm sorry," she whined as if she were about to cry. "But I had him sign the register."

"Okay, we'll take a look," Abrams said. "So you let him go to Mr. Montgomery's room."

"Yes. He came out a little later with Mr. Montgomery in a wheelchair and said he wanted to take him outside for some fresh air. Mr. Montgomery waved at me and had a blanket wrapped around him. The sun was out, so I thought it would be okay. Besides, it was really busy yesterday, and…"

"And they never came back?" Giorgio said.

"No," she said, slumping her shoulders. "They went out the front doors, and I saw them turn to the right along the pathway that goes to a nice bench out there. I thought that's where they were headed. A lot of people go out there to smoke. I took a break and didn't notice whether Mr. Montgomery came back inside. Then, the nurse came looking for him, and I realized they had been gone for over an hour. So I reported it."

"We looked outside, but of course didn't see them," the administrator said. "So we searched the building. It wasn't until the maintenance man went to throw something into the dumpster that he found him."

"Is there anyone else who may have seen the two together, or talked to either one of them?"

Abrams asked. "A nurse, perhaps? Or a roommate?"

"He had a roommate," Ms. Felton said, lighting up a bit. "Mr. Cornwall." She stood up. "He should be awake. I'll walk you down there," she said. "You can return to the front desk, Irene."

The girl left and the three of them moved past the front desk into the patient wing, where the newly waxed floor gleamed. The smell of urine, however, made Giorgio's nose twitch. It reminded him too much of the place his grandfather had stayed just before he died of colon cancer. Giorgio didn't have good memories of that. His grandfather had suffered terribly, making Giorgio glance through open doorways as they passed, wondering momentarily about the patients here.

They stopped at #32 and Ms. Felton knocked and then slowly opened the door. She stepped in first and spoke quietly to Mr. Cornwall. Then she swung the door open wide and allowed the two officers inside.

"Mr. Cornwall said he'd be happy to talk with you. Let me know if I can be of any more help."

Lying in the first bed was a little, wrinkled old man. His face was covered in age spots, and his blue eyes had turned milky. There was a small explosion of white hair on the top of his head. He greeted them with a smile.

"What can I doose for you boys?" he asked with a fake New Jersey accent.

Detective Abrams shot a glance at Giorgio and smiled. The curtain was pulled back, so he moved to the bed that must have been Montgomery's, which sat next to the window. It had been remade and all of Carson Montgomery's belongings removed. Abrams sat down, while Giorgio remained standing.

"We were wondering if you remembered a young man coming to see Mr. Montgomery yesterday."

His expression immediately became somber. "Too bad about old Montgomery. He was a good egg."

"Were you here when someone came to visit him?" Abrams tried again.

"Yeah. I was asleep, but whoever it was closed my curtain," he said, gesturing to the circular curtain that could be pulled around the bed. "And that woke me up. I don't hear too good anymore, so I probably can't tell you too much. But I did hear him say the name Freddie."

"Freddie?" Giorgio repeated. "Nothing else? A last name, maybe?"

"Naw. Just the name Freddie. They were whispering. Then my nurse came in."

"Did you see them when they left the room?" Giorgio asked.

"No. I was pretty focused on Hannah," he said with a smile. "She likes to wear her uniform pretty tight, if you know what I mean."

Giorgio smiled. "Is there anything else you can think of that might be helpful?"

The old man shook his head. "Naw. Sorry." He glanced up at the two men, his eyes beginning to water. "I'll miss old Montgomery. He was a cantankerous old coot, but he wasn't so bad. And now I'll never have a chance to find out what he knew about that girl."

"Girl?" Giorgio said, his nerves on alert.

"Yeah. We were out in the activity room watching the news day before yesterday. CNN had a report about that girl's skeleton they found down in Southern California. Montgomery mumbled something and when I asked him about it, he said I'd have to beat him at poker to find out." The old man shrugged his skinny shoulders. "Now I'll never find out."

Abrams and Giorgio glanced at each other.

"You couldn't hear what he mumbled?" Abrams asked.

"It was just something like, 'ruined my life,' or 'my wife,'" he said apologetically. "Like I said, I don't hear too good no more."

Abrams stood up. "Thank you, Mr. Cornwall. We appreciate your time." He handed over his card. "Please let me know if you think of anything else."

The two men headed down the hallway toward the entrance.

"So, it looks like you were right. Someone wanted him dead because of your cold case," Abrams said.

Just then, the ringtone on Abrams' cell phone chimed and he answered it. He listened for a moment and then exclaimed, "Shit. Okay. Thanks."

He flicked off the phone and turned a grim expression in Giorgio's direction.

"The M.E. hasn't cut him open yet, but says we need to be looking for a syringe."

"Why?" Giorgio asked.

"Because Montgomery has a big, ugly puncture wound in his neck."

Abrams immediately dialed his phone to call someone else. "Tim," he barked into the phone.

"Get a forensics team out to the Cascades Nursing Home up by Green Lake pronto. Yeah. It looks like that old guy we tracked down today was murdered. Meet me in the parking on the west side of the building." He hung up and put the phone back in his pocket. "Let's go give the good news to the lovely Mrs. Felton. I want to see if anyone found a syringe when they cleaned out his room, and then check the register."

They were nearly to the lobby when they passed double doors leading to a large activity room. There were several round tables filled with people chatting, playing board games or cards. Giorgio glanced across the room to the floor-to-ceiling windows that overlooked the side yard and the parking lot.

"You go see Felton," he said to Abrams. "I want to talk to a few people in here."

Abrams nodded and disappeared. Giorgio pushed the door open and crossed to the window. The front walkway looped around the corner of the building and back along the side street to a parking lot. The front half of the parking lot was right in front of the rec room windows. But from where he stood, he couldn't see the dumpsters.

Two women sat up against the windows, playing cards. One was wearing a blue robe. The other woman was dressed in a polyester pantsuit. He interrupted them.

"Excuse me, ladies," he said. "But by any chance, were you here playing cards yesterday?"

The woman in the polyester suit looked up over her glasses. The other one either ignored him, or hadn't heard him.

"Yes, we were, weren't we, Sister?"

"Hunh?" the one in the robe mumbled. "Weren't we what?"

"Playing cards here yesterday."

Sister looked up at Giorgio as if she just noticed him. "Who are you?"

He pulled out his badge. "I'm a police officer, looking into the death of Mr. Montgomery. Did you know Mr. Montgomery?"

"Knew a Montgomery when I was a kid. Kent Montgomery. He was a real pain in the ass," she said.

"No, Sister," the woman in the pantsuit said. "Did you know a Mr. Montgomery here at the nursing home?"

"Bethany, you know I hate it when you call me Sister all the time. I may actually *be* your sister, but my name is Corinne. Call me Corinne. You'd think we were Mormons or something," she said to Giorgio. "No. I didn't know Mr. Montgomery. Why are you looking into his death? People die around here all the time."

Giorgio had to suppress a smile. "We believe someone may have taken him out of here against his will yesterday. Did you happen to see a young man pushing an older man in a wheelchair yesterday, down the walkway into the parking lot?" He gestured toward the walkway outside the big window.

They both turned and looked out the window as if Mr. Montgomery would be out there now. Then the one named Bethany turned back to him quickly.

"Yes, I did. We were just beginning our second hand of cribbage, and I glanced outside. He was a blond kid. Not a kid really, a young man – maybe in his late twenties."

"Did you see where they went?" Giorgio asked.

"No," Bethany said. "They disappeared into the parking lot. But he wasn't gone long. He came jogging back a few minutes later."

"What do you mean? Like he was running away from something?"

"Not like he was scared or anything. Just in a hurry," she said. "Then he jumped into a van that was parked right there and drove off," she said, pointing into the parking lot.

"That's right, and he wasn't blond anymore," Corinne said, moving cards around in her hand.

Bethany's head snapped around. "You saw him, too?"

Corinne looked up. "I know you think I'm half dead, Bethany, but I'm actually quite alive. Yes, I saw both of them." She looked back at Giorgio. "There was a blue van parked in the second or third spot. He got into that."

"That's right, officer," Bethany said. "But it was gray, not blue."

"Dammit, Bethany! I know what the color gray is. It's the color of my hair. And I know what the color blue is. And it's the color of yours."

"Ladies," Detective Abrams said, interrupting them.

They both looked up at the tall detective who had come up quietly from behind. Their eyes said it all – even at their age, they recognized sex appeal when they saw it.

"Did either of you see anyone else in the van? Or a license plate number, maybe?" he asked.

They looked at each other and shook their heads.

"No," Bethany said. "We were arguing over the card game, so I'm afraid I didn't pay much attention."

"Me neither," Corinne admitted. "Now, if it had been either one of you..." she said with a seductive wink. "I would've paid more attention."

Giorgio smiled. "But you're sure it was the same person," he stressed. "One minute he was blond. And the next minute, what?"

"His hair was black," Bethany said.

"That's right," Corinne confirmed.

"And it was the same young man?" Giorgio asked again.

"He was wearing the same clothes," Bethany said. "Black pants and a black hooded sweatshirt."

"And he had glasses," Corinne added. "Which he threw away as he got in the car."

Bethany stared at her sister in shock. "I didn't see him do that."

"No, you were too busy trying to cheat." Corinne looked up at the two men as Bethany gasped at the remark. "I saw him reach up and take the glasses off as he climbed into the van and toss them away."

Giorgio was impressed. "Thanks. You've been very helpful."

Detective Abrams pulled out his notepad again. "Can I get your names?"

"I'm Bethany Ames," the woman in the pantsuit said. "And this is my sister..."

"I think they have that part," Corinne said with a sneer. "My name is Corinne Paulson."

"Here's my card," Abrams said. "If you can think of anything else, would you give me a call?"

Corinne looked at his card and then back up at him with a mischievous smile. "Is this your home phone?"

"Sister!"

Corinne turned an evil gaze on her sister. "I swear I'm going to rip out your tongue if you call me that one more time."

The detectives left the two sisters arguing and stepped into the hallway.

"Let's walk around to the side," Giorgio said.

They went out the front entrance and followed the path to the side street and the parking lot. The street ended in a cul-de-sac, with the entrance to the parking lot in the middle of the circle. Giorgio stood at the curb, looking back at the windows along the activity room. He couldn't see the two sisters because the windows were heavily tinted. But he assumed that they could see him.

"From here," he said, "you can't see the people inside. You wouldn't know if someone was watching you or not."

"Which might make you careless," Abrams said.

They turned and walked to the dumpsters, which sat some twenty yards back into the lot, up against the exterior wall of the building. They moved to the far side, where they were protected from view.

"So this is where they must've found him." Abrams looked around. "Pretty private. It's probably where he was killed, too."

The two men surveyed the ground around the dumpster, but all they found were empty candy wrappers and cigarette butts. Giorgio opened the dumpster.

"When your guys get here, they should probably go through this, just in case," he said to the tall officer.

"I'll have them check around Montgomery's bed, too," he said. "In fact, I'll check with Mrs. Felton and get a hold of all his personal belongings."

"Let's go see if we can find those glasses," Giorgio said, heading back towards where the van had parked. "Hopefully, someone didn't drive over them with their car."

CHAPTER NINETEEN

The sun had set by the time they were finished. The forensics team had combed the parking lot, the dumpster and Montgomery's room, but found nothing of consequence.

Giorgio did find the killer's cheap glasses under the tire of a car, but they'd been pretty much smashed to smithereens. Abrams still had them bagged and tagged, just in case. The registration book had revealed that the killer had signed in as one Trent Wagner. A quick check of public records showed that Trent Wagner had died in Afghanistan in 2013.

"Well, we're hitting a dead end here," Abrams said, stretching his arms above his head.

"What time does your flight leave?"

They were standing at Abrams' car and were ready to leave.

"It's an open ticket," Giorgio answered.

"Good. Let's get something to eat."

They stopped at a local Applebee's. While they waited for their orders, the two detectives got to know each other.

"So I decided it was time to move to a smaller town," Giorgio said, finishing the story in which his partner had been killed in New York. "I thought maybe my wife wouldn't have to worry so much. Then there were three murders up at this monastery in town, and now, I'm following up on yet one more murder that took place decades ago. All in a town where murders are supposed to be rare."

"Well, at least the weather is better in Southern California," Abrams said with a smile. "I've been thinking of doing the same thing. Switching to a small town, I mean."

"Why?" Giorgio asked.

The big man shrugged. "I got divorced about a year ago. My wife…" he paused, tapping his fingers on the table. "Let's just say I haven't been too easy to live with at the department. I've burned some bridges."

"You should think about Southern California," Giorgio said.

Abrams laughed. "Naw, too many actors down there. If I collared one, I wouldn't be able to tell if he was acting or telling the truth."

"Some actors are okay," Giorgio said with mock insult.

"Is your brother an actor or something? Am I offending a family member?"

"No," Giorgio said with a grin. "Just me."

Giorgio paused, allowing the remark to register. Abrams eyes grew wide.

"Really? No shit?"

Giorgio shrugged. "I did a lot of acting in high school and found I was pretty good at it. It's relaxing, if you can believe it. Kind of keeps me sane."

The waitress brought their meals. As Giorgio cut his patty melt in half, he said, "How long do you think it will take to get the drug screens back?"

Abrams shrugged. "Couple of days at least. So...anyone in this case of yours named Freddie that you know of?"

Giorgio shook his head. "No. But you can bet we'll be checking on that."

"So, what's your next move?" Abrams asked.

Giorgio sat back and wiped his chin. "We started out just confirming information from the original investigation. But two suspicious deaths in two days changes everything. Someone out there doesn't want us to find the truth and is willing to kill again to keep it secret."

Abrams reached for his drink. "Cold case, meet current case. But the kid who killed Montgomery certainly didn't murder your vic way back in 1967."

"No," Giorgio said. "But he must be connected somehow. And it tells me that the kid they actually convicted back in 1967 was probably innocent."

"He was set up," Abrams agreed.

"Yeah. And Montgomery knew enough about that set-up to get him killed."

"But why wait to off him forty years later? Why didn't they just do it back then?"

Giorgio pushed a fry into a glob of ketchup on his plate. "I don't know. My guess is that whoever asked Montgomery to plant that evidence had an unusual hold over him. They had to be pretty confident all these years that he wouldn't spill the beans."

"But why would they lose confidence in him now?"

Giorgio looked over at the detective. "It could be because the players have changed over the years. Some of them may have died. Perhaps whatever influence they had over these two has softened. Plus we have better forensics today. Or maybe it's just as simple as the killer being afraid that since both of these guys were old, one of them might want to clear his conscience before he died."

"Well, I'll have my guys canvass all the rental car agencies looking for either a gray or blue van. Plus we'll check all the flights coming into SeaTac from LAX."

"Or Burbank," Giorgio added. "Sierra Madre is close enough that they could have used either airport. But maybe the kid drove."

"Pretty long drive," Abrams said skeptically.

"Yes, but we don't know if he was alone. And a flight would have been easier to trace."

"Except if they drove, they'd have out-of-state plates, which stand out," Abrams suggested.

"True. But that's easily remedied. If the kid had a fake ID, he could have used fake plates. I think we should also consider that whoever did this could have hired someone up here to do the job."

Abrams shrugged his broad shoulders. "Maybe. But unless this is organized crime, most people can't just call up a bunch of thugs in another city and pay them to do a job. It's not like they're in the phone book."

"Good point," Giorgio shrugged.

There was a moment of silence between them while Abrams twirled the ice in his drink.

Finally, he said, "You know, I have a friend who might be able to help."

"Who's that?"

The tall officer paused, looking uncomfortable for the first time that afternoon. Giorgio didn't
think this guy suffered a lack of confidence .

"You might think I'm crazy, but she's a psychic," Abrams said quickly and then shut up.

Giorgio stopped and gave him a curious glance. "Seriously? You believe in that sort of
   thing?"
The big cop pursed his lips and shrugged again. "I don't know if I believe it or not. I met her in a class over in Ballard a while back. She's helped me in a peripheral way on a couple of cases."
"What would she do?" Giorgio asked, taking a bite of his sandwich.
"She's really good at finding connections between people. Especially if there's been something traumatic between them."
Giorgio swallowed. "Traumatic – like a killer and his victim?"
"Exactly like that," Abrams responded.
"So, you're thinking that maybe she could find a connection between Montgomery and the girl we found?"
"Couldn't hurt to try," the big cop said.
"I'm all for trying," Giorgio nodded, knowing full well that he had enough paranormal things going on in his life that he couldn't very well scoff at the idea of using a psychic. "I'll fax you a picture."

CHAPTER TWENTY

After the trip to Seattle, Giorgio got to the office early the next day, anxious to get back into the investigation. He got a pot of coffee going before Rocky sauntered in.

"The Captain said to bunk with you temporarily," Rocky said, a personnel file clasped in his hands.

"Sounds good. Swan'll be back next Monday, and we can figure things out then."

"I heard you went to Seattle yesterday. What was that all about?"

Giorgio leaned back in his chair, clicking a retractable pencil as Rocky rolled Swan's chair out and sat down.

"Let me grab a cup of coffee and I'll bring you up to speed. It's a long story. Want one?"

"Sure," Rocky said.

Giorgio filled two mugs and put one on the desk in front of his brother.

"Seriously?" his brother quipped. "I'm gone only three weeks and you forget that I take it with half a pound of sugar?"

Giorgio flinched. "Sorry. I'm used to giving it to Swan, who takes it black and no sugar."

He went back to the small table that held the coffee pot and grabbed the sugar canister and slid it across the desk to Rocky.

"Been to see a dentist lately?" he said with a sneer.

"You know damn well I have the only straight teeth in the family," Rocky said, pouring a generous amount of sugar into his mug.

Giorgio returned to his desk. "Yeah, but it's what's under the hood that counts," he said. "If they're rotting out from the inside, you'll look like Gumby before you know it."

"By the way, when did you get into the holiday spirit?" Rocky said, nodding towards the Santa sitting on the corner of Giorgio's desk.

"Oh, Swan gave that to me. It was my Christmas present," he said with a sardonic smile. "Speaking of which, I need to get some time to do some Christmas shopping. Tony wants a pair of those night vision goggles. Know where I could get them?"

"Probably any toy store," his brother said, taking a sip of his coffee. "What'd you get Angie?"

Giorgio sat back and put his feet up on his desk. "We decided the new washer and dryer were our presents to each other. And now, as it turns out, we didn't even need to buy them."

He allowed a little puff of air to escape his lips in a sign of displeasure.

"What do you mean?" Rocky said, blowing on his mug of coffee.

"The whole day care idea is off. The consortium's attorney says that what with guns on the property and a psychologically impaired dog, we'd never get the license."

"Jeez, Joe, I'm sorry," his brother said. "How's Angie taking it?"

"Probably better than me," Giorgio said.

"That's not surprising," Rocky said with a shrug. "She always accepts things better than you. In fact, most people I *know* accept things better than you."

"That's not true!" Giorgio complained. "I take things in stride."

"Oh, pleeez," his brother retorted. "What about that summer we were supposed to go to Sleepy Hollow Lake for a few days and got rained out? You moaned and groaned about it all weekend because you wanted to use the sword you'd made out of wood to kill the headless horseman…who, by the way, doesn't even exist!"

Giorgio lifted his chin in disdain. "Who's to say he doesn't exist?"

"I do," Rocky said in finality. "And that toothpick of a sword wouldn't have left a scratch on him anyway."

"So, do you want to solve real crimes or not?" Giorgio snapped. "Or do you want to reminisce about childhood memories all day?"

Rocky chuckled. "No, let's solve the real ones. At least for those you've moved up to using a real weapon."

"Funny," Giorgio said with a sneer. "Get your notepad out."

Rocky grabbed a legal pad, still brandishing a smile. Then, Giorgio took the next few minutes to fill him in on how Springer and

Montgomery had died. When he was finished, Rocky sat back thoughtfully, the notepad and a cooling cup of coffee sitting in front of him.

"Well, there's not much to go on," Rocky said. "I mean, technically nothing points to anyone else but Jimmy Finn, at least in the case of Lisa Farmer. But…that could have been Ron Martinelli's car that Finn saw in the alley that night. Maybe he and Lisa got into an argument right there in the backyard. He killed her, dumped her in his trunk and drove away."

"Jimmy Finn was positive that wasn't Ron's car in the alley."

"But didn't you say that Ron said he borrowed his dad's car that night?"

Giorgio shrugged. "Yeah, you're right. But how would Ron have known there was a well at the monastery?" Giorgio countered.

This time, Rocky shrugged. "He could have hung out up there as a kid. You and I used to climb the fence all the time at that big old power plant near the house."

"Maybe," Giorgio said. "But Ron Martinelli didn't seem to be faking his reaction when we told him how Lisa died. It was instantaneous. I'm not sure he could manufacture that so quickly, especially after forty years. That kind of acting takes practice."

"You should know," Rocky grinned at him.

"I *do* know," Giorgio said. "The biggest part of making acting believable is to make the line you read sound as if you just thought of it. I don't think Martinelli was acting. And now we know that Jimmy Finn had a girlfriend named Cheryl. And we know that Cheryl's brother didn't like Lisa."

McCready appeared in the doorway and interrupted them.

"Welcome," he said to Rocky and then turned to Giorgio. "I tried to locate Lisa Farmer's step-dad. Turns out he died a couple of years ago. And the Farmer's duplex is also long gone. There's a new housing tract up there. Apparently, they've even reconfigured some of the streets. But I have an address on Leroy Lincoln," he said to Giorgio.

Giorgio's eyes lit up, making him pause with the coffee mug halfway to his lips. "Let's take a trip," he said to Rocky, putting the mug back down.

÷

Leroy Lincoln lived in a rundown single-wide mobile home next to the 210 Freeway. There was a small fenced yard that hadn't seen water or fertilizer in years and a beat-up old Chevy pickup parked under an awning by the back door.

The brothers opened the squeaky front gate and climbed the well-worn steps to a front porch littered with dead plants, cigarette butts and empty beer cans. A broken screen door hung off one hinge, and the sound of heavy metal music from inside actually vibrated the porch floor under their feet.

Rocky reached out and rang the doorbell. Thirty seconds passed before the door opened. An older overweight black man wearing nothing but red boxer shorts poked his head around the door.

"Yeah?" he grunted.

Both detectives held up their badges. The man's eyes opened wide.

"Shit!" he yelled and slammed the door shut, disappearing inside.

"Go around the back!" Giorgio shouted to his brother.

Rocky jumped off the porch and ran out the gate. Giorgio threw open the screen door and burst inside, weapon drawn.

Leroy Lincoln had just disappeared out the back door as Giorgio came through the living room. He followed him out the door and down another set of steps into the driveway, but Rocky was already hot on Lincoln's heels.

By the time Giorgio got to the back of the trailer, Rocky was pulling Lincoln off the fence that led to the freeway. Between the two of them, they quickly got the man's wrists into zip ties and flipped him around.

"What the fuck?" Lincoln said. "I ain't done nothin'."

He fumbled with his wrists, trying to get his hands loose.

"Cool it," Giorgio ordered. "We just want to talk. Let's go back inside, or we may have to arrest you for indecent exposure."

Giorgio glanced down. Lincoln followed his gaze. The fence had torn his shorts, leaving his manhood flopping out for all to see.

"Shit," he said. "You owe me a pair of shorts."

They pushed him toward the back steps and into the trailer. When they got him into a chair, Giorgio found an old blanket and tossed it into his lap.

"Here. Cover up. I just had breakfast" he said. "Anyone else here?" he asked, glancing around.

"No," Lincoln grumbled.

Giorgio nodded for Rocky to look down the hallway. Rocky pulled his weapon and walked to the back of the trailer, while Giorgio waited.

Leroy Lincoln had a round head, with short cropped gray hair. Little squinty eyes peeked out from folds of flesh set close to a wide, flat nose. His stomach ballooned out like a beach ball, stretching his skin tight.

Giorgio eyes roamed the room while he waited for Rocky, taking in stacks of flat screen TVs, flat screen computer monitors, several laptops, and boom boxes along one wall of the shabby living room. A few iPads were stacked on the kitchen counter.

"Well, well, well. I guess I know why you ran. It looks like you're running a little business here," Giorgio said, walking over and lifting up an iPad.

"I got all that stuff legally," Leroy said.

"Sure you did. But that's not why we're here," Giorgio said, turning back to Lincoln. "We're here about Lisa Farmer."

Rocky returned and they both holstered their weapons.

The man just stared at Giorgio. "Lisa who?" he grunted.

"Lisa Farmer," Giorgio repeated. "Jimmy Finn went to prison for her murder."

The proverbial light bulb went off in his bowling ball head. "Oh, that chick. That was a hundred years ago."

"We found her body," Rocky said.

He glanced over at Rocky and then back at Giorgio.

"No shit?"

Giorgio feared this was quickly deteriorating into a wasted trip.

"Your sister used to date Jimmy, is that right?"

"Yeah," he snarled. "So what? She didn't have nothin' to do with that chick's death."

"Did Jimmy?"

"How the hell should I know?"

"Where were you the night she disappeared?" Giorgio asked.

"Fuck! That was a long time ago."

"Think," Giorgio encouraged him. "Her disappearance was a big deal. You must remember

where you were that night. A new pair of boxer shorts might depend on it."

Lincoln shifted uncomfortably in the chair, forcing the blanket to slide precariously off one leg.

"Jimmy and Cheryl didn't go to the prom that night. So, I drove her over to his house so they

could hang out."

"Did you pick her up later?"

He shook his big head. "She usually walked home."

"What were *you* doing that night?" Rocky asked.

"Hell, I don't know," he snarled again. "I was twenty-one, and it was a Saturday night. I was probably out drinking."

"So you weren't anywhere near the house around midnight that night?" Giorgio asked.

"Why would I be?"

"What kind of car did you drive?" Rocky asked.

His eyes darted toward the younger detective. "Back then? Um...a beat-up old Ford."

"Color?" Rocky asked again.

"White," he said.

Rocky and Giorgio exchanged glances.

"Jimmy said you didn't like Lisa," Giorgio said.

"Jimmy's still alive?" Lincoln asked with surprise. "I heard he died in prison."

"He's alive," Giorgio confirmed. "So why didn't you like Jimmy?"

Lincoln shrugged his massive shoulders. "He had a crush on that skinny little white bitch. But he was dating my sister. Cheryl wasn't what you'd call popular, back then. She was a little slow herself. Her and Jimmy were made for each other. Then he got her pregnant."

That was news. Giorgio felt the familiar increase in his heart rate.

"Your sister was pregnant?" he asked.

"Yeah."

"By Jimmy?" Giorgio wanted clarification.

"Yeah."

"You're sure?" Rocky said.

He looked over at Rocky. "Well I'm not positive," he retorted. "She could've been handin it out to others, but that's what she told me."

"What did Cheryl think of Lisa?" Giorgio asked, thinking that maybe they were talking to the wrong Lincoln.

"Well, obviously, she didn't like her. She thought Lisa flirted with Jimmy, leading him on. After all, Jimmy couldn't date her –

him being black and all. So she thought Lisa was just playing with him."

"Was your sister jealous enough to do something about it?" Giorgio asked.

He snorted. "Cheryl? No. She was a ditz. Not too much between the ears, if you know what I mean."

Giorgio snuck a glance at his brother. "Yeah, I think I know what you mean," he said.

"Where's Cheryl now?" Rocky asked.

"She lives in Florida. Married some trucker."

"Did she ever have Jimmy's baby?" Giorgio asked.

Lincoln stuck out his lower jaw. "Naw. She got rid of it. But if you're looking for someone who might have killed that girl, I'd be looking at Jimmy's brother, Marvin."

"Why?" Giorgio asked.

"He was home on leave from the Army back then. He'd watch her through the window... thought she was hot. That made Jimmy mad, and I guess they argued about it. Cheryl told me that Marvin said something like, 'If you're not going to take her for a ride, then I just might.'"

"Where would we find Marvin?" Rocky asked.

"Hell if I know."

"I'll need your sister's contact information," Giorgio said to him.

The man shrugged, indicating he couldn't write while his hands were tied. Giorgio released him; they got the information they needed and left.

As he and Rocky climbed into the car a few minutes later, Giorgio called McCready to find Marvin Finn, and then dialed the local police department. He told them they might like to pay a visit to Mr. Lincoln within the next few minutes if they wanted to retrieve some stolen property.

CHAPTER TWENTY-ONE

When Giorgio walked through his front door that night, he felt as if he could sleep for a week. Too many early morning wake-up calls by the ghost of Christian Maynard, along with the frustrating trip to Seattle.

"You're home early," Angie said, as he walked into the kitchen.

The aroma of cheese had saliva flooding his mouth again. He came to stand next to his wife at the counter. She was cutting up vegetables for a salad.

"We've kind of hit a wall on this cold case. I'm waiting to hear if they've learned anything more on those two recent deaths."

He reached around her and nabbed a sliced carrot and popped it into his mouth. She slapped the back of his hand.

"Stop that. Dinner will be ready in about a half hour."

"Smells like macaroni and cheese. Please let it be macaroni and cheese."

She smiled indulgently. "You're so transparent. I know darn well you only married me for my cooking."

He threw his arms around her waist and hugged her. "That and your mother's apple pie recipe," he said, kissing her cheek. "Is there any chance we're having *that* for dessert?"

Laughter bubbled up in her throat. "No."

He leaned in and nibbled her neck.

"Joe, stop that," she said, trying to push him away.

"We could go upstairs, you know," he whispered. "You said we have half an hour. I'm tired, but not *that* tired."

"You're incorrigible," she chided. "Now go say hello to the kids and let me finish."

He gave her a pat on the rear. "Okay, but if there's no apple pie, I expect your own special dessert later on."

He gave her a double lift to his eyebrows as he exited into the hallway. She smiled and shook her head.

Tony and Marie were in the den, each huddled over their electronic tablets. Grosvenor was sprawled in front of the cold fireplace.

"What are you kids doing?" he said.

"Playing games," Marie murmured without looking up.

Tony didn't even respond.

"Hey! Tony!" Giorgio bellowed. "Did you go deaf?"

Tony looked up, his dark eyes devoid of expression. "What?" he said.

"Do you guys ever talk to each other anymore?"

Marie rolled her eyes. "Geez, Dad. What's the big deal?"

Grosvenor struggled to his feet and lumbered over, pushing his head in between Giorgio's legs.

"The big deal is no one ever talks to each other around here anymore. When I asked you the other day to find out what Tony wanted from McDonald's, you sent him some sort of message through your tablet. He was only in his bedroom!"

"Gee, Dad, you used to complain that all we did was watch TV," Tony said, already refocused on the electronic screen again.

Giorgio paused. Tony had a point. It wasn't that long ago that he'd force them to turn off the TV. Now he wanted them to put down their tablets. But he was beginning to worry that an entire generation was forgetting how to actually speak to each other.

"Tell you what, why don't we do some Christmas shopping later? We could all go down to the mall."

That had their attention.

"Really?" Tony exclaimed. "Can I look for night vision goggles?"

"We'll talk about it later," Giorgio said. "We're going to eat in about thirty minutes."

And they went back to their games.

Giorgio sauntered back to the kitchen, Grosvenor following at his heels.

"I'm beginning to think we should never have let your parents get them those tablets," he said to Angie. "It's all they do."

"Tony asked for a cell phone yesterday," she said, pouring salad dressing over the salad.

"No way!" Giorgio said, opening the refrigerator. "It's bad enough that Marie has one."

"She's only a year older than him, Joe."

"Yeah, but he doesn't need one. He's in the third grade. Who's he going to call?"

He reached into the refrigerator and grabbed a beer.

"First of all," she said, turning to place the filled salad bowl on the table, "Kids don't call anyone anymore. They only text." She smiled. "I think we'll just have to get used to it."

"I don't like it," he said, pulling out one of the chairs and sitting down as he popped the top to the beer can. "It's not normal. What happened to kids going outside to play after school? That tree house I built for Tony last year has hardly been used."

"I know, Joe," she said patiently.

"I told them we'd go to the mall later. I want to find those night vision goggles, anyway. Can you keep him busy while I try to find them?"

She smiled indulgently. "I thought you told him you weren't going to get those."

"Well, if I told him I was, it wouldn't be a surprise. Are we getting that hair dryer for Marie?"

"Sure," Angie said. "Maybe a curling iron, too."

Giorgio rolled his eyes. "Oh God, you're encouraging her."

Angie laughed lightly. Then she gave Giorgio a lifted eyebrow. "You know, you could help set the table rather than just sitting there like the lord of the manor."

He grimaced. "Sorry." He got up and reached into a cupboard to grab four plates. As he put them on the table, Angie spoke.

"By the way, Joe, I talked with Elvira again today."

He stopped on his way to get the silverware. "Is the state inspection on again?"

"No," she replied, pulling the casserole dish out of the oven. "I think that's a lost cause. But she had an offer for me."

Angie put the dish on a trivet in the middle of the table and went to get a serving spoon.

"She wants me to work for her," she said, grabbing a large spoon out of an old ceramic pitcher on the counter. She turned to Giorgio. "I'd work at one of the bigger day care centers teaching letters and numbers to the smaller children. Simple stuff. What do you think?"

He was placing forks and knives around the table. "What about Tony and Marie? Who would be here when they got home from school?"

"Don't worry, Joe. I'd only be working in the mornings. I'd be home when the kids got home. You're worse than my mother," she said, going back to the stove to get a sauce pan with green beans.

"Ha!" he exclaimed, finishing his job. "No one could be worse than your mother. If she had her way, you'd be married to Marty Friedberg just because he's a dentist and is home every night by five o'clock."

"Marty Friedberg is a nice man," she said, draining the beans.

"He's the biggest bore I ever met," Giorgio said, taking his place at the table again. "When we were at your cousin's wedding two years ago, he actually cornered me and asked me if I'd thought about getting my teeth whitened."

She chuckled as she dumped the beans into a dish. "You could stand to have your teeth whitened. You drink too much Coke."

"Humph," he groaned. "Teeth whitening is for models and pretty boys. If I flashed a big pearly white smile at some of the guys I come into contact with, they'd die laughing."

"Better than shooting you," she said. "Now, call the kids."

CHAPTER TWENTY-TWO

Giorgio relaxed into his pillow feeling a soft glow from the rich dessert served up in bed that night by Angie. She snored softly next to him, her auburn hair sprayed across the pillow. He'd known Angie since before high school. Deep down, he'd always known she was the one, even though there had been a few other girlfriends along the way. But once she had corralled him, he'd never turned back.

They say you shouldn't look for a relationship to complete you, but there was no doubt that Giorgio was nothing without Angie. She didn't just complete him – she made him a better person.

Clink!

His head jerked toward the window.

Clink!

He glanced at Angie, but she hadn't budged.

He got out of bed and moved quietly to the curtains. Big white clouds dotted the sky, outlined by an iridescent moon. A breeze moved the branches of the elm tree, and hovering by the garage was the image of Christian Maynard.

Giorgio shivered.

How many more times would this happen? And what the hell was Christian's message this time?

He glanced at the clock next to the bed. It was only a little after midnight. Damn! He hadn't even been to sleep yet.

Angie didn't wake this time when he got dressed. He slipped into the hallway and into Marie's room, where Grosvenor was sleeping. A few minutes later, man and dog were once again going for a late night walk.

It was colder tonight, and the air was damp. He pulled up the collar to his coat, took a deep breath to quiet his nerves and began to follow the boy again.

This time, the boy took him straight to the Pinney House, which loomed large in Giorgio's mind now. There was obviously something about this place, something the boy wanted him to know. And the queasiness in his midsection told Giorgio it wasn't going to be good.

Giorgio stopped again at the walkway that led to the porch. He didn't want to go any further. Not because he might get caught, although that was a risk. But because his intuition was screaming at him that this wouldn't turn out well.

The big building sat silently, like a brooding teenager in the dark. The boy had disappeared, but heavy clouds slipped across the sky in quiet procession, throwing deep, animated shadows across the yard.

When Giorgio caught a movement to the right of the porch, he saw that Christian had reappeared at the north side of the building. He was a pale shimmering form against the backdrop of bushes that separated the properties.

Giorgio glanced up at the big house again. All windows were dark, and a quick glance up and down the street told him he was alone. With a deep sigh, he hurried up the steps and cut across the lawn to where the boy's image glistened in an unearthly light.

Giorgio had to step over a deep trench that ran from the back yard to the street. Then he ducked around the corner of the house. The boy had moved to a pair of French doors, but as soon as Giorgio got there, his image disappeared again.

Frustrated, Giorgio studied the side entrance to the house. Then he turned and eyed the trench that ran along the planters.

The trench was new. It was a couple of feet wide and looked to be about the same depth. It ran down the side yard, connecting to the house with a shorter trench that cut off at a forty-five degree angle right where the French doors opened. It did the same thing further back. Probably sewer lines, he thought to himself.

Flash!

Giorgio's head jerked around and his heartbeat skipped. What the heck was that?

Something white had flashed at the back of the house.

He backed up a step.

Was it Christian?

He stared down the side yard, as a breeze slipped past him to flutter the leaves of the bushes nearby. When he didn't see or hear anything, his instincts took over and he reached for his gun.

But of course he'd left the house without it.

Gathering up the leash in his left hand, he pulled Grosvenor and crept along the side of the house. As he approached the back yard, all he could hear was a frog croaking and the soft rustle of leaves. He cornered the house and found a square brick pond in the middle of a square yard, moonlight reflecting off the water's surface. A short brick wall surrounded the pond, and framing that were trimmed hedges.

Without the holiday lights, the back yard was steeped in deep shadows. Fortunately, as the clouds moved past, the moon revealed parts of the yard to him.

Compared to the size of the house, the yard was small. Tall hedges enclosed the north and west sides of the yard, and hedges extended behind the garage to the far side of the property. This created a barrier that gave the area complete privacy. The trench turned the corner and was connected again to the back of the house near the kitchen.

So, what the heck had caused the streak of white he'd seen?

It could have been his imagination, but then again, it could have been a cat. He was about to retrace his steps, when he realized the frog had stopped making racket. The yard was deathly quiet.

He glanced nervously around.

Grosvenor jerked at the leash and began to dig in the trench under the basement window.

Giorgio yanked him back.

"Grosvenor!" he snapped in a hoarse whisper. "Come here."

But Grosvenor was already flinging dirt up into the air.

Giorgio forcibly dragged him away from the trench and moved back toward the pond. He stood for a moment, wondering what to do next.

Once again, he caught something out of the corner of his eye. Something glistened in the water at his feet, and his heart seemed to short-circuit.

Giorgio glanced down. An image began to materialize, like a photo developing in a photographer's tray.

It was a young woman – naked from the waist up – standing behind him.

He spun around. And that's when he nearly lost it.

The woman wasn't standing as much as hovering behind him. The outline of her body shimmered in the moonlight, as if lit by some inner source.

Giorgio took an involuntary step backward, bumping into the wall of the pond. He caught himself just before he fell. His heart pounded and a prickly heat spread across his skin.

God, now he was seeing two ghosts!

Grosvenor took the opportunity to lie down. Apparently dogs didn't see ghosts. But Giorgio couldn't help gawking at this new apparition.

A large cloud had finally covered the moon, blotting out any natural light. The darkness accentuated Giorgio's isolation, making him feel incredibly vulnerable.

He didn't like this. He didn't like it at all. But as he kept staring, his cop's eye for detail kicked in.

The girl had short, dark hair and she wore old-fashioned glasses. Her upper torso was bare, exposing a set of full breasts – well breast. There was only a gaping hole where her left breast would have been and blood streaming down her torso. She was slender and wore a nurse's cap, but nothing else.

And then more unsettling details began to emerge.

She had what looked like knife wounds across her chest and arms. One eyebrow was completely gone. Her mouth sagged at one corner, and one side of her neck was smeared with something dark that ran across her shoulder.

He zeroed in on this and felt bile seep into his mouth.

Her ear was missing.

And when he glanced down to her feet again, he realized that both big toes were gone, leaving ragged skin behind.

He felt the sudden urge to run, but the appearance of a second apparition stopped him.

This time, he let out an involuntary gasp and dropped down onto the wall surrounding the pond, using one hand to steady himself.

What the hell was happening?

As the second girl's image sharpened, he realized that she was completely naked and probably not more than fifteen. She hovered near the back door of the house, near the basement window where Grosvenor had been digging.

Her head had been shaved, and dark stains extended down her abdomen in sweeping curves, as if her skin had been peeled away in large splotches. And it looked like she was missing the fingers on her right hand.

Giorgio began to feel sick to his stomach, and it seemed as if his hearing had shut down. The only sound he was aware of was the blood pounding through his eardrums.

A breeze scattered some leaves across the lawn at his feet, but he just stared at the two girls. When he became aware of something next to him, he turned to his left.

A hand was reaching for him out of the darkness.

Giorgio bolted sideways and tripped over Grosvenor's leash, landing sprawled on the lawn.

A third girl hovered over the pond.

Bile actually poured into his mouth now, and he had to control his gag reflex.

He sat up and leaned forward, dropping his head between his knees, forcing himself to take deep breaths. After two or three, he glanced up.

The third girl was also naked and had shoulder-length hair and small breasts – but her nipples had been removed, leaving bloody gouges behind. She had other wounds, too – multiple cuts all over her body.

With growing alarm, he watched as she gestured to the ground beneath her feet, her face an expressionless mask.

Giorgio was puzzled, but glanced back at the girl by the tree. She was also pointing to the ground below her.

They were buried here, he thought to himself.

He looked up at the girl by the back door, and his insides shifted. She wasn't pointing at the ground. She was pointing through the basement window.

"Shit!" he whispered. That could only mean one thing.

There were more buried in the basement.

And then all three were gone. All of them. The moment he had that thought. The cloud passed from in front of the moon, and he and Grosvenor were alone.

He sat for a moment, allowing his breathing and heart rate to return to normal. Moments later, the frog began to croak again.

Giorgio got unsteadily to his feet.

These girls had been tortured, murdered and then buried here. His question had finally been answered. He knew why Christian Maynard had brought him to the Pinney House.

But now what the hell was he supposed to do about it?

CHAPTER TWENTY-THREE

Giorgio woke the next day to a forbidding sky and a dull headache. Once he'd made it home the night before, he'd lain awake staring at the ceiling thinking about the three girls, their wounds, and their horrific deaths, finally falling into a restless slumber.

As a New York cop, he'd seen gang murders, killings for revenge, greed, and power. He'd even seen his share of torture. When he'd adopted Grosvenor and realized that someone had used a cigarette to burn his skin, he'd immediately thought of a four-year old boy who had been tortured in a similar way in New York. But Giorgio hadn't seen anything like what this appeared to be – the wanton, repeated torture of young women.

There was a problem, though. No one even knew about these women, and he had no idea who they were. How was he supposed to investigate crimes that no one in *this* world even suspected? He couldn't very well approach a judge and ask for a search warrant based on visions he'd had of ghosts.

He made it to the office frustrated and bleary-eyed. He spent the morning valiantly trying to focus on the current investigation, when the phone rang. It was Detective Abrams from Seattle.

"Maybe some good news," he said. "Our guys found a syringe in the gutter about a block from the nursing home. There were only partial prints on it, and there's no way to tell if it was the one used to kill Montgomery, but this isn't a normal neighborhood for drug paraphernalia. So we're having the lab run it anyway. Maybe we'll get lucky and it will match whatever we find in Montgomery's system. I should have his tox screen back this afternoon."

"Anything from your psychic friend?" Giorgio asked hopefully, his thoughts returning to the images of the girls the night before.

"Yes, but I'm not sure it's helpful," Abrams replied. "I took her up to the nursing home and then down to the morgue. She kept seeing a cabinet."

"A cabinet?" Giorgio said.

"Yeah. A wooden cabinet and something about a rose. Also, when she placed her hand on the puncture wound on Montgomery's neck, she said she felt as if she was drawn through a tunnel of sorts. Back in time, through several decades of the same family."

"Montgomery's family?" Giorgio asked.

"No. She didn't think so. She thought it was whoever held that syringe," Abrams replied.

"What do you suppose that means?" Giorgio asked.

Abrams sighed loudly. "Hell if I know. I don't profess to understand how this works. Or even *if* it works. But she grew very weak and almost passed out as a result."

"Huh, I wonder why?" Giorgio murmured as he wrote notes on a pad of paper.

"She said she saw a whole lot of death – painful deaths."

"Murders?" Giorgio asked, looking up, his heart rate increasing.

"She thinks so. At least they were traumatic deaths. She said these people are all connected somehow through very painful deaths. It was enough to make her physically ill."

Giorgio's body was humming. "Did she see any details? Like faces?"

"Only that they were all women. That's why I said it might not be much help." Abrams said.

"Okay, thanks," Giorgio said, sitting back with disappointment. "Let me know about the tox screen."

"Will do," Abrams replied.

Giorgio hung up and stared at the opposite wall for a moment, unable to quiet the raging thoughts in his head. Traumatic deaths going back a long time. All women. It made him wonder – how long had those girls been buried at the Pinney House?

He had to know more.

While Rocky went out to interview Jimmy Finn's brother, Marvin, and McCready tracked down Cheryl Lincoln in Florida, Giorgio drove to a small white bungalow a block off Colorado Boulevard in Pasadena. He'd seen the house many times on his way to his favorite Mexican restaurant.

He parked at the curb and turned to study the entrance for a moment, questioning whether he really wanted to do this. He didn't know anything about the place, other than what the sign said. And his better judgment was telling him to just turn around and go back to the office.

And yet, he hesitated.

The sign outside said, "Psychic. Palm reading. Tarot cards. Walk-ins welcome."

When he'd first seen Christian Maynard's apparition at the monastery, he'd ignored it, telling himself it was his imagination. When he saw the boy again, he felt a little confused and embarrassed. After all, he was the lead investigator on a major murder case. How could he explain such a strange phenomenon? So he'd never told anyone. But when he saw the boy a third time, he began to question his sanity, at least until it was clear that Christian's ghost was actually trying to help.

He'd thought many times about stopping here to see if the psychic could help explain his experience at the monastery. But his cop brain had always stopped him. Psychics were for kooks or gullible women trying to connect with long-lost lovers. But the boy was back, and it couldn't be a coincidence that he had taken Giorgio to the Pinney House, the exact place where the Martinellis had lived when Lisa Farmer went missing. He didn't know if the deaths of all those girls were connected to Lisa Farmer, but the psychic in Seattle seemed to think they were connected to Montgomery's death, and Giorgio needed to know for himself what was going on. He only hoped that he wasn't making a big mistake.

With a sigh, he got out of the car and strode up the walkway to the front door of the little bungalow. He started to knock, but then noticed a small sign hanging from a beaded wire on the door that said, "Please Enter. Madame Mirabelle will see you."

The name was an instant turnoff, and he thought about leaving. But he took the doorknob in his hand and turned it, springing a small bell as he entered a waiting room.

The room was furnished in comfortable overstuffed furniture. Two chairs were draped in quilts, while a wooden rocker sat in the corner. The tinkling sound of water drew his attention to a small water feature that sat on a stack of old suitcases now serving as a side table.

His nose twitched at the deep floral scent of incense, and in the background was the sound of harp music. All in all, he felt like he'd walked into a New Age bookstore and wondered again if he'd made a mistake. The only normal things in this place were several copies of *Vogue* and *Good Housekeeping* scattered across a coffee table made out of an old wicker picnic basket.

As he stood uncomfortably in the entrance, a side door opened and two women emerged.

"Give it some time, Mrs. Fanning," a young woman said to the plump, middle-aged woman by her side.

The older woman just nodded and used a tissue to wipe her eyes. Giorgio stepped out of the way as she passed by and left. He shifted awkwardly back onto his heels as the young woman turned her gaze upon him.

"May I help you?" she said in a gravelly voice.

She was probably twenty-three or twenty-four, of medium height. Her short, spiky black hair had a red streak that swept from front to back on the left side. Although it was December, the young woman was wearing a tank top and baggy jeans.

It seemed that everywhere he looked she sported either a tattoo or piercing of some kind. She had two rings pierced through her lower lip, a stud in her nose, three or four small hoops up each ear, and a bar through one eyebrow. Giorgio felt his skin prickle at the thought of so many holes punched through his skin, and he couldn't help but flash momentarily on the girls from the night before with their many cuts and missing parts.

He had to forcibly switch thoughts.

She smiled as she watched him take it all in.

"You're a cop," she said matter-of-factly.

His eyebrows shot up. "You know that because you're psychic?"

"No," she laughed. "I can see you assessing me. Cops read people like me," she said without any animosity. "They map the tats and remember how many rings I have through my lip, just in case they have to ID me later for something – you know, as either a suspect or a victim."

"*Have* you been ID'd before?" he smiled.

"Only as a suspect. I'm never a victim," she said confidently. Her lips parted into a self-satisfied grin. "You don't believe me," she said.

Giorgio shrugged. "I don't know whether to believe you or not. I guess that's why I'm here."

"Right. Because I see things. You want to see things, too."

He stuck his hands into his pockets. "I want to talk to you," he said. "I have questions."

"I get paid by the hour," she said. "Read the sign, and then I'll meet you inside."

She returned to the other room. He glanced over at a sign that said, "Reading Fees." According to the chart, a half hour reading was $35. A full hour was only $60. Even psychics cut deals, he thought.

He got out his wallet.

When he stepped into the next room, he was enveloped by a feeling of claustrophobia. The curtains were drawn and a single dim light hung from the middle of the ceiling. The walls were draped in white, gauzy fabric. Although the room was carpeted, a second, round area rug had been laid on top of the wall-to-wall.

Once the door closed, there was utter silence.

A square table, flanked by two chairs, took up the center of the room. Several straight-back chairs sat against one wall. Underneath the curtained window was a narrow table with a pitcher of water and a stack of plastic glasses.

His skepticism must have registered on his face.

"This is normally my aunt's gig," she said. "She likes all of this...ambience. Me? I could take it or leave it."

"So you're not the...you're not...?"

Her laughter rang like a pair of church bells. "Madame Mirabelle?" She lowered herself into the chair on the opposite side of the table. "Why don't you have a seat?"

He pulled out a wooden captain's chair and sat down.

"No, I'm not Madame Mirabelle," she smiled. "That's my aunt. Her ex-husband died in Atlanta, so she went to the funeral. I'm filling in."

Giorgio started to get up again. "I'm sorry, then. I think I'll..."

"Whoa! Whoa! Whoa!" she said, putting a hand up. "Not so fast. You have questions. I have answers."

"No, I think I've made a mistake," he said, turning for the door.

He was just about to step out when she said, "The boy's here, you know. He came in with you."

Giorgio whirled around. "What?"

"The boy…the one in the knickers and the white shirt. He came in with you. He's over by the window," she nodded to her left.

Giorgio's heart rate went into overdrive. He stepped back to the table.

"Why can't I see him?" he asked. "I usually see him."

"I don't know," she shrugged. "We could ask him," she said, holding out her hand.

He paused, but then fished out thirty-five dollars in cash and handed it over. As he sat down, he asked, "What should I call you?"

"My friends call me Flame."

His eyes drifted up to the red streak in her hair.

"And you are?"

"I'm Detective Salvatori."

"So, do you want to know who he is?"

"No. I know who he is. I want to know why he's still here. I thought I…released him."

She gave him a quizzical look, but then shrugged again.

"Okay, I'll try. But they don't come through the way you and I are talking right now. I sometimes hear voices, but it's usually just snatches of conversations. I mostly get impressions, which I then have to interpret. Sometimes I'm right. Sometimes I'm wrong. And they don't usually appear like this," she said, glancing to the window. "This is unusual. Anyway, why don't we try something easy first?"

"Like what?"

"Like how old he is."

"I generally know how old he is," Giorgio said.

She sighed in frustration. "Is there something else?"

"No. Go ahead – ask him how old he is. I don't know for sure."

"Do you know his name?"

"Christian," Giorgio replied, glancing at the water table again.

The girl closed her eyes. He watched her, wondering again at his sanity. He even glanced around the room, wondering if there was any kind of special effects apparatus built into the ceiling.

But then Flame leaned back in the chair and her breathing slowed. He watched her again, hoping she wouldn't start speaking in tongues or try to levitate.

"Ten, I think," she said. "He's ten years old. He's holding up all of his fingers."

She paused again and tilted her head, as if listening to something. Giorgio waited.

"He's showing me a big Spanish-style building. He seems very sad about it. I think it's where he died." She paused and the room went still for several seconds. "Oh, yes," she said. "He jumped out a window to hang himself." Her voice reflected sadness, and she shook her head slightly at the mental image. There was another long pause. "Now he's showing me...I'm not sure. I think it might be his father. Yes, his mother, too. He also had a little brother. He left them all behind, when he..." She paused. "When he hung himself." She swallowed as if whatever she was seeing was difficult. "Anyway, now he's...he's somewhere else. He's surrounded by several young girls. I think they're people who haven't crossed over." She wrinkled her brow. "I'm not sure why they're with him."

There was a long pause, while Giorgio waited, almost holding his breath.

"He's taking me to a big house now," she said. "It's very old. Very pretty." She paused again. "The young women are there...I can't see their faces, but there is a man, too. He's holding a long knife and – oh God!" she exclaimed. Her breathing became ragged and her entire body tensed. "I don't understand," she cried. "What...what is this?" Her eyes popped open and she sat forward in the chair, breathing hard. "Oh my God," she said again. "He...he cut off...he...oh shit! And then I saw the girl as she died," she choked out.

She got up and almost ran to the table to pour a glass of water. Her hands were shaking uncontrollably. She took a long drink and then just stood there, staring at the draped window and taking deep breaths.

"Did he show you who killed them?" Giorgio asked, now sitting forward in his seat.

She spun around. "You knew I'd see that, didn't you?"

"No," he said, standing up. "I didn't. At least not for sure. But I thought that's what you do –see dead people. Why is this so different?"

"Because these are young girls," she snapped. "Torn up with flesh wounds and...missing parts."

He paused a moment and then said, "I know. I saw them last night. And yes, I hoped you would see them. It's really why I came. I need to know more about them. I need to know who they are."

"Where?" she asked, wiping her eyes. "Where did you see them?"

"At a house the boy led me to. Probably the big old house you saw. I think he wants me to do something, but I don't know how to help them. No one even knows they're buried there."

"You're a cop," she said, as if that should fix things.

"Yes, but no one's going to believe me if I say I know they're there because I saw their ghosts. Please, I need your help."

Flame paused as if weighing an internal decision. She returned to the table, but stayed standing. She stared at the water glass in her hands as if contemplating something. Then she nodded once, took a deep breath, and sat down.

"What do you need to know?"

"Anything," he said, resuming his seat. "Anything that might help to either identify the girls or the man who killed them. Did you see him?"

"Not his face," she said, her hands beginning to shake again. "I don't want to see his face."

"I understand," Giorgio said.

"Okay," she said with a deep breath. "One more time."

She sat down and watched him for a moment, as if still uncertain she would do this. Then her eyes closed, and the room went silent again. Giorgio waited.

After a moment, she inhaled sharply, and the fingers on her left hand closed into a fist.

"The boy," she finally whispered. "The boy keeps pointing from the girls to the house, as if there is something important about the house." Her breathing began to accelerate. "I'm not sure what he means. Wait. He's showing me something else. Another girl. Different from the rest. She's dressed in a fancy dress. Long dark hair. She's not like the others."

"She's at the house?" Giorgio asked.

"Yes. There's also a young man…no!" she cried, shaking her head. "No. Not again."

Her eyes opened again and this time there were tears in them. "He showed me one of the naked girls again. Her breast…" she gulped and then stopped speaking. "God, how do you do what you do?" she asked, using her hand to wipe her eyes. "How do you investigate crimes like that?"

"I don't usually. He only showed the girls to me last night. That's why I'm here. I wanted confirmation. I guess I got it."

They shared a long moment of silence without looking at each other. Finally, she spoke in almost a whisper, her voice shaking.

"Look, I've been able to communicate with the dead since I was a little girl," she said quietly. "It started when I began seeing my grandfather after he died in a car accident. My mother freaked out and took me to a shrink. So, I learned to suppress this so-called gift. But then I found out that my aunt had some of the same abilities. Maybe that's what frightened my mother – she didn't want me to be like her sister. But my aunt helped me develop the talent, and, well, here I am. But I don't see things like this." She looked up at Giorgio. "How did you come to meet the boy?"

"On a case a couple of months ago," Giorgio said. "A woman was murdered at a monastery in Sierra Madre where he'd been a student a long time ago. He'd killed himself because he and other boys had been abused by the attending priests."

She seemed to consider this. "The monastery murders," she said. "I read about all of that. You were the lead detective."

"That's right," he said, shifting in his chair. "Christian made himself known to me early in the investigation. But I...I..."

"You denied it...thought you were seeing things," she said as if she'd heard it a million times before.

He nodded. "But then he actually led me to a couple of important clues."

"And then?" she asked.

"I hadn't seen him since we closed that case. Then, a few days ago we found the skeleton of a young girl in an old well at the monastery. We think it's the remains of a girl that disappeared the night of her prom back in 1967."

A momentary flash of recognition passed across her face. "A girl in a fancy dress," she whispered.

"Yes. With long dark hair," he said. "Her name was Lisa Farmer. All of a sudden, a couple of nights ago, Christian showed up again." He reached into his pocket and drew out the metal coin with "Big Bear Lake" stamped on it. "He...delivered this to me," he said, handing it over to the young woman. "I don't know how he does that. But he did it before – with an old button. I know it must mean something. But I don't know what. And I don't know how or even *if* these young girls somehow fit into the Lisa Farmer case."

She took the metal coin and studied it for a moment, rubbing her fingers across its surface. Her eyes seemed to sink back into her head as her eyelids closed halfway. She grew very quiet. A tear formed and ran down her cheek. The tick tock of a clock in the corner marked the passage of time. She dropped her head and then raised it again suddenly, her eyes open.

"I'm not quite sure what I'm seeing," she said, dropping her chin and wiping the tear away. "First I saw the color amber. I don't know what that means. But this is all related somehow. I think that's what the boy is trying to tell you. That's why he brought you to the big house. But it didn't all happen there. He keeps showing me young girls being…tortured. It happens over and over again." She handed the coin back. "You're right, though. Something happened in Big Bear. Something you're supposed to know. And somehow these women are connected to you. The house is connected to you. Big Bear is connected to you. It's all connected to you now."

"To me?"

"Yes. Whether you like it or not, it seems you've stepped into a gruesome quagmire of some sort. And he's trying to help you sort it out."

"Was there anything about a cabinet?" he asked.

Her eyebrows clenched together. "No. Not a cabinet. Just what I told you."

"I just wish I knew what it all meant."

"He's trying to help you," she said with a shrug. "You just have to get quiet and follow his lead."

He glanced over at her. She seemed so young and innocent, despite all the tattoos and piercings. Her dark eyes shone in the dim light with a disquieting sense of wisdom for someone so young.

"What about you?" he said. "Would you be willing to help?"

He asked it cautiously, knowing the answer was uncertain at best. She took a deep breath and brought her hands together on the table in front of her.

"I don't know."

"Look," Giorgio began, feeling desperate. "I would need a search warrant in order to find the bodies at this house. But no one's going to give me one. I have no reason to ask for the warrant. But I'm pretty sure I could get permission to visit the property since it's connected to the Lisa Farmer case; her boyfriend lived there. You could go with me and just... see what you see."

He stopped and watched her, hoping he hadn't overstepped his bounds. She drew one of the rings that pierced her lower lip into her mouth, thinking. Finally, she exhaled.

"I'd like to help. But, let's face it. I mostly help people who want a last chance to communicate with someone they loved. Or want some kind of confirmation that their loved ones are okay on the other side. Mrs. Fanning, the woman you saw leaving? She wanted to communicate with her husband of thirty-five years who died recently when he was hit by a drunk driver. I deal with simple stuff, Detective. I make people feel better. I don't *do* horrendous murders," she said, her voice beginning to shake. She took another cleansing breath and then exhaled. After a long pause, she said, "My mother was murdered, Detective. Almost six years ago. She was beaten and then shot by a burglar. That's why I'm living here with my aunt. I don't have any other family." She paused. "I'm sorry. I…I just can't. It brings up too many memories." She drew her hands into her lap and dropped her chin. "I can't help you."

His body sagged with disappointment.

"I understand," he said. "You've already been very helpful. Is there anything else you can tell me, though? Anything that Christian might know?"

She glanced up at him and after a pause, closed her eyes once more. As he watched her, her eyebrows furrowed and she bit her lip again. After thirty seconds, she opened her eyes.

"It's difficult," she said, rubbing her eyes. "I get snatches of pictures, sometimes moving pictures. Sometimes just flashes of color or a blurred image. Here and then gone. He kept showing me a baby, an adult and an old person. So maybe someone who grew up and then grew old. I don't know who that is, though. And he kept showing me a rose."

Giorgio started. "A rose?"

"Yes. I don't know what it means, though."

Giorgio contemplated this, a buzzing in his ears. Abrams' psychic had said something about a rose, too.

"Okay, thanks," he said. "Thanks very much. I can show myself out."

He stood up and started to leave, but she stopped him.

"By the way, Detective. This might not mean anything. But I also kept seeing a dog. I think the dog is important somehow."

Giorgio's heart rate picked up again. "What kind of a dog?"

She shook her head. "It's hard to tell." She closed her eyes a moment. "Long ears, long snout," she said.

Giorgio nodded. "Thanks. By the way, do you know why the boy appeared to me in the first place and not someone else?"

She took a deep breath. "Because you're a police officer."

Giorgio just stared at her.

"His father was a police officer," she said.

CHAPTER TWENTY-FOUR

The moment he walked back into the office that morning, his phone rang again. This time is was Lieutenant Pearson.

"One of the neighbors ID'd a Jeep Wrangler parked around the corner from Alex Springer's home the night he was killed," she said. "No one had ever seen it before, and it doesn't belong to anyone in the neighborhood. Unfortunately, no one got a license plate number.

At the mention of a Jeep, Giorgio's antenna went up. Jeep Wranglers weren't that common, and yet he'd seen one outside his own home the night he went to meet with Monty Montgomery. And as Lieutenant Pearson continued to talk, the image of the retreating taillights at the Christmas tree lot had his adrenalin flowing.

"The housekeeper also reported that nothing of value was stolen from the home," Lieutenant Pearson was saying. "Hopefully, we'll get DNA off the cigarette butts, but that will take some time. Anything on your end?"

He shared information about his trip to Seattle and the speculation that the two murders were connected.

"Okay, thanks," she said. "Let's keep in touch."

Giorgio hung up and sat staring off into space.

"Who was that?" Rocky asked from the doorway.

"The Lieutenant handling Alex Springer's murder," he replied.

"Anything new?" his brother asked.

Giorgio looked up at his brother as if he'd just noticed him.

"Let's go get some lunch. My treat."

Rocky lifted his eyebrows in surprise.

They walked down the street to Mama's Café. Mama's was a central gathering place for anyone who worked downtown, and all the officers were well known there.

While they waited for their chili dogs and fries, Giorgio spied Mia Santana at a corner table, hunched over and furiously punching out a story on her small laptop. He scooted further into the booth so that she wouldn't see him.

"So, what's up with Alex Springer?"

"Not much. But they ID'd a Jeep Wrangler that was parked around the corner from his house that night, and no one in the neighborhood knows whose it was."

"Hmmm," Rocky murmured. "Well, Marvin Finn, Jimmy's brother, is a bust," Rocky said. "He never actually met Lisa. He was only home for a short time on leave from the Army and was back on base the day before Lisa went missing."

"Okay. Let's see if we can confirm it," Giorgio said.

"We also found Cheryl Lincoln," Rocky said. "She'd moved twice since that address her brother gave you. But she wasn't home. Truck driver hubby was, though. Said she was at work."

Rocky was playing with an advertisement for apple pie on the table. He turned it over and over in his hands as he talked.

"You guys didn't tell him why you were calling, did you?"

"No. McCready called the local PD down there and asked one of their detectives to go out and interview her. They said they'd get back to us tomorrow. So, are you convinced now that Jimmy Finn didn't do it?" Rocky asked, dropping the advertisement and sliding the salt shaker over in front of him instead.

Giorgio sat back in the booth and sighed. "Pretty much," he said. "Think about it. The girl went missing the night of her prom. So the department began an investigation, but didn't do much real investigating. Then a tip comes in out of the blue telling them to search the lockers at the school. And surprise! They find the girl's underwear and shoe in Jimmy Finn's locker – who just happened to be black, defenseless, and infatuated with the victim. How much more perfect could it get?"

"He could've done it," Rocky said, spinning the salt shaker on the table.

"Yes, but now we have two more murders," Giorgio said. "Springer and Montgomery were probably killed because of what they knew. We don't know yet what Springer might have known, but most likely Montgomery was killed because he was asked to plant the evidence against Jimmy Finn. If he did, then the odds are pretty high that Finn didn't kill Lisa Farmer. Besides," Giorgio said, "if

Finn *was* the killer, why are these other guys showing up dead *now*? He's already served his time."

"Maybe they were in on it," Rocky speculated.

"You haven't met Finn. He isn't sophisticated enough to have been working with anyone else. Besides, in what world would he be connected to either Springer *or* Montgomery? Especially back in 1967?"

Rocky raised an eyebrow. "The plot thickens, as they say."

"Yes," Giorgio sighed again. "But things keep coming back to the Martinelli family somehow. I want to know more about them. I just don't buy it that Lisa Farmer was never at that house. She and Ron were talking about getting married. What if she was there that night?"

"Technically, we don't know *where* she was just before she got killed," Rocky said, finally pushing the salt shaker away. "Although we think she made it home."

"But it would change the dynamics if she'd been to the house," Giorgio said. "Otherwise, as far as we know no one saw her after the prom except Ron. If he dropped her off at home, like he said, the killer *had* to be waiting for her when she got there."

"Unless she went out again," Rocky suggested.

"Maybe. But why? Something doesn't add up. I want to go check out the Martinelli house," Giorgio said.

He took a sip of water, hoping Rocky wouldn't question his idea.

"What do you hope to find?"

Inwardly, Giorgio swore, as the moment arrived when he would have to lie to his own brother.

"I've just never been inside it, have you?" he said after swallowing.

Rocky shook his head.

"And yet it's a landmark in this community. I just have a feeling about that old building," he said as he exhaled. "The Martinellis lived there when Lisa disappeared. His mother said the girl never came to the house because they didn't approve of her. Yet, they didn't care if their son took her to the prom? I'm telling you, something's wrong here."

"You and your 'feelings,'" Rocky quipped. "If we could only bottle them."

Just then, a little bell rang and McCready strolled through the front door. He gave a brief wave and crossed over to the table.

"You hungry?" Giorgio asked him.

"No. I grabbed a sandwich already," he said, sliding into the booth next to Rocky.

The waitress arrived with two chili dogs, and McCready waited while Giorgio and Rocky each got a first bite.

"That'll give you heartburn," McCready said with a smile as he eyed the slop in front of Rocky.

Rocky swallowed, allowing some sauce to run down his chin. "Yeah, but after more than three weeks of cardboard chicken in rehab, I don't care," he said, going for a second bite.

"So what have you got?" Giorgio asked the young cop, shoving a napkin across the table to his brother.

Rocky grimaced and wiped his chin. McCready was about to answer, when someone appeared at the end of their table.

It was Mia Santana.

"Have you interviewed Ron Martinelli yet, Detective?" she asked in a loud voice.

Giorgio had reached for a few French fries, but had to stop.

"Good afternoon to you, too, Ms. Santana," he said, glancing up at her.

She was dressed in a wool coat and checkered scarf and carried a black messenger bag over her shoulder. She ignored the sarcasm.

"I want to know if you've interviewed Lisa Farmer's boyfriend," she said.

Giorgio wiped his hands on a napkin.

"First of all, Ms. Santana, I'm not in the habit of discussing ongoing investigations with the press," he said with an edge to his voice.

"So this *is* an active case again?" she said triumphantly.

Giorgio grimaced. "Look, why are you so worried about Ron Martinelli?"

She put one hand on her hip and sighed. "Because I discovered this morning that his father was on the building committee at the monastery when Lisa Farmer went missing. The same building committee that approved the plans for the new west wing and patio up there. The *same* concrete patio that covered over the old well."

Both Rocky and McCready glanced at Giorgio, who was taking a moment to process the information.

"Thank you, Ms. Santana. We'll look into it."

He lifted the French fries again and prepared to stuff them into his mouth. She turned and marched out the door.

"Well, that's a piece of information we didn't have," Rocky said, watching her disappear.

"Yes, dammit," Giorgio said, holding the fries between his fingers. "How did we miss that?"

He leveled a measured look in McCready's direction.

McCready shifted uncomfortably in his seat. "Sorry."

"Why does that make a difference?" Rocky asked, negotiating another sloppy mouthful.

"Because that means that Ron Martinelli *might* have known about the well," Giorgio said. "The contractors would have had to have permission to cover it up, so the entire building committee would have known about it. And maybe Royce Martinelli talked about it at home."

"Who else was on the committee?" Rocky asked.

"Good question," Giorgio said. He looked at McCready again. "Make sure you find that list. We need to know who else might have known about that well back then."

The young cop nodded and Giorgio finally popped the fries into his mouth.

÷

McCready returned to the station, while Giorgio called the Pinney House to get permission for a visit. Since it was considered an historical building and served as a bed and breakfast, he was sure tourists often stopped by to take a look. But he felt a twinge of anxiety at the thought of returning so soon after the horrifying encounter the night before. Maybe having Rocky there would help to mitigate the stress he was feeling.

On his way to the car, his cell phone rang. It was Angie.

"Can you take Grosvenor to the groomer's at three o'clock?" she asked. "Elvira just called and asked me to come in to talk to the Consortium owners about working there."

A shiver ran down his spine as Giorgio remembered what Flame had said about the dog.

"Um, yeah, I guess," he said, unlocking the car.

"Well, he's beginning to smell, and before you suggest it… the answer is no, the kids cannot give him a bath in the middle of winter."

"Not a problem, I'll go get him," he said, thinking that a bath for Grosvenor was the last thing he was worried about.

"Oh, and by the way," his wife said, "someone delivered an envelope for you. I left it on the desk in the den."

"Uh…okay," he said, wondering what it could be.

"What?" Rocky said after Giorgio hung up and they got into the car.

"We have to pick up Grosvenor."

÷

It was early afternoon when they pulled into the driveway at the Pinney House. The elegant building stood proudly in the afternoon light, a magnificent example of Victorian architecture.

Giorgio left Grosvenor in the car with the window open. They met a tidy woman in her forties at the door. Her short gray hair was cut close to her head, and she wore a gray jumper over a long-sleeved white blouse.

She introduced herself as Veronica Johnson, current owner of the house. She couldn't have been over five foot two, but exuded enough energy to fuel a person twice her size. When Giorgio made an admiring comment about the house, she responded.

"My husband and I bought and renovated the property several years back, with the intention of opening a bed and breakfast. It's been a real labor of love," she said with pride. "It has a long history, you know," she continued. "It's even haunted."

Giorgio froze.

"Haunted?" he said.

"Yes," she prattled on. "A little nine-year-old girl from the turn of the century appears from time to time at the back staircase. But I've been reading in the paper about that girl *you* found. So her boyfriend lived here back then, did he?"

Giorgio relaxed when he realized she wasn't referring to the young women in the yard. Mrs. Johnson crossed her arms across her chest to ward off the chill in the air, but her gray eyes were alight with enthusiasm at owning the home where Ron Martinelli had lived. Apparently she liked the idea of having the house in the spotlight.

"Yes, he did," Giorgio replied. "The Martinellis. Have you heard of them?"

"Actually, I have," she said. "We found a small box of things hidden in the wall of the basement when we remodeled down there. There were a couple of bills, I think, that had the Martinelli name on them. Plus, of course, I did some research on the house when we bought it so that I could tell guests about its history. Well, why don't you come in?"

As she stepped aside to let them in, she happened to look past Giorgio and spy Grosvenor sticking his nose out the open window of the car.

"Is that a Basset Hound?" she cooed.

Giorgio glanced back at the car. "Yes," he said innocently, knowing full well he'd left the window open hoping Grosvenor would show himself. "He's on his way to the groomer's."

She stepped out onto the porch to get a better look. "Well, why don't you bring him in? It's cold out here, and we love dogs. I used to have a Basset when I was a little girl. I'd love to meet him."

Giorgio shot a look at Rocky. It seemed at least once a week someone mentioned that they'd owned a Basset. He returned to the car, clipped on the dog's leash and let the dog out.

Grosvenor ambled up the walkway, stopping once to lift his leg on a rose bush that lined the walk. Giorgio jerked the leash, shot a sheepish smile at Mrs. Johnson, and Grosvenor reluctantly hefted his heavy body up the steps. He approached the woman with his head down and his tail wagging.

"This is Grosvenor," Giorgio said.

"Well, aren't you the sweet thing?" she said, reaching out and petting him.

Grosvenor knew a soft touch when he met one and wiggled his entire body in response. Mrs. Johnson was charmed.

"Grosvenor, that's an odd name," she said, her eyes dancing.

"He was a rescue dog. It was on his tag. But it seems to fit," Giorgio said, looking down at his short-legged companion.

"Yes it does," she said. "Well, c'mon, Grosvenor – let's go inside."

She led them into a richly carpeted entryway and then closed the big door behind them.

"Welcome to the Pinney House," she said with a broad smile.

Giorgio glanced around, impressed with the grandeur of the décor. The walls were painted a soft crème color accented with brass wall sconces. Pine wainscoting wrapped around corners and all the way down the hallway, and a handsome oak staircase extended to the second floor. Holiday garland and red bows accented the bannister. An elegant crystal chandelier hung from the center of the foyer ceiling.

"It's lovely," he said.

"We're very proud of what we've accomplished," she said. "It wasn't in very good condition when we bought it. What you see is the result of a lot of blood, sweat and tears. And money," she joked.

Giorgio had explained on the phone that he wanted access to the home to get a better sense of the layout.

"We'd like to look around if you don't mind," he said.

"We're full right now, so I'm afraid the guest rooms wouldn't be available," she said, reaching down to pet Grosvenor again.

"That shouldn't be a problem," Giorgio told her. "We just need to see the study and the basement."

"Of course. The study is down here."

They followed her past a set of beautifully carved wooden doors that opened up onto a large room that looked out onto the front porch. It was filled with antique furniture and fresh flowers tastefully arranged in large cut-glass vases. A floor-to-ceiling Christmas tree stood in the corner, decorated with Victorian bows and glass ornaments.

"If we go back here, behind the staircase," she said, leading them back into the entryway and past a guest bathroom, "this would probably have been the study. We use it as a library today."

She stopped across from the foot of the staircase and opened the door to a room the size of a large bedroom. On the far wall was a fireplace framed by an oak mantle inlaid with blue Moroccan tiles and flanked by two tall, leaded windows. In the far left corner were heavy green floor-length drapes.

Giorgio moved into the room and went directly to the set of drapes. He pulled them aside and found the French doors, picturing himself standing outside the night before.

"I have a photo taken the night the girl went missing," he said, pulling out the photo Claire Martinelli had given him. "Can you look at it and tell where it was taken."

He showed her the photo.

"Yes, that's this room," she said. "You can tell because of the French doors."

"Okay, the desk would have been here," he said, pointing to the center of the room. "Facing that wall." He pointed to the bookshelves.

"Yes, it looks that way," she confirmed.

Giorgio went back to the door leading to the hallway, glanced at the photo and back at the room. He backed up until he was at the foot of the stairs.

"So Mrs. Martinelli must have been standing about here when she took the photo."

Mrs. Johnson followed him, looking at the photo in his hand and then back at the room.

"That seems right," she agreed.

"From what I understand," Giorgio said, "the master suite used to be at the south end of the building. I suppose at the end of the hallway up there," he said, pointing up the stairs and to his left. "Do you know?"

"I believe that's right," she said. "But the Pinney House has been renovated several times since then."

"Then the master suite would have been closest to the garage. And if you were sleeping in that room, you could hear someone pull up the driveway into the garage, couldn't you?" he asked.

"I would think so," she said with a nod of her head.

"May we see the basement?" he said.

"Of course."

As she led them to the back of the house and into the updated kitchen, Rocky pulled Giorgio aside.

"Why are we looking in the basement?"

Giorgio turned quickly. "I just want to understand the building," he said quietly, following Mrs. Johnson again.

Mrs. Johnson led them down an old set of wooden stairs off the kitchen.

"I'm afraid we just use the basement as an extra pantry and laundry room now," she said. "But I understand that there was a root cellar somewhere at one time which was used for fruits and vegetables."

She pulled the string for an overhead bulb that illuminated a small room, maybe five hundred square feet. The walls had been lined with sheet rock and painted brown. The floor was untreated concrete.

Aged, but sturdy wood shelving lined the far wall and held canned fruit and canisters of flour and sugar. A large washer and dryer sat against the right wall, flanked by a sink and a set of cupboards and a long counter. Storage boxes and a couple of old chests were stacked against the wall under the small horizontal window that faced the backyard.

Giorgio felt a tingling at the back of his neck as he glanced out that window. He could see a few bushes close by and imagined the girl hovering there and pointing through the window.

"You said you remodeled," Rocky said to her.

"That's right. There used to just be old paneling that covered the walls. We tore that down and put up the dry wall and added a dropped ceiling. The bookcases were here when we moved in. We just painted them over."

The center of the room was empty, except for an old rickety table, a support pillar and a drain in the middle of the floor.

Giorgio wandered the perimeter, surveying the walls. Grosvenor followed him partway and then stuck his nose to the floor and made a beeline for the drain. He then headed straight for the bookcases at the far end of the room.

Giorgio looked up from where he was staring at the drain in the middle of the floor and watched the dog intently. "What's Grosvenor doing?"

They all turned. Grosvenor was running his nose along the bottom of the center bookcase at the far end of the room, sniffing with loud snuffling noises.

"He must have found some food under there," Rocky said with a chuckle.

Grosvenor suddenly backed off, sat down and let out a "woof."

"What's the matter, Buddy?" Giorgio said, moving over and reaching out to touch him.

Grosvenor whined and backed up even further, his mouth open now in a rapid pant.

"What's wrong with him?" Mrs. Johnson asked with concern.

Giorgio knelt down, stroking the dog's back. "Hey, G, what's up? You okay?"

Grosvenor leaned into Giorgio and licked his hand, and then went back to panting. Giorgio looked over his shoulder at the bookcases.

"Why don't I take him upstairs?" Mrs. Johnson offered.

Giorgio stood up. "That's okay. I think we're done down here anyway. Maybe we could look at the backyard."

"Of course," she said with a smile.

Grosvenor led the group back up the stairs, with Giorgio bringing up the rear. He couldn't help a final glance back at the basement. He'd learned to trust Grosvenor's nose and his own instincts. And both were screaming for attention.

Once they were outside, Grosvenor's demeanor changed immediately. He watered a nearby bush and began to aimlessly wander around the yard, completely relaxed again.

Giorgio watched him for a moment and then began to concentrate on the yard.

Everything seemed innocent in the afternoon sunlight. There were no ghosts, just a well-groomed yard with winter bare trees.

Giorgio moved to the garage and turned to look up to the second-story corner window, trying to focus on the Lisa Farmer case and not the other dead girls.

"What are you thinking?" Rocky asked.

"That someone sleeping in that corner bedroom would have heard a car pull in."

"I thought the mother said she was asleep when her son got home that night," Rocky said.

Giorgio studied the yard some more. "She seemed confused by that the other day," he said.

His eyes involuntarily drifted over to the planter beneath the small basement window.

"From what I read, the Martinellis only had the one son. Is that right?" Mrs. Johnson asked.

"Yes," Giorgio replied, turning his attention to her. "Ron Martinelli."

"Does he still live in the area? I was just wondering because there was something in that box we found that might belong to him."

Giorgio turned to her. "What was that?"

"The box is filled with mostly girl stuff, but there is a St. Christopher. I know a lot of the boys back then wore those. My brother did. Anyway, I just thought it might be his."

Once again, Giorgio's antenna went up.

"Could we see that box?" he asked.

He felt a slight humming in his ears. It happened every time he was about to discover something important. He felt the familiar accompanying adrenalin rush.

"Just a minute. I'll go find it," she said.

Mrs. Johnson bustled into the house, leaving the brothers to themselves.

"It looks like they're having some sewer line problems," Rocky said, eying the trench.

"Yeah," Giorgio replied. "Probably costing them a fortune."

Grosvenor had moved over to the trench that ran under the basement window, and Giorgio purposely turned his back on him.

"So what are we looking at here?" Rocky asked impatiently.

"I'm just kind of mapping the building," Giorgio replied. "So, there are two exits in addition to the front door," he said, trying to sound as if he was really trying to make a point.

"Yeah? So?" Rocky said.

"Well, it's important to know how people get in and out of a building," Giorgio said, stalling for time.

Meanwhile, he waited for Grosvenor, hoping against hope the dog would find something. He'd done it up at the monastery when he'd found a body buried in the vegetable garden. Maybe he would do it again.

Rocky stuffed his hands into his pockets, clearly bored.

"I think it's interesting that you two are brothers," Mrs. Johnson's voice called out as she came out the back door again. "And you're both police officers." She scurried across the lawn, holding something in her hands. "My uncle was a security guard on a university campus," she continued. "He loved that job."

When she reached them, she stopped and said, "Here you go." She handed an oblong tin box to Giorgio. "There's just a lot of old trinkets in there. But you'll also find the St. Christopher."

"Thank you," Giorgio said, taking the box.

He popped the lid and glanced inside. There was a layer of random pieces of jewelry, hair clips and things like shoe strings and old tubes of lipstick. But his heart stopped when he saw a pair of old-fashioned eye glasses with winged tips and accented with rhinestones. They looked just like the ones the first ghost was wearing the night before. Giorgio forced himself to ignore them, and used a finger to search through the junk until he found the St. Christopher. He lifted it up by its chain.

"That's it," Mrs. Johnson said. "It might be that boy's, don't you think?"

"Could be," Giorgio murmured, glancing back into the box, knowing that this box had just become evidence. He dropped the medal back into the box and pulled out a folded piece of paper from the bottom. It was a deposit slip for Heritage Bank from 1966; Royce Martinelli's name was on it.

"What's that?" Rocky asked.

"A bank deposit slip for Royce Martinelli," Giorgio said, studying the slip of paper.

"That's how I knew the box belonged to the Martinellis," Mrs. Johnson said.

"May we keep the box?" he asked.

"Of course. I've almost gotten rid of it several times because there's nothing of value in there. But, I don't know, I tend to hold onto things," she said with a chuckle. "My husband says if I hadn't married him, I'd be a hoarder."

She finished with a loud chortle, as if this was a common joke between the couple. Giorgio was about to put the lid back one, when something tucked in the corner of it caught his eye.

"Wait a minute," he said, quickly slipping the lid beneath the bottom of the box and holding them together.

He reached in to pull out a small, heart-shaped silver earring.

"Well, I'll be damned," he swore softly.

"What is it?" Rocky asked, moving in to look over his shoulder.

"I do believe we just found Lisa Farmer's matching earring."

"No shit?" Rocky exclaimed. "Oh, sorry," he said to Mrs. Johnson.

"That's quite all right," she said. "Is that the case you're investigating?"

Giorgio turned a wary expression to Rocky.

"Yes," Giorgio said to her.

As Giorgio dropped the earring back into the box and put the lid back, Mrs. Johnson suddenly cried out, "Uh, oh!"

She'd glanced around Giorgio's shoulder and noticed Grosvenor, who was knee deep into a hole. Her eyes opened wide and Giorgio responded.

"Grosvenor!" he yelled, as if surprised by his actions.

He ran over and grabbed the dog by the collar, pulling him back. Grosvenor was covered in dirt.

"I'm so sorry," Giorgio said to the woman.

Grosvenor twisted away from Giorgio's grasp and went right back to his work.

"I'm sorry, Mrs. Johnson, he doesn't usually do this," Giorgio said.

But Mrs. Johnson dismissed the whole incident as Grosvenor continued to dig.

"Oh, not to worry," she said. "What's one more hole?"

"Rocky, take this," Giorgio said, handing off the box to his brother.

Giorgio stepped forward and grabbed the dog's collar. He pulled Grosvenor back and pushed him away. Then he stepped forward and squatted down.

"Let me clean this up a bit," he said, peering into the hole.

He reached in and pushed the dirt around, as if he was filling in the hole. Mrs. Johnson moved over to his shoulder.

"Oh, don't worry, Detective. My husband will take care of that...oh, but wait," the little woman exclaimed.

Giorgio glanced up at her. She was pointing into the hole near the window.

"What could that be?" she asked.

He glanced down. Buried deep within the hole next to the basement wall was something white. Something that shouldn't be there. The hairs on the back of his neck stood up.

Giorgio reached in and pulled away more dirt. When the jawbone of a human skull emerged, he glanced up at Rocky.

Mrs. Johnson's hand flew to her mouth. "Oh my..."

Giorgio sat back on his heels. "I'm afraid the question isn't what, Mrs. Johnson," he said. "But who?"

CHAPTER TWENTY- FIVE

It took several hours to organize a recovery team. Most of the resources had to be brought in from other cities, including a forensics team and a cadaver dog. Since it got dark by six o'clock, Giorgio scheduled the recovery for 9:00 a.m. the next day and then stationed a pair of uniformed officers to guard the burial site. Meanwhile, the Johnsons and their guests were asked to leave the premises.

Back at the station, Giorgio compared the earring from the tin box to the earring that came out of the well with Lisa Farmer's remains. They were a match. He logged the box into the evidence locker at the police station for safekeeping.

The earring meant that Lisa Farmer had either been to the home the night of the prom, or that someone in the Martinelli family was involved in her murder and had kept it.

But first things first. Giorgio had to focus on the bodies buried at the Pinney House.

It was late by the time he got home that night. He had to explain to Angie why Grosvenor not only didn't make it to the groomer's, but looked worse for the wear.

"What was in the envelope?" she asked, sliding a dinner plate with a cheese enchilada and rice into the microwave oven for him.

"Oh, I forgot," he said, turning around and heading for the den.

He found a large manila envelope in the middle of the desk. It was addressed to 'Detective Joe Salvatori' with no return address. He was immediately suspicious.

Giorgio grabbed a tissue from a Kleenex box on the corner of the desk and used it to pick up the envelope. He pulled out a letter opener from the desk drawer and slit the envelope open. It was empty.

"Who delivered this?" he said, taking it back into the kitchen.

Angie turned around and glanced at the envelope in his hand.

"Um…I don't know… Some young man in a uniform."

She went back to working at the counter.

"What did he look like?" Giorgio asked, trying to appear as casual as he could.

She talked as she pulled his dinner from the microwave.

"I don't know, Joe. He had long blond hair in a ponytail. Just a kid with tattoos."

Giorgio's insides had begun to churn.

"Do you know what company he was from?" he asked, trying to conceal his concern.

She turned to him momentarily. "Joe, I didn't pay attention. Why all the questions?"

"But was it FedEx, or UPS?"

"Why is it important?" she said, putting his plate on the table.

His head was spinning. It appeared that the same person who might have killed Carson Montgomery had delivered the envelope to his house.

"Um…it's empty," he said. "Somebody screwed up. I just need to track it down. Do you remember what it said on the side of the truck?"

She was already busy back at the counter putting the leftovers away.

"He wasn't in a truck. I saw a Jeep at the curb."

÷

Giorgio spent a restless evening at home, replaying details in his mind about the Montgomery case in Seattle and what he knew about the young man who had killed him. His mind kept jumping back and forth between the various threads of the investigation and the intrusion on his family's safety. In the end, he slept very little. Something was wrong. Very wrong.

The next day he rolled out of bed feeling strained and grumpy, and yet anxious to get going. Instincts told him something big would break today.

The weather outside matched Giorgio's mood perfectly – cloudy and dreary.

Giorgio took the envelope with him to the police department to log it into evidence and have it checked for fingerprints. Then he went to see the captain.

It felt as if the Lisa Farmer case had morphed into something out of his control. Two new murders. At least one body buried on the Pinney House property. Someone had fondled his daughter in public. And now a strange delivery to his home by the man who might have committed one of the murders.

He needed to get control of the situation before it spun completely *out of control.*

"I need eyes on my house," he said, after explaining the situation. "Something's going on, and I can't be everywhere at once."

The captain thought a moment and then nodded. "I'll put an unmarked car outside. You take care of the Pinney House."

÷

A team of officers converged on Lima Street, rerouting traffic with their police cruisers at Grandview and at Sierra Madre Boulevard. Then they cordoned off the Pinney House property with yellow crime scene tape from neighbors and passersby.

Extra help came in the form of a ground-penetrating radar unit, the lead forensics technician from the Pasadena PD and his assistant, the county medical examiner and two cadaver dogs. Grosvenor was home, his job done.

Giorgio led the recovery process, bringing the forensics technicians to the back of the house.

"That's where we found the skull," he said, pointing to the hole under the basement window.

Forensic Tech, Gerald Fong, was in his late thirties and dressed in a white jumpsuit. Giorgio had worked with him on the Mallery Olsen case. Although he didn't display much personality, Giorgio found him incredibly thorough.

"Okay," Fong said. "We may need to remove this bush," he said, pointing to a nearby rhododendron bush. "But let me see what we've got first. Let's get your photographer over here to take pictures before I get started."

Giorgio called Mulhaney over, who took several photos. Fong brought a metal tool box from his car and knelt down. He pulled out a thick brush and a small trowel.

"This will take some time," he said. "The dirt is soft, but it will be a problem if the body extends underneath the steps to the kitchen or has been tangled up in the roots of this bush."

"Okay, let's see how it goes," Giorgio said. "I'm going to get the dogs started."

Giorgio walked over to the detached garage where Todd Atwater, a stout man with broad shoulders and a trimmed beard, stood next to a black Labrador retriever.

"How ya' doin', Todd?" Giorgio said, as he shook the handler's hand. "Thanks for coming. What do you think?"

"This is a pretty small area, so I'll take Molly here," he said, indicating the Lab, "and do an initial sweep of the yard. But there are a lot of things that can affect how well she'll perform," he said, cautiously.

Giorgio nodded. "I know. The type of soil, air temperature, humidity, etcetera."

"Right," the handler said. "But also rodent holes can do what they call 'vent' the scent. So it's best to use the dogs first to find the general area and then bring in the GPR to pin it down," he said, nodding to the strange apparatus sitting in the driveway.

"Okay," Giorgio said. "Sounds good," Giorgio said. "Who's this little guy?"

Giorgio leaned over and stroked the head of a young Golden Retriever, who began to wiggle in joyful appreciation of the attention.

"This is Bones," the handler said. "He's only a couple of years old, but we're training him as an archaeological cadaver dog."

Giorgio arched his eyebrows in question, and the handler smiled.

"Dogs find human remains based on scent. But, once decomposition has stopped and only bones are left, there's less scent for the dog to detect."

Giorgio's eyes opened in recognition. "I get it. And we found bones. Okay, great. I'll let you get to work."

"We'll do it in quadrants," he said. "She'll lie down if she finds anything."

Giorgio watched while the handler and his assistant used string and tent spikes to mark off four large areas of the yard. Rocky came over and stood by him.

"Why don't you oversee this," Giorgio said, "and I'll hang out with Fong, while he unearths the bones?"

Rocky nodded and Giorgio went back to where the technician was using a small trowel to gently remove dirt from around the skull. Mulhaney was hanging over his shoulder, taking photos.

Giorgio stayed with the forensics man, watching as he began to unearth the shoulder bones and torso of the skeleton. Mulhaney kept the camera clicking away as individual bones were removed. A second technician stood by with boxes and tissue paper to accept them.

As Giorgio watched, a cool breeze rose up. He glanced at the sky, hoping it wouldn't rain.

After a while, he began to pace impatiently back and forth. As the clock inched towards noon, Fong finally called to him.

"Detective, we'll have to remove the bush," he announced. "Most of the body extends under it."

Giorgio nodded and waved to a waiting officer.

"Get some shovels," he said.

The officer left and soon, two officers were carefully digging around the roots of the big bush. The neighbors had accumulated along the street in front of the big Victorian, and officers were kept busy keeping the lookey-loos away.

"Can you tell yet if it's a man or a woman?" Giorgio asked, hovering over the technician.

"Might be a female," the man replied. "Just from the size and shape of the jaw. But it's the pelvis that will tell us for sure. We can't know more until we get it all the way out of the ground."

"Okay," Giorgio said, stepping back and crossing his arms.

"Giorgio!" Rocky called.

He turned.

"The dogs have found something."

Bones had lain down in front of Atwater in the corner of the yard, near the garage, exactly where Giorgio had seen the image of the girl in the rhinestone glasses. His heart rate picked up. The dog's face was alight with enthusiasm at his find. Giorgio walked over.

"Someone's buried here," the handler said, nodding to the dog.

"Someone? Or something?" Giorgio asked. Even though he knew there were multiple bodies buried on the property, he had to sound surprised.

The handler turned a grim expression in Giorgio's direction. "They're both cadaver dogs, Joe. They find human remains."

"Okay," Giorgio said with a sigh. He turned to the officers who had just finished pulling out the rhododendron bush. "Guys!" he called. "Over here."

The two officers shook out the bush, tossed it to the side and moved over to begin to break ground next to the tree.

"Take it slow," he ordered. "And dig shallow until we know what we've got."

Giorgio moved over next to Rocky, who was standing next to the M.E. The coroner was a tall, thin man in his forties. He watched from under the tent, a look of solemn resignation on his face.

"Looks like you might be busy, Doc," Giorgio said to him.

"It's happened before," he said fatalistically.

Giorgio had always been fascinated by people who chose to study the dead. He had a hard enough time trying to identify dead people and find their killers. The thought of slicing them open and picking them apart gave him the heebie-jeebies.

"How did you know we'd find something here?" Rocky asked, catching his attention.

Giorgio turned back to the activity in front of him. "I had a feeling," he replied.

Rocky glanced at his brother skeptically. Giorgio saw the look and shrugged nonchalantly.

"Hey, I *had* a feeling," he insisted. He glanced at Atwater, who had moved to another section of the yard with Molly. "And something tells me we're not done yet."

÷

They brought in pizza for a late lunch; most everyone took a break and grabbed a slice. Giorgio called home to let Angie know he wouldn't be there for dinner. He also asked if any more deliveries had been made. The answer was no.

While he and Rocky grabbed some lunch, Giorgio told Rocky about the empty envelope.

"Whoa!" Rocky exclaimed. "And you think it's the kid who killed Montgomery?"

"I'd bet on it. The captain has put a car outside the house."

"What does Angie think of that?"

Giorgio grimaced and glanced around. "I haven't told her. The less she knows the better."

"Jeez, Joe. If you're right, someone you think is a killer has been to your house and looked Angie right in the eye."

"Don't you think I know that?" Giorgio snapped. "But after what happened to Marie, I don't want to freak her out. I've got eyes on the house and we'll increase the patrols in the neighborhood. It's probably just someone trying to scare me off this case."

Rocky shrugged. "Okay. You're the boss."

Giorgio inwardly cringed. It had only been a few days before that he'd told Angie that *she* was the boss. Although it had been a playful exchange, now he'd forcefully taken that away from her.

But he couldn't tell her about the envelope. When he'd almost lost his life in the gun battle in New York, something had changed between them. Angie's demeanor had become guarded every time he left for work. She'd stopped asking about his cases, and she would turn away whenever he removed his gun and holster in her presence. He loved his job, but he loved his wife, too. Somehow, he had to find a way to balance the inherent danger in his job with his family life.

By that afternoon, the body buried next to the basement window had been removed, and they'd found a skeleton wrapped in an old tarp under the tree. McCready had also found anomalies in the ground beneath the pond with the GPR unit, which meant the pond had to be drained and removed. Tents and teams of police officers and forensics personnel had overrun the property, and the Johnson's nice backyard now looked like a mining operation.

There was a crime investigation van pulled up in the driveway, along with the medical examiner's van and several police cars parked at the street. Uniformed police officers were positioned along the front sidewalk.

A tent sat in front of the garage, complete with work tables and forensics equipment, while an ambulance was ready to transport the remains. The M.E. called Giorgio over at one point to look at the girl who had been buried by the tree.

"I wanted you to see this," he said. "The bones are still pretty dirty, but right here, in her left chest cavity, there are several nicks consistent with knife wounds."

Giorgio flinched, remembering that this was the girl who looked as if her breast had been removed. The doctor looked over at him.

"And there are similar marks on other bones in places that wouldn't kill her – at least right away."

"You think she was tortured?" Giorgio said without emotion.

The man's gray eyes didn't waver. "Yes," he said. "But also, she's missing her big toes. Someone hacked them off."

"Can you tell how she died?" Giorgio wondered out loud.

He shook his head. "Too early to tell."

The doctor gestured to his assistant to bring a body bag and then he moved over to where they had laid the body that came from the back door.

As the M.E. carefully sorted through the jumble of bones, he gestured to Giorgio.

"Look here," he said. "More cuts on these bones. These are her rib bones. And it looks like she's lost at least a couple of fingers.

The M.E. studied the bones a moment, and then said, "I'd say this is also a young woman."

He turned with a resolute expression. "I'll get as much information as I can about these girls and their deaths," he said. "And then I hope you fry the bastard who did this."

Giorgio nodded. "Thanks. We've got to get busy on that pond," he said, and turned to find McCready.

They drained the pond and used sledgehammers to disassemble it. More officers were brought in to remove the bricks and plaster. Then the dogs were brought in again. Bones immediately marked a spot right where the middle of the pond would have been.

The news that there was a body beneath the pond flat lined all activity for a moment. Everyone stood and stared.

They'd been working for so many hours that the gravity of the situation hadn't sunk in. Finally, it did. They'd found three bodies buried in someone's back yard. A backyard that kids and families had probably played in over the years. How many others would they find?

"C'mon," Giorgio finally said to everyone. He looked at the darkening sky. "We need to get this done before it rains."

That reanimated the group, and they went back to work. Giorgio walked over to where Todd Atwater was resting the dogs.

"Ready to go back to work?" Giorgio said.

The handler looked up, a bottle of water in his hand. "Sure. Front yard?"

"No," Giorgio said. "We have a search warrant for the basement."

The man's eyebrows shot up, but he just nodded and stood up. "Okay, let's go."

Giorgio led Atwater, his assistant and the two dogs to the basement, with Rocky trailing behind.

"My own dog seemed nervous about being down here yesterday," Giorgio explained as they went down the steps. "He sniffed those bookcases and then acted like he was scared of something."

Giorgio pointed to the wall of shelves at the opposite end of the room when they reached the bottom. Atwater regarded the bookcases and then approached them, Molly in tow.

"They won't smell anything underneath the concrete," he said, glancing down to the floor.

"I know," Giorgio responded. "But Grosvenor sniffed the drain first and then made a beeline for the bookcase. Whatever he picked up really bothered him."

Atwater turned to the bookcase again, leaned over and patted Molly's head, released her leash and then gave her the command to search. She immediately put her nose to the floor and started moving back and forth.

Her nose took her to the drain in the middle of the floor. Then, just like Grosvenor, she followed a trail back across the floor to the center bookcase. She pushed her nose right up to the bottom and sucked in several breaths. Then, she lay down and looked up at Atwater, allowing a whine to bubble up from her throat.

His eyebrows arched. "I'll be damned," he said. "Looks like you're going to have to move those bookcases."

Giorgio turned to one of the other officers. "Call Mulhaney. We need pictures first."

There were three sets of shelving units in all, set side by side. Each was about four feet wide and made of heavy oak, but painted a deep gray. Each unit had five shelves equally spaced apart. The bottom shelf on all four units ended about two inches above the floor, with a faceplate of wood that capped it off, hiding the unit's underbelly.

After Mulhaney had taken photos, Giorgio found a crowbar and removed the faceplate on the center unit. Then, using a flashlight, he got down on the floor on his right shoulder and flashed the beam underneath.

"There are rolling casters down here."

Rocky knelt down, bent over and examined the area Giorgio had illuminated.

"Damn. What about the others?"

Giorgio removed the face plate on the right bookcase and shined a flashlight underneath.

"No casters here."

"So only the center one moves," Rocky said. "Maybe there's a hidden door or something back there."

"Well, no one's ever found the root cellar," Giorgio said, standing up and wiping dust off his hands.

Giorgio bent over and studied the floor. "Look at this," he said to Rocky.

He pointed to faint grooves in the concrete that curved away from the center bookcase.

"If I'm not mistaken, these grooves will match up to those casters under the bookcase."

Rocky nodded. "No mystery there," he said.

Giorgio called to one of the officers who had come down with them.

"We need an electric screwdriver," he said.

The officer disappeared up the stairs, while he and Rocky began removing the boxes and canisters from the shelves. When everything had been removed, they yanked on the bookcase. It didn't budge.

A moment later, the officer returned with the screwdriver. Rocky took it, gauged the size of screw head they would need, plugged in the driver and went to work in the upper right corner of the bookcase.

"It's bolted right into the concrete wall," Rocky said, straining to get the first bolt out.

Because the screws had been painted over several times, it took some time to get them loose. What finally dropped out were 3 inch concrete screws. They found two more at the bottom corners. When those two came out, the entire unit seemed to relax.

"Someone didn't want this thing moved," Rocky said. He put down the screwdriver and glanced at his brother. "Ready?"

Giorgio took a deep breath. "Not really. I'm not sure what we're going to find."

While the handlers, three officers and Fong looked on, the brothers each took a side of the massive unit. On the count of three, they pulled.

The unit hesitated, as if held back by fifty years of secrets. Then it released and inched forward.

It took some grunting and groaning, but the bookcase finally cleared its neighboring units, and Rocky was able to swing the whole unit out from the wall to the left. When he did, the rollers skated across the concrete floor almost exactly where the indentations were.

Behind it was a mass of cobwebs, dirt, and bugs. And behind all of that was an old, rotting wooden door that hung off its hinges.

"Shit!" Rocky said as he stared at the door. "Now even *I* have a bad feeling."

Giorgio turned and asked Fong for a towel. A moment later, he was wiping away the bugs and cobwebs.

"Don't forget to glove-up," Fong said, handing over a couple of pairs of latex gloves.

"You really think there will be fingerprints left after all these years?" Giorgio said.

"Don't know," the man said. "But it's better to be careful."

Giorgio put on the gloves and then grabbed the flashlight.

"Okay, let's go," he said to Rocky.

The door hung inwards off one metal hinge. They pushed it all the way open, nearly pulling it free from the bent metal casing. As Giorgio stepped onto the landing of the old, rickety staircase, he was met with a flood of musty, damp air from below. He flicked on the flashlight, revealing a set of old wooden steps and a railing that led down.

Rocky peered around the corner and down the steps with a shudder. "I wonder how many rats are down there. I don't much like rats. After you, Sherlock," Rocky nodded to Giorgio.

Giorgio paused, feeling a heavy weight in the middle of his chest. This was the yin and yang of police work. There was the exhilaration of finding something that could blow a case wide open, and the chilling anticipation of what that find might actually mean.

He paused and took a deep breath. Then he began his descent.

The staircase shifted under his weight and the ancient steps creaked and groaned, sounding like the sound effects from every horror movie he'd ever seen. He waved the towel in front of him to remove cobwebs and dust motes, as he dropped into a well of inky blackness.

The flashlight beam bounced around, revealing snapshots of a small empty room with brick walls and a hard-packed dirt floor. The cellar was only about ten feet square. A sagging ceiling was held up by solid wooden columns in each corner and one in the center of the room.

Giorgio stepped off the last step and glanced around. An old dangling light bulb socket hung from the center of the ceiling, its bulb long gone. The floor was uneven and there was no furniture, no shelving, nothing that spoke to the sordid past Giorgio firmly believed it had. But as the flashlight splayed across the dirt floor, it revealed darkened splotches.

"It's okay," he called up to Rocky. "C'mon down."

He moved into the room, as he heard Rocky come down behind him. Giorgio crouched down to examine an area by the far wall.

Something had seeped into the dirt, leaving a jagged demarcation between it and the surrounding soil. He reached out and touched it and then rubbed his index finger and thumb together. It wasn't oily. Whatever it was had dried completely. And he knew by instinct that it couldn't be anything but blood.

"What'd you find?" Rocky said from behind him.

Giorgio straightened up.

"Not sure. We need some lights down here. Then we'll need Molly and maybe Bones."

CHAPTER TWENTY-SIX

As late afternoon became evening, the team brought in electric generators and scoop lights to allow them to work outside after dark. They also strung long extension cords into the basement to set up pole lights. Finally, they brought the dogs down. Molly signaled four spots on the packed dirt floor. For training purposes, Atwater allowed Bones the same opportunity and he hit every spot.

"The earth is much damper down here," Atwater said to Giorgio. "I think that's why there's still the scent of human decomp."

Giorgio nodded and called in the forensics team.

By the time Giorgio emerged from the house to get some fresh air, they had found four more skeletons, along with the partial skeletal remains of two others. It had been dark outside for some time and the scene in the backyard reminded him of a night-time movie set, minus the actors. The lovely pond had been removed and was now just a pile of concrete rubble. A big hole had been dug right in the center, where the third body had been found. The area under the basement window had also been dug up and the second body removed.

A tired and haggard-looking Mulhaney cornered Giorgio, a haunted look etched into his normally friendly features.

"You know, Joe, I've worked for this department for more than seven years," he said grimly, "In all that time, I think we only worked four murder cases. Now, between the monastery murders and this, we've encountered more dead bodies than in my whole career here."

"I know," Giorgio replied, feeling his own spirits weighted down by the enormity of it all. "But now we need to focus on finding out who these remains belong to and then work to bring whoever did this to justice."

"How the hell are we going to do that?" Mulhaney said, glancing back at the chaos behind them. "These bodies are so old. The perp must be long gone. Maybe dead."

Giorgio looked up at Mulhaney, who was a good three inches taller than him.

"Maybe. But we owe it to the families to try."

Mulhaney nodded and went back to work, videotaping the remains as they came out of the ground.

Every inch of the backyard and side yards had now been scanned twice, and the dogs had signaled one more location along the side of the house. Cops and forensics techs were busy digging up that location and the basement. Both dogs had been allowed to go home. News vans had lined Lima Street for hours, and pools of onlookers strained to catch a glimpse of something they could record on their cell phones.

But by ten-thirty that night, the curious spectators had dispersed and the team was packed up and ready to leave. They would resume their work the next day, when they would scan the front yard for good measure. Giorgio felt confident they wouldn't find anything there, since the yard was too visible to prying eyes. But it had to be done. He stationed officers overnight at the front corners of the property and in the back yard.

Once the chaos had died down and the big house was dark, with only a few security lights illuminating the back yard, Giorgio and Rocky stood side-by-side as the rest of the police personnel dragged themselves down the long driveway to their cars.

"Wanna get something to eat before you go home?" Rocky asked.

Giorgio turned bleary eyes in his direction. "Yeah. That pizza we ate tasted like cardboard. Mama's should still be open if we hurry."

They took separate cars and met at Mama's Café a few minutes later. The place was almost empty and would be closing in less than twenty minutes. But Eve, the waitress on duty, allowed them in.

"You guys must be exhausted," she said, following them to a table. "Everyone's been watching it on the news." She handed them menus and then took out her order tablet. "It's too late to do anything like fried chicken, but there's meatloaf left and it was pretty good. It's on the house," she said proudly.

Eve stood poised and ready to write. Giorgio just slid the menu back to her without even looking at it.

"The meatloaf sounds great."

"Me, too," Rocky said.

"Okay," she said. "And two Cokes?"

"Just water for me," Giorgio replied. "I need to sleep tonight."

"Same for me," Rocky concurred.

Eve left to get their dinners, and the brothers sat motionless for a few moments. Giorgio felt like someone had poked a hole in him and drained him of any life-giving fluids. To say he was exhausted was putting it mildly.

"So how did you know?" Rocky suddenly said. "I mean, really?"

Giorgio glanced over at his brother. Rocky's eyes were dull and lifeless with fatigue.

"I've never thought this was just about Lisa Farmer," he replied.

"Why?" his brother asked.

"I don't know. Maybe because of the people involved. Maybe because of the way she was disposed of. It just didn't seem like a random murder. Someone went to a lot of trouble to hide her body. There had to be a reason."

"But we don't even know yet whether all of these other murders have anything to do with Lisa Farmer's death," Rocky said.

Rocky normally couldn't stop moving. If his knee wasn't bouncing up and down, his fingers were reaching for something to touch, grab or move. Right now, his left hand reached out for the salt shaker, but this time more out of habit. When his fingers wrapped themselves around the shaker, they stopped. He didn't seem to have enough energy to even give it a twirl.

"The earring proves that Lisa was at the Pinney House that night," Giorgio said. "What if she found something, heard something, or saw something that got her killed? Finding all those bodies at the house can't be a coincidence," he said quietly.

"Maybe," Rocky said. "But I know you. And I watched you today. You were never really surprised by any of the finds. In fact, the only time you seemed surprised was when you found the earring. You didn't expect that, did you?"

Giorgio watched him cautiously. "No."

"But you did expect everything else. Including finding the root cellar."

"Grosvenor signaled the root cellar," Giorgio replied quickly.

"You know, when we were at the monastery, investigating Mallery Olsen's murder, you seemed to know things there, too. I know you get hunches, but…" Rocky paused, thoughtfully regarding his brother for a moment.

"I do," Giorgio cut in. "I can't explain it."

He wasn't ready to reveal the boy to his brother. He didn't know if he ever would.

Fortunately, Eve returned with their meals, forcing them to forego the conversation for the moment.

"Sometimes I hate my job," Giorgio said after a few bites. "Even though we're cops, I can never seem to accept how someone can appear so normal on the outside and yet be such a sick bastard on the inside. Most likely whoever killed those women, tortured them, murdered them, and then went on about their business like nothing had ever happened."

"Do you think it was one of the Martinellis?"

"I'd bet one of them did Lisa Farmer. But we won't know for a while if the other bodies were buried before or after the Martinellis lived there."

"Do you like Ron Martinelli for Lisa Farmer's death?"

Giorgio shrugged and reached for his water. "I don't know. Right now, I'm too tired to think."

"So how *did* you know about these women?" Rocky asked, unwilling to give up on his question.

Giorgio stopped mid-bite. He'd hoped they'd moved off the topic of ghosts. He put his fork down again.

"I had a weird dream," he said, grabbing a napkin. "No big deal. It happens sometimes."

He *had* had a dream about the women, running from a faceless man in a stocking cap.

"So, you're a psychic now?" Rocky said with a snort.

Giorgio had to tread lightly.

"No. I just get dreams sometimes."

Rocky shifted in his seat. "You'd better not tell anyone else. Cops don't accept that sort of thing very easily."

Giorgio leveled a serious look at him. "I don't plan on talking about it. And neither should you."

Rocky held his hands up in defeat. "Don't worry. I have no plans to mention it to anyone. They'll think you're crazy."

"Thanks," Giorgio said with irritation. "I didn't think you were so closed-minded."

Rocky glanced at him under hooded lashes. "I'm just realistic," he said. "Ghosts don't exist. And there's no such thing as psychics. It's all fakery."

"Well, then, you'd be surprised to learn that Detective Abrams uses a psychic," Giorgio said.

"The guy up in Seattle?"

"Yeah. He works with a psychic up there. He brought her in when Montgomery was killed."

Giorgio avoided mentioning the fact that he'd also been to see a psychic, and that it was Flame who had confirmed the fact the girls were buried at the Pinney House.

Rocky blew out a dismissive breath. "Bunch of malarkey."

"Well, Abrams seems pretty convinced she's the real deal."

Rocky's eyebrows shot up. "Shit, Joe, we'd better be careful. I don't want to get laughed out of the department before I even get started."

"Don't worry," Giorgio said, his voice reflecting caution. "This conversation stays between us. I'm just telling you that Abrams asked her to see what she could see."

"And?" Rocky said skeptically.

Giorgio shrugged. "She didn't see much, other than something about a cabinet and a rose."

"Well, that's helpful," Rocky said sarcastically.

"Yeah, I don't know what it means. It's probably nothing," Giorgio said.

"So what would you do if you thought you saw a ghost?" Rocky asked quietly.

Giorgio wondered whether Rocky was testing him.

"I don't know," he shrugged, taking a bite of his mashed potatoes. "It would be freaky, that's for sure."

He swallowed, hoping that Rocky would change the subject. He didn't.

"I thought I saw Grandpa Reno when I was little," he replied.

Giorgio shot his brother a look. "Seriously?"

Rocky tensed. "Yeah, but I didn't. Mom just said it was my imagination. A kid thing."

"But you had an invisible friend when you were little, too," Giorgio said. "What was that all about?"

"Nothing!" Rocky said defensively. "I had a vivid imagination. I always have. Not like you. You're the dull one."

Giorgio let the comment ride. They continued to eat for a moment.

"Remember fat 'ole Craig Melbourne?" Rocky asked all of a sudden. "He told me once that he saw his dead mother."

"No shit?" Giorgio said, wide-eyed. "He was a no nonsense kind of guy. He didn't even have a sense of humor as I remember."

"I know," Rocky said with a chortle. "But he said that his mom would appear to him in dreams and help him with his tests."

Giorgio laughed out loud. "Damn! I could've used that kind of help back then."

"Me too," Rocky said. "Who knows, maybe your dreams are…you know…maybe there's something real about them."

Giorgio glanced at his brother. "Maybe," he said. "I don't think it's any big deal, though."

"You do get hunches, though," Rocky said. "And your hunches are usually spot on."

It seemed to Giorgio that Rocky was trying to say something. Make some kind of point. But his gut said to let it go.

"Well, next time I have one of those weird dreams, I'll call you."

Rocky smiled. "Okay. But what if it's a ghost?"

"Then I'll send him to your house. You need all the help you can get."

CHAPTER TWENTY-SEVEN

By the time Giorgio made it to the office the next day, the police station was overrun by reporters. He pushed his way through the crowd in the parking lot, ignoring the shouts:

"Detective, will there be any more bodies dug up?"

"Detective, is this Sierra Madre's first serial killer?"

He ducked inside, only to find a similar scene. Phones were ringing off the hook, and the lobby was filled with people crowding the front desk, holding pictures of loved ones that had gone missing and clamoring for attention.

"Hey, Joe," McCready said, as he appeared through the doorway. "Glad you're here."

McCready took Giorgio by the arm and guided him through the melee just as an officer called out that CNN was on the phone. Sam Waters, their public information officer, hurried over from his desk to grab the call.

"Damn, it feels like aliens have finally landed," Giorgio said, looking around.

McCready followed his gaze. "Yeah, it's been this way since early this morning. We have officers set up in the two conference rooms doing interviews. They're coming from all over the valley."

"Okay, but let's be careful," Giorgio said. "I don't want it released yet that all the bodies were female."

McCready nodded. "I already sent an email out to everyone."

"Is the captain in?"

"Yeah, he's in with the mayor. I think the governor has even weighed in. They want this all wrapped up soon."

Giorgio rolled his eyes. "Yeah, well, good luck with that. These *aren't* fresh kills. We're going to have to dig for clues." He grimaced when he realized what he'd said. "Sorry. No pun intended. While I go see the captain, I want you to go to public records. We know the Martinellis owned the Pinney House from 1955 until 1968. I want to know who owned it for the ten years before the Martinellis moved in and also up until the present day. And I want to know about any building permits or digging permits issued for that property during that time period."

McCready nodded. "Will do."

Giorgio grabbed a notepad off his desk and then stepped into the captain's office.

Captain Alvarez was sitting behind the desk, while Mayor Brunwell had stuffed his stocky frame into a captain's chair facing the captain. Brunwell considered himself a fashionista and liked to dress in black pin-striped suits with brightly colored silk ties. Today the color was crimson to match the handkerchief in his pocket.

"Joe," Captain Alvarez said, when Giorgio poked his head in. "C'mon in. You know the mayor," he said, gesturing stiffly to the man in the chair.

"Good to see you, Joe," Brunwell said. "You've got your work cut out for you on this one."

"Have a seat, Joe," Captain Alvarez said, indicating a second chair.

Giorgio sat down, acutely aware of the nervous energy in the room. He glanced at the mayor, who was shifting uncomfortably in his seat.

"Joe," the captain began, "what do we know so far?"

Giorgio brought them up-to-date on the ten bodies they'd found, and the two men listened quietly. But when he mentioned the M.E.'s speculation that the women had been tortured, the mayor's face flushed to match his tie.

"What do you mean?" he blurted.

"The medical examiner noted that some of the bones had multiple knife cuts, as if the person had been repeatedly stabbed. But the stabbings were in places that *wouldn't* have been life threatening. And...some of the fingers and toes had been severed." Giorgio paused and glanced at the captain.

"When the girl was dead, you mean?" the mayor said, with an encouraging nod of his head.

Mayor Brunwell's presence had a tendency to make people uncomfortable. He had a curt manner and liked to jump to conclusions. Like now.

"We don't know that yet," Giorgio said carefully.

The mayor got up and went to the window, his hand searching his pocket. When he found his handkerchief, he pulled it out and held it to his mouth. The captain watched the mayor but didn't say anything.

"God in heaven," the mayor murmured from the window. "Between this and what happened at the monastery, Sierra Madre is going to be known as the murder capital of the Los Angeles basin. No one will want to move here."

"Are these murders connected to the Lisa Farmer case, Joe?" the captain asked, redirecting the conversation.

He was tapping a pencil on his desk, something he did whenever he was processing information.

"I don't know for sure," Giorgio replied. "But we found one of Lisa Farmer's earrings in a tin box that was found hidden in the wall of the basement. Her mother gave her the earrings on the afternoon the day she went missing. So, either she was *in* the home on the night of her murder, or whoever murdered her is connected to the Martinelli family."

Both men seemed to freeze in place and just stared at him.

"But you don't know that for a fact?" the mayor almost stuttered. "They *can't* be connected," the mayor stated flatly, returning his handkerchief to his pocket. "If they were, Lisa Farmer would have been buried on the property, just like the others. But instead her body was found blocks away."

"There's a lot we don't know yet," Giorgio said.

"Then let's not waste any time," the mayor snapped, moving toward the door.

Both the captain and Giorgio stood up, as the mayor stopped and turned.

"The Governor called me at home this morning," he said. "He offered his help, which I can tell you I don't want unless it's absolutely necessary. The last thing we need is to have some *other* law enforcement agency butting in." He paused and turned to look directly at Giorgio. "And let's not put out any speculation about the Martinelli family. While they don't live here anymore, they are still a prominent family in Pasadena. I don't want to ruffle feathers before we have something concrete."

Giorgio winced, thinking he'd already ruffled many of those feathers and would ruffle as many more as he had to in order to get to the truth.

"We'll tread lightly," the captain said. "We'll schedule a press conference for this afternoon. Will you be there?"

"Yes, of course," Brunwell said. He regarded them for a moment and then left the room, taking the negative energy with him.

"He's not cut out for this sort of thing," the captain said with a sigh.

"Who is?" Giorgio replied.

Captain Alvarez turned to Giorgio. "Okay, tell Sam to schedule a press conference for four o'clock. And, Joe, I want you there, too."

Giorgio returned to his desk and had just sat down when his phone rang. He picked it up and was surprised when Detective Abrams greeted him.

"Our M.E. ruled Montgomery's death a homicide," Abrams reported. "No surprise there. He'd been injected with a large dose of Fentanyl right into his carotid artery. It's an analgesic. And guess what? It's exactly what they found in the syringe we found in the gutter. But no clear fingerprints."

"Wow," Giorgio murmured. He sat back. "Any news on the van?"

"Yeah, a neighbor saw a van pull towards the curb as it turned the corner and saw the driver toss something out the window. He didn't get the license plate number, but was sure they were California plates. So it looks like you were right. Whoever did this drove into town."

"Any more about the driver?"

"Same description as before. But I went back out and interviewed the sisters again. They remembered that the van wasn't a passenger van. It was one of those box-shaped commercial vans."

"So what's your next move?" Giorgio asked.

"I have someone calling gas stations along I-5 to see if we can get a hit on where he might have stopped for gas. Maybe he used a credit card. And we're interviewing the neighbors whose homes border the parking lot and street. Maybe they saw something."

"Sounds like you have it covered. Thanks for letting me know."

"Anything new on your end?" Abrams asked.

Giorgio ran his fingers through his hair. "More like where to begin?"

He spent the next five minutes filling Abrams in on the new crime scene. Afterwards, he joined the others in helping to interview distraught relatives.

÷

Over the next two and a half hours, the duty officer managed the interview process like a triage nurse in a hospital emergency room. Giorgio took a quick break around 11:30 to grab a soda and stretch his legs. He came back to find an old man who had to be in his early nineties sitting at his desk. The man was dressed in gray slacks and a crisp white shirt. He wore glasses and was just wiping off the lenses when Giorgio stepped into the room.

"I'm Detective Salvatori," Giorgio said, moving behind his desk.

The man looked up. "Oh, I'm...uh...Phil Carr. They told me to come on back. I'm here about my daughter."

"Can I get you anything to drink?" Giorgio offered.

"No. Thank you. I was just wondering if...if," he said and then stopped.

"If one of the bodies we found is your daughter," Giorgio said.

The man nodded and Giorgio noticed a tear glistening in the corner of his eye. He took a deep breath and sat down.

"Why don't you tell me about her?"

The old man raised a hesitant finger to his eye to wipe away the tear and then sighed. Giorgio noticed that his hand shook.

"Her name was Pat Carr. Patty," he said, a sob getting stuck in his throat. "She disappeared back in 1963. She was twenty-one and had just gotten a job at the hospital. We only lived six blocks away, down on Mariposa Street. She would walk home every night after work. And one night..." He stopped and shifted his gray eyes to Giorgio's, fifty years of pain etched into the folds of his face.

The nurse, Giorgio thought with alarm.

"And one night she didn't come home," Giorgio said.

Tears flooded his eyes. "No," he murmured, shaking his head. "We never saw her again. The police said she probably ran away. Since she was over the age of consent, they wouldn't do anything."

"Had she ever run away before?" Giorgio asked.

"No," Mr. Carr said, pulling a handkerchief from his pocket. "My wife and I married very young, but we doted on Patty. She was everything to us."

"Was there a boyfriend in the picture?"

"No. Nothing like that. Patty always wanted to be a nurse. She was so excited about her new job. There was no reason for her to leave."

"Mr. Carr, we won't have any definitive information about these bodies until the medical examiner has had a chance to examine them. Is there anything you can tell us about Patty that might help? For instance, did she have any accidents growing up? Broken bones? Dental work? Any abnormalities?"

His eyes seemed to light up. "She broke her right ankle when she was in the seventh grade. She fell running down some steps."

"Okay, that's good," Giorgio said. "I'll let the examiner know. Anything else? What was she wearing the night she disappeared?"

"Her work outfit. A nurse's uniform. And she wore glasses."

The hairs on Giorgio's neck bristled.

"Glasses?" he said.

"Yes. I have a picture," Mr. Carr said, reaching into his pocket.

He pulled out an old picture and passed it over to Giorgio. Giorgio stared down at the picture of Pat Carr. She had short, dark hair and wore a nurse's cap and glasses. It was the girl whose body was buried next to the tree, he was sure of it, and Giorgio's skin went cold.

"May I keep this for now?" he asked with a slight waver to his voice. "I'll be sure you get it back."

The old man nodded. "She also wore her grandmother's opal ring," he said. "She just loved that thing. Do you think one of those bodies you found is my Patty?"

The ring raised additional hairs on the back of Giorgio's neck. They had logged a small opal ring into evidence from the tarp that had encased the body by the tree.

Giorgio wanted to tell the old man, but he couldn't yet. He had to let the facts come out naturally. Until then, he would have to make Mr. Carr wait.

"I don't know," he said with difficulty. "But I'll be sure to let you know as soon as I have more information."

"Please, Detective," Mr. Carr said. "I've waited for over forty years. I need to know."

Giorgio felt the pressure build in his chest. He pushed a yellow pad across the desk.

"Why don't you give me a description of the ring and leave your contact information?"

When Mr. Carr had left, Giorgio sat back, staring at the picture of Patty and wondering what her last moments had been like. Had her killer made her cry for mercy? Had she been tortured and raped? Had she screamed out for her father, wondering why he didn't come to rescue her?

Giorgio thought back to the night the man in the stocking cap had reached out and fondled Marie. If Grosvenor hadn't been there, he could have grabbed her and been gone. Tony couldn't have stopped him, and the thought churned Giorgio's insides.

"I'm starving. Wanna get some lunch?" Rocky said from the doorway.

÷

The diversion was a welcome relief. They walked across the street to Mama's Café, but it was filled with press people. They took a sharp turn and went to a pizza place around the corner instead.

"You're pretty quiet," Rocky said, fingering the napkin holder in a red leather booth.

Giorgio looked around to make sure they had privacy, but the place was nearly empty. "I think I just ID'd one of the girls."

"Really?"

"It would have been the one buried under the tree," Giorgio said, careful to keep his voice down. "They found an opal ring with her, a ring her grandmother gave her. And her father said she was a nurse. He showed me a picture and she was wearing glasses like the ones in that tin box."

A young waitress came to take their orders. When she left, Rocky leaned into his brother.

"So, who was she?" he said quietly.

"A young girl named Patty Carr."

Rocky's eyes went wide. "Did you tell her father?"

"No. We'll have to wait until the M.E. gives us more information. He described an ankle break – that might help us."

"Detective," a female voice chirped.

They both turned to find Mia Santana standing at the end of the table. Rocky glanced at Giorgio and slipped out of the booth.

"I have to hit the head. Be back in a minute."

Abandoned by his brother, Giorgio turned to the reporter.

"What do you want, Ms. Santana? I don't have any information on the bodies yet."

"Oh, c'mon. You have an opinion. Are they connected to the Lisa Farmer case?"

The young reporter was only about five foot four and couldn't have weighed more than 110 pounds, and yet had the tenacity of a combat veteran. He turned around to look for her cameraman, who was usually attached to her like an umbilical cord, but she was alone.

"We don't know much of anything about them. The coroner has the remains and will let us know how they died and approximately when they died," he said curtly.

She sat down in the booth across from Giorgio, uninvited. "Yes, but Ron Martinelli lived in that house and those bodies could have been buried during that time. If they were, then this is all connected to Lisa Farmer's death."

Giorgio sighed, reaching for his glass of water. "We don't know that. Detective work can be slow and tedious. And most likely, the medical examiner won't be able to give us an exact date as to when they went into the ground, anyway."

"I know that," she spat.

"Look, there will be a news conference this afternoon," he said.

"No kidding?" she said bluntly. "Listen, I was hoping to get a scoop."

"I don't have a scoop," he said in frustration.

"What about Jimmy Finn? We know he's still alive. I tried to talk to him yesterday, but the manager wouldn't give me access."

Giorgio arched his eyebrows. "You've done your homework."

"Yes, I have. I'm actually pretty good at what I do."

"I don't doubt that," he said.

"But you don't approve," she said, a look of reproach in her eyes.

He shrugged. "It's not that. I just have a job to do, and the press is always…interrupting me."

"We have a job to do, too," she said with all the confidence her twenty-plus years could muster. "So are you officially reopening the Lisa Farmer case?"

He sighed. "Let's just say that at this point we're not satisfied with the information we have."

She had no way of knowing about Carson Montgomery's death up in Seattle, Alex Springer's death, or the earring. And he wasn't about to tell her.

"Will you let me know if you do reopen the case?"

Her enthusiasm was palpable. Giorgio couldn't help but admire her. She was young and ambitious and trying to make it in a big media market.

"Look," he said. "If something breaks on the Pinney House case, I'll let you know. But right now, we're treating the two cases separately."

"That's great. Thanks. Here's my card," she said, passing it over. "That's my cell phone. Day or night."

He glanced at the card and then at her.

She couldn't have been much older than Patty Carr was when she was killed. And like Patty Carr, Mia Santana was pretty and petite – just like all the victims found buried at the Pinney House.

"I'll give you a call," he said.

CHAPTER TWENTY-EIGHT

After lunch, Giorgio made a quick trip to the Prairie Café to see Carson Montgomery's son again.

"I'm sorry about your father," Giorgio said when the man sat down. "I meant to come see you sooner, but…"

"That's okay," Monty said with a dismissive wave of his hand. "I heard about the bodies you discovered yesterday." He stared at the table a moment, his eyes glazed over. With a deep sigh, he said, "I never meant to put my dad in danger when I told you about the phone call."

"You didn't get your father killed," Giorgio reassured him. "Whoever did this was in motion before you ever contacted me."

That brought a glimmer of hope to his eyes. "You think so?"

"I know so," Giorgio said.

He nodded. "I guess I was right, though. My dad knew something about that locker check – something he'd been carrying around for over forty years. And it finally got him killed."

"It looks that way," Giorgio said. "Monty, do you know anyone who owns a blue or gray van?"

He looked up. "Um…no. Not that I can think of."

"Think hard. Have you seen a van like that lately? Maybe around your neighborhood or outside the café?"

He shook his head. "No. The detective from Seattle asked me that, too. I haven't seen anything like that."

"How about a Jeep Wrangler?"

He thought a moment and then shook his head.

"Well, your father was visited by someone driving a van the day he was killed. A young man wearing a blond wig came to see him – said he was your dad's great nephew."

Montgomery furrowed his brows. "Like I told Detective Abrams, I don't know of any great nephews in the family."

"Did Detective Abrams ask you about tattoos?"

"No. But to be honest, I had to cut the conversation short. My daughter fell in her gymnastics class, so I had to go. I was supposed to call him back, but I've been too busy," he said, shrugging his shoulders.

"The guy who came to visit your father had at least one tattoo on his neck. He was wearing a turtleneck, so witnesses couldn't see more."

"Wait a minute," Montgomery said, his expression brightening. "On his neck? I talked with my mom the day before I talked to you. She called to tell me that someone had tried to deliver something to the house for my dad. She said the guy had a row of skulls tattooed around his neck. Could that be him?"

"A delivery guy?" Giorgio's adrenalin began to pump. He pictured the same delivery guy delivering the empty envelope to Angie. "Did your mother tell him where your dad was?"

"I don't know. She just mentioned it to me because it's been so long since they lived together, she thought it was weird. And the skulls creeped her out."

"I'd like to go see your mom. See what else she can tell me," Giorgio said.

Montgomery gave Giorgio his mother's address.

÷

Mrs. Montgomery lived in a small house on the grounds of an assisted living facility in Arcadia. When she answered the door, she appeared to be in her late seventies, a bit younger than her now deceased ex-husband.

"There was something wrong with that young man," she said, when they'd taken a seat. "He couldn't stop moving. He kept tapping his fingers against his leg and had kind of a wild look in his eyes."

"Can you describe him in any more detail?" Giorgio pressed her.

"Of course. He wasn't more than five foot ten, black hair, like it was dyed. He had a slight build and skin that looked like he'd never been out in the sun." She rolled her eyes as if she was slightly offended by this. "He had bad teeth, too. And he reeked of smoke. Anyway, he had dark eyes, and I think he wore makeup."

"You mean, like eyeliner?" Giorgio asked.

"Yes. And he had on some kind of uniform, like he was a delivery man. But I remember thinking that no delivery company I knew would ever hire him."

"What was it he was trying to deliver?"

Giorgio's mind was whirring now. The sisters had said the man who had pushed Montgomery into the parking lot had been blond, but had come back with black hair. Angie said the delivery man who had delivered the envelope had been blond.

"He just said he was delivering a box of something," she said. "He said it was perishable, though, and he had to get it delivered quickly."

"Did you tell him where to find your ex-husband?"

For the first time, she paused and just stared at him.

"Oh, my," she said quietly. "I...uh...oh dear." She began to wring her hands. "Yes, I gave him the name of the nursing home in Seattle. He said he would get the box to him right away." Tears suddenly glistened in her eyes. "I shouldn't have done that. I haven't spoken to Carson in over four years. I only knew he was in the nursing home because his wife sent me a note. Things didn't end well between us, you know. He just became a different person over the years. But I would never wish him ill," she said. She shook her head as the tears began to flow. "Oh, do you really think I was responsible for his death?" She reached over to a table and grabbed a tissue.

"You couldn't have known, Mrs. Montgomery. You were clearly tricked," Giorgio said, trying to console her. "I need to ask you though, if Carson ever said anything about the Lisa Farmer case to you while you were married?"

She glanced up at him and took a moment to wipe the tears from her eyes.

"Yes, once. It was a couple of years after that boy's trial. We'd been arguing, and I told Carson that if I'd known he was an alcoholic I would never have married him. He snapped at me...said he wasn't a drunk when he married me, that Lisa Farmer had made him that way."

"What did he mean by that?"

"I'm not sure. But he finished by saying that he wished Edmond Martinelli had never saved his life."

Giorgio's heart rate went from zero to sixty.

"He *knew* Edmond Martinelli? Ron Martinelli's uncle?"

"Oh, yes. I believe they lived next door to each other growing up. And then he and Edmond served in Vietnam together."

"And Edmond saved his life?"

She shrugged. "Well, that's what Carson said. He would never explain how. But when Carson got back from the war, he was a wreck. He couldn't keep a job. Edmond ended up hiring him to clean some of his brother's apartment buildings at night. And then when Monty was born, Edmond's brother, Royce, got Carson the job at the high school. It allowed him to work normal hours and have weekends and holidays off."

"Thank you, Mrs. Montgomery. You've been a big help," Giorgio said, feeling for the first time like the pieces of the puzzle were coming together.

Giorgio returned to the station, his adrenalin pumping. The connection had been made. Carson Montgomery had worked for the Martinellis *and* Edmond had saved his life, all the leverage he would need to force Montgomery to do something he didn't want to do. That meant that it had to be a Martinelli who had killed Lisa Farmer – how else would they have had her shoe and underwear to plant in Jimmy Finn's locker?

CHAPTER TWENTY-NINE

Giorgio took Rocky off his research task to accompany him to Edmond Martinelli's home. They called in advance, and thirty minutes later pulled up in front of his sprawling ranch-style home, with its perfectly manicured lawns. They parked next to a spouting fountain in the middle of a circular drive. A four-car garage sat off to one side. One garage door was open, revealing a vintage Mustang.

"I guess it pays to be a Martinelli," Rocky sniped as they approached the front door.

Pushing the doorbell resulted in a melody of chimes, which hadn't finished playing before the door was opened by a middle-aged woman in a uniform. Giorgio introduced himself and his brother, and the woman led them to the living room overlooking the front drive.

The room was decorated in rich leather, dark cherry woods, and thick brocades. Very male. A group of family photos was carefully arranged on a finely polished table in the corner. Laid out on a glass coffee table was a plate of dessert bread and coffee.

"Mr. Martinelli is just finishing up his afternoon massage. He'll be right in. Please help yourself," she said, gesturing to the food. She smiled and then left.

Rocky cocked his head. "Afternoon massage. Must be nice."

He helped himself to some of the lemon bread, while Giorgio studied the family photos. Royce and Edmond Martinelli looked enough alike to be twins. They were both tall, with dark hair and heavy features. Ron Martinelli, Royce's son, was shorter and had a slender build and lighter coloring. Edmond's son, Fritz, looked just like him – tall, with dark hair, imposing eyebrows and a strong jaw. A young boy and a small girl at his side were probably the youngest of the Martinelli clan. Giorgio didn't know if Ron Martinelli had kids.

Even in photos both the elder Martinellis had a disquieting quality. It was partly the way they held themselves, as if they owned the world and everything in it. But those dark eyes held secrets, as if there was something lurking beneath the surface of all that wealth.

As Giorgio gazed at the photos, he wondered momentarily about Ron. There was a different quality about him. He was more relaxed and didn't look like the others. Just then, a woman came into view from around the far end of the house. Giorgio turned to watch her through the front window.

The woman was dressed in high heels, a short, flouncy skirt and a skin-tight blouse. She carried a messenger bag over one shoulder and had her wallet in her hand.

Giorgio watched her walk to the end of the driveway, adjusting her skirt as if it wasn't on properly. A black sports car was waiting for her at the end of the drive. She got in and the car sped off.

A moment later, an older gentleman strode confidently into the room, one hand in his pocket. He was over six feet tall and walked slightly stooped at the shoulders. His hair was white now and he wore glasses, but there was agility and power still contained in his frame. He extended a hand to Giorgio.

"I'm Edmond Martinelli," he said.

Giorgio studied the man as he introduced both himself and his brother. Martinelli's face was flushed and his lips moist. He remained standing, so Giorgio did, too.

"I understand you're here about the Lisa Farmer case," he said.

"That's right," Giorgio nodded. "We're following up on some loose ends."

"I'm not sure I can help much," he said. "I wasn't involved."

"Well, since your brother, Royce, is gone, we thought perhaps we'd take a long shot and see if he'd ever said anything to you about it."

"Like what?" the man asked.

Since Edmond still hadn't offered them a seat, it was clear he didn't intend for this to take long.

"Did he mention anything about that night?" Giorgio said. "For instance, we understand he'd been out of town."

There was a momentary tensing of the man's lower jaw.

"That's right," Martinelli said.

"Do you know where he'd been?" Giorgio asked.

"What difference does it make where Royce was?"

"We're not sure it does," Giorgio was quick to say. "We're just trying to fit all of the pieces together."

He seemed to relax slightly. "He was with me. We'd been out-of-town on a fishing trip. Something we did about that time every year."

"I see," Giorgio said with a big smile. He turned to Rocky. "My brother and I like to fish. What do you go after -- carp, walleye?"

The man froze momentarily.

"Really, Detective. Can we get on with this?"

Giorgio's smile faded. "When did you get home?"

"What does it matter?" he said impatiently.

"Your nephew's girlfriend went missing. It's important to know where everyone was."

He sighed. "As I recall, the fish weren't biting and Royce had some pressing business back in town, so we came back early."

"The night of the prom?" Giorgio asked.

"Yes."

"And how did you travel? Fly? Drive?"

"We drove. Actually, Royce drove," the man said. "Is this going to take long, Detective?" he said, shifting his weight impatiently. "I have…"

"Not much longer," Giorgio said, cutting him off. "What car did you take?"

The man glared at Giorgio momentarily before answering. "As I recall, we took Ron's car. An old Chevy Impala. Ron had asked to use Royce's car for the prom."

"I see," Giorgio mused. "So where did you go fishing?"

"Why does that matter?"

"Just routine," Giorgio said.

"I don't know. We fished every year. I really don't remember where we went that particular year."

Giorgio paused, as if to weigh the veracity of his statement. Just then, the front door opened and another man came in.

"Dad, we need to talk…"

The man stopped the moment he saw two strangers standing in his father's living room. Edmond Martinelli took immediate control of the situation.

"This is my son, Fritz," he said, gesturing to the younger Martinelli.

"Yes, we've met," Giorgio said, remembering the chance meeting in Ron Martinelli's outer office.

Fritz Martinelli was dressed in crisp slacks and a silk shirt. He merely nodded to the police officers as a way of acknowledging them.

"They're here about the Lisa Farmer case," his father said, eyeing Giorgio.

"Yes, they came to see Ron, too," Fritz said. "Well, I'll be in the kitchen," he said and started to leave.

"Just a minute," Giorgio said, stepping forward. "Would you mind answering a few questions?"

He turned and leveled a critical gaze at Giorgio. "I don't know anything about Lisa Farmer."

"But you're Ron's cousin, and you're about the same age, aren't you? You would have been in high school back in 1967," Giorgio said.

His eyes narrowed. "Ron was a year ahead of me. Why?"

"I thought maybe you might have heard things…from kids at school back then. Maybe comments about Lisa or someone who didn't like her."

He glanced at his father before replying. "We lived in Arcadia, so I went to a different high school. I didn't even know her."

"I see," Giorgio said. "Were you and Ron close back then?"

"Not really."

"But you work together now?" Giorgio said.

His father stepped in. "Fritz runs the real estate side of the business," he said. "He took over for me when I retired."

Giorgio turned back to Fritz. "Would you know anyone who might own a blue or gray van?"

Fritz Martinelli flinched ever so slightly.

"No," he said with a snap. Then he turned to his father. "I'll be in the kitchen."

He hadn't liked the question, and by Edmond's demeanor, Giorgio could tell the welcome mat would soon be pulled out from under him.

"Now, if that's all, Detectives," Edmond was saying as he began to usher them to the door. "I have some business…"

"Just a couple more questions," Giorgio said quickly, stopping in the foyer. "We were curious about the locker search at the high school. The one that resulted in finding Lisa's underwear and shoe in Jimmy Finn's locker."

Martinelli seemed to freeze in place. "I don't understand. Why are you curious about that?"

"There was a tip; someone called the police department a couple days after Lisa went missing and suddenly there was a full locker check at the school. We're trying to find out who might have placed that call."

He shrugged. "How would I know?"

"Ron said you oversaw the maintenance of the buildings in the Martinelli Company back then."

"That's right."

"Did you know a Carson Montgomery?"

He blinked the moment Giorgio uttered the name.

"Carson Montgomery," he repeated slowly, as if deciding how to respond. "Yes, we served in Vietnam together."

"He was the janitor at the high school," Giorgio continued.

The man began to rub his thumb and index finger together as his hand hung by his side.

"So?" Martinelli snapped.

"He was the one who conducted the locker check," Giorgio said, watching him closely.

"I see. I don't think I knew that. But I believe Royce knew the school principal. I think he got him that job. I'm not sure what year it was," he said cautiously. "That was so long ago."

"But you knew Carson Montgomery well?" Giorgio prodded him.

He paused before answering. "Yes. We grew up together. In fact, we served in Vietnam together. I just said that." He was growing exasperated.

"And you saved his life?"

His eyes opened wider. "If you know all about me, Detective, I'm not sure why you're here."

"I need to hear it from you," Giorgio replied matter-of-factly.

Martinelli drew his large hands in front of him and clasped them together. He had long, straight fingers that seemed to match his overly large feet splayed out to the sides.

"I saved more than his life," he said with exasperation. "I saved his reputation. He panicked one day when we were on patrol together. A young Viet Cong appeared out of nowhere. I called for Carson to take cover, but he turned and ran. The Viet Cong raised his gun and would have shot him in the back, if I hadn't shot him first."

"And you never told anyone about Montgomery's reaction," Giorgio said. "Because they would have called him a coward."

The big man shrugged. "Yes. It was the least I could do. Wouldn't you do that for a friend?"

Giorgio had the sense this man didn't have any real friends, only people who owed him things.

"Were you or your brother close to anyone in the police department at that time?" Giorgio asked nonchalantly.

This time his reaction was pronounced. He straightened up as if Giorgio had just accused him of some indiscretion.

"What are you suggesting?"

"Nothing. We're just trying to fit some pieces together."

"You just heard my son say that we didn't even live in Sierra Madre at the time. But my brother was probably its most prominent citizen. I believe he was even a member of the City Council. So, yes, Royce must have known people in the police department, probably even the Chief of Police. So what?"

"We're not accusing anyone of anything, Mr. Martinelli."

Martinelli turned towards the door, signaling that his patience was at its end. "That girl disappeared over forty years ago and last I heard, someone has already been convicted of the crime," he said, opening the door. "Poking your nose into people's business isn't doing anything for anyone. I suggest you focus on current crimes instead."

Giorgio stood directly behind him, but didn't move to step past him.

"You must be aware of what's been happening at the Pinney House – the house where your brother lived at the time Lisa Farmer went missing."

Martinelli paused and took a deep breath.

"The Pinney House has a long history," he said with an exhale. "I understand it was once even a sanitarium. Those bodies could have been buried there at any time. My brother had nothing to do with any of that. He and Claire lived there for only five or six years. There's no telling when those young women were killed."

"Actually, they lived there from 1955 until just after Lisa Farmer went missing," Giorgio corrected him. "So it's quite likely they *were* living there when those bodies were buried. And just for the record, what did *you* do after your brother dropped you off the night Lisa Farmer disappeared?"

It appeared that no one had ever asked him that question. He stopped for a moment, and an awkward silence prevailed as his eyes darted toward Rocky. Then he regained his composure.

"Again, that was forty years ago."

"Mr. Martinelli," Giorgio said patiently. "Your nephew's girlfriend went missing and he became the prime suspect. Think back."

He regarded Giorgio with a look of anger now firmly planted on his face.

"As I recall, it was late when Royce dropped me off," he said in a monotone. "I wasn't feeling well, and so I went straight to bed. He called me the next day to let me know about Lisa."

"Thank you. We'll let you know if we need anything else."

Giorgio and Rocky stepped past the man and they heard a loud click, as he firmly closed the door behind them. They returned to the car, and Giorgio sat still for a moment staring at the big house.

"What's bugging you?" Rocky asked.

"He's an arrogant son-of-a-bitch," Giorgio said, turning to Rocky. "Did you see the hot young thing that left through a side entrance just after we got here?"

Rocky's eyes lit up. "No."

"So even though he knew we were on our way, he didn't let our visit interrupt his scheduled *massage*."

"Still, not a convictable offense," Rocky countered.

"No, but I'd like to know how he knew all the bodies we found yesterday were young women. That won't be announced until the press conference this afternoon."

CHAPTER THIRTY

By five o'clock that afternoon, the press conference was over and Giorgio, Rocky and McCready were huddled in the War Room, a large conference room off the main hallway. It was pretty bleak as conference rooms go. There were two long tables that sat end to end, surrounded by metal folding chairs. A few battered file cabinets were tucked into the corner, and one wall was covered by a large chalk board and two maps, one of the city and one of the entire San Gabriel Valley. Two swivel white boards were pushed up against the front wall.

They spent twenty minutes taping up photos of the crime scenes onto one white board, including the well and every hole a body had come out of at the Pinney House. They posted photos of the cast of characters on the other white board – including pictures of Lisa and Ron, Jimmy Finn, Alex Springer, Carson Montgomery and the entire Martinelli clan. Then Giorgio began drawing lines between related photos, writing in dates and notes on relationships as he went. When he was done, both white boards were filled.

"So, do we think these two cases are related?" McCready asked as he sat back into one of the chairs. "Lisa Farmer and the women found at the Pinney House?"

It was quiet for a moment as Giorgio took a seat, and then he said, "My gut tells me they are. Same time period. Same family. Same house, even. And I think once we solve Lisa Farmer's murder, we solve the others."

"So what do we know?" Rocky said, sitting at the end of one of the tables with a toothpick in his mouth.

McCready pulled out his notes. "Ron Martinelli says he dropped Lisa off at her home around midnight the night of the prom. And Lisa's mother said that Lisa always came in through the back door and that she found the gate open the next morning. So Lisa probably at least made it into the backyard that night."

"Where someone was waiting for her. Jimmy Finn said he saw a car in the alley behind her house," Giorgio said, tapping the table. "And even though both Ron and his mother said that Lisa had never been to their home, we found an earring her mother had given her *that afternoon*. It was in a box hidden in a wall at the Martinelli home."

Rocky sat forward. "So, maybe Lisa was at the Martinelli home earlier that evening and lost the earring. Or…maybe the earring was taken from her *after* she was killed…as a trophy."

He looked around the table.

"In the second case, she may not have been at the Pinney house at all," Giorgio said.

Rocky nodded and stuck the toothpick back into his mouth, while Giorgio began to tap the table with one hand again.

"But if the killer took the earring as some kind of trophy, then maybe we could ID some of the other bodies with what else is in that box," McCready said, perking up at the idea.

"Exactly," Giorgio said, turning to him. "So let's contact any of the people we interviewed who reported young women missing during that time period and ask them about signature pieces of jewelry, hair clips, or clothing. But don't tell them what we have in the box." He sat back again.

Rocky looked up at the white board and sighed. "The two sets of crimes could be related, but Lisa Farmer was different than the girls at the Pinney House. She wasn't buried on the property, for one thing. There were no signs of torture. And it looks as if she was buried fully dressed."

"I agree," Giorgio said. "So we need to find out for sure whether or not Lisa was at the Martinelli home that night." He turned to his brother. "Sounds like another trip to see Ron Martinelli. We have a lot to ask him about the bodies buried in his backyard, anyway."

"By the way, I got the full list of the monastery's building committee from back in 1967," McCready said, pulling out a folder. "And both Royce Martinelli *and* Alex Springer were on it."

Giorgio arched his eyebrows. "That's interesting. I wonder if that gives us a clue as to why Springer was killed."

"Didn't you say that Claire Martinelli said her husband hated Springer because of the school board race or something? But then

Martinelli suddenly hired Springer to run a part of the company." Rocky asked.

"Yeah, she did," Giorgio replied.

Rocky used the toothpick in his hand to gesture as he talked. "Well, you don't hire someone you hate unless you have to," he said with a lift to his eyebrows. "Springer must have had something on Royce Martinelli. Something important enough that Martinelli paid him off with an executive level position."

"And then Springer gets killed when Lisa Farmer's body is discovered, because at his age there's nothing to pay him off with anymore," Giorgio speculated.

"Okay, so it looks like Carson Montgomery was killed up in Seattle because he was the one who planted the evidence in Jimmy Finn's locker," Rocky said. "And that means that Jimmy Finn didn't kill Lisa Farmer."

"Right. And, I'll bet that Edmond Martinelli is the one who made the call to Montgomery. His leverage was Vietnam," Giorgio said.

"So if Edmond Martinelli forced Montgomery to plant evidence," McCready said, staring at the board, "he must have been covering up for someone in his family." He turned to Giorgio. "After all, how else would they have had her shoe and underwear to plant in the locker?"

Giorgio pointed his index finger at the young cop. "Bingo. Ron said he had sex with her that night after the prom. Maybe they got into an argument and he killed her. Then his father and/or uncle helped him get rid of the body. But we can't rule out that either Royce or Edmond killed her for some reason and then took those items after she was dead."

"But why would either one of them kill her?" McCready said.

"Who knows? Maybe something as simple as they found out Ron planned to marry her," Giorgio said with a shrug. "I learned a long time ago that the reasons for murder don't always make sense to those of us investigating. So if Edmond planted the evidence, we have to figure out who he was protecting. Ron Martinelli. Ron's father, Royce. Or himself."

"Or the mother," Rocky spoke up. "Didn't you say she was a real piece of work? Maybe she's capable of killing someone."

"I have no doubt that Claire Martinelli could kill someone under the right circumstances," Giorgio said, getting up and going over to look at the picture they had of the Ice Queen. "Especially if her family's reputation was at stake. But she would have needed help."

"So we're thinking that Carson Montgomery planted the evidence, but Alex Springer didn't have anything to do with Lisa's death. He just knew something about it?" Rocky speculated.

"I'd bet on it," Giorgio replied, turning to his brother.

"And his son, Joshua Springer, is dead?" Rocky said.

"Yeah, from an overdose or something, ten years ago," Giorgio said. "What are you thinking?" Giorgio asked as he sat down again.

"I don't know. This whole thing seems so incestuous," Rocky said, using the toothpick to gesture to everyone on the board.

He got up and took hold of one of the white boards and flipped it around. Then, grabbing a marking pen, he began to write.

"If you start from the center, you start with Lisa and Ron. Right? They're the nucleus." He wrote their names in the middle of the board and put a circle around them. "Now, let's look at how others are related to each of them."

He wrote Jimmy Finn's name off to the right and then drew a straight line from Lisa's name to Jimmy name.

"Jimmy Finn is *only* connected to Lisa," he said. "He's not related to Ron other than he knew him at school. Now, let's keep going on this side. Connected to Jimmy are his girlfriend, Cheryl, and Cheryl's brother, LeRoy, along with Jimmy's brother, Marvin," he said, writing their names. "That's it. And so far nothing points to any of them as the killer."

Rocky turned to look at the others and both Giorgio and McCready nodded. Rocky turned back to the board.

"So let's start on Ron's side." He drew several lines from Ron's name off to the left. "Ron is connected by blood to his father, Royce, and his mother, Claire. He's also connected to his uncle, Edmond, and his cousin, Fritz," he said, writing up all of their names. "He's directly connected to Alex Springer because of the rivalry with Alex's son, Joshua, when they were in high school. And once Royce gave Springer that job, Alex Springer is connected to both Royce and Edmond through the company," he said connecting their names with dotted lines. "Carson Montgomery is connected to Edmond because of Vietnam, and even eventually connected to Royce because Royce got him the job at the high school," he said, writing up their names, connecting them with more dotted lines.

"And since both Springer and Montgomery are now dead, we believe they're connected because of something they knew," Giorgio said.

"Right. They didn't commit the crime, but knew something about the crime – which means they had to be connected to the killer somehow. But if you look at this," he said, gesturing to all the names on Ron's side of the board, "except for Springer and Montgomery, Ron is connected to everyone on this side in a big way. And all of these guys," he said, drawing a circle around all the names on Ron's side, are connected to each other by blood, school or business."

"Just one big incestuous cesspool," Giorgio murmured.

Rocky turned to him. "Exactly."

"It's enough to give you a headache," McCready said.

Giorgio got up again to join his brother at the board.

"So even though Lisa was the victim, it doesn't come back to her. It all comes back to Ron." He turned to his brother, his eyes alight. "Time to go see Ron again."

CHAPTER THIRTY-ONE

It had been one week since they'd found Lisa Farmer's skeletal remains, and only five days since they'd first interviewed Ron Martinelli. When they were given entrance to Ron Martinelli's home now, his change in appearance in that short time was alarming.

They found him sitting in a big leather wing back chair, staring into the fireplace, a glass of bourbon in his right hand. Although it was after six o'clock in the evening, he hadn't shaved and looked like he'd barely dressed. He was wearing loose fitting jeans, an old baggy t-shirt and slippers. He didn't stand up when they came in. Nor did he greet them.

"So how many bodies did you find, Detective? I stopped watching after five."

"Ten in all," he said.

Martinelli shook his head. "How do you do your job?" he said in a flat voice, still staring straight ahead. "How do you sleep at night?"

Giorgio moved further into the room and to Martinelli's right, flashing a cautious look at Rocky. Rocky stood behind Martinelli.

"I find the bad guys," Giorgio said.

"And you think I might be one of them."

"You lied to me." Giorgio reached into his pocket and pulled out the evidence bag holding Lisa's silver earring. "We found this at the Pinney House."

Martinelli finally looked up, dark circles smudging the area underneath his eyes. He stared at the small piece of jewelry for a moment, and a glimmer of recognition momentarily lit up his face. He turned back to the fire.

"Yes. I lied," he said with a cleansing exhale. "I've been lying for over forty years."

Ron took a sip of his drink, while Giorgio sat down slowly, never taking his eyes off of him. Rocky remained standing behind Martinelli's chair.

"Tell me about it," Giorgio said.

Ron swirled the remaining alcohol around in his glass. "I did take Lisa to the house that night," he said in defeat. "I knew my father would be gone, and my mother took sleeping pills because she often got bad headaches. It was prom night. I thought just once, it would be nice to…" He paused and took a deep breath. "To make love to the girl I hoped to marry inside, where it was warm and comfortable," he said. "We went into my father's study. He had a big leather sofa in there. But when I heard my father drive in, we panicked. I told Lisa to hide behind the curtains, while I went out to talk to him."

"And what happened?" Giorgio asked

He looked up again, his eyes dull and lifeless. "I met my dad in the entryway. As usual, he was completely preoccupied and just ordered me to bed. I went upstairs, but stayed at the head of the stairs, wanting to make sure he didn't go into the study. But the phone in his study rang, and he went in to answer it. As he closed the door, I heard him say my uncle's name. I was sure he'd find Lisa, so I stuck around to take the heat. But he was only in there a few minutes, and then he came out again. He locked the study door and stopped to use the phone in the front hallway for some reason and then went out the front door."

"Why do you say for some reason?" Giorgio asked.

"Because he'd just left the phone in his study. Anyway, I could hear him talking on the phone by the front door, but I couldn't hear what he was saying."

"What happened after that?"

"He left and I ran back downstairs. I knew where he hid an extra key to the study, so I used it and went in, but Lisa was gone and the French doors were open. I ran out into the side yard. I thought maybe I could catch her, but my dad was just pulling up the street, so I ducked back inside." He let out a deep sigh. "I never saw her again."

Giorgio glanced down at the baggie holding the earring. "So how did she lose this?"

Martinelli looked up. "I have no idea. As far as I know, she didn't take any of her jewelry off. I swear. But she was really spooked that night. She was afraid of what my father would do if he found her there. She had initially wanted to run out the French doors, but I'd talked her into hiding instead. I thought my dad would go right up to bed. So, I think she panicked and just ran. Maybe the earring got caught on the curtains or a bush as she went past."

"Did your father ever tell you where he went that night?" Giorgio asked.

His head snapped up. "You think my father killed her?"

Giorgio shrugged. "I don't know. He didn't want you dating Lisa. Maybe he knew you planned to marry her."

"He wouldn't kill someone for that," he said incredulously.

"But he might kill them for some other reason?" Rocky asked quietly, stepping forward.

Ron looked over at Rocky as if he'd just noticed him.

"I'm sorry," Giorgio said. "This is Detective Rocky Salvatori, my brother."

Ron Martinelli swallowed nervously. "No...I...no, my father wouldn't kill *any*one," he said, shaking his head.

But his voice lacked the confidence that comes with the truth.

"Ron," Giorgio began. "Did you know about the root cellar?"

Martinelli's face muscles tensed, as if he'd swallowed a spider. And then he looked away.

"Ron! We found a root cellar behind the big bookcases in the basement. Six bodies were buried down there. Four more in the yard – we believe all during the time you and your family lived there."

A tear began to make its way down Martinelli's cheek.

"I know," he whispered with all the finality the truth brings with it.

"You know?" Giorgio snapped.

"Yes. Somewhere in my heart," he said softly. "I knew...not everything. Not even very much. But I knew," he said. "I've known for a long time that something was very wrong in my family."

That made Giorgio think of the photos. "But they're *not* your birth family, are they?" he said.

Martinelli looked over sharply at Giorgio. "How did you know?"

"I've seen a multitude of family photos over the past few days. There's a distinct family resemblance between everyone...except you."

He nodded. "My mother only told me I was adopted when my father died. I'd always suspected, but I didn't know for sure. I was relieved, of course," he said, with the hint of a smile.

"Because you weren't one of them?" Giorgio speculated.

"No. I didn't have to claim any of their bad traits. I was my own man."

"So, tell us what you know," Giorgio said as his heart rate increased.

Ron stared into his glass for a moment, and then said, "My father was a monster."

He glanced over at Giorgio and then turned back to stare into the fireplace. The hand holding the bourbon had begun to shake.

"When I was five, maybe six years old," he began slowly. "I did something I wasn't supposed to do. My father used to build furniture in the basement. I was told never, *ever* to go down there. Too many sharp tools, he told me. But one afternoon, my father had gone out. My mother was upstairs, and my nanny was asleep. I was bored. My father always locked the basement door, but I knew where he kept the key. I was a smart kid," he said with a brief smile. "So I got the key and went down to the basement. There wasn't much to see. He had two wooden work tables set up, with electric saws and stuff. It looked like he was working on a rocking chair. The pieces were lying about and part of the chair sat on one of the tables. But then I noticed drops of red paint on the floor, and one of the slats from the chair had red paint on the end of it."

He took some deep breaths and had another sip of his drink. His hand was visibly shaking now.

"It wasn't red paint, was it?" Giorgio made the statement for him.

He shook his head slowly as he swallowed. "No. But the drops led across the floor, all the way up to the big bookcase, which was pulled away from the wall. I could hear moaning or something coming from behind it. So I peeked around the corner and realized there were stairs. I really wasn't a very brave kid, but my curiosity got the better of me. The light was on down below, so I crept down the stairs, afraid that my dad might be down there. But he wasn't."

A tear had begun to trickle down his cheek as he spoke.

"There was a girl," he said, choking on his words. He coughed to clear his throat before continuing. "She was on a bed, tied to the bed post. And she was naked," he said with a sigh. "She heard me and looked over at the staircase where I was peeking through the railing.

She looked…she looked weird to me, until I realized that parts of her face and body had…had been stripped of skin."

He paused as he gulped some air. Giorgio thought he might be sick.

"One of her eyes was swollen shut, and she had cuts and horrible bruises all over her body," he said, continuing. "The sheet was covered in blood, and there was another piece of the chair down there. And then she spoke to me. 'Please,' she said. 'Help me. He'll kill me.' But suddenly, my dad was there, behind me." Ron was taking in big gulps of air now. "He grabbed me by my collar and threw me up the stairs. I landed on the top step and cried out. But he came after me and grabbed me again. He pulled me into the workroom and held me up to his face. He was livid."

Ron took a deep breath and paused at the memory, his whole body vibrating.

"He got so close I could smell his breath, and he was shaking he was so mad. He told me that if I ever told anyone what I'd seen, the same thing that had happened to that girl would happen to me. He put me down and I ran upstairs and into my room. About a half hour later, he came to see me. I just huddled in the corner of my bed, scared to death that he was going to beat me and peel my skin away. Instead, he closed the door and went over to where I kept my little pet turtle, Pepper. Pepper was the only pet my parents ever allowed me to have. He lived in this little bowl with rocks and a little house."

Martinelli stared straight ahead as he spoke, as if living in the moment. Tears began to stream down his cheeks.

"My father reached in and grabbed Pepper, and then came over to my bed and held him out so that I could see him. And he said, 'I want you to understand how serious this is. You are never to tell anyone about what you saw, or this will happen to you.'" Ron paused, and then in a monotone, he said, "And then he dropped Pepper to the floor and crushed him with his foot."

Martinelli took a deep breath and hunched forward in the chair and groaned as if he was going to throw up.

A moment later, he stammered, "Oh God. I'll never forget that. I'll never forgive him."

He disintegrated into tears and Giorgio just waited, feeling a mixture of sadness and rage build inside him. But he had to let Martinelli play out the memory. It was a full thirty seconds before Martinelli regained his composure. He reached for a napkin to wipe his nose before continuing.

"All these years," he said through sobs, "I convinced myself that what I just told you wasn't real, that it was just a little kid's nightmare. I told myself it never really happened. But I can't fool myself any longer. My father really *was* a monster."

"Mr. Martinelli," Giorgio said through clenched teeth, controlling the anger he felt. "We need to know everything you might know that could help us."

Ron looked up, his face swollen and red. "But I don't know any more than that," he said. "That's the only time I ever actually saw anything."

"You probably know more than you think you do. What was your relationship like with your father *after* that?" Rocky said.

Giorgio looked over at his brother. Rocky's grim expression was a signal that the story had affected him as well.

"We were *never* close," Ron said. "It was always about appearances with them. I was just the kid that made our family look normal."

"Did you ever do things with your father – you know, father-and-son kinds of activities?" Rocky asked.

"No. Not really. I joined the Boy Scouts, but the nanny always took me. My parents would show up at the requisite awards ceremonies, and when I was in high school they came to a few football games."

"Did your father have women on the side?" Rocky asked.

Martinelli looked over at Rocky with a haunted expression.

"He and your mother..." Rocky let the sentence lapse.

"No. There was no intimacy between them that I ever saw," he said, finishing Rocky's thought. "They were like automatons with each other."

"How much do you think your mother knew?" Giorgio asked.

He shook his head. "I don't know. They had such a strange relationship. I do know that when I was fifteen, something changed, though. I'm not sure why, but my father stopped going down into the basement. He had all his equipment removed, and he took up fishing."

"Fishing?" Giorgio said, his heart rate increasing. "Had he been into fishing before?"

"No. Not that I know of. But suddenly he and Edmond would go fishing once a year."

Giorgio's ears perked up. "Did Edmond ever go down into the basement with your father?"

"Uh, yeah. They called it their man cave," he said, the realization dawning on him. "Oh, God, they were working together, weren't they?"

The glass of bourbon slipped out of Martinelli's hand and fell to the floor, emptying its contents onto the rug. He turned toward the fire again.

"Ron," Giorgio snapped, trying to get his attention. "We think your uncle is the one who had the evidence planted in Jimmy Finn's locker."

"Edmond?" he said, turning to Giorgio. "Why?"

"Did you know that Alex Springer was shot to death in his home a few days ago?"

"No. But why would someone kill Mr. Springer?"

"Your mother told us how your father hated Alex Springer because of the campaign he ran against your dad for the school board. And yet not too long after Lisa disappeared, your dad hired him to take over a major part of the company. We think Springer knew something and may have blackmailed your father in order to get the job. He sat on the building committee for the monastery, and so did your father. They both would have known about the well where we found Lisa's body. Is there anything else you can think of that might have given Alex Springer leverage over your father?"

Ron shook his head slowly. "No. Nothing."

"How about his son, Joshua?" Rocky asked.

Ron thought a minute and seemed to sit up straighter.

"Well, Joshua liked to hang out at the monastery," he said. "In fact, he used to take all of his girlfriends up there to have sex. He had a favorite spot out in the garden; he kind of claimed it as his own. He even got mad one summer night when Pete Cameron got there before him. They got into a big fight about it, and Pete had to leave."

"What are the chances that Joshua would have gone up there the night of the prom?"

Ron froze and stared at Giorgio. Then he murmured, "*Every chance.*"

Giorgio glanced at Rocky who merely arched his eyebrows. Joshua's connection to the monastery provided at least a possibility for how Alex Springer could have blackmailed Royce Martinelli. Joshua Springer could have been up there that night and seen either Royce or Edmond Martinelli or both throw Lisa Farmer's body into the well. But they'd never be able to prove it.

Ron began to rub his hand up and down the arm of the chair as he stared off into space. Giorgio could tell he was losing him again.

"Ron, we were at your uncle's house earlier today. He confirmed that he and your father had gone fishing the weekend Lisa went missing. They came home early for some reason. You said your father went into the study that night to answer the phone."

He nodded, his eyes glazed over.

"And Lisa was in there behind the curtains, is that right?"

"Yes. Yes," he said.

"Where did your father go after he left the study?"

He looked up, his face a blank slate. "Like I said, I don't know for sure. He told me the next day that he had gone back to the office."

"And his office was in Pasadena back then?" Giorgio pressed him.

"Yeah. Why?"

"The direct route back to his office would have been to go south on Lima to Sierra Madre Boulevard," Giorgio said. "But you said you had to duck out of sight when he pulled *up* the street, to the north? Is that right?"

"Yeah," Ron replied, still confused as to where Giorgio was going with this.

"*Up* the street," Giorgio said, "in the direction of Lisa's house?"

"Oh, God," Ron said, sucking in air. He seemed to waver in the chair for a moment and then put a hand across his stomach. "I…think I'm going to be sick."

He lurched out of the chair and stumbled from the room. Giorgio followed him into the hallway and saw him duck into a bathroom. There was the sound of gagging and a moment later the toilet flushed.

Ron Martinelli came back into the living room, wiping his hand across his mouth, his face deathly pale. He stood uncertainly in the middle of the room, breathing heavily.

"My father killed Lisa," he said, his bleak eyes rimmed with red.

"Let's stick with what happened that night," Giorgio said. "When your father left the study, you said he made a phone call from the front hallway."

Ron nodded.

"But he had his own phone in the study?"

Ron nodded a second time, wringing his hands. "Yes. We were one of the few families back then who had two separate phone lines."

Two separate phone lines? That gave Giorgio an idea.

"So why would he stop to call from the hallway phone?" Giorgio asked.

Ron took a deep breath and a tear began to make its way down his cheek. "There's only one reason," he said. "She heard something, didn't she? When he was talking to my uncle the first time. Then, because he saw Lisa behind the curtains, he had to hang up and use the phone out front."

All three men were silent for a moment, and then Ron dropped into a nearby chair.

"Ron, when you were fooling around, had you gotten undressed?" Rocky asked.

He wiped the tear away. "Yes, pretty much."

"Had she taken off her underwear?" Giorgio asked carefully.

Ron stared at him. The muscles around his mouth had begun to sag and his brown eyes had lost all luster.

Finally, he said, "Yes. When we heard my father pull into the driveway, I told…her to get dressed and hide behind the curtains, and then I ran into the hallway." He started to shake his head slowly. "She probably didn't have time to put them on. They would have been stuck in the sofa or were maybe even on the floor. Oh God, I can't believe this," he said, leaning forward and putting his head into his hands.

"Ron, do you know where your father and uncle went fishing that weekend?" Giorgio asked.

He took a deep breath, wiped his mouth and sat up. "No. But my mother might."

Giorgio glanced at Rocky and nodded. He felt that they had gotten all the information they could out of Ron for the moment.

"Okay," he said. "Please don't tell anyone about this conversation until I've had a chance to check out some details."

Ron looked over at Giorgio, his face ashen and his muscles slack. "Do you really think my father killed Lisa?"

"I don't know. But I need to know one more thing. You drove your father's car to the prom, is that right?"

Ron nodded.

"What car did your father use when he left again that night?"

"His car," Ron said.

"And what kind of car did your father drive?"

Martinelli's eyebrows curled up into a question. "A black Lincoln Town Car. Why?"

CHAPTER THIRTY-TWO

They were forced to wait until the next morning to pay a second visit to Claire Martinelli. Her big Bentley was just pulling through the gate when they came to a halt in front of it, blocking its departure. Giorgio got out and approached the driver's side and ordered the driver back to the house.

"Don't you dare, John!" Mrs. Martinelli ordered from the back seat.

"If you'd prefer," Giorgio said through the open back window. "I can arrest you."

"On what grounds?" she said with a sneer.

"For aiding and abetting a murderer."

Her eyes opened wide, and she stiffened. "It's all right, John. Take me back."

Ten minutes later, they were situated in Claire Martinelli's living room again. There was no offer of lemonade this time, and there was no sign of the maid.

"What do you mean by invading my home?" she blustered.

"Where were you going?" Giorgio said, ignoring her question.

"I was going out of town for a while. Obviously, things have gotten rather ugly over at the Pinney House. That reporter, Mia Santana, has been all over the news pointing fingers at us. And she's been calling the house. I need to get away."

"Gotten rather ugly?" Giorgio said angrily. "Is that what you call it? We found the skeletons of several mutilated bodies buried in the yard and in the basement during the time you lived there."

"You don't know that," she spat.

"Mrs. Martinelli, let's stop beating around the bush. You knew perfectly well what your husband was doing down in the basement.

Down in the root cellar. Why didn't you tell anyone? Why didn't you stop him?"

She held herself erect for a brief moment and then the tension released. Her rigid figure became lax and the ramrod back finally bowed in defeat. She dropped her hands into her lap.

"Yes, I knew. Or at least I suspected. I never saw anything firsthand. But I knew he wasn't

down there making furniture."

"What *did* you know?"

She glanced up at him, her face looking suddenly very old and haggard.

"Not much, really. We slept in separate rooms. I had the master suite at the corner of the house, closest to the garage. I was a very light sleeper and saw him on several occasions bring a girl into the house through the back door."

"The girls came into the house willingly?" Giorgio couldn't quite believe it.

"Yes, but they were either drunk or drugged. They hung on his arm as if they could barely walk. One night, I sat by that window, waiting for him to bring the girl out again. But he never did. Instead, hours later, I heard him come up the stairs and go into his bedroom. And then for several days, he was very busy in the basement. Neither Ron nor I, nor any of the servants were ever allowed down there. When it happened again, I slept during the daytime, and at night I'd sit at the window and watch, waiting for him to bring the girl out. Days went by, and then finally, I saw him carry something out of the kitchen..." she stopped and swallowed. "He buried whatever it was in the corner of the backyard."

There was a long pause. The clock on the mantle ticked quietly in the background.

"What did the *something* look like?" Giorgio asked, nearly spitting at her.

"It was hard to tell," she said. "It was quite dark. We only had a single light above the garage. But whatever he was carrying was long and heavy, and he carried it over his shoulder."

"And you thought it was a body?" Giorgio asked.

She started to object, but then nodded, all sense of pride gone.

"And then what happened?" Giorgio asked.

"I know you think I'm a cold bitch, Detective," she said suddenly. "But I actually married Royce because I thought I loved him. My

father was a state senator, and I was brought up to know my place."
She stopped and took a deep breath. "Royce had an unusual sexual
appetite. I…couldn't make myself do the things he wanted me to do.
He…he seemed unable to perform unless he could hurt me. Twist
the skin on my arm or put pressure on a bone. I couldn't take it. So
we made an agreement. We would stay married, and I would allow
him to do what he needed to satisfy his urges. But, when I saw this,
well, I couldn't put up with it. So I told him, 'not in my house.'"

Giorgio couldn't believe what he'd just heard. This woman's
answer to her husband murdering young women was to just tell him
to do it somewhere else.

"And so he stopped?" Giorgio asked, feeling adrenalin pump
through his veins. "Around the time Ron was fifteen?"

"Yes," she said, contemplating the comment about Ron. "And as
far as I know Royce never brought another woman into the house."

"Nor buried anyone else in the back yard," Giorgio said.

"No," she murmured. "He started going fishing instead."

She went very still for a moment, watching him. His hands had
turned into fists in his pockets as he tried to control his anger.

"And you knew he wasn't fishing?"

She stared at him. "I never asked," she said with a slight turn of
her head. "I preferred not to think about it."

He slammed his fist onto a table, making everyone in the room
jump.

"Why didn't you tell anyone!?"

She stiffened again. After a moment she replied, "Royce assured
me they were girls he pulled off the street. They were prostitutes and
drug addicts. In fact, he said he was very careful to select girls no
one would miss, so the family name would never be drawn into
his…fantasies."

It was all Giorgio could do not to hit her. He turned and paced to
the other side of the room, thinking. She wasn't just a cold bitch; she
was a selfish cold bitch. The perfect partner. As long as her husband
left her alone and maintained the family reputation, she didn't care
who he murdered.

"Mrs. Martinelli," he said through clenched teeth, when he came
back. "You just said a minute ago that you were a light sleeper. Are
you telling me that you *did* hear your son come home the night of his
prom? Perhaps your husband as well?"

"Yes," she replied quietly. "I heard them both."

"And you listened in when your husband made the phone call from the hallway before leaving again, didn't you?" Giorgio said, not giving her a chance to deny it.

"Yes," she said after a pause. "The phone in his study was a private line, but the one in the hallway had an extension in my room. I don't know who he was talking to. I only heard what he said."

"Which was what?" he said patiently.

She didn't reply right away.

"Mrs. Martinelli, tell me what your husband said," he said forcefully.

"He said, 'Meet me at the entrance to the monastery right away. We have a problem.' And then he hung up."

Giorgio felt his voice vibrate with anger. "So you've known for over forty years that your husband was the one who probably murdered Lisa Farmer, and you never told a soul."

"No," she said plaintively. "I didn't know back then that the monastery had anything to do with Lisa's disappearance. I just heard him say he was going to meet someone up there."

"But you knew something was up?" Giorgio pressed her.

Once again, her hackles were raised.

"You make it all sound so easy, Detective. As if all I had to do was tell the police what I knew. Think about it. If I had, my life would have been ruined."

She made this last comment as if the quality of her life was the most important thing in the world – not just for her, but for all of mankind.

"Mrs. Martinelli, do you know where your husband went fishing the weekend Lisa Farmer went missing and why he came back early?"

"I don't know why he returned early. But I do know where they went. Only because…the next day I found the coat he'd worn. He'd left it hanging on the coat tree next to the front door. I went through the pockets, and there was a receipt for gas from a town outside of Big Bear."

"Big Bear Lake?" Giorgio asked. The hairs on the back of his neck tickled.

She nodded, and Giorgio felt suddenly cold all over. Without thinking, he reached into his pocket and fingered the souvenir medallion.

"Last question – do you know anyone who drives a Jeep Wrangler?"

She looked up at him, surprised at the change in questioning. "Uh...well, yes. I think my nephew Fritz's son does. Why?"

"Fritz's son? What's his name?"

"Perry...Fitzgerald. His mother was Fritz's first wife. She went back to her maiden name after they got divorced," she said.

That answered why the Jeep had never come up under the Martinelli name when they'd searched the DMV.

"What does Perry look like?"

"He takes after his mother," she said. "He's kind of small and pale, and he wears all those disgusting black clothes and heavy jewelry."

"Tattoos?" Rocky said.

She looked up at him. "Yes. Around his neck."

"And Fritz," Giorgio said. "Is that his real name?"

"No, it's Frederick," she said. "Why?"

"And he was called Freddie?"

"He was Fritz in the family, but, yes, I think he was Freddie to his friends. Yes, why, Detective?"

The cacophony of bells going off in Giorgio's head made it hard for him to hear her last question.

"We're done for now, Mrs. Martinelli," Giorgio said. "But you are not to go anywhere or talk to anyone about this, especially other members of your family. If you do, I'll send an entire squadron of police after you and lock you up, do you understand?"

She blanched. "Yes, I understand."

They returned to the car and Giorgio called McCready and told him to put APBs out on Perry Fitzgerald and Fritz Martinelli.

"So, what do we do now?" Rocky asked.

Giorgio started the car and looked over at his brother. "We're going to Big Bear Lake."

"But it seems like all the action is down here," Rocky said.

"Yes, but we don't have any real evidence to implicate either Fritz or Perry, other than the fact that Perry owns a Jeep."

"The girl at the nursing home could ID Perry," Rocky said.

"Yes. But only for Montgomery's murder. We'll get him for that. And my guess is that Fritz killed Springer. But I want Edmond, and I doubt either Fritz or Perry will give him up for any role he played in those two murders," Giorgio said as he took off the emergency brake. "But if we can get Edmond on a different murder…"

Rocky's eyebrows went up. "You mean one of the girls they picked up on one of their fishing trips?"

"I want to know what went wrong up in Big Bear," Giorgio said, preparing to pull away from the curb. "So wrong that those two had to come home early. I think whatever it was got Lisa Farmer killed."

CHAPTER THIRTY-THREE

Giorgio had been to Big Bear Lake only once when the family had taken a summer vacation there. The lake sits in the middle of the San Bernadino National Forest. In the late 1800s, a trip to Big Bear by buggy would have taken over two days. By car, they'd be there in just under two hours.

"Apparently Big Bear is good for trout, catfish, and bass fishing," Rocky said, reading from his smart phone. He glanced over at Giorgio. "Too bad Royce and Edmond Martinelli didn't actually like to fish."

The brothers arrived at the San Bernadino County Sheriff's office just before noon. Fortunately, the sheriff was in and welcomed them into his office.

Sheriff Williams was a small man with razor cut hair, a receding hairline and a thin smile. The brothers sat in wooden arm chairs on the other side of his desk, staring out a window at a stand of pines trees.

"What can I do for you boys?" the sheriff asked amiably.

"We're looking into a murder case that may be connected to something that happened up here back in 1967," Giorgio said.

The Sheriff shrugged. "Whoa, 1967? You're not going to find much information going that far back. What was the incident?"

Giorgio snuck a glance at his brother. "We don't know. But two men who we believe are involved in the murder of a number of young women came up for a long weekend and probably rented a cabin."

The little man had leaned way back in his chair and tapped the fingers of his right hand on the desk. "This have anything to do with all those bodies that were dug up down your way?"

Giorgio reached into his pocket and pulled out pictures of Royce and Edmond Martinelli.

"Yes. These are the two men. We believe something happened up here that made them pull up stakes suddenly and go back home. We're trying to find out what that was."

The sheriff studied the pictures a moment. He tapped his fingers again before saying, "You'll need to talk with Sheriff Masters. He's retired now, but he would have been sheriff back then."

"Do you know where we can find him?" Rocky asked.

"Sure. He has a home over in Fawnskin by Dana Point Park."

He popped his chair forward and punched something into his computer. Then he grabbed a sticky note and wrote it down.

"Here's his address." He glanced out the window. "But the sun's out, so most likely you'll find him down by the marina even. Even at this time of year, he likes to take his Kindle and sit down there and read."

Giorgio nodded. "What's he look like?"

The sheriff smiled. "Oh, you can't miss Tubbs Masters. He lives up to his name."

Giorgio smiled back. "Thanks for your time."

As promised, they found Sheriff Tubbs Masters sitting on a bench at the end of the dock, a Kindle held loosely in his hands. He wore sunglasses and a straw hat. A heavy corduroy jacket was stretched tight over an enormous belly, and he had a wool scarf around his neck. The lake lapped gently against the pilings, while a few clouds floated across the sky.

"Sheriff Masters?" Giorgio said, coming up to the side of the bench.

He turned and looked up.

"Who's asking?"

"My name is Giorgio Salvatori. Joe to my friends," he said with a smile. "I'm with the Sierra Madre Police Department, down in the San Gabriel Valley." He lifted up his jacket to show his badge, which was attached to his belt. He pointed to Rocky. "My brother, Rocky. Also with the Sierra Madre PD."

Rocky nodded to him and also flashed his badge.

The sheriff glanced at the badges and closed his Kindle. "I know Sierra Madre," he said. "I have a sister who lives in Arcadia." He eyed Giorgio for a moment. "The monastery murders. You were the lead detective."

"Yes, sir. I was," Giorgio said.

"Nice job on that one."

"Thanks," Giorgio replied.

"Well, what can I do for you?"

The brothers moved in front of him and leaned against the dock's railing, both squinting against the glare off the water.

"We need to know if you remember if anything significant happened up here back in May of 1967."

A short chuckle erupted through his lips. "Like what? A forest fire? A boating accident? A celebrity sighting?"

"No, sir," Giorgio said. "We have two suspects in a case we're working from back then. They were supposed to be on an extended fishing trip up here, but came home after only a few days. They've been implicated in a string of murders – young girls. We think something happened up here that sent them packing – scared them away."

The heavyset man sat up a little straighter at the mention of young girls.

"Tell me more about the murders," he said, removing his sunglasses.

"The women were tortured," Rocky said. "And murdered."

The sheriff dropped his gaze to the water behind them for a long moment. He took in a deep breath and then said, "I think you'd better follow me to my home."

He stood up and led them back to the parking lot, where he hefted his big bulk into an old Ford pickup. They followed him out of town and up a winding road, through the forest. Ten minutes later, they pulled off the paved road onto a dirt road that wound around a natural pond to a large log cabin.

He welcomed them into a warm living room filled with leather furniture, big throw rugs and a rough-hewn wooden dining table. Instead of dead animals gracing the walls, however, framed oil paintings of the lake hung there.

"Why don't you have a seat, and I'll make some coffee," he said.

He disappeared into the kitchen, while Rocky and Giorgio made themselves comfortable. A few minutes later, the sheriff returned with a tray of steaming coffee mugs and a plate of chocolate biscotti.

"I make the biscotti myself," he said proudly.

He dropped his bulk into a big chair and leaned back, holding his coffee cup on his chest. Giorgio dipped the hard cookie into his coffee and then took a bite. His eyes lit up. "Mmmm," he murmured. "That's good stuff."

"Thanks," the big sheriff said. "I'll send some with you. Okay, I suppose you'd like to get to the topic at hand. So here's what I know. It was late May back in 1967. I don't remember the exact date. There was a young girl by the name of Amber Riley who was picked up by a couple of guys when she was hitch-hiking."

As soon as he mentioned the name, Amber, Giorgio's antenna went up. Hadn't Flame mentioned seeing the color amber?

"They took her to a remote cabin," the sheriff continued. "They raped her and tortured her over a period of a couple of days. But she escaped."

Giorgio's heart skipped a beat. "Did you find out who the men were that picked her up?"

"No. They burnt the cabin to the ground when they left. There was nothing left behind, and the owner said she was paid in cash by mail. So she never knew who the renters were. It was different back then. People trusted more. There were no computer trails. No cell phone records. Anyway, the girl wasn't found until the next morning about a mile and a half away, naked, bleeding and pretty mangled up."

"Did you launch an investigation?" Giorgio asked.

"Sure we did. But Amber said she had been on a road trip with some friends. She and her boyfriend had gotten into a big fight and she'd left by herself. These men picked her up on the way into town. They never gave her their names and never called each other by name. And from what we could tell, they never utilized any services in town, either. No gas. No food. No nothing. So they came and went like ghosts," he said, dipping his biscotti into his coffee.

At the mention of ghosts, the muscles in Giorgio's chest tightened. But he let his hands drop to the table in disappointment.

"Did you get a description from her?"

"Sure," the big sheriff replied. "Tall, dark hair, dark eyes. But as I said, no one but Amber ever saw them."

"What about the vehicle they used?" Rocky asked hopefully.

"She was pretty traumatized by the time she was found. Not long on details," Tubbs recalled.

"Damn! I was hoping we could somehow confirm it," Giorgio exclaimed.

"Well, you could talk with Amber," the sheriff said casually. "You might learn a little more. You have the luxury of having someone in mind. We didn't."

"She's still around?" Giorgio asked, flashing a look at his brother.

"Yeah. She stayed in town and runs the area's only homeless shelter. It's over in the City of Big Bear, off of 3rd. But I need to warn you, she may not want to talk to you. What they did to her was awful. They broke two of her fingers, used an electrical probe on her genitals, and…" he paused. "They pulled her eyelashes out…one by one." He swallowed hard and shook his head. "Amber's case was one of the few times when I hated my job."

"We'll go slowly with her," Rocky promised.

The sheriff stared at Giorgio for a moment and then nodded. "I'd better give her a call."

He stood up and went into the kitchen again. They heard his voice, but not what he said. A moment later, he was back with a piece of paper and a paper bag filled with biscotti.

"She said she'll talk to you," he said handing Giorgio a bag of biscotti and a slip of paper. "But as you said, take it slowly. I doubt any of us could fully understand what she went through."

CHAPTER THIRTY-FOUR

When Giorgio and Rocky walked into the shelter, Amber Riley was standing behind a counter, folding towels, making sure all the corners matched. She was a petite woman with short brown hair and glasses.

Giorgio noticed that her left hand seemed stiff, as if the fingers didn't work so well. Then he remembered what the old sheriff had said about how her kidnappers had broken two fingers on one hand.

She looked up as the two men strode in and instantly stiffened. Her hands stopped moving.

"You're the police officers," she said before they could even introduce themselves.

"Yes," Giorgio said. "I'm Detective Giorgio Salvatori, and this is Rocky Salvatori. We're with the Sierra Madre Police. We're here to talk to you about what happened back in 1967. We think we know who abducted you."

Her eyes opened wider and slowly, her hands began to shake.

"I know this is difficult, Ms. Riley. But we need your help," he said, modulating the tone of his voice. "One of the men we believe did this to you is dead. But we need help in identifying the second man. We'd like to put him behind bars."

She paused for a moment, and Giorgio held his breath hoping she wouldn't just turn and walk away.

Then she exhaled and said quietly, "Come with me."

They followed her down a short hallway, where she handed off the towels to another woman. She led them into a small office at the end of the hallway, where she sat behind the desk, bracing her hands on the arms of the chair. Her body was tense and she looked as if she was afraid they were going to assault her. In a way, Giorgio thought, they were.

Giorgio and Rocky sat facing her.

She'd been pretty once. Her face had good bone structure, and she had few wrinkles, but she also had two dark splotches that stretched across one cheek, like dark birthmarks. And a small chunk of her left nostril was missing, along with her left earlobe. These were just some of the physical scars left behind from her ordeal. Giorgio couldn't help but study her eyes, thinking about what Sheriff Masters had said about having her eyelashes pulled out one by one. When she noticed him studying her, he dropped his gaze.

"What do you want to know?" she said.

"Everything," Giorgio replied, glancing back up at her. "Even if you think it's not important. We believe these men have a long history of doing what they did to you. But you're the only one we know of that got away."

That raised an eyebrow. She clasped her hands in front of her on the desk, twisting her fingers into a knot. When she spoke, her voice was barely above a whisper.

"I've spent my entire life trying to understand what happened to me," she said, her voice shaking. "I was young and so damn carefree. I trusted everyone. The world was my oyster. Isn't that the saying?"

She looked at them with a haunted expression.

"I know this is difficult, Ms. Riley. We don't need to know the details of...of the physical abuse. We want to know about the men who abducted you. How they behaved with each other. How they even found you."

She glanced down to her hands again and pressed her lips together. Then she began to speak as if it took every ounce of strength she had to get the words out.

"Two men offered me a ride one night." Tears formed in her brown eyes, and she used her good hand to wipe them away. "They looked normal. Like my own dad. In fact, one of them said he had a daughter about my age and wouldn't want her out hitchhiking alone. They said they'd drop me off at a motel. So I said okay." She shook her head. "Such a simple act – getting into the wrong car."

"What happened next?" Giorgio asked gently.

"The one in the passenger seat got out to open the back door for me. As I was about to get in, he grabbed me from behind and put something over my nose and mouth. It smelled awful and I passed out."

She started to breathe heavily as she relived those moments.

"I woke up tied to a bed...naked."

She had to stop for a moment. Giorgio just let her tell it at her own pace.

"I tried to get them to let me go, but of course they only laughed. One of them started to hurt me almost immediately."

She shook her head, as if even now she couldn't believe it.

"At first, he just pinched my skin, twisted my fingers, things like that. I could tell it got him excited. Eventually...eventually, he raped me."

Tears began to stream down her cheeks, and Rocky reached over and pushed a box of Kleenex forward to her.

"Take your time, Ms. Riley," Rocky said.

She took a tissue and wiped her eyes and nose and then continued.

"They kept me there for two days. They did awful things to me," she said, choking out a sob.

"We know, Ms. Riley," Giorgio said. "You don't need to repeat that."

"Why would someone do that?" she said, crying and wiping her eyes.

Giorgio let the moment play itself out as he waited patiently. Finally, he asked, "How did they refer to each other?"

She took a deep breath to gain control again. "Believe it or not, they called each other Batman and Robin. The shorter one was Batman. He seemed to be the one in control."

"What did they talk about? When they weren't..."

"They didn't, for the most part," she interrupted him. "If they wanted to have a conversation, they went outside."

"How did you get away?" Rocky asked.

"It was the third day. I was slipping in and out of consciousness. But I could tell that Robin was getting sick. I heard him say that he'd forgotten to pack his medication. Batman swore at him, and kept saying that he could just eat something. But by nightfall, Robin was really ill. So Batman finally said he'd go back and get his medication. I was tied to a chair and pretty out of it by that time, so I guess he didn't think I was a threat. Anyway, he said he'd be back in a few hours and gave a gun to Robin. He told him to shoot me if I moved. I think that was more for my benefit, because Robin was really sick. Anyway, it had to be at least a couple of hours after

Batman left that Robin finally passed out. I could barely see him, because…" she stopped and sucked in some air. "There was blood caked in my eyes and they were really swollen."

She was breathing heavily and Giorgio waited for her to get control again.

"But the chair I was in was close to a counter where they'd left the knife they'd used to…to…" She had to stop and take another deep breath. "I was able to push my chair back and knock the knife onto the floor. Then, I had to tip my chair over, and I remember being really scared that Robin would wake up. But he didn't. I somehow got a hold of the knife with my good hand. It was hard and it kept slipping out of my grasp. Anyway, I tipped the knife up and slowly cut my ropes. I almost passed out several times myself. The pain in my left hand was terrible, but I used my good hand and finally cut myself loose."

She looked up at Giorgio with a renewed sense of purpose.

"I had to wash my eyes out, and I was shaking so bad that I kept dropping the towel. But then I just ran. No shoes. No clothes. I just wanted to get as far away from that cabin as I possibly could. I had no idea where I was, but I couldn't take the road in case Batman came back. So I stuck to the forest. I fell several times and finally rolled down a steep hill and passed out. A couple of hikers found me in the morning and got me to a hospital."

"We need to know whatever you can tell us about the man who got sick. It sounds like he was a diabetic."

She nodded. "Yes, I think so. When I recovered, I studied up on it."

Giorgio nodded. "We can check that out," he said, remembering what Edmond had said about feeling ill the night they had returned early from their fishing trip. "Anything else you can remember about him?"

"For instance, can you describe them for us?" Rocky asked.

She glanced at Rocky. "Both of them were very tall and had dark brown hair, almost black. On the slender side. Robin was taller than Batman, but by only an inch or two. Dark, blank eyes," she said, stopping again. "Dead eyes."

"Any unusual things about how they looked or how they moved?" Giorgio said.

She looked up at him. "Unusual in what way?"

He shrugged. "Anything that made you think to yourself, 'Hey that's weird.' Or when you saw it you commented on it in your mind."

She thought a moment and then her eyes lit up. "Yes. Robin's feet."

"His feet?" Rocky said.

"Yes. He had enormous feet. I had to look at them for hours when I was in that chair. Sometimes he was sitting in front of me, toying with me. Other times he was sitting on the bed close by. His shoes looked custom-made. Very expensive. And when he walked, he walked like a duck, his toes pointed way out to the side. He sat like that, too. It was like his feet weren't his own, you know what I mean? Like someone had stuck someone else's feet on him. Does that help?"

"Yes," Giorgio said quietly. "That's exactly what we were looking for, Amber."

"Do you know who he is?"

Her voice had taken on a plaintive quality.

"Yes," Giorgio said.

Giorgio pulled out several pictures. Three were of local cops they used in line-ups. The other two were of Royce and Edmond. He cautiously slid them all across the desk. She stared at them for a moment and then slowly picked up the ones of Royce and Edmond. Her face had gone pale, and she suddenly looked like she might be sick.

"Oh my God," she whispered.

She dropped the photos and glanced up at Giorgio, her eyes filled with tears.

"Who were they?" she asked, as if even now, she feared them.

"Brothers. I can't give you their names, because they haven't been charged with anything. But we think they have a long string of murders on their hands. You were very lucky. You *do* recognize them, I take it."

She seemed to shudder. "Yes. That's them," she said, pointing to the pictures of Royce and Edmond. "That's Batman," she said pointing to Royce. "And the other one was Robin. But it doesn't feel like I was lucky. There were many times over those few days that I prayed for death." Her right hand fluttered to her face. "I lived, but I'm covered in scars." She touched one of the places where they'd peeled skin away. Her fingers were shaking. "Will I have to testify in a trial or anything?"

Giorgio glanced at his brother. "I don't know. As I said, one of the brothers is already dead. He died several years ago. The other one is in his eighties."

"But...how did you find me?" she asked.

"We're following up on the murder of another young girl who was killed the same night you escaped. Her body was just recently discovered. She hadn't been kidnapped and tortured like you. It looks as if these men had been doing this for a very long time, and there had never been any problems. Then you escaped. That became a very big problem. They came home earlier than expected, and we believe this other girl overheard something, perhaps a discussion about what happened with you."

"And that got her killed?" she almost screeched.

Giorgio drew his lips together and nodded.

"Oh," she said. "I'm so sorry."

"It wasn't your fault," Rocky said quickly.

Giorgio stood up. "Ms. Riley, I'm going to ask the sheriff to send an officer over to stay with you. I believe we're very close to solving this case, but things are at a critical juncture right now. I want to make sure you're safe."

She straightened up. "From who? The guy who's in his eighties?"

"We don't know. But two *other* people connected to the family involved have recently died under suspicious circumstances."

"Why come after me now?" she asked, standing up. "Why didn't they try to find me all those years ago?"

"Maybe you can answer that better than we could," he said.

She thought a minute. "Well, they didn't know *my* name, either."

"You didn't have your purse with you?" Rocky asked.

"No. I stormed out when my boyfriend and I got in a big argument. I didn't take anything with me. I was kind of stoned, to be honest. I just started walking. And when I was finally found, Sheriff Masters purposely kept my picture and name out of the papers. He's been very protective of me over the years."

"Sheriff Masters said that no one in town ever saw them, so they may have felt that if they could just lay low, no one would ever be able to ID them. They must have brought everything they needed with them to the cabin. Food. Gas. Water."

Her eyes lit up. "Yes. They had several coolers and boxes lined up along the wall."

"They were very smart," Giorgio said. "They just didn't count on Robin forgetting his insulin. If they'd tried to go to a hospital or a doctor's office to get that, it would have stood out. Somebody would have remembered that. So Batman had to go back home to get it."

"But why didn't they just kill me? Then both of them could have left."

"Because it would have taken too long," Rocky said. "Killing you. Burying you. And then cleaning up the cabin. They couldn't leave a trace. It sounds like Robin was too sick to help, and he needed the insulin too quickly. He must have been close to what they call diabetic shock. My guess is that they were in a big hurry when they left. That's why they burned the cabin down. They had to make sure they destroyed any evidence."

She extended her hand. "Thank you," she said. "I've been looking over my shoulder for over forty years."

Giorgio shook her hand and then gave her his card. "We'll wrap this up as quickly as we can, Ms. Riley. And if we can, we'll keep you out of it."

Giorgio and Rocky left and climbed into their car. Giorgio called Sheriff Williams and arranged protection for Amber, and then they stopped for a quick dinner on the way out of town.

It was just getting dark when they finally pulled onto Highway 18, heading for the valley. Rocky was driving.

"What's our next move?" Rocky asked, keeping his eyes on the road.

They were on a two lane stretch of road with the mountain to their left and a deep ravine to their right.

"I'm going to call the captain, but I think it's time we go arrest Edmond."

"Shit!" Rocky snapped, looking up into the rearview mirror.

"What?" Giorgio said, twisting around and looking out the back window.

"Some dumb ass behind me. He's right on my tail."

The headlights from the other vehicle glared into the sedan. The car began to pull around them.

"Idiot," Rocky snarled. "Where does he think he's going? There's not enough room to pass."

Rocky pulled over to the right as much as he could to allow the other car to pass, bringing the guardrail alarmingly close.

"Jeez, I hope no one comes the other way," Giorgio said, glancing ahead of them.

The vehicle pulled up alongside the sedan. Rocky waved him by, but it stayed where it was. Rocky glanced over.

"Shit!" he exclaimed again.

Giorgio turned, just as the van plowed right into them.

The sedan swerved to the right, smashed through the guardrail and flew over an embankment. It came down hard on the front end, and then bounced down the slope, banging over rocks and logs. Both men were thrown around inside, forced to hold on to whatever they could find.

Ten seconds later, it was all over.

The car slammed into a tree. The air bags deployed, exploding into their faces, while steam burst from the battered hood.

Things remained still for several moments. Both men sat, dazed.

"Your nose is bleeding," Rocky said, pushing the bag away from his face.

Giorgio looked over at his brother, waiting until his eyes could focus. Then he lifted the back of his hand to his nose and felt the warm blood. He wiped it off.

"Who the hell was that?" he exclaimed.

Rocky glanced into the rearview mirror. "It was a blue van. That's all I know," he mumbled.

Giorgio's head snapped around. "Then let's get out of here."

Both men disentangled themselves from the airbags and seatbelts and began to climb out of the car.

The car had landed in the center of a bank of bushes that encircled the tree, making it difficult to open either door. Giorgio pushed his door and finally had to lean his weight against it to get it open. He fell out and pushed his way through the branches until he was behind the tree. Rocky slid through a small opening between his crumpled door and the frame, and climbed through the bush on his side. Just then, a shot rang out and clipped the low hanging branch of the tree.

Rocky scrambled through the bush and slid on his butt down to where Giorgio was. They both removed their weapons.

"Can you see anything?" Giorgio said, peering through the bush, past their steaming car and up to the road.

"No. It's too dark."

Giorgio pulled out his cell phone. "Thank God!" he said when the phone lit up.

Another bullet winged the side mirror of the car, and they both ducked.

Giorgio dialed the Sheriff's office. "Sheriff, this is Detective Salvatori!" he barked into the phone. "Someone's shooting at us. We're pinned down on an embankment about a mile or two out of town on Highway 18."

Another bullet ricocheted off the tailpipe. Rocky crawled up underneath the side of the bush and squeezed off four rounds in the direction of the incoming fire.

Giorgio came up behind his brother.

"Can you tell if it's Fritz or Perry?"

Giorgio had his own gun out now.

"No," Rocky said, peering through the darkness. "Whoever it is up there behind those boulders."

He nodded to the turn in the road where several giant rocks cradled the edge of the pavement.

A bullet whizzed past Rocky's shoulder, embedding itself into an old log behind them. Giorgio flinched to the side as it flew past.

"Shit, he's getting too close. C'mon."

Giorgio backed up and scuttled to the other side of the tree. Rocky followed him. They positioned themselves behind the rear wheels of the car, facing up the hill. Giorgio lay on his stomach, with his arms stretched out under the car chassis, the gun clasped between his hands. When a gun flash lit up the night and a bullet hit the other side of the car, he fired. A voice cried out and a moment later, the sound of screeching tires echoed through the canyon as the car sped away into the dark curves of the mountain.

CHAPTER THIRTY-FIVE

Giorgio and Rocky spent the next hour and a half at the sheriff's office in Big Bear, filling out a report. Since it was clear they'd been followed, Giorgio called Sheriff Tubbs, who volunteered to take Amber Riley into his home until he got an all clear from Giorgio.

It was almost eight o'clock when he and Rocky hit the road again in a rented car. It had been a long hour and a half, in which both men had been chafing at the bit to get going. Their adrenalin was flowing and they wanted to end this.

Giorgio called Ron Martinelli.

"Is your uncle a diabetic?" he asked.

"Uh...yes, why?" Ron replied.

"I'll explain later. I also need to know if Perry or Fritz might have access to a commercial van through your company. An old blue or gray one?" he asked Ron.

There was a moment of silence on the other end of the phone. "Not through *our* company. But Fritz has a separate recycling business. He drives one for that," Ron said.

"What color?"

"Blue."

"Okay. Stay close to the phone," Giorgio said. "I may need you again."

He hung up and called Captain Alvarez at home.

"Captain, we have a positive ID on Edmond Martinelli as one of the men who abducted, tortured and raped a young woman up in Big Bear back in 1967."

"A positive ID?" the captain said.

"Yes, sir. Her name is Amber Riley and she still lives there. We interviewed her and showed her four photos. She picked out both

Royce and Edmond Martinelli's pictures. We're on our way to Edmond's house now to arrest him. We're about two hours away."

"So how is all of this connected to Lisa Farmer?"

"When this girl escaped," Giorgio said, "Royce and Edmond came home early. Lisa was hiding in the study that night when Royce took a phone call from Edmond. Lisa must have overheard them discussing the girl who got away up at Big Bear."

"And that's what got her killed," the captain stated.

"Right. But there's more. As we were leaving town up here, a blue van ran us off the road and then someone opened fire on us. We're pretty sure it was either Fritz Martinelli, or his son, Perry. I think I hit whoever it was. I've already put out APBs on both of them. We don't know which one tried to kill us, but Ron Martinelli just told me that Fritz owns a blue van. This is all coming to a head, Captain."

"Good work, Joe," Captain Alvarez said. "If you're going straight to Edmond's house, I'd better call in the Altadena police and tell them to meet you there."

"Okay," Giorgio agreed. "But no lights or sirens. We'll meet them half a block up the street. Have them bring the warrant."

"I'll have McCready and a couple of our officers meet you at Martinellis. Be careful," he said and hung up.

Rocky's eyes darted toward his brother. "Do you think Fritz will be there?"

"Hell if I know," Giorgio snarled. "But I have no doubt that Edmond is the puppeteer in all of this. I doubt the others do much of anything without his blessing. He's a man who likes to be in control."

When they pulled up to the intersection closest to Edmond Martinelli's home, they encountered three other police cars – two from the Altadena Police Department and one from Sierra Madre. Giorgio and Rocky got out and Giorgio explained the situation. They were told that the lights were off at the home, but Edmond Martinelli's car was in the garage.

After conferring with the officer in charge from Altadena, the group of eight officers got back in their cars and pulled into the big circular drive. Car doors opened and officers emerged with guns drawn, fanning out to surround the home. While two officers planted themselves behind their vehicles in the driveway, Giorgio and Rocky approached the front door.

Giorgio pounded on the door.

"Edmond Martinelli! Police. Open up."

Nothing.

"Mr. Martinelli, come out with your hands up!"

Still nothing.

Giorgio counted to five and was about to call one more time when the porch light finally flicked on. He and Rocky stood back, their hands cradling their weapons.

The front doorknob clicked, and the door opened about an inch.

"Mr. Martinelli," Giorgio called through the door. "We don't want a confrontation. Please come out with your hands up."

"No, Detective," a voice called from inside. "I know the game is over. At least for me. But you'll have to come inside to arrest me."

"Mr. Martinelli, the house is surrounded."

There was a mirthless chuckle from inside. "Don't you think I know that? No, Detective. This will be on my terms."

"Damn!" Giorgio said under his breath.

"What do you want to do?" Rocky whispered.

"I don't trust him. He could have booby-trapped the entrance," Giorgio said, glancing around them. "Step back," he ordered Rocky.

Rocky backed off and Giorgio lifted his left leg and kicked in the door. The door swung all the way open, but nothing happened.

Giorgio signaled to McCready to have a team enter from the back. He waited a moment as the men got into position. When he heard glass shattering, he counted to five and then entered the house, his gun held firmly in front of him. He crossed through the entryway and cautiously entered the living room where an officer had just relieved Edmond Martinelli of a pistol and a cell phone.

"I caught him with these, Detective," the officer said, handing the gun to Giorgio. Rocky took the cell phone.

"He had the gun pointed at his temple," the officer said.

"Check the phone," Giorgio said to Rocky.

Rocky scrolled through the call log.

"He just talked to Fritz," Rocky said.

Edmond slumped into a high-backed, leather chair as Giorgio tucked the weapon behind his back.

"Stand up!" Giorgio ordered him.

Giorgio nodded to the closest officer to move in. But Martinelli ignored the officer and remained where he was. He turned to Giorgio instead.

"I'm an old man, Detective. I'm not going anywhere. By the way, how was your little trip to Big Bear?" he said, as if this was just a casual visit.

"Fritz told you we were coming," Giorgio said, matter-of-factly.

"Yes," he nodded.

"So this is a family affair," Giorgio snarled. "First you and your brother. And now your son and grandson. Which one of them tried to kill us up in Big Bear?"

Edmond turned and gazed out the window, his heels together on the floor, his large feet turned out to the side.

"There's really nothing in life more important than family, wouldn't you agree, Detective?"

"You didn't answer my question."

The old man remained silent.

"You son-of-a-bitch," Giorgio said, advancing. "We met the woman you tortured up in Big Bear – the one that got away."

"The one that got away," Edmond said with a wistful smile. "A rather colloquial way of describing it, don't you think? I told Royce we should have gone back and taken care of her. But he was convinced there was no way anyone could trace us. We were so careful, you know. We didn't talk to one person in that town. We brought everything with us and then burned the cabin down when we left. Royce thought that going back would have only served to put us at risk. So we just moved our little hobby to other locations." A smile played across his lips at the thought.

"Where? Where else did you go?"

"Oh, Detective," he said, glancing at Giorgio. "I'm afraid I'm not going to just give up that kind of information. I know my time is up. I'm an old man. And an old man has to have a few memories that are his alone."

Giorgio was near the fireplace and kicked out with his foot and sent the wrought iron fireplace set crashing to the floor.

"They're not just your sordid little memories! These were young women!"

Edmond Martinelli merely glanced at the iron tools now splayed across the floor and then turned to Giorgio with a smile.

"Careful, Detective. You'll have to pay for anything you break."

Giorgio flinched and Rocky stepped in front of his brother.

"We know Perry killed Carson Montgomery," Rocky said.

The octogenarian glanced up, his eyes reflecting a momentary surprise. Then he rested his

elbows on the arms of the chair and brought his hands together, fingers touching in a church pose.

"You're all going to jail for a very long time," Giorgio said, anger searing his voice.

"I don't think so," Martinelli murmured.

"What?" Giorgio blurted, moving forward again. "What do you mean?"

"No one's going to jail," he said in a casual voice. He turned very calm eyes in Giorgio's direction. "I'm afraid that's not in the game plan."

"And I suppose it's *your* game plan, isn't it?" Giorgio said.

He flashed a confident smile. "It's *always* my game plan, Detective. You…standing here in *my* living room is part of my game plan. The Martinellis have always had a game plan. Starting with the family motto and right up to the end. No one will be going to jail. But the world *will* remember us," he said with a smile.

"Joe!" a voice called out.

Giorgio and Rocky turned. McCready burst into the room.

"I just heard it on the radio! That reporter, Mia Santana…she's been abducted right off Sierra Madre Boulevard. Two men pulled her into a van."

A voice shouted, "No!' and a shot exploded behind them, shattering the silence.

Everyone dropped into crouches, guns aimed at Martinelli.

But Edmond Martinelli had slumped sideways in the chair, a gaping wound in the side of his forehead. Blood ran down his neck into his starched white shirt. A 45-magnum pistol had dropped from his hand to the floor. The smell of sulfur hung in the air.

Giorgio ran forward and kicked the gun away and then checked his pulse.

"Shit, he's alive! Call an ambulance!"

Rocky pulled out his cell phone.

"What the hell happened here?" Giorgio spun around on the young cop assigned to guard Edmond.

"He…he must've had a gun tucked into the chair," he said, his voice shaking. "I'm sorry. I glanced away for just a moment…and…"

"Never mind," Giorgio snapped.

He leaned over and observed the elder Martinelli. The man's breathing was shallow and his mouth had dropped open. But he was still alive.

"McCready!" Giorgio yelled.

McCready appeared behind him.

"Secure this area and wait for the ambulance. When you get this guy to the hospital, put a guard on him." He glanced up at the young cop. "Someone who will actually watch him. We're going after Fritz Martinelli."

CHAPTER THIRTY-SIX

Giorgio and Rocky converged on Ron Martinelli's home one last time. He was waiting for them, Ms. Brinson, his attractive and able assistant by his side.

"What's going on?" he said, from the entryway to his home.

"Your uncle just shot himself," Giorgio said.

"What?" Ron Martinelli said, the blood draining from his face. He reached out for Ms. Brinson's hand and clasped it tightly. "So we were right," he said. "It was the two of them together, wasn't it? My father and my uncle?"

"Yes," Giorgio replied. "But now Fritz and Perry are involved. One of them tried to kill us tonight."

Ron Martinelli's eyes widened. He backed up, allowing them inside.

"Why...would Fritz try to kill you?" he mumbled.

"Because we think he killed Alex Springer, and Perry killed Carson Montgomery up in Seattle," Giorgio said.

Ron looked from Giorgio to Rocky and then turned and walked into the living room. He stopped at the fireplace as if in a trance.

"Mr. Martinelli!" Giorgio called, following him. "I need some answers. Another young woman was abducted tonight...a female reporter who has been covering the Lisa Farmer story. We think Fritz and Perry have her. They're desperate. Your uncle knew we were coming, and he was on the phone to Fritz when we got there. He said something about having a game plan."

"Game plan?" Ron muttered. "Shit!" he said, slamming his fist onto the fireplace mantle. He turned to Giorgio. "It's my father again. His legacy lives on. My father lived in New Hampshire for a while. Their motto there is, 'Live free or die.' My father coined his own motto, 'Live *big* or die.' It was all about excess to him. He prided himself in never having lost at anything. He even once forced me to play in a football game even though I'd ripped my Achilles tendon." Ron glanced up at Giorgio. "He told me that the Martinellis don't give up, ever! They die trying."

"Where would Fritz have taken her?" Giorgio demanded.

"I don't know," Martinelli said, exasperated. "Really, I don't. But this is probably his last stand. Fritz used to fantasize about going out in a hail of bullets. He admired the guys who died at Ruby Ridge and Waco. I've always thought he was a little nuts."

"But you know him. You grew up with him. He runs your real estate business. He knows every nook and cranny of this area. Where would he be likely to take something he wanted to hide? Something he wanted to *play* with?" Giorgio said with distaste.

Ron thought for a moment and then his expression changed. He slowly stood up.

"Wait, I do know. When we were kids, his family had a big tree with a tree house out in their backyard. Fritz loved to go hide up there."

"So we're looking for a tree house?" Rocky said with a sneer.

"No," Ron said. "I climbed up there once when we were teenagers. I found him with a little bird." He cringed at the memory. "He was pulling the feathers off the little bird one-by-one. The bird kept trying to get away, and he would just laugh. Then I noticed that there were two dead birds lying on the floor. One had its feet cut off, and the other had its wings broken." He shuddered at the thought. "I asked him what he was doing, and he just turned to me with this horrible, self-satisfied smile and said, 'This is my little hobby. Leave me alone.'" He inhaled and then said, "Fritz took her to the old Pottinger Sanitarium up in Monrovia. It's been empty for decades."

"Why there?" Rocky asked.

"Because he bought it a few years ago. He said he wanted to salvage what he could and then turn it into a luxury hotel." He paused and looked from Giorgio to Rocky. "When I asked him why he would sink so much money into something so risky, he gave me that same self-satisfied smile and said, 'Because it's my little hobby.'"

Giorgio and Rocky turned for the door, but Martinelli stopped them.

"Detectives!" he said. "I've been up there. You'll need bolt cutters to get through the gate. And it's a monstrosity of a place. It has three stories with three separate wings. There's no electricity. He'll have the advantage. And he has nothing to lose. He'll just kill her if he hears you coming."

"What do you suggest?" Giorgio asked quickly.

Ron ran fingers through his hair. "I don't know. But unless you have an army, you're going to need a bloodhound just to find him in there."

Giorgio turned to Rocky with a self-satisfied smile of his own.

"I think we have that covered," he said. "But we'll need something of his for scent. And I need the address."

"Hold on," Martinelli said. He turned and left the room. A moment later, he was back and handed Giorgio a baseball cap. "This is Fritz's. We had a company picnic here a few months ago. He left it behind."

CHAPTER THIRTY-SEVEN

Giorgio raced back down Colorado Boulevard towards Sierra Madre. As he swerved to pass other cars, Rocky shouted, "So what's *our* game plan? Should we call Captain Alvarez?"

Giorgio shot him a look. "No. You heard Ron. If he hears a cavalry coming, he'll just kill her. We go in quiet and alone."

"Are you kidding me?" Rocky exclaimed.

"We've got one chance to get her out," Giorgio said, leveling a somber look in Rocky's direction. "One chance. Are you in or are you out?"

Rocky turned to look out the front window as they sped forward. "I'm in. But as usual, you're insane."

"Okay, call Angie and tell her to have Grosvenor ready. We'll be there in less than ten minutes. And tell her to make sure the kids are up in their rooms."

"Why?" Rocky said, taking the phone.

"Because we need to raid my gun cabinet," he said with a grim expression.

Rocky pulled out his phone and dialed Giorgio's home phone.

"Hey, Angie, this is Rocky... No, no, everything's okay," he said quickly. "We're...we're on a case and we need to pick up Grosvenor. Can you have him ready?" Rocky paused as he listened to the response. "Really? Shit," he responded. "Um...okay, thanks. But, well, we need you to get the kids up in their rooms. Can you do that?" He listened for a moment. "Like I said, Ange. We're on a case. We need extra firepower. The kids don't need to see that. Okay? What's that? Okay, thanks."

"Why'd you say shit?" Giorgio said, glancing toward his brother.

Rocky flicked off the phone and threw it onto the console. "Grosvenor's not there."

"What?"

"Angie said he ate a whole rash of chicken bones earlier. She took him to the vet and they wanted to keep him overnight."

"Damn!" Giorgio swore, hitting the steering wheel.

"Now what do we do?" Rocky asked.

"I don't know," Giorgio said. "It's too late to try and get a search and rescue dog."

Rocky shrugged. "Guess it'll just be you, me and those hunches of yours."

"What did you say?" Giorgio said, glancing at his brother in surprise.

"When we get there," Rocky said. "We'll have to rely on your hunches."

"No," Giorgio said, turning back to the road. "We need something more reliable than that."

He suddenly switched lanes and made a tire-screeching U-turn in the middle of the street. As Rocky flew against the door, he snarled, "What's going on?"

"We need to pick up someone."

"By the way," Rocky whispered, as they raced down Colorado Boulevard. "Angie said something about Detective Abrams coming down. I guess he called."

Giorgio's eyes lit up. "How soon?"

Rocky shrugged. "I don't know. She didn't say."

Two minutes later, Giorgio was pulling up to the small white bungalow. The porch light was on, as well as a light in the front window. The brothers got out and hurried up the walk. Rocky spied the sign for Madame Mirabelle on the door.

"We're picking up a psychic? You've got to be kidding!"

"You have a better idea?" Giorgio said as he rang the doorbell.

A moment later, the front window curtain was pulled aside. Dark eyes glared at them through the window until the individual recognized Giorgio. Then, the latch was released and the door opened. Flame stood there, dressed in sweat pants, a pajama top and a pair of baggy socks.

"Detective," Flame said, standing back to let them in. "What's going on?"

He and Rocky stepped into the reception area.

"We need your help. We need you to come with us."

Her eyes opened wide. "What? Why?"

"A young woman has been abducted," Giorgio said breathlessly. "By the son and grandson of the men who killed those girls. We don't have much time," Giorgio said. "Please, get dressed quickly."

She hesitated. "Detective, it's after eleven o'clock. I..."

"PLEASE!" Giorgio barked. "This time it's to *save* a life."

She flinched at the intensity in his voice.

"But I don't understand. Why... do you need *me*?"

"Get dressed and we'll explain on the way. Please," he said in a softer tone. "I wouldn't ask if I didn't think it was critical."

She glanced at Rocky and seemed to make a decision. She turned and disappeared through a door behind her. It was only a few minutes later when she re-emerged dressed in jeans, boots, a turtleneck sweater and a hoodie jacket. She held a backpack over one shoulder.

"Okay, let's go."

÷

On the way to the house, Giorgio filled Flame in on the situation.

"So, I'm your bloodhound?" she said without animosity. "Okay. I get it."

Flame was sitting in the front seat. Rocky was in the back.

"I don't mean to gloss over the seriousness of what's happening here," Giorgio said gravely. "Or the risk. This is a very dangerous situation. But we won't expose you any more than we have to. We just need help in finding where these guys have her in this building. Then you're done."

She glanced at him and then back through the front window. "I'm not afraid, Detective. I want to help. I'll be okay."

Giorgio pulled into his driveway a few minutes later, and the three of them emerged from the car and moved quickly toward the front door. Angie met them.

"What's happening?" she asked, alarm written all over her face.

"Mia Santana, that reporter, has been abducted. We're going after her."

Angie paused momentarily and then nodded and stepped back to let them in.

"The kids are upstairs," she said.

"Angie, this is Flame. She's...she's helping with the case."

Angie nodded and smiled briefly at the young woman. "Joe, there's someone..."

"Evening, Detective," a voice cut in.

Giorgio turned to find Detective Abrams standing in the middle of his living room.

"Hey," Giorgio responded, stepping forward with his hand out. "Boy, am I happy to see you! I don't know why you're here, but I don't care. We can use you," Giorgio said, giving Abrams' hand a quick shake.

"From what you said on the phone yesterday you're getting close to nailing the guy who killed Montgomery," Abrams said. "I thought I could help. Besides," he said, reaching into his pocket, "I have some new evidence I thought you should see."

He pulled out a grainy photograph of a van parked in the nursing home parking lot. The California license plate was clearly visible – XTC 434.

"Where did you get this?" Giorgio said.

"Turns out there's a domestic violence shelter right next door to the nursing home. It sits on the other side of the parking lot. They have security cameras everywhere. They got this shot. They also got a shot of the kid who wheeled Montgomery out there. It's not too clear, but we're working to clean it up."

"Good to go," Giorgio said. Giorgio handed the photo back. "By the way, my brother Rocky just joined the force," he said, nodding towards his brother. "Sean's with the Seattle PD," he said to Rocky. He turned back to Abrams. "We believe the guy who killed Montgomery and his father have now abducted a young woman – a reporter." He strode into the hallway and started moving toward the back office. Everyone trailed after him. "It's a long story, but this is all part of the same family. Their modus operandi is to torture the women and then kill them. We have to find her *tonight*. We just stopped to get armed."

"Okay, I'm in," Abrams nodded. "Just tell me what you want me to do."

"Are you carrying?" Giorgio asked as the three men moved into the back office.

"Yeah," he said patting his waistband.

"Okay," Giorgio said, stopping at the gun cabinet.

Giorgio turned and saw both Flame and Angie standing silently in the doorway, Angie with her arms crossed. He paused.

"It's going to be okay, Ange. We have plenty of back-up. We just need to save this girl."

Angie's pretty features were drawn into a mask of defeat. A look of resignation he'd seen before. She knew the drill and knew she had no hope of changing his mind.

"Just be careful," she murmured, and she disappeared up the stairs.

Flame watched her go, her hands hanging onto the backpack strap slung across her shoulder.

"What back-up?" Rocky asked quietly after Angie had left. "The psychic?"

Giorgio shot him an angry look.

"By the way," Giorgio said to Detective Abrams. "This is Flame. She'll be our way finder."

Abrams nodded, as if having a civilian along was no big deal. Giorgio unlocked the gun cabinet. Standing on end were three rifles, two for hunting and one Remington Arms M24. Held in drawers below the rifles were two Glock pistols and loaded magazines.

He and Rocky each pulled out a second handgun and two extra magazines, and Giorgio grabbed a high-beamed flashlight.

"Mind if I take one of the rifles?" Abrams said, studying the weapons. "I'm pretty good with a rifle."

"Suit yourself," Giorgio replied.

"This is nice," Abrams said, pulling out the Remington Arms. He held it up and pointed it toward the far window, adjusting the scope.

Giorgio turned to his brother.

"Can you get the bolt cutters from the garage? They're hanging above the workbench."

Rocky nodded. "I'll meet you at the car."

As Abrams grabbed extra cartridges for the rifle, Giorgio pulled out his cell phone and dialed McCready.

"Drew, where are you?"

"I'm at the hospital. They just took Edmond Martinelli into surgery."

"Okay, do me a favor. We're going after the girl. I need you to come watch and my house, just in case."

"Uh...okay. What about Martinelli?"

"Get an officer to stand in for you. Edmond won't be going anywhere for a while," Giorgio said. "I don't trust these guys, and they know where I live."

"I'll be there in fifteen minutes," the young officer said.

"Okay, just park outside. Don't let my wife know you're here unless it's absolutely necessary."

"Got it," McCready answered.

Giorgio hung up and turned to Flame. Her dark eyes were staring at the rifle in Abrams' hand.

"You sure you're okay with this?" Giorgio asked her.

She glanced up at him. "Of course I'm not okay with this. But we're wasting time."

She turned on her heel and led them back outside.

CHAPTER THIRTY-EIGHT

It was after midnight by the time they reached the gravel road that led to the old sanitarium. The sky was clear, and they followed the deeply rutted road as it wound its way through a forest of old oak and eucalyptus trees back into the foothills. As the car bounced along, it was quiet inside. The four occupants sat contemplating what lay ahead.

Giorgio had to slam on the brakes when a deer bounded across the road. A moment later, it was just a fleeting image of bob tail as it disappeared into the darkness.

After six or seven minutes of straining to keep the car on the road, the locked gate in a tall chain link fence blocked their way. Barbed wire topped the fence. The monstrosity of a building, as Ron Martinelli had described it, sat a hundred yards beyond, camouflaged by trees and looking every bit like something out of a gothic horror movie.

Giorgio cut the headlights and the four of them just stared.

"Shit," Rocky murmured. "Ron Martinelli wasn't kidding. This place is huge."

Giorgio turned to his brother.

"Wire cutters?" he asked.

"In the trunk," Rocky said.

Giorgio sighed deeply. "Let's go, then," he said.

He killed the engine and they all got out. The air was crisp and the moon shone brightly onto the ground below.

Giorgio grabbed Fritz Martinelli's baseball cap off the seat and stuck it into his jacket. He came around the back of the car. Rocky had opened the trunk.

"Do you have a plan?" Abrams asked Giorgio, as he pulled the rifle from the trunk.

Giorgio glanced at Flame, as if she could provide the answer.

Flame was staring at the building, one hand to her ear, a pained look on her face.

"What's wrong?" Giorgio asked.

She looked up as if coming out of a trance.

"I'm getting images from hundreds of spirits," she said. "A lot of people have died here. It's coming across like a buzzing in my ears. I can't focus on any single one. I need to get closer. I think I need to connect with the building itself," she said.

Giorgio had no idea what the heck she was talking about, but he didn't care.

"Okay, let's go in from the back. They're less likely to expect that. If she can, Flame
will tell us where to look once we're in there. We'll split up and try to come at them from two directions." He looked from Rocky to Abrams, and they both nodded. "Wait a second," Giorgio said, reaching in and removing a box from the trunk. The box was wrapped in Christmas paper and a bow.

"What the heck is that?" Rocky snarled.

"It's Tony's Christmas present," Giorgio said, ripping off the wrapping paper. "I just bought it the other day."

He finished removing the wrapping and quickly opened the box. It held a pair of kid's night vision goggles. Rocky took one look and snorted.

"Jesus, Joe. First a psychic and now a toy!"

"Just shut up and grab the batteries," Giorgio said, pointing to the box.

Rocky did as he was told and handed them over. "Joe, those are made for kids."

"We only have one flashlight," Giorgio said. "These might help."

"I doubt it," his brother said skeptically.

"These will work okay," Abrams said, looking at the box. "My nephew has a pair. They just might not fit too well."

Giorgio put the batteries in and adjusted the strap as wide as it would go. When he put them on, Rocky chuckled quietly.

"You're an idiot, you know that?" he said, shaking his head.

Abrams was smiling. "Here, flip this," he said, turning the switch to 'on.' Then he helped Giorgio adjust the straps so that it fit snugly onto his head.

"Okay, I'm good. Here," he said to Flame, handing her the baseball cap. "You'll need this. It belonged to Fritz. Let's go."

The four of them moved to the gate. Rocky used the wire cutters to clip the chain holding the gate closed. The heavy chain and big padlock dropped to the ground with a *whack.*

Giorgio pushed on the metal gate and it creaked open. As they passed through, an owl hooted somewhere up in the trees. A light breeze picked up the scent of sagebrush and swirled it around them. They followed the pitted road until they reached the circular drive that led to the main entrance.

The Pottinger Sanitarium loomed before them. It was a three-story, C-shaped building, with broken windows and graffiti sprayed across each wall. Its once pristine stucco exterior was chipped and peeling. The red-tiled roof seemed intact, but there were three chimneys, one in each wing of the old hospital. Two of the three had crumbled into piles of rubble.

Tall arched windows extended across the central wing, all of them protected by bars. Several large trees hugged the exterior of the building, tall enough to bump up against the eaves of the uneven roofline, while overgrown bushes and sagebrush obscured most of the first floor.

The fence that surrounded the property was set to within six feet of the west exterior wall. The barbed wire extension faced outward, preventing all but the most ardent vagrants from gaining access. Only two security lights played across the front entrance, leaving most of the old sanitarium to sit like a monster in the dark, waiting to swallow them up alive.

"Well, at least the electricity is on," Rocky said, spying the security lights.

"Yeah, but Martinelli was right," Giorgio exclaimed, glancing around him. "This isn't going to be easy. This place is enormous. There are even some outbuildings over there."

He pointed to where two smaller, single-story buildings sat off to one side.

"He's not in one of those," the girl said, holding the cap in her left hand. "He's in there."

She still had a strained look on her face, but pointed confidently to the big building. The three men turned in unison toward the direction she pointed.

"Let's go," Giorgio said.

He began moving up the driveway, his shoes crunching the gravel beneath his feet. They passed chunks of broken concrete, lumber and rocks. The lawn had been reduced to brown patches of dead grass and weeds.

The building faced south, with the San Gabriel Mountains standing in the background. When they passed the front entrance, Giorgio motioned for them to cross the lawn to get up close to the building. Weapons drawn, they did as he instructed, moving quietly across the front of the east wing.

They rounded the southeast corner and hugged the building, darting from bush to bush. Rocky and Abrams peered into windows as they passed, while they both kept a check on their rear flank.

Each wing of the old building was about half a football field long, so it took them several minutes to traverse the distance, avoiding bushes, broken benches, and a few sections of old fencing that had been thrown into a pile. The once grand building was nothing more than a trash heap now, overgrown and forgotten by all but a serial killer.

At one point, Giorgio stopped them with a finger to his lips.

They froze and listened. There was only the rustling of trees and the occasional whoosh of a low-flying bat.

"This place gives me the creeps," Rocky murmured.

Giorgio waved them on.

The grass along the building had long since died. It had been replaced with a tangle of weeds, broken bottles and trash. Everyone stepped carefully. Flame's foot got caught once, throwing her into Detective Abrams' back. Everyone stopped. He turned and helped her back on her feet.

"Didn't see that one coming did you?" Rocky quipped.

"You okay?" Abrams whispered.

She flashed Rocky an irritated look and nodded.

"Let's keep going," Giorgio ordered.

When the group finally came up to the northeast corner of the building, Giorgio glanced to where the driveway wrapped around to the back. He stopped them with a raised hand and then pointed to where the front end of the blue van poked its nose out from the corner of the building.

Giorgio edged carefully around the corner, his weapon held firmly in front of him. Detective Abrams made a wide arc around the front of the van with the rifle aimed at its interior, while Giorgio advanced toward the rear. Rocky hung back with Flame.

The back of the vehicle had been left open, and Giorgio whirled around the open door, but the van was empty. No sign of Martinelli. No sign of the girl. But the now familiar license plate was in full view. Giorgio lowered his gun and pulled the goggles up. He glanced at Abrams, who had come up the other side and then nodded at the license plate. Abrams nodded back.

The van was parked next to the loading dock, which at one time accepted the delivery of everything from food to pharmaceuticals and medical equipment. It extended for some thirty feet with stairs on both ends.

All was dark and quiet.

Giorgio gestured to the girl. "Okay, Flame, you're up."

The breeze played with a wisp of hair at the crown of her head. She turned toward the building and held out the hand with the baseball cap.

"Here," she said, handing it to Giorgio.

"But don't you have to..."

She stepped past him without a word and moved to the back of the building, where she reached out and placed both hands on the exterior wall. She kept her hands flat and dropped her head for a moment, as if listening to something. The three men watched her quietly. After almost a minute, Giorgio became impatient and was about to say something, when she nodded once and spun around to face them.

"They're in the morgue," she whispered. "In the basement. They showed me a main hallway that leads to the center of the building."

"They?" Rocky said, his voice filled with sarcasm.

She shifted her gaze to Rocky. "The spirits. As I said, the building is filled with them. Some of them are children. But a few know why you're here, and they want these men gone." She turned back to Giorgio. "They've done bad things here...things the spirits don't like. I saw more women..." she stopped and took a breath. "I think they want to help you. But I don't know how. Just be open to it."

The three men looked at each other, an unspoken question between them.

"They showed me several sets of stairs," she continued. "But I think they want you to go all the way to the other end of the building, because one of the hallways is blocked." Then she turned to Detective Abrams. "And, they also showed me a tall man with a rifle out front. That seemed very important."

Abrams gave her a questioning look. "Do you trust what you're seeing?"

A breeze drifted through the portico, swirling dust and leaves around their feet.

"Yes, I do. These people died of natural causes. This is their home now, and these men have invaded it."

Abrams paused and turned to Giorgio with a shrug. "Okay, with me," he said in a hushed tone. "I'll position myself at the entrance in case either one of them comes out that way. What do these guys look like? I don't want to shoot the wrong person."

"Fritz Martinelli is tall, maybe your height, with dark hair and dark eyes. Perry, his son, is shorter with black hair and tattoos around his neck."

Abrams nodded. "What do you say when you're about to go on stage?" he asked.

"Break a leg?" Giorgio replied.

He chuckled. "Okay. *Don't* do that," he said. "I'll see you in a few." He turned and started to leave, when Giorgio stopped him.

"Sean," he said. "The moment you hear gunshots, call it in. By that time, they'll know we're here and we'll need back-up."

Detective Abrams nodded and left for the entrance. Giorgio turned to Flame.

"You need to go with him," Giorgio said.

"I will," she replied. "But first...you need to know...the boy is here," she said.

Giorgio's heart skipped a beat. "He...why can't I see him?"

"He doesn't belong here," she said quietly. "So he won't come in close. But he showed me a
big tree. The tree is important for some reason."

"There are big trees all around here," Giorgio said in frustration. "Okay," he sighed. "You need to go back to the car. And stay there. No matter what. The keys are in the ignition. If something happens...if you get scared, just leave."

She gave him a weak smile. "The girl is still alive, Detective, but you need to hurry. Her captors know you're here," she said, and then she turned and followed Detective Abrams.

Giorgio and Rocky glanced at each other, sharing a somber moment.

"What boy?" Rocky said.

"Never mind. Let's do this," Giorgio replied.

CHAPTER THIRTY-NINE

Rocky flicked on the big flashlight. The metal door to the loading dock was up, revealing a large, dark interior. Everything smelled of age-old dust, with just a hint of motor oil.

Across the room, a metal staircase extended up to a door with a glass window. Directly ahead of them was an old industrial lift.

They approached the lift. The two doors to the lift stood open. Rocky flashed the light down and saw the lift sitting below ground. The ancient electrical box sat on the right wall, and Rocky reached out and was about to push the button, when Giorgio stopped him.

"Wait. He might hear it. Let's take the stairs to the main hallway, just as we were told."

They turned and hurried up the short flight of stairs and quietly opened the door, slipping into a darkened hallway. Giorgio pulled the infrared binoculars back down over his eyes.

"Be careful," he whispered. "Remember, there are two of them."

The stairwell in the east wing of the old Pottinger Sanitarium was dark and cold, and the air was filled with dust. The stairs switched back and forth, extending up and then down to the basement. Directly in front of them was a door. Giorgio peeked through a small window. A long hallway ran along the first floor of the east wing. Another door to their right led to a hallway that appeared to run the entire width of the building, along the back. So, they had three choices. Take a hallway or go down the stairs to the basement.

"Eeeney, meeney, miney, mo," Rocky whispered. "Which way do we go?"

Before Giorgio could respond, the door directly in front of them popped open. They both snapped around with their guns out. No one was there.

"I guess we go that way," Giorgio said, as a chill inched its way down his back.

He stepped into the hallway. The infrared glasses allowed him to see everything bathed in a red light.

The two brothers moved quietly forward, their senses on alert. They passed darkened doors to their left and some old broken furniture stacked against the wall on their right.

Halfway down the corridor, the right wall opened up to a nursing station. An old metal sign on the wall said, "Ward B." Behind the nursing station was a set of swinging doors. The room beyond was as dark as a coffin.

They kept going.

They turned a corner and entered a hallway that cut off to the right. They passed an old broken gurney and some boxes lined up along the right wall. The hallway extended into the heart of the building, deep enough to swallow the flashlight beam.

"This must be the main hallway," Giorgio whispered.

They passed another nurses' station and stopped to listen for any revealing sounds. But all they heard were the occasional knocks and pings of a huge empty building.

It took them a couple more minutes to make it to the main entrance and lobby, where moonlight streamed through the front windows, illuminating a few old benches and a central staircase in the rear. To the left of the staircase were the main elevators. Across the room was an old, oak reception counter. To the right of the counter was another set of double swinging doors.

"What now?" Rocky whispered.

"I think we're supposed to cross through," Giorgio replied.

"Okay, let's go," Rocky said. "You take the left. I'll take the right."

They hurried through the open space of the lobby. Rocky covered the front half of the large room, while Giorgio took the back half.

When they got to the door, Giorgio flattened himself against one side of the wall, while Rocky did the same on the other. Giorgio nodded and Rocky used his left hand to swing open one door. He slipped through, with Giorgio coming through behind him.

They found themselves in the west wing. Halfway down the hall, they passed a door marked 'Stairs.' Rocky started to turn for the stairs, but Giorgio stopped him and waved his hand forward. Giorgio moved to the end of the hallway and glanced to the right. This hallway mirrored the one in the east wing and extended to the rear of the building, where the windows allowed moonlight to bathe the area in light. He signaled to Rocky and they turned the corner and crept forward.

They stopped when they got to the hall that ran along the back of the building.

"Now what?" Rocky whispered.

"I'm not sure," Giorgio replied, looking around.

Metal doors stood at each end of the long hallway. The door to the right was positioned near the center of the building, probably near the main staircase, and each door was marked for a stairwell.

"Flame said the morgue was in the basement," Giorgio said.

"Then either staircase will probably take us there," Rocky whispered.

"But she also said to go to the far end. That would be to our left," Giorgio said, turning in that direction.

He flinched back. A weird glow had appeared through the window in the door to their left. Giorgio felt a full blown chill run the length of his body. He nodded toward the door.

"Who needs a bloodhound?" he said.

"I guess we won't be putting this in the duty report," Rocky murmured, staring at the light.

"C'mon," Giorgio said, moving into the hallway and towards the far left door.

They traversed the distance quickly. When they passed through the door, the glow evaporated.

They descended the stairs as quietly as possible, their weapons held out before them. At the bottom was one more metal door.

Giorgio slowly reached out and grasped the door handle, turning it carefully. The door was locked.

"Shit," he murmured.

He was about to turn around, when a faint light appeared through the window, and the door handle began to silently rotate.

Giorgio backed up, bumping into Rocky. His heartbeat thumped wildly.

"Grab it," Rocky hissed.

Giorgio reached out, just as the door quietly clicked open. He grabbed the doorknob and pulled the door wide. They slipped through as the light on the other side faded.

Rocky caught the door behind him, not allowing it to close all the way or to make any noise. Giorgio nodded.

The rear basement hallway extended away from them. An electrical light emanated from a door halfway down the hall. A small sign on the wall said, 'morgue' and an arrow pointed forward.

Giorgio signaled to Rocky to move quietly.

They inched forward until they reached an intersecting hallway to their right. Giorgio glanced around the corner and pointed to a stack of gurneys and chairs that blocked the space. Rocky nodded.

This was the blocked staircase Flame had mentioned, the same one they'd passed above. Add to that the locked door they'd just come through, and Giorgio understood the current game plan. The men they were chasing didn't want anyone coming at them from this end of the building. They'd blocked the hallway and locked that door. That could only mean one thing – they had planned an ambush.

Giorgio glanced past the morgue.

The door to the central staircase was propped open down here, and he could just barely see the last step of the staircase leading up to the next floor.

As Giorgio watched, a brief flare lit up the stairwell. Someone had just lit a cigarette.

He alerted Rocky, who nodded that he'd seen it, too.

A faint sound of movement came from that direction, confirming his belief. Someone was waiting for them.

Giorgio signaled for Rocky to pass in front of him and move towards the other stairwell. Rocky tip-toed forward, ducking under the windows of the morgue door. He stopped on the other side, ready to engage whoever was waiting for them in the stairwell.

Giorgio approached the morgue doors. There were double swinging doors with small windows in each. He lifted up onto his tiptoes to peek through.

A battered, old wooden desk, with an L-shaped counter behind it sat just inside the doors. A floating retaining wall stood behind the desk. The room opened up on either side of the wall, revealing old metal gurneys in various states of disrepair.

To the left of the center wall was the end of a gurney with someone on it. Bare feet twitched as a moan echoed through the room.

Giorgio flinched, his nerves on fire. He pulled up his goggles. He wouldn't need them in there since there was a light.

As he contemplated his next move, a man's elbow came into view, and suddenly he was looking at the back of Fritz Martinelli, who was just about to lift something above a bare leg.

Giorgio tapped Rocky and pointed towards the man in the stairwell. Rocky nodded and began to inch that way.

A moment later, Mia Santana's pained scream cut through the silence, forcing Giorgio to push through the swinging doors.

He broke to his left, making a wide circle to come around so that he could see the gurney.

Fritz Martinelli was gone.

Two shots rang out from the stairwell. Rocky had encountered Perry.

Giorgio crouched down. He was near the end of the gurney. A drain in the floor was awash with blood, and Giorgio's insides churned.

A few more shots in the hallway. And then it was quiet.

Giorgio moved further into the room, glancing around, looking for Martinelli.

A metal sink and counter stood on the other side of the room. Metal shelving hung on the wall above.

In the far left corner was a huge door that led to the cooler, the room where they would have laid the dead bodies.

Giorgio's eyes roamed the walls. There were no windows in the morgue, just the way Martinelli would want it. No prying eyes.

The cooler door was open and the light was on. Giorgio guessed that Martinelli hoped he would move in that direction. But something told him it was a ruse.

Instead, he moved further into the room along the left wall of counters.

A noise made him jerk to his right just as a bullet whizzed over his head, slamming into the wall.

He leapt forward and behind the end of the counter.

The only light was directly above Mia Santana. The rest of the room was cast in shadow.

There was no movement. And Giorgio couldn't see anything that resembled a human form other than the woman on the gurney.

He took a chance and scuttled into the center of the room, and then towards the back wall, where there was a long counter that ran horizontally. As he was about to turn the corner and hide behind the counter, his foot rolled over an old test tube on the floor. He was thrown off balance and toppled awkwardly into the counter just as a loud crack shattered the silence.

A second bullet ricocheted off the countertop, just missing his shoulder.

He hit the floor, rolling behind the cabinetry.

Giorgio glanced up and took a deep breath. To his left was the cooler door. To his right, an alcove disappeared into a black well of darkness, like a hallway, making him think there might be a second door back there.

But the bullet had come from the nurses' station by the front door. Martinelli had probably slipped around the far side of the floating wall and behind the L-shaped counter when Giorgio burst into the room. If there wasn't a second door, he was trapped in here.

Giorgio heard a faint shuffling of feet, and then a bullet took out the fluorescent light bulb above Mia's gurney, raining shards of glass onto the floor and onto her.

The room dropped into complete darkness.

Giorgio pulled down his goggles again and the room came alive.

"C'mon, Martinelli," Giorgio shouted. "You're not going to get away."

He crouched around the edge of the counter. A human form appeared from around the corner of the floating wall, on the other side of Mia's gurney. Giorgio watched him in the goggles' crimson light. Martinelli lifted his right hand and discharged another bullet. It hit the metal shelving and glass beakers on the wall behind Giorgio. Shards of glass sprayed out, forcing him to duck.

Then suddenly, there was a loud crack and gun flare from Giorgio's right.

Giorgio spun in that direction.

Rocky had come in low from the darkened alcove and had taken a shot at Martinelli.

Giorgio heard the sound of running feet and a hand hitting the swinging door. Martinelli had fled into the hallway.

Giorgio got up. A moment later, Rocky was by his side with the flashlight on.

"What happened to Perry?" Giorgio asked.

"He won't be a problem," Rocky replied.

"Okay, take care of the girl," Giorgio said, gesturing towards the gurney. "Get her out of here. I'll take care of Fritz."

Giorgio ran for the double doors.

He came into the hallway and scanned both directions. A sound to his left made him turn that

way. Martinelli had gone up the stairwell they'd just come down.

He sprinted in that direction, just catching the door before it close and ran up the first set of stairs.

When he hit the first landing, he hung back to the side and threw the door open. A bullet seared past him from above.

He flinched as the sound of running feet echoed up the stairwell.

Giorgio followed around the foot of the staircase and began to climb again, his weapon pointed up. He saw Martinelli's heels as they turned onto the next flight of stairs. A moment later, a jiggling sound reverberated in the small space.

Giorgio listened. Martinelli was yanking on a locked door on the second floor. Giorgio climbed cautiously to the next landing. But Martinelli was headed up again.

Giorgio tried the door, and it turned effortlessly. A glow of light through the window told him all he needed to know.

A door closed above him, making him spin around. He ran up the final flight of stairs.

When he got to the third floor, he was breathing hard. He stopped at the door and pulled it open slowly.

A shot rang out, hitting the door casing.

Giorgio ducked down and rolled forward into the hallway.

He came up onto his feet in a crouched position and saw Martinelli duck into a room about a hundred feet in front of him. Giorgio stayed close to the interior wall, but hurried forward.

Martinelli had ducked into the cafeteria, and the door was still swinging when Giorgio got there. He looked through the window and saw a figure dart across the room towards a door at the far end.

Giorgio pushed through the door and immediately broke to his left as Martinelli went out the rear door.

Giorgio scrambled through the room, past broken tables and chairs and the long serving counters. When he got to the rear door, he edged through. Martinelli was just disappearing over a guardrail and up a metal ladder attached to the exterior wall.

Giorgio came out onto a small patio and pulled up the goggles. He got to the guardrail and paused. He'd be a sitting duck on that ladder; all Martinelli would have to do is lean over from the roof above and shoot him. Giorgio waited until a roof tile tumbled over the edge and fell to the ground.

Martinelli wasn't waiting for him. He was trying to climb over the roof.

Giorgio tucked his gun into his holster and followed Martinelli up the metal ladder. The ladder crested the roof and kept going, following the angle of the roof to the chimney, where there was a small service platform.

But Martinelli wasn't there. He had struck out across the peaked roofline, sliding and kicking tiles off as he went.

Giorgio climbed to the chimney platform, just as Martinelli slid down the roof to a second ladder near the front of the building. He grabbed the handrails, pulled his gun and fired back at Giorgio.

Giorgio ducked and the bullet hit the bricks directly over his head, sending out a spray of plaster dust.

Martinelli dropped over the edge and was gone.

Giorgio took off after Martinelli, scrambling across the pitched roof, nearly losing his footing twice. Each time, he stopped, hyperventilating at the thought of sliding off to drop three stories to the ground.

He made it to the spot where Martinelli had slid down to the second ladder and wondered again if he would be waiting for him.

But his gaze landed on what Martinelli was aiming for: an escape route.

A large oak tree stood right next to the barbed wire fence. One large branch extended over the fence and came right up to the building. If Martinelli could reach it, he could use the branch to climb over the fence and drop down on the other side. From there he could take off in any direction into the surrounding hills.

And suddenly Giorgio knew why the spirits had locked the second floor door – to keep Martinelli off the second floor and without access to the tree. It also explained what Christian Maynard had meant about the tree. Too bad Martinelli knew the building so well. He'd made it to the tree, anyway.

Giorgio didn't hesitate.

He lay on his belly and began to slide down the roof just as Martinelli had done. His foot caught once, dislodging a roof tile.

He kept going.

Giorgio made it to the ladder and began to descend. When he got to the bottom of the ladder, he reached for his weapon and glanced to his left.

There was a wide, open-air patio here. It extended fifteen feet away from the building and ran half the length of the west wing of the hospital. The patio was cluttered with old, broken chaise lounges and chairs, a couple of bent metal tables, and several enormous broken planter boxes that seeped rivers of dirt onto the tarred roofing. At the other end of the patio, the branch from the big oak tree had pushed its way right through the metal railing and into the patio space.

But Martinelli was nowhere to be seen.

Perhaps Giorgio had been wrong. Maybe Martinelli had gone inside again instead of heading for the tree.

Giorgio swung around and jumped off the ladder at a spot where the metal railing had been broken and been twisted away from the building.

There was a shuffling of feet, and then a figure emerged from the dark and slammed into him, knocking the gun out of his hands and throwing him back towards the edge of the patio.

Giorgio reached out and grabbed the railing just before he flew off the edge. He balanced precariously, his torso hanging over empty space, with only his legs planted on firm ground.

Martinelli came at him again, kicking his legs off the platform. All of a sudden Giorgio was hanging by one hand in midair.

The railing had at one time extended the width of the patio. But over time, much of it had been broken or removed. Now Giorgio was holding onto one of the last pieces still anchored to the building, but his weight had pulled the railing further away from the building and was beginning to bend the whole piece down.

Martinelli growled in frustration and began rocking the remaining section back and forth, trying to pull it loose at the base.

Giorgio vainly reached out with his left hand, attempting to grab Martinelli and pull him over the edge instead, but the man kept just out of his reach.

Finally, Martinelli gave up and fell to his knees, panting.

"Too bad, Detective," he laughed, sucking in deep breaths. "You're in a bit of a predicament, aren't you? A couple more minutes, and that pretty little daughter of yours will grow up without her daddy."

"You bastard!"

Giorgio tried to kick at Martinelli, his rage igniting a frantic attempt to kill the man. It only served to loosen the railing even more, making his situation that much more precarious.

Martinelli finally stood up and took a deep breath. He looked down at Giorgio, laughing at his futile efforts. He reached behind his back and pulled out his gun.

"Sorry, Detective. I can't wait. I have to get going. I have a car waiting."

"You won't get away," Giorgio said, stalling for time. "Perry is already dead."

Martinelli flinched. "All the more reason to kill *you*," he said, his dark eyes glaring.

"Your father is dead, too," Giorgio said quickly. "He shot himself *after* he told us where to find you."

A flash of surprise registered on Martinelli's face. Then he smiled.

"No he didn't. Ron told you. Ron was always the weak one. The goody-two shoes. The star athlete. The one who got all the breaks. He told you." He paused. "He was never really a part of this family. His own father would have disowned him if he could have. Instead, he willed the cabinet to my father, and now it's mine. Passed down from generations," he said smugly. "Not money, but memories. Far more important, don't you think?"

Giorgio cringed at the word 'memories,' remembering what Edmond Martinelli had said about an old man needing to have his memories.

Martinelli raised the gun and pointed it directly at Giorgio. "And now I'll have the memory of killing *you*."

A smile played across his lips as his index finger flexed.

And then a tiny *poof* made him freeze.

A small hole opened up in the middle of Martinelli's forehead, and his dark eyes glazed over, as a small trickle of blood flowed down between his eyes.

Ever so slowly, his body tipped forward. Giorgio ducked, as Martinelli fell over him and off the building.

The body hit the ground below with a thud.

Giorgio swallowed.

Martinelli had to be dead. But so was he if he couldn't get back onto the patio.

And suddenly, there was a strong hand reaching out for him.

"Here, little brother," Rocky said, holstering his weapon. "Take my hand."

Giorgio looked up at him. "I'm not your little brother," he grunted.

"Not a good time to argue," Rocky grinned. "C'mon. Let's get you back on solid ground."

Rocky reached out and pulled Giorgio to safety.

As Giorgio stood up and dusted himself off, he turned. The brothers stood shoulder-to-shoulder, gazing to the ground below.

Detective Abrams was kicking at Martinelli, his rifle pointed at the man's head. Behind him, glowing in the darkness was the shimmering image of Christian Maynard.

"What the hell's that?" Rocky whispered breathlessly.

Giorgio glanced at his brother and then to the ghost in the trees. "Just another friend."

The boy lifted a hand as if in a solemn wave and then his image faded.

Abrams glanced up at the same moment and gave the brothers the thumbs up signal. Fritz Martinelli was dead.

"Damn," Rocky said. "He wasn't kidding."

"Who?" Giorgio said, shifting his gaze from Christian Maynard to his brother.

"Abrams. You know, when he said he was pretty good with a rifle. There's very little light out here and a pretty brisk breeze, and yet he hit the nail on the head...literally."

"Yeah," Giorgio smiled, glancing down to the ex-Army Ranger. "Apparently, he was only being modest. You could learn a thing or two from him."

Rocky gave him an incredulous look. "Are you kidding me? I was just about to shoot the bastard," he said, gesturing below. "And I just saved your sorry ass, don't forget that."

They turned away from the scene below and moved toward the doors that would lead them back into the building.

"Yeah, and you'll never let me forget it," Giorgio quipped, throwing a hand up onto his brother's shoulder. "By-the-way, thanks."

CHAPTER FORTY

The next ten days dawned sunny and clear, as if the world had been washed clean of a dark disease. During that time, Giorgio kept track of the various elements of the case.

The Monrovia police converged on the Pottinger Sanitarium and found blood evidence from multiple victims in the morgue and the bodies of seven young women buried just outside the fenced perimeter. Meanwhile, five of the young women buried at the Pinney House were identified through the jewelry and trinkets found in the small tin box, including Patty Carr, the young nurse. Their families were notified and the remains released.

Mia Santana spent two days in the hospital recovering from her ordeal, and then took a leave of absence from her TV station.

Giorgio had Claire Martinelli arrested at her home for aiding and abetting her murderous husband. Even though they would never be able to prove the charge, Giorgio treated the Ice Queen to all the humiliation she deserved, including a 48-hour hold in a cold cell, with a full interrogation. Under the threat of incarceration for providing false information during the Lisa Farmer case, she gave them one more critical piece of information they didn't have – the existence of a wooden cabinet handmade by her husband the year they moved to Pasadena. She claimed ignorance as to what was in it, but told them that when Royce died, he willed the cabinet to his brother, who moved it immediately to his own home.

They found the cabinet tucked inside a secret wall in the back of Edmond's garage. It was a four-foot tall oak cabinet enclosed by a single, beautifully carved domed door, inlaid with mother of pearl in the shape of a rose.

The rose, Giorgio thought when he saw it. The rose seen by both psychics.

When they opened it, they were met with the immediate stench of decay and formaldehyde. And just like some of the more bizarre cabinets of curiosities in the late 1800s, which sought to preserve medical oddities, tumors, and strange anatomical and pathological specimens, this cabinet preserved the trophies extracted from a string of young murder victims.

The cabinet had three drawers. The first held thirty-nine individual rings, bracelets, necklaces, earrings, and buttons, they presumed from different victims. A second drawer was devoted entirely to photographs, which documented in horrid detail some of the monstrous deeds done to these women. And the third drawer held journals written by Royce Martinelli as he gave a play-by-play account in several cases of unspeakable experiments conducted as part of the women's captivity.

But it was the three shelves above the drawers that would haunt Giorgio for some time to come.

Floating in mason jars of formaldehyde were human body parts: ears, women's genitalia, nipples, fingernails and even a set of milky blue eyeballs. Royce Martinelli described the piercing blue eyes in one journal as belonging to a young girl named Phoebe, who he'd picked up on a downtown street in San Pedro. He was captivated by her eyes, and so, after raping and torturing her to death, he saved them to remember her whenever he wanted.

Although Giorgio had almost gone into the seminary at one point in his life to please his mother, it was moments like this that tested his faith. It left him to wonder if there even was a god. Because if there was, why hadn't he, or she, interceded? Why had these girls been forced to endure such unspeakable horrors? And why had Royce and Edmond Martinelli been allowed to live full lives, while these girls had never even had the chance to grow up?

In Giorgio's mind, the only good news out of the case was that Edmond Martinelli survived as a quadriplegic, unable to talk, eat or care for himself. He would be forever forced to rely on someone else to feed him and clean him while incarcerated in prison.

Perhaps there *was* a god.

÷

A week after their ordeal at the sanitarium Giorgio left his house dressed in a dark suit and tie. He picked up Rocky, and they drove to the Evergreen Cemetery, where an open grave stood waiting for a cedar coffin filled with the remains of Lisa Farmer.

Mrs. Farmer stood next to the gravesite, her oxygen tank by her side. She was dressed in a violet-colored polyester pant suit and white blouse. She looked so small and frail against the surrounding pine trees, that Giorgio thought a brisk breeze might blow her away.

As Giorgio and Rocky began to tramp across the lawn to join her, a clunky old truck pulled up to the curb. Cal Birmingham, the original detective on the Lisa Farmer case, pulled his lanky frame out of the driver's side, and a woman who looked to be his same age got out of the passenger seat. They clasped hands and approached the grave.

"This is my wife, Sara," he said, when he met up with Giorgio.

"Nice to meet you," Giorgio said. "It's nice of you both to come. My brother, Rocky, is also with the department" Giorgio said, gesturing to his brother.

Birmingham's eyes had deep circles under them, and his wizened face had a haunted expression.

"I can't believe we never saw any of this," he said, shaking his head and glancing toward the grave. "All those girls. Poor Lisa was just one of them."

Giorgio followed his gaze, and said, "I knew a priest once who told me that we all have a purpose in life, even if that purpose isn't discovered until after we die." He looked back at the old detective. "Maybe this was Lisa's purpose – to get the ball rolling so that we'd finally stop these bastards."

"So it was Royce Martinelli all along that killed Lisa?" Birmingham said.

"Yes," Giorgio said as they began moving slowly toward the gravesite. "His brother Edmond helped cover it up. All because one of their many torture victims got away."

"And did the wife know about Lisa?" he asked.

"She says she didn't know, but we arrested her because she knew about other women that Royce had killed and she impeded the investigation. We got her on aiding and abetting. Of course, it won't stick. There's no evidence. But it did *my* heart good to handcuff her and take her away in front of all her neighbors. After all, protecting her reputation was all she ever cared about."

Cal Birmingham chuckled. "I think I'd hate to get on your bad side, but I like your style."

They joined the few people assembled in front of the coffin. It was a short service, but a heartfelt one. Lisa's senior class picture had been blown up and mounted on foam core and placed on a tripod in front of the group of chairs. The director from the facility where Jimmy Finn lived had brought the man who had served time for Lisa's murder. He sat rocking back and forth in his chair, never taking his eyes off the coffin.

Monty Montgomery was also there, holding a handkerchief to his nose. And Amber Riley had driven down from Big Bear to pay her respects to the young woman who had died the same night that she had escaped.

But there was no sign of Ron Martinelli. Giorgio kept glancing over his shoulder, hoping that he'd make an appearance. But he never did.

"He's not coming," Rocky said at one point. "Would you, under the circumstances?"

Giorgio sighed with disappointment, turning back to the service. "Probably not."

When the service ended, Giorgio approached Amber Riley. She held a tissue in her hand and dabbed at her eyes.

"It's nice that you came," he said to her. "Would you like to meet Mrs. Farmer?"

She glanced over at Lisa's mother and shook her head. "No. I don't think I can. I was responsible for the death of her daughter."

Rocky put a hand on her shoulder.

"Those guys were going to kill you. You had no other option and no way of knowing how your escape would impact someone else," he said.

She nodded. "I know. But I'll always feel like a kindred spirit to her. She took my place, you know? She died *instead* of me."

"At least now it's over," Giorgio said. "It's really over."

She seemed to relax. "Yes. After you called the other night to tell me, it was the first night in forty-seven years that I truly slept soundly. Thank you," she said to Giorgio. Then she turned to Rocky. "Thank you both."

After Amber left, they approached Mrs. Farmer, who was thanking Detective Birmingham for coming. As Giorgio appeared,

Cal Birmingham nodded to him, and then he and his wife left. Mrs. Farmer turned watery eyes to Giorgio.

"She wasn't hurt, like those other girls, was she? The ones I read about in the paper?" she asked plaintively.

"No," he shook his head. "The medical examiner thinks she was struck on the head. He thinks she died instantly."

The little woman dropped her head. "I'm glad," she said, as a sob escaped her throat. "I don't think I could have lived with that. She'd already been through so much. But why did that man kill her?"

Giorgio rocked back on his heels before answering. "We believe she heard something that night in Royce Martinelli's study. Something about a botched attempt to kill a young girl up at Big Bear Lake."

As he said this, his eyes followed Amber Riley across the lawn to her car. Giorgio reached into his pocket and pulled out a white handkerchief and held it out to Lisa's mother.

"We didn't need this after all," he said. "And I'll get her jewelry back to you as soon as I can."

She stared at the crumpled handkerchief with the cherry red sucker stuck inside. Tears began to flow. She reached out with a shaky hand and clasped onto it, as if it was a life preserver thrown to a drowning victim.

"Thank you," she choked out. She looked up at Giorgio. "At least now she'll be buried and I can come visit her grave. We have lots to talk about, you know," she said, with the briefest of smiles.

They left Mrs. Farmer at the gravesite and started back towards the car. Giorgio was just about to slide in behind the wheel, when Rocky stopped him.

"Look over there," his brother said.

Giorgio followed his gaze to a small hill about fifty yards away. Tucked into the shadow of the trees was Ron Martinelli, dressed in a black suit and black turtleneck, staring blankly toward the gravesite. He was alone. No Miss Brinson. No Claire or Royce Martinelli to hold him up. Just the adult version of the eighteen-year-old kid who had lost the girl of his dreams.

"I wouldn't want to be him," Rocky said cynically.

"No," Giorgio said, getting into the car. "I wouldn't want to be any of these people. There were no winners here."

CHAPTER FORTY-ONE

It was opening night of *Arsenic and Old Lace*. Detective Abrams had flown down for the occasion, and he and Flame had joined Angie and the kids in the front row.

The theater was filling quickly, and the electricity of opening night crackled in the air. Backstage, the actors and stagehands were busy getting ready. Giorgio was just powdering his face makeup when Rocky sauntered in, threw a long leg over the bench and sat down facing him.

"I never get used to seeing you in makeup, you know?" Rocky said with a smile. He leaned over to peer at Giorgio's eyes. "Weird," he said, spying the eyeliner.

"Forget it," Giorgio retorted. "Comes with the territory. If you want to act, you have to wear makeup."

"Well, everyone's pretty excited," Rocky said, reaching out to toy with a makeup sponge. "Abrams can't believe he's going to see you strutting your stuff on stage, and Flame has predicted a standing ovation."

He grinned and Giorgio grimaced. "I bet," he said, cynically.

"Well, at least Tony's excited," Rocky said. "He thinks he'll get to see a bunch of dead bodies."

Giorgio sighed loudly. "Did you tell him most of them are buried in the basement...off stage?"

"Naw," Rocky smiled. "I didn't want to spoil it for him. Besides, he'll love the Boris Karloff character. Are you going to stick a fork in his leg like they do in the movie?"

"Ten minutes!" a voice called out.

Giorgio looked up to where the stage manager was just disappearing out the door.

"No, no fork," he said

"By the way," Rocky continued, "I asked Abrams where he learned to shoot like that. He said he went to Army Ranger *sniper* school," Rocky said with a laugh. "Can you believe it? But I'm glad he was on *our* side."

"Well, it might be a dumb name for a school, but here's to Army Ranger sniper school," Giorgio said, giving a fake toast. "It sure saved *my* ass."

Giorgio went back to finishing his makeup.

"You're not going to tell Angie, are you?" Rocky suddenly said.

Giorgio stopped and looked over at his brother. "What do you mean?"

"You're not going to tell her that the guy who fondled Marie in the Christmas tree lot, was from a long line of psychopathic serial killers."

The air went dead between them, and then Giorgio exhaled.

"No. I'm not going to tell her that. Why should I? It would just haunt her the way it haunts me."

"But keeping a secret from her isn't good," Rocky said.

Giorgio sighed as he began to put his makeup away.

"There are a lot of things I don't tell Angie, Rocky. She doesn't need to know about some of the ugly stuff we see. Hell, my job already puts a strain between us. I don't want there to be more. If you were married, you'd..."

He stopped and looked over at his brother.

"I'm sorry, Rocky. I didn't mean..."

Rocky waved him away, a pained look on his face.

"It's okay. I get it. Even though Rebecca was training to be a cop, there were things I didn't tell her, either." He took a deep breath. "By the way, I'm...I'm thinking of going to see that psychic."

"Flame?"

"Yeah." He paused again and then took a deep sigh. "I've seen Rebecca, Joe. Since she was murdered. I've seen her several times, in fact. It's one reason I started drinking."

Rocky looked at his brother with a haunted expression, and Giorgio knew immediately that he wasn't joking.

"I'm sorry, Rocky. I had no idea."

"I saw her again last night. Her image," he corrected himself. "And it was everything I could do not to reach for a beer."

"Do you have alcohol in the house?" Giorgio exclaimed.

"No. You know what I mean. I just wanted one. I've never said anything before because…"

"Because you were afraid people would think you were crazy," Giorgio said, finishing his thought.

"Yeah. Do you? Think I'm nuts, I mean?"

Giorgio contemplated his answer, thinking back to when he'd first see Christian Maynard and thinking the same thing.

"Are you kidding? After what we saw at the sanitarium? No. I may be dull, as you put it. But I've learned recently to be a lot more open-minded about things like this. I think Flame is the real deal. I think ghosts probably are, too. Maybe Rebecca is trying to communicate with you somehow."

He approached the subject slowly. He didn't want to freak out his brother at a time when he was clearly so vulnerable.

"I thought maybe Flame could help me," Rocky said shyly. "Maybe she could find out why Rebecca keeps appearing to me. What do you think?"

The air in the room felt suddenly heavy as Giorgio contemplated what it took for his brother to admit all of this.

"I don't know, Rocky. I don't profess to know how any of this stuff works. Maybe it will help. Maybe it won't. I wouldn't get your hopes up."

The door opened and Mia Santana walked in with a bouquet of flowers. Rocky saw her and quickly stood up.

"Listen, I'll see you after the show," Rocky said, ending their conversation.

He passed the young woman with a brief smile and slipped out the door. She moved over next to Giorgio.

"How are you?" he said.

She tried to smile, but came up short. "I'm okay. Not 100%, but okay."

He turned to her. "Sit down," he said, gesturing to the bench.

She sat down and handed him the flowers. "I brought you these…for opening night."

He smiled and took them from her. "Thanks. I didn't know you covered the theater, too."

"I don't. But I wanted to see you…before I leave."

"You're leaving?"

She glanced down to her hands, which still carried the scars from where Fritz Martinelli had sliced each finger open.

"I'm moving back to San Diego – to live with my parents for a while. I'm going to go back to school. To become a teacher."

"No more reporting?"

A tear glistened in the corner of her eye. "No. I think I'm done with that."

He regarded her for a moment. This woman, who had at one time been so full of confidence and raw energy, was now cowed and timid. It made him sad.

"You're very good at what you do, you know," he said.

Her brown eyes lit up at that. "You mean that?"

"I do. You were a pain in the ass, but you were a good journalist. I admired you."

A wave of relief seemed to wash over her. "Thanks. I appreciate that. You're good at what you do, too." Now more tears glistened. "I wouldn't be here if you hadn't...I..." she said, and then stopped.

He reached out and placed his hand over hers.

"We each did what our jobs demanded. What we were trained to do. Listen, Mia. If you're half as good a teacher as you were a reporter, your students will be very lucky."

"Thank you," she said.

She smiled, leaned forward and gave him a brief kiss on the cheek, and then she was gone.

He sat for a moment, gazing at the flowers and thinking of his daughter, Marie. In a few years, Marie would look a lot like Mia. She might even be as stubborn. He chuckled at the thought, and then a dark cloud passed before his eyes.

What he hadn't told Rocky was that he'd followed Marie's bus home from school twice in the last few weeks – scanning each and every person who dropped their kids off or picked them up. He knew he couldn't protect his children from everything, but he wanted to, because the world was actually a pretty ugly place. And Fritz Martinelli had reminded him of that.

"Curtain in five," the stage manager announced over the intercom.

Giorgio rose and quickly got into costume. He adjusted the fake monocle in one eye that would help make him look like Teddy Roosevelt and studied his image in the mirror, running his fingers through the empty pockets of his wool vest.

He was alone now in the dressing room, and the period costume made him think of the boy.

Giorgio had to admit that young Christian Maynard had done them all a great service. He'd given closure to so many people. But Giorgio's heart fluttered at the thought that the boy – dressed in his knickers and starched white shirt – might remain a permanent part of his life. What other ghastly things would he have to look forward to?

Just then, he felt a tug at the pocket of his vest.

Giorgio jerked around, but he was alone.

Curious, he looked down and reached into the vest pocket with two fingers again, expecting to find it empty. Instead, he drew out a folded piece of paper, and his heart jumped. He opened the paper and took a deep breath.

It was a torn flyer, depicting the twisted face of a vampire, blood dripping from his fangs, and a snarling dog in the background. Splashed across the top were the words, "Fangtasia – March 18th."

"Shit," he murmured, a queasy feeling in his stomach. Where the hell had this come from?

He glanced up and stuffed the flyer back into his pocket.

He couldn't deal with this now. He had a play to do.

÷

A few minutes later, Giorgio stood backstage, ready to go on stage. Through discipline, he forced thoughts of Christian Maynard from his mind. He had only thoughts of *Arsenic and Old Lace* – the story of two spinster aunts who poisoned lonely old men and then had their crazy brother bury them in the basement.

While *Arsenic & Old Lace* made for great fun and laughter in the theater, Giorgio couldn't help but think about the real bodies buried at the Pinney House. So many young lives cut short.

Laughter bubbled up from the audience, and he glanced out on stage.

Tonight, the antics would only be make-believe – just make-believe, he reminded himself. The characters would *talk* about bodies buried in the basement, but there would be no tortured souls lain to rest.

Unless, of course, someone dropped a line. Then all bets were off.

The End

AUTHOR'S NOTES

The idea to set the story at the Pinney House came from my high school friend, Cindy Warden, whose family used to own it. Cindy and I graduated together from Pasadena High School in 1967, just like the characters in the book. So I decided to not only set the story at the local landmark, but during the time when we grew up there.

THE PINNEY HOUSE

The Pinney House is currently owned by Greg and Judy Asbury, who describe it on their website this way:
"Welcome to The Pinney House! Built in 1887 as one of the original railroad hotels, the house features eight suites, up to three of which are available for short-term rental (the rest are rented out on a yearly basis)."
I'm sure the Asburys would appreciate your business. Please visit their website at www.pinneyhouse.com. They have my sincere appreciation, not only because they gave me permission to use their home in the book, but they offered up the cover photo and the tale about its current resident ghost.

THE POTTINGER SANITARIUM

The Pottinger Sanitarium (I found it spelled both Pottinger and Pottenger) was built in 1903 by Dr. Frances Marion Pottinger, after his wife contracted tuberculosis. The hospital, called Pottinger Sanatorium for Diseases of the Lungs and Throat closed in 1955, when Dr. Pottinger retired at 88-years old. But Dr. Pottinger and his ground-breaking treatments were world-famous by that time for treating diseases of the lung. While the building no longer exists, you can see pictures of it online.

DETECTIVE ABRAMS

For those of you who have read *Inn Keeping With Murder*, you will recognize an earlier version of the handsome Detective Abrams in this book. I created his character in a short story called *A Palette for Murder*, which appears in my book of short stories, *Your Worst Nightmare*.

Thank you so very much for reading *Murder In The Past Tense*. If you enjoyed this book, I would be honored if you would go back to Amazon.com and leave an honest review. I do read them. We "indie" authors thrive on reviews and word-of-mouth advertising. This will help position the book so that more people might also enjoy it. Thank you so much!

About the Author

Ms. Bohart holds a master's degree in theater, has published in Woman's World, and has a story in *Dead on Demand*, an anthology of ghost stories that remained on the Library Journal's best seller list for six months. As a thirty-year nonprofit professional, she has spent a lifetime writing brochures, newsletters, business letters, website copy, and more. She did a short stint writing for Patch.com, teaches writing through the Continuing Education Program at Green River Community College, and writes a monthly column for the Renton Reporter. *Murder In The Past Tense* is her fourth full-length novel and the sequel to *Mass Murder*. She is already hard at work on the third Girogio Salvatori book.

Follow Ms. Bohart

Website: www.bohartink.com
Twitter: @lbohart
Facebook: Facebook @ L.Bohart/author

24754565R00158

Made in the USA
San Bernardino, CA
06 October 2015